The Silk Merchant's Daughter

The Silk Merchant's Daughter

DINAH JEFFERIES

VIKING

an imprint of

PENGUIN BOOKS

VIKING

UK | USA | Canada | Ireland | Australia
India | New Zealand | South Africa

Viking is part of the Penguin Random House group of companies
whose addresses can be found at global.penguinrandomhouse.com.

First published 2016
001

Copyright © Dinah Jefferies, 2016

The moral right of the author has been asserted

Set in 12/14.75 pt Dante MT Std
Typeset by Jouve (UK), Milton Keynes
Printed in Great Britain by Clays Ltd, St Ives plc

A CIP catalogue record for this book is available from the British Library

HARDBACK ISBN: 978–0–241–26116–3
TRADE PAPERBACK ISBN: 978–0–241–26126–2

www.greenpenguin.co.uk

History of Vietnam Timeline

1787

French involvement in Vietnam begins. Versailles Treaty creates alliance between French King Louis XVI and the Vietnamese Prince Nguyễn Ánh.

1840s–1890s

French colonization of Indochina (Vietnam, Cambodia and Laos). France divides Vietnam into three areas: Tonkin, Annam, Cochin-China.

1927–30

In the north two heavily repressed communist groups are formed to resist the French.

1940

During World War II, Japan invades and occupies Vietnam, allowing French colonial government to continue for a time.

1941–4

The Vietminh Independence League is organized by Ho Chi Minh who emerges as a leader of anti-Japanese resistance.

1945

The Japanese take over government from the French (briefly). After the Japanese surrender, the Vietminh, led by Ho Chi

Minh, take control (also briefly). British and US military forces assist the French to re-establish colonial rule.

1946

The Vietminh resist. French forces shell the port of Haiphong. The first Indochina War (or French War) begins.

1946–54

During the Indochina War, China and the USSR support Ho Chi Minh; the US supports France in order to halt the spread of communism.

1954

With popular support the Vietminh forces surround an isolated French military outpost in the town of Dien Bien Phu. Twelve thousand French troops are trapped. France surrenders. The Geneva Accords are signed dividing Vietnam into North and South, with national elections to be held in two years.

1955–6

With support from the US, Ngo Dinh Diem declares himself president of South Vietnam, refusing to hold national elections.

1957–9

Weapons and men from North Vietnam begin infiltrating the South. Beginning of communist insurgency in the South.

1960

The Vietcong, or National Liberation Front, are formed to fight the US in the South.

1964

A North Vietnamese patrol boat attacks a US destroyer.

1965

US combat troops arrive in Vietnam, beginning the American–Vietnam War. The US drop more tonnage of bombs than are dropped in the whole of World War II.

1973

The US withdraws troops following Paris Peace Agreements negotiated by Nixon and Kissinger but hostilities continue in the South.

1975

Communists take Saigon. Last remaining US citizens are evacuated. Vietnam is unified under communist rule and Saigon is renamed Ho Chi Minh City.

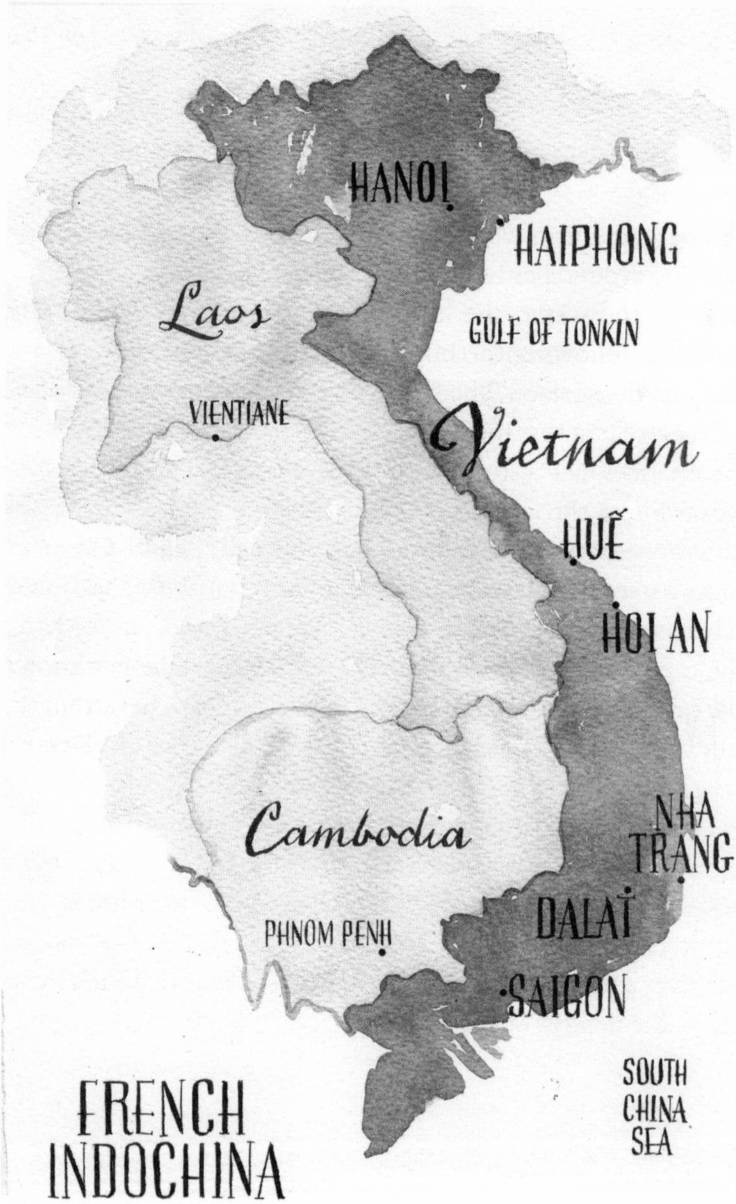
HANOI
HAIPHONG
Laos
GULF OF TONKIN
VIENTIANE
Vietnam
HUẾ
HOI AN
NHA TRANG
Cambodia
DALAT
PHNOM PENH
SAIGON
SOUTH CHINA SEA
FRENCH INDOCHINA

Prologue

Submerged, she moves in tumbling slow motion, her long hair swirling around her head. Spellbound by golden light pouring through the water, she kicks her legs and thrusts her body upwards, following the bubbles of her breath as they stream towards the surface. The flat sun splinters, spreading droplets glittering far across the water. She throws back her head, gasps for air, sees her sister's face. Seconds pass. Dazzled, as the world filters through, she raises a hand to wave, opens her mouth to shout. But the water swallows her again. The river roars as she treads water, its voice echoing with thuds and thumps. *Thwack. Thwack.* Despite the need to shout for help, she can't make a sound. She's desperate to breathe but knows she cannot. She tries to swim, but something saps her strength. Above her, the iridescence fades. She starts to sink. Deeper down, the darkening river is cold, and as each pulse of light grows fainter, it is happening too fast. She tries to roll over, tries to climb a watery ladder to the top, but the river is too powerful and her feet are slipping through the gaps. Images of home begin flooding her mind, her legs grow heavy and, as the river sucks the struggle out of her, she feels as if she's floating in the depths. She is not floating, but drowning.

I

Threads of Silk

May to early July 1952

I

Hanoi, Vietnam

Nicole sniffed air heady with the scent of wild gardenia, the shiny green leaves and fragrant white flowers of the shrub carpeting the partially shaded area of the garden. She glanced down from her bedroom window and spotted her father checking that everything was perfect outside. Still a handsome man, his well-cut dark hair, with just a scattering of silver, made him seem especially distinguished and, although it was irritating that he was using her eighteenth birthday party to show off the garden, she had to admit how pretty he'd made it. Incense burned at the French windows of their honey-coloured villa and the garden ponds reflected bright colours from strings of paper lanterns hanging from the branches of two enormous frangipani trees.

Nicole took one last look in the mirror and deliberated. Should she pin a single fuchsia at the side of her long black hair to match the Chinese-collared dress she'd had made for today? The bodice clung to her slim frame like a second skin and, as she moved, the skirt swirled and fell just short of the floor. She listened to Edith Piaf singing 'Hymne à l'amour' on the wireless, glanced out of the window again and, deciding against the flower, saw that her sister, Sylvie, was now walking at their father's side, the two of them with their heads close together as they so often were. For a moment Nicole felt left out and swallowed a brief flash of envy. She ought to be used to it by now, but even before she'd combed her hair or brushed her teeth, her sister looked beautiful; wavy auburn hair, chiselled cheekbones and a perfectly tilted French nose saw to that. Tall, willowy Sylvie had inherited their French father's looks, while Nicole resembled their long-dead Vietnamese mother and felt conscious of her amber complexion. She drew back her shoulders, shrugged the moment off and left the bedroom; she wasn't going to let anything spoil her day.

As she strolled through the large, high-ceilinged room leading to the garden, two shining brass-bladed fans freshened the air. The room, like the rest of their home, was elegant and stuffed with exquisite antiques. From her spot in the open doorway she caught sight of a couple of old school friends, Helena and Francine, self-consciously fiddling with their hair in a corner of the garden. She went over to be kissed and hugged. As they chattered about boyfriends and the exams they'd passed, the garden was filling; by the time Nicole finally made her excuses, she saw the French guests had already arrived and were now smoking and drinking, while some of the wealthy Vietnamese had started to promenade in their silks. She noticed a tall, broad-shouldered man in a pale linen suit approach her sister and something about him made Nicole stare for a moment or two. Then she smoothed her hair, drew back her shoulders and went across.

Sylvie touched the man's arm and smiled at him. 'Let me introduce you to my sister, Nicole.'

He held out a hand. 'I'm Mark Jenson. I've heard a lot about you.'

She took his hand and glanced up at his face, but the intense blue of his eyes startled her and she had to look away.

'Mark's from New York. We met while I was over there,' Sylvie was saying. 'He travels all over the world.'

'It's your birthday, right?' he said, and smiled at Nicole.

Nicole swallowed and struggled to find her voice but luckily

Sylvie interrupted. 'There's somebody I just need to have a word with.' She waved at a dumpy woman on the other side of the garden, then turned to Mark and giggled as she touched his hand. 'I won't be long. Nicole will look after you.'

Mark smiled politely. For a moment the air seemed too thin and Nicole's breath failed her. She shifted her weight from one leg to the other, then looked up at him properly and tried not to blink too much. His eyes were the colour of sapphires, made even brighter by the contrast with the deep tan of his skin.

'So,' she said eventually.

He didn't speak but was still gazing at her.

Suddenly self-conscious, she touched her chin. Was there something on her face?

'I didn't expect you to be so pretty,' he said.

'Oh,' she said and felt confused. 'I'm sure I'm not.' But what had he expected and why was he expecting anything at all?

'Sylvie spoke of you when we were in the States.'

Her thoughts slowly untangled. Of course Sylvie had spoken about her. It was only natural to talk about your family, especially when away from home.

She smiled. 'Then you know I'm the black sheep.'

He flicked away a lock of hair that kept falling over his right eye. 'Fire and marquee do come to mind.'

At his gentle teasing, Nicole's hand flew to her mouth. 'Oh God, no! She didn't tell you about that?'

He laughed.

'I was only thirteen and it was an accident. But this isn't fair, you've already heard stories about me yet I know nothing about you.'

An impulse passed through her. As if he too felt it, he reached out a hand, but she realized it was only to indicate the way. 'Let's pick up some champagne and then why don't you show me round? I'll tell you everything you want to know.'

As they moved on, a little of the inner tautness she'd felt since being introduced released its grip, though at just five foot two, she felt tiny beside him and wished she'd worn higher heels.

A waiter in a white suit approached with a tray. Mark accepted two glasses and handed them both to Nicole. 'Do you mind me smoking?'

She shook her head. 'You don't sound as if you're from New York.'

He took out a packet of Chesterfields, lit one and then held out his hand for a glass. Their fingers touched and Nicole felt a jolt run up the underside of her bare arm.

'I'm not. My father has a small dairy farm in Maine. I grew up there.'

'What took you away?'

He stood still. 'Thirst for adventure, I suppose. After my mother died my father did his best but it was never the same.'

The tone of his voice had changed and she recognized the suppressed sadness in it. 'My mother died too,' she offered.

He nodded. 'Sylvie told me.'

There was a moment's silence.

He sighed again and smiled as if remembering. 'I did all the usual country things – fishing, hunting – but my passion was motorbikes. Dirt-track racing. The more dangerous the track the more I loved it.'

'Didn't you get hurt?'

He laughed. 'Frequently! But nothing too serious. It was mostly the odd broken ankle and a few cracked ribs.'

She was close enough to him to smell a warm spiciness on his skin. Something about him made her feel happy, but she twisted away slightly and looked up at a sky shot with stars, listening to the sound of cicadas and night birds shuffling in the trees. Mark had taken a step away and she saw that

8

his height gave him that loose-limbed way of walking Americans had in movies; a nonchalant walk conveying ease and confidence.

'People say May is the last month of spring in Hanoi, but it's so warm tonight it feels like summer already. Would you prefer to go indoors?' she said.

'On a night like this?'

She felt exhilarated and laughed. His short light-brown hair had a curl to it and was now tinged with gold. Someone had lit the torches and the light from the flames flickered on his face and hair.

'Where are you staying?'

'At the Métropole, on the Boulevard Henri Rivière.'

At that moment Sylvie reappeared and drew him away. After he'd gone Nicole felt his absence and, despite all the people milling around, the garden seemed empty. She remembered one of their cook Lisa's favourite sayings: *Có công mài sắt có ngày nên kim* – if you polish a piece of iron long enough you can make a needle. Though Lisa was French she spoke enough Vietnamese to get by in the markets, and took pride in quoting Vietnamese sayings. Perhaps it was time to apply a little polish to herself, Nicole thought as the live music started up. Time, too, for dancing the night away.

2

The next morning Nicole made her way down to the labyrinth of rooms on the lower ground floor. At the bottom of the narrow stairs, she walked along a long corridor and pushed open the door to the kitchen. There she glanced around at walls lined with white brick-shaped tiles and at a row of gleaming copper pots hanging from an iron bar in the centre. The new green roll-up blinds gave the kitchen a cool feel, and four big wall arches, smelling of paint, divided the room into sections.

Lisa had already made herself comfortable in her armchair, right beside the conservatory doors where she could watch over her precious vegetable plot. From the moment of Nicole's birth, Lisa had been the one constant. She looked just the way you'd want a cook to look: plump. Only in her forties, with her flyaway, greying hair tied in a topknot and her hands red from washing dishes, she had both feet up on a footstool. She fumbled in the pocket of her apron for the first cigarette of the day; a woman whose only concerns were rabbits, lizards or birds, and making sure the longan fruit were brought in safely in July, ready for preserving.

'You okay to get your own coffee?'

Nicole nodded, poured the coffee into a large mug then threw herself into a chair opposite the cook. 'I need this.'

'Hangover?'

'I suppose.'

'I saw you with an interesting-looking man last night.'

'Which one?' Nicole tried to conceal her smile but knew there was nothing she could hide from Lisa.

'I take it you like him?'

Nicole laughed. 'It felt extraordinary. I'm probably being silly, but I felt as if I'd just met the person who might change my whole life.'

Lisa smiled. 'He looked very handsome. I'm happy for you, *chérie*. Did you dance?'

'Not with him. He didn't stay long.'

But Nicole couldn't properly communicate the feeling of being changed, as if all her old feelings of inadequacy were disappearing. The brief meeting with Mark had slid inside her and she couldn't help but think it was the start of something very different.

'What does he do?'

'I didn't ask.' She grinned at Lisa and got to her feet. 'He's American.'

'A friend of Sylvie's?'

There was a noise coming from the housekeeper's room along the corridor and Nicole pulled a face. 'Bettine is here then?'

Lisa nodded. Though they had worked together for years, Bettine and Lisa could not have been more different. While Lisa was plump and round, Bettine was stiff and thin as a rake. Lisa's cosy bedroom and little sitting room of her own next to the kitchen were always a source of strife between the two women; the housekeeper lived out in rooms. The scullery and laundry room were the domain of the housemaid, Pauline, and there was a food preparation room for the part-time kitchen maid, only called in when Lisa needed extra help.

Nicole opened the conservatory doors and, smelling May air thick with the scent of wet earth, she listened to the creaking *cyclo pousse* as it drew up at the back of the house. She wrapped her silk dressing gown across her body, glanced at a few early yellow persimmon lying on the grass – where Sylvie maintained the bodies had been buried – and spotted Yvette, the baker's daughter, climbing out of the rickshaw, the ribbons of her dark plaits flying in the breeze.

The smell of freshly baked brioche drifted across.

Nicole beckoned the child over and, once inside the kitchen, drew up two chairs at the scrubbed pine table. Lisa had already laid out plates for Nicole's two pains au chocolat and Yvette's slice of soft white bread, spread with butter and honey.

Although she was only ten, Yvette usually delivered their Saturday patisserie treats: crème anglaise tarts, fresh loaves to eat with jam and preserves, the breakfast brioche, croissants and pains au chocolat. Her Vietnamese mother had died at the hands of the Japanese during the war, but Yves was a doting parent, who tried to be both mother and father to his little girl, and Nicole was very fond of her.

Nicole folded her legs under herself and kept an eye on Yvette's puppy. Trophy was already nosing around and, in a flash, leapt on to a chair.

'Bad dog.' Yvette shook her fist, but too late, for the pup had stolen a croissant and retreated beneath the table to wolf it down.

Nicole laughed. 'But he is adorable.'

'I wish I'd been old enough to come to your party. Did you have dancing?'

'Later on, though the evening was so beautiful, nobody really wanted to come inside.'

Lisa glanced at her watch. Yvette wasn't really supposed to have breakfast in the house but it was a little routine the three of them enjoyed. 'You'd better be off,' Lisa said and glanced upwards.

Nicole was set to disagree, but Yvette jumped off her chair, Trophy barking at her heels.

'Quiet or you'll wake up the house,' Yvette said, and picked up the puppy, who smothered her face with licks. She dashed out through the back door by means of the conservatory, where the spicy smell of ginger from Lisa's reed-like plants infused the air.

As soon as Yvette had gone Nicole kissed Lisa on the cheek.

'I can't believe you're eighteen, my darling girl,' the cook said and sniffed. 'It seems like only yesterday . . .'

Nicole grinned. 'Now don't you get all soppy. I have important things to do.'

'Like?'

'Like planning the rest of my life.'

'Something to do with that American chap you've got your eye on?'

'I don't know when I'll see him again.' Nicole paused at the sudden realization that she had no idea how long Mark would be in Hanoi. But she hoped that the Paris of the Orient, as the French liked to call the watery city, would cast its seductive spell on him.

It was only the three of them at table for supper. The smaller of the two dining rooms in the Duval villa fronted a small thatched pavilion where oversized wicker chairs and a glass coffee table sat beside a lily pond. A pretty carved lacquer screen sat in one corner, partitioning off a small desk and sofa where Sylvie liked to write. As Nicole had wasted what little time she'd had to tidy up before supper, reading a book, she combed her hair with her fingers and glanced at the ceiling. Painted blue with fluffy white clouds and cherubs flying round the central ceiling fan, she'd never liked it.

From the garden next door, Nicole heard the sound of peacocks.

'Damn things,' her father said. 'Dreadful squawking racket.'

'But they are beautiful,' Nicole said. 'Don't you think?'

'Why does she have to keep them in her garden? They drive me crazy.'

'Father's right,' Sylvie said. 'They are terribly annoying.'

After that they ate in silence. Despite the slow movement of the fan it was too hot. The heavy silk curtains, restrained with gold tasselled cords, had not been closed, and light muslin drapes fluttered through a mere suggestion of air. More peacock shrieks only served to darken their father's mood.

They were finishing the dessert when he glanced at Sylvie and Nicole before speaking. 'I'm glad you're both here.'

The sisters exchanged looks. There had been an uneasy atmosphere in the house lately: messages delivered by thin, tense men in army whites, the phone ringing off the hook and Papa looking increasingly strained. Nicole had noted the rapid rise in the number of Americans visiting the house and had come to the conclusion they must be from the Central Intelligence Agency. When she'd asked Sylvie, however, her sister had been non-committal. It seemed neither girl knew the reason behind it.

Their father shifted a little in his seat. 'Now that you're eighteen, Nicole, I want to explain my plans. I had expected to be talking about this when you were both over twenty-one, but as I'm taking on a role with the government now, that has changed.'

'In what way?' Sylvie said.

'In a way that means I won't be available to take care of the business.'

'What role is this, Papa?' Nicole asked.

'The exact nature of the task is classified, but with all my Vietnamese contacts they seem to think I'm the right man for the job. It is a great honour to be selected to work for the good of France.'

'But you do mean here in Hanoi?'

'Mainly.' He paused briefly. 'This may come as a surprise, but I believe it's in the best interests of the company that only one of you should be in charge. As Sylvie is the elder, I have decided to make over control of the business to her, with immediate effect.'

14

Nicole glanced at her sister, but Sylvie lowered her eyes and fiddled with her napkin.

'By the end of the year everything will be in Sylvie's name, but I have saved the small silk shop for you, Nicole.'

'I don't understand. Why can't we share? I always thought that one day Sylvie and I would run the business together.'

He shook his head. 'Sylvie is older and wiser. She has more experience, especially of the American markets, and it's only right that she should take control. If you had learnt all your lessons at the lycée, as your sister so diligently did, you would have had many more opportunities. You surely must see that.'

Nicole frowned. 'So Sylvie will be in charge of Paul Bert?'

He nodded.

Nicole swallowed rapidly, picturing the imposing Maison Duval, with its wonderful domed ceiling, polished teak staircase and elegant balconied upper floors. It was on Rue Paul Bert, often nicknamed the Champs-Élysées, and Nicole loved it.

'What else?' she said.

He stared at a spot above her head as he counted off on his fingers. 'The import and export business, and the emporium in the French quarter.'

Nicole knew much of the silk they supplied came from Huế, where the export side of the business operated, and where she had focused her hopes. 'But I was hoping to become the chief buyer one day. I thought that was why you took me with you to the silk villages while Sylvie was in America.'

He reached into his pocket for a cigar then tapped it on the table. 'Look, I'm sorry if it disappoints you, *chérie*, but there it is. You still have the option of finishing your education or you can take up my offer of the old silk shop; otherwise I'll have to find you a nice Vietnamese husband.'

It was a joke but Nicole couldn't prevent the tears of distress welling up. 'I thought the old shop had been abandoned.'

Another squawk reached them from outside. Her father's cheeks puffed out and his knuckles turned white as he gripped the table. Nicole could smell his scent – the leather wax, brandy and cigars – as she watched his nostrils flair.

'Damn those birds,' he said.

Nicole felt devastated. It had been exactly the same over Europe. Sylvie went and she didn't. Though of course that had been soon after she'd accidentally set fire to the marquee on Sylvie's eighteenth birthday.

Their father got to his feet. 'You two stay and finish your supper. Lisa will be bringing in the coffee any moment now. I shall take mine in my study.'

Nicole managed to hold back the burning at the backs of her eyelids.

'As for the business, do remember that Sylvie is your senior by five years and she is extremely reliable.' As her father reached the door, he glanced back. 'If you will drop out before your exams and disappear for days, what else do you expect me to do? The entire police force was out looking for you. And all the time you and that idiotic friend of yours had decided to get on a bus for Saigon. You must have known we'd be worried. Anything could have happened.'

She hung her head. Were they ever going to let her forget it? 'I know. I'm really sorry. I didn't think.'

'Well, you need to think now and I can only hope you've learnt from your mistakes.'

'I have, Papa. Truly.'

'So make a success of the shop and prove it. Then we'll see what else you might be able to do.'

3

The next day the temperature must have touched thirty-two or thirty-three degrees. As Nicole watched a bulging-eyed lizard run up the wall to hide behind the tips of a fern, she knew it would be horribly humid outside, though with a cool tiled floor, giant indoor ferns and the light shining down from a high glass cupola, the hall felt like a shady garden. She glanced down as she picked up her keys from the mother-of-pearl tray, pulled down the skirt of her tight-fitting dress and slipped on the matching high heels. She needed to get away from the house to think over her father's announcement and had decided to walk into the centre.

As she left the house behind, she twisted back to see Lisa throwing open the deep green shutters. Their three-storey house was gleaming, its ochre plaster freshly painted, and the overhanging eaves of the roof shaded the sweeping verandah circling the exterior. An entirely French exterior disguised the fact that indoors Indochinese style had made its mark in the form of red-lacquered panels placed either side of the ground-floor doors and decorated with gold leaf.

Nicole walked in the direction of the town centre but, a few turnings past their road, she was dimly aware of a shout. She hesitated, but hearing another shout and then a shriek coming from a lane running at an angle behind the main road, she took a step back. Glancing down, she saw nothing. It must be children playing, she thought, and began to move on. The shrieks grew louder and more alarming. Without making a conscious decision, she turned into the lane where several houses with shattered windows overlooked ruined tarmac. After the Second World War and the battle afterwards with the Vietminh, a few streets still awaited repair. She removed her shoes and, as far as her tight dress allowed, jumped over the rubble at the bend where trees hid the remainder of the narrowing lane from sight.

Now she could see half a dozen overexcited French boys. When she drew closer, she was horrified to see they were driving a little girl back against the wall behind a tree. The child, trapped with no escape from the circle of boys, looked younger than her tormentors, who seemed about thirteen. Nicole took it all in and ran closer.

'Métisse, métisse!' one of the boys chanted.

The others joined in, sneering at the girl, their faces twisting in contempt.

'Dirty métisse.'

'Go back where you belong.'

Nicole tensed, recognizing the child's tear-stained face as she was spun round, her bright blue skirt billowing out – Yvette! She didn't stop to think but tore down the lane. The boys saw her coming and most backed off, though the two biggest stood firm. One of Yvette's blue hair ribbons came loose and a boy snatched hold of her plait.

'Let her go,' Nicole commanded in her most authoritarian voice, trying to appear in control. She was vaguely aware of the sounds of the city around her: car horns, the creak of rickshaws, human voices, though she was more aware of her pounding heart.

'She's a métisse herself. Don't listen to her,' the tallest boy said.

Nicole smelt alcohol and glanced at the ground where wine bottles and cigarette ends lay discarded among the leaves and clumps of cement.

'But her father . . .' one of the smaller boys piped up.

Nicole raced towards the tallest boy, grabbed his collar and hit him with her shoes. 'My father will report you!'

Full of himself, he fought back, but one of her heels caught him in the temple. He stood still and, like any bully, began to whimper as he touched his head and saw the blood on his fingers.

Nicole narrowed her eyes. 'You ever touch her again . . .'

The boy gave her the finger but began to back off.

'That's it, run away like the cowards you are. Picking on a little girl! Very brave.'

Another boy turned to come back; one of the quiet ones at the back, whom she hadn't even noticed. He was thin and well-dressed and, now that she looked, seemed familiar. When she caught the glint of a knife in his hands, she glanced at Yvette.

'Run, Yvette,' she yelled and pointed behind her. 'Back that way. Run home, fast as you can.'

Yvette hesitated.

'Go. Now!'

As the little girl turned on her heels Nicole squared her shoulders and stood with her legs apart.

The boy sniggered before making a sudden dash at her, waving the knife in the air. She dodged but managed to catch him by the arm and twisted it roughly behind his back.

'Ow! You're hurting me!' he shouted.

'Drop the knife!'

He struggled and managed to free himself, but not before the knife had caught her on the cheek. He pushed her to the ground and she touched her face in shock, only vaguely aware of a man running past her. When she looked up she saw the man was now holding the boy by his throat. She was even more shocked when she saw him clearly and recognized Mark Jenson.

'Drop the knife, you little bastard,' he was shouting, while the boy made a terrible choking sound, his eyes wide with fright.

Nicole looked on in horror. For a moment it seemed as if the American might throttle the boy. She opened her mouth to shout out before things got any worse but then Mark released the youth, pushing him away at the same time. The boy staggered backwards but did not fall.

As boy and man stared at each other, she felt the touch of air on her skin. It seemed suddenly colder, the way it did when the sun went behind a cloud, and yet the sky remained a startling blue. The boy was still waving the knife in front of him and Nicole, feeling the sweat breaking out on her forehead, was certain that in a split second he would run at the older man. But then the moment went on too long and, clearly thinking better of it, the boy took a step back, dropping the knife.

Mark stepped forward and raised his fist. 'Now get the hell out of here.'

The boy ran off.

For a few moments everything had been too quiet but now she was aware of the sounds of the city breaking through.

Mark turned to her. 'Here,' he said and wrapped an arm round her waist. Then, as he lifted her up, she felt the warmth of his hand through her thin cotton dress.

'I was dealing with it,' she said, but they could both see she was unnerved.

She hardly dared examine her own feelings about being called a *métisse*, the now unsavoury name for mixed-race children, and smothered the burst of shame. It hadn't been like that before the Vietminh had taken power, albeit briefly. But now, as far as the French were concerned, being mixed-race and looking Vietnamese meant suspicious glances and whispers. It never happened to Sylvie, who looked almost entirely

French, but it wasn't the first time Nicole had been taunted, and it instantly exposed her own deep-felt insecurities.

The wind got up as Mark wiped the blood from her cheek with his fingers, then cleaned them on a handkerchief.

'Thank you,' she said. So much for looking polished, she thought, while attempting to repin a chignon that had never been right. She smoothed down her dress and paused, remembering who the boy was: Daniel Giraud. His father was the chief of police, a friend of her father's. That wouldn't go down well.

'Come on,' Mark said. 'I think we both need a drink.'

He helped her climb over the craters in the road before they headed towards the Boulevard Henri Rivière, where they walked beneath the shade of tamarind trees. Nearer the hotel, he slowed his pace. 'Are you feeling all right?'

'A bit shaken.'

She stopped to look at him properly. He wore a softly coloured checked shirt with linen trousers and was as clean-shaven as you'd expect an American to be. He looked as good in casual clothes as he had in a smart suit; better perhaps, she thought. She glanced across the street at the French high commissioner's residence, and hoped her father wasn't there, then they went through the large glass doors of the Métropole Hotel.

Mark ran his hand over the front of his hair, smoothing it back, then indicated the tea tables. 'Tea or something stronger?'

She smiled and gestured to the French windows at the back of the hotel.

Mark glanced out at the wide porticos surrounding the hotel gardens.

'Tea, out there in the shade,' she said. From the verandah they'd be able to listen to the band rehearsing old-fashioned dance music interspersed with the songs of Nat King Cole.

Once outside he pulled out her chair and she smelt something bitter-sweet, like anise and lemon, and felt his warm breath on the back of her neck.

They settled at a table next to three French army officers, one of whom laughed, raised a cigar in the air and waved it in Nicole's direction. She sniffed the smoke as it curled towards her and smiled at him.

'What about Hanoi? Do you like it here?' she asked Mark.

'It's a fantastic place for silk.'

'Is that what you do?'

'Indeed. I'm on a silk-finding mission.'

'We do have wonderful silk, though I'd love to go to China and India too. Have you been?'

As they drank their tea, Nicole examined him from beneath her heavy fringe. His face was not completely even. Head on, he was good-looking, but sideways you could tell his chin was slightly too angular. He had a straight nose and she had already noticed the faint lines fanning his eyes that deepened when he smiled. He seemed to be figuring things out as he surveyed the verandah. She knew all about that. Desperate to appear as French as her sister, she'd learnt to look for the little giveaways: the toss of a head, a certain aloofness, though she had never really been able to pull that off; above all, to be properly French, you needed to ooze an absolute sense of entitlement.

When his eyes focused on her face, she noticed the dark shadows beneath them making him seem older. He was a man, not a boy, and the first Nicole had been drawn to.

'So what about you?' he asked.

'Well, we used to live by the river in Huế and only came to Hanoi for Christmas, but we've lived here for five years now. You're lucky. All I ever wanted was to see the world and buy silk.' She shook her head and laughed at herself. 'I just don't want to stay in Hanoi all my life.'

At that moment a man came over with an unlit cigarette in his mouth. He spoke in a foreign language that Mark understood. He drew out his lighter, snapped it open and offered the flame to the other man before replying. A stream of what sounded like Russian then followed as Mark took control. Though Mark remained cool, the other man seemed to argue – or at least his voice was raised – but eventually he shrugged and walked away. Whatever it had been about, it looked like Mark had won the argument.

'Well,' Nicole said when the man was out of earshot, 'you speak Russian? What was that about?'

'It wasn't important.' Mark paused. 'My mother was Russian. White Russian. Her father was a university professor and when he and his wife were killed during the revolution, my mother fled the Bolsheviks for America.'

'But your father is American?'

'Yes. She married him soon after arriving in America and they had me straight away.'

Something about his tone prevented her from asking more. 'So how long are you here for?' she said, and twisted a lock of her hair round a finger.

'As long as it takes.'

The waiter appeared carrying a silver tray with a white pot of jasmine-scented tea and matching cups and saucers. She narrowed her eyes and glanced at Mark's hands as he thanked the man. They were not elegant office hands, but big hands accustomed to physical work.

It went quiet between them and once they'd finished their tea he sighed, checked his watch, then gazed at her, the skin around his eyes crinkling. 'I've really enjoyed seeing you, Nicole Duval. You're like a burst of fresh air.'

She pushed herself back in her seat and found she couldn't meet his eyes. They seemed to see right into her, and she didn't want to give herself away. Would a man like him ever be interested in her? When she did glance up she saw him straightening his tie and running a hand over his hair.

'Leaving already?'

He nodded. 'Sorry. I have a business engagement and I'm already late. It was great to see you again. If you're sure you're fully recovered I'll call you a taxi.'

She laughed. 'Do you know, I'd forgotten all about those boys.'

'If you like we could meet again, for coffee?'

'I like.'

'Morning coffee in three days' time? Shall we say nine thirty? Let's meet at the fountain outside the hotel.'

4

Nicole stood gazing at the swirling colour of a market in the Vietnamese quarter. It was easy to wander into the heart of the ancient streets, laced together by alleys aromatic with the smell of ginger and charcoal. She watched women traders shouting out their wares in shrill voices, their socks, shawls and cotton reels displayed on trolleys covered with straw and tarpaulin, while the men sat cross-legged on low stools, rolling dice on the pavement. Canaries sang in bamboo cages hanging from canopies outside narrow shops and the sun lit up particles of dust, making the air shimmer.

Despite all that, Nicole felt a little heavy-hearted. After the Japanese left at the end of the Second World War and Ho Chi Minh proclaimed Vietnam independent, a Vietnamese government had briefly been in power. But the French had fought back and, supported by Britain and America, regained their Indochinese empire. The silk shop had been closed all that time and it remained shut now, but she had decided to look it over anyway. She knew most girls of eighteen would be glad of a shop of their own to manage, but she'd been hoping, and had been given to believe, there would be so much more. She couldn't help feeling disappointed and hurt by the favouritism.

The history of the French in Indochina since they'd established their colonies in the nineteenth century had been drummed into Nicole all her life; they had elevated the country with their *mission civilisatrice*, their civilizing mission, building roads, schools, hospitals. But because Nicole had inherited her Vietnamese mother's looks, she looked too Vietnamese to fully belong with the French, and too French to belong with the Vietnamese. Before the war it hadn't mattered, but now, with so much suspicion in the air, it did. She searched the eyes of the young Vietnamese girls, whose conical hats bobbed up and down as they sold fried onions and broth, and saw herself in their bland but pretty faces. A high-pitched squealing came from behind. She twisted round to see a piglet running free from its makeshift pen. The creature scuttled across the street, past a row of chickens in cages and between the legs of traders and shoppers alike. The birds started squawking and flapping and a woman shrieked as she raced after her pig. Nicole watched the little drama play out and smiled. It might not be so bad to be based here. There was something happening all the time and it would never be boring.

Deeper into the old quarter the undulating rooftops of the narrow houses crowded together like drunken dominoes. She liked the thirty-six ancient streets, each devoted to selling one single thing: hats in Hang Non, copper plates and trays in Hang Dong, silk fabric on Hang Gai where the silk dyers lived, known to the French as Rue de la Soie.

She bought a sticky bun flavoured with coconut from a stall in Hang Duong, chewed it slowly, and carried on until she arrived at the oldest of their family's three Hanoi shops. She sat down on the step. It was midday in May and, apart from the humidity, the exuberance of a sunny day had now infected the place. There was laughter, the sound of a radio playing discordant music, and the constant movement of people, bicycles and animals mingling together as the fragrance of lotus flowers drifted in the air. Her spirits lifted.

A young woman, not much more than a girl, who sold silk thread with her mother, came out from the shop next door.

She was tiny, delicately pretty, her plaited hair hanging down her back in one thick rope. 'Hello,' the girl said. 'Is the shop yours?'

Nicole stood and gave a little bow. 'It is mine now, yes.'

'Will it open again soon? It is not good to leave it empty so long.'

Nicole glanced at the bales of fading fabrics still displayed in the upstairs window that, without a blind, kept an eye on the outside world. 'Maybe.'

'My name is O-Lan,' the girl said. 'Would you like a coffee?'

Nicole hesitated but the girl was beaming at her and waiting for a reply. 'Thank you. I'd love one. Can I just take a look inside and then come over after that?'

Nicole watched the silk birds twirling in the window of the shop and pictured the place bursting with racks of shiny new fabric, fresh upstairs curtains billowing in the breeze. The girl next door was friendly and although the silk shop itself looked a little shabby it didn't seem as bad as she'd expected. Much to her surprise, she was enjoying herself.

Once inside the shop she switched on the lights, then tugged on the front blinds. They rolled up with a snap, releasing clouds of dust. She held her nose, hurrying through the tube-like ground floor to the doors at the back, to throw them open. In the inner courtyard beyond the doors, she pulled at some of the yellow blooms of creeper populating most of the courtyard walls and obscuring part of the upper windows. The courtyard, open to the sky, was inhabited by a dozen cats who lay sleeping on the flagstones, soaking up the sun's warmth. Cats kept vermin down. The extinguished earthen oven, the broken pots on a bench and the well in the middle of the yard signalled the courtyard had been used as an outdoor kitchen. She took a quick look at a basic bathroom on the left and, accessed via the courtyard, an indoor kitchen and the servants' rooms beyond, currently in darkness. When she spotted a door at the back of the kitchen storeroom, she unbolted it and saw it led to a narrow alleyway. She glanced back at the main building where an exterior staircase curled up to the next floor, and saw that O-Lan had orange and red *hoa cuc*, chrysanthemum, growing in pots on her balcony. She made a mental note to buy some plants.

5

After a disturbed night, Nicole was woken far too early by the recurring dream. Only this time it wasn't a clammy nightmare. This time it happened on a windless day, when the lilac mist lay suspended over the river like an endless ocean. She had felt as if she was sinking beneath the surface of a lavender-coloured pool; above her the sunlight shimmered on the water growing ever stronger until the yellow globe of the sun filled the entire horizon. The key was not to struggle. The worst thing about the dream was the awful smell of fish and the fact that, for a second, Sylvie was in the dream too. It left Nicole feeling unsettled and that remained, even after the dream ended. They say you never die in a dream but, if you do, it means you won't wake up – so death, even in a dream, will always remain a mystery.

The day they'd left Huế to come to live in Hanoi had been one of those glorious bright blue days with a cool wind blowing down from China, and not the least bit muggy. Nicole had glanced at the icy morning water of the Perfume River that divided Huế and, despite everything, knew how much she'd miss their home on the southern tree-lined riverside.

No river to gaze at here in Hanoi, but the banyan and frangipani trees blew about in the breeze, the rain had gone, and with the sun settling over the garden, the peacocks next door were sleeping. She slipped down the stairs and found Lisa, who habitually rose at five to stoke the boiler. Today it was sluggish, unwilling to cooperate, and the room had filled with smoke. Lisa wiped the hair from her eyes, leaving smudges of coal dust on her face as she knelt beside it.

'Damn the old bastard!'

Nicole laughed. 'Are you talking about father?'

Lisa straightened up and rubbed her back. 'Course not. It's this bloody monster!'

'Language,' Nicole said as she opened the back door to let out the smoke.

'Why you up so early, little flower?'

'Couldn't sleep.'

Lisa carried on stoking and finally the heat began to build. She stood with her hands on her hips, still in an attitude of exasperation. 'Now that's done, I'll put on the coffee. So, any news?'

Nicole shrugged. Every time she thought about the unfairness of her father's decision, it brought her close to tears. 'I've been given the old silk shop, that's all.'

Lisa clucked and muttered, then, with wide sweeping movements, wiped the table as she spoke. 'Well, I suppose we all have to start somewhere. Now sit.'

Nicole pulled up a chair. 'Except for Sylvie. She's been handed the whole lot on a plate, and she doesn't even know as much about silk as I do. Why is he so unfair?'

Lisa puffed out her cheeks and tucked the wisps of straggling hair behind her ears. 'Some things are . . . I don't know, but after your mother died –'

Nicole interrupted. 'He blames me, doesn't he?'

'Not any more.'

'But he did?'

Lisa hesitated, as if there was something she wasn't ready to divulge. 'Darling girl, it was all so long ago. Why not look to the future? Prove to him you can do well.'

'I went to see the old shop.'

Lisa drew a sharp breath.

'What?'

'Well, there has been talk of a bomb going off in the old quarter. I just hope it's safe there.'

'Are the Vietminh close to Hanoi?'

'Probably not. You know what gossip is like.'

There was a brief lull.

'Shall I do your shoulders?'

Nicole nodded and Lisa came round to stand behind her, beginning to massage the knots away. 'Up to you to put the life back into the shop then.'

'I suppose. I did quite like it there.'

Lisa stopped rubbing and Nicole twisted round to look up at her. Something flickered across the cook's face and Nicole noticed her eyes were moist.

'I've always loved you, little one.' Lisa hesitated again. 'I know it's been difficult.'

Nicole felt a lump forming in her throat.

Lisa sighed. 'I think your father has his own guilt to bear and maybe sometimes he takes it out on you.'

'Why would *he* feel guilty?'

Lisa shook her head. 'Nicole, don't be too hard on your sister. She suffered too. Don't let that cool exterior fool you . . . And I've done my best to make up for what happened.'

'What happened in Huế wasn't your fault.'

'You have to make the best of it, my love. Come on, come here.' She held her arms out wide and Nicole got up and went to her.

With Lisa's arms embracing her, Nicole couldn't halt the flood of tears. Lisa patted her back and, when Nicole drew apart to wipe her cheeks, the cook smiled. 'There, that's better. A good cry never did anyone any harm. It's not as bad as you think.'

'Really?'

'You know this might still turn out for the best.'

*

Sylvie's bedroom was painted the palest shade of yellow, with white rugs and pale brocade drapes at the window. That evening Nicole tapped at the door, went in and sat down on her sister's satin bedspread.

Nicole sniffed as a light breeze from the garden blew in the mingled scent of smoke and mown grass. The room was still sunny and only the sound of a branch brushing the outside wall interrupted the silence. Sylvie had already changed into white silk pyjamas and smoothed down the curtain of wavy auburn hair she'd been growing for years, proud that it now reached her waist, without a split end in sight. As she began writing in her journal over by the dressing table at the window, Nicole gazed at the neat row of books on the bookshelf, the glass ornaments on the shelf above Sylvie's bed and the yellow and white roses on her dressing table, then she unwrapped a toffee and sucked on it. Her sister's room was sacrosanct, with a precise place for everything; if you valued your life, you didn't touch.

'I had tea with Mark Jenson yesterday,' Nicole said. 'At the hotel. There were officers and music.'

'I'm concentrating.'

'I rather like Mark. Doesn't he have the most amazing blue eyes?'

Sylvie bent her head and paused before she spoke. 'Isn't he a bit old?'

Nicole looked up at the ceiling. Was he too old? She turned to look at Sylvie again. 'What do you write about?'

'Are you bored, Nicole?' Sylvie closed the leather-bound journal and began filing her nails.

Nicole envied her sister's perfect nails, each one filed to the exact same curve. Her own split too easily, but with the summer ball fast coming up – the first Nicole would go to – she had to attend to them.

'What are you going to wear to the ball?' she asked.

'My secret.'

Nicole decided to wait until her sister was out and then search the room.

'I know what you're thinking and it's not in here!'

Nicole laughed. 'When did you become a mind reader?'

Sylvie shook her head and gazed at her sister, her hazel eyes a perfect mirror. 'You wear your heart on your sleeve. You're too transparent.'

Sylvie was the exact opposite. The two of them couldn't have been more different. You never knew what Sylvie was thinking or feeling.

'Have you never felt the impulse to rush into the street and dance naked under the stars?' Nicole said.

Sylvie laughed. 'Have you?'

Nicole stared at her sister. Why did she always look so calm? While Sylvie seemed barely aware of the unfairness of their current situation, Nicole was consumed by it.

'Tell me why Papa gave you the entire business.'

Sylvie shook a bottle of pink nail varnish and began to paint her nails. 'You know why. He's focusing on his governmental work.'

'And you know what that is?'

Sylvie looked up again and Nicole watched a single drop of nail polish drip on to the floor. Sylvie took out a tissue and wiped the polish away. She spotted Nicole's toffee paper, crouched down to pick it up and threw it in the bin.

'So?' Nicole said again.

'*Chérie*, I don't know any more about it than you.' Sylvie continued painting her nails. 'What I want to know is are you going to accept the offer of the silk shop or not? Because if you are we need to organize some protection there.'

'Protection?'

'Just a precaution.'

Nicole gazed at her sister's impassive features and took in the perfect symmetry of her face. Everyone envied Sylvie's flawless complexion and chiselled cheekbones; she was the girl who had everything. Sylvie seemed to be studying Nicole's face too, but then lowered her eyes and finished the final nail.

Suffocating black clouds gathered over the city the next day and time hung heavy. Nicole could hardly wait for the following morning when she would meet Mark and she wandered about the house and garden in a state of suspense. She wanted to talk to her father about the shop, but he seemed more distant than usual; when Nicole felt she could wait no longer, she walked into his office expecting him to be alone. Unfortunately she'd interrupted a visit from a high-ranking Vietnamese mandarin just as he was speaking about an underground network in Haiphong.

'Well? What do you want now?' her father snapped. 'This is a private conversation.'

'I didn't hear anything,' she said, feeling embarrassed. 'I only wanted to say I will accept the offer of the shop.'

'All right. Talk to Sylvie about it.'

The words 'French puppet' rang in her head as she backed out of the room. They had been daubed in red on their neighbour Madame Hoi's garden wall more than once. Could it be her father who was the puppet master? She was surprised when he seemed to change his mind and followed her out to the hall, closing the office door behind him.

'I had a phone call complaining about you,' he said in a lowered voice, 'and I must say I am not impressed.'

'What complaint?' She ran over all the things she'd done that her father could reasonably object to.

'It concerns Daniel Giraud. Apparently you pulled a knife

on him the day before yesterday. What on earth were you doing with a knife?'

She felt herself grow hot. The little sod hadn't wasted any time snitching. She tucked her hair behind her ears. 'That is not what happened. He had the knife. Look, I've still got the cut on my cheek! It wasn't me.'

'He is a small boy, timid too.'

'He may seem that way –'

She was cut short by her father's voice. 'I will not have my daughter behaving like a ruffian. You must write a letter of apology.'

'They were bullying Yvette. The boy's a racist, like his father.'

'Nevertheless, it is what you will do,' her father said. 'His father may be racist but he is the new chief of police, and this would have gone further had he not been an acquaintance of mine.'

He pointed outside. 'The best thing you can do with a knife is to cut the throats of those wretched birds.'

He turned on his heels and went back into his office.

She listened to the sounds of the world through the open window after he'd gone, then a little later she heard him showing his visitor out before going round to the back garden. His footsteps grew loud, and then they faded, so she tagged after him and saw he was sitting on a bench overlooking the pond, now covered in blossoms. Their sweet scent drifted over but he was holding his head in his hands, oblivious. He looked up, snapped off a rose from a nearby bush, sniffed it, then threw it on the path where he ground it down with his heel.

Despite their differences, and his increasingly short fuse, she knew he was worried about the unrest in the country. He didn't care to call it a war, though it was common knowledge that, not so very far beyond the city of Hanoi, battles were being fought and lost.

The flying insects were out in force now and the garden was in constant motion with a breeze rustling the leaves. She watched the wide branches of the pipal tree blowing sideways and the birds flying about in the area overlooking the ponds. A light mist wafted over the water as she picked a few wild daisies and then chatted to the gardener in Vietnamese while he watered the hedge of hydrangeas.

When her father noticed her he beckoned her over and moved to leave space for her beside him on the bench.

'I'm sorry I was brusque. I'm glad you've decided to take on the shop.'

'And I'm sorry to be ungrateful.' She paused. 'Papa, can I ask you something?'

'Of course.'

'Is it true the Vietminh are creeping closer to Hanoi?'

He stared at her. 'Why would you say that?'

'Because of the rumours. Lisa heard something about a bomb in the ancient quarter. And you've been so preoccupied, I thought it might be that.'

'It's nonsense. And even if the Vietminh do win the support of some rural villages, they will never beat the French army.' He drew a newspaper from his jacket pocket. 'See, no bomb.'

Nicole read the headlines. True enough, the bombing was denied, but she read that a French official had been assassinated by a Vietminh hiding in a bamboo grove.

She pointed at it. 'What about this assassination?'

'Unfortunate, but the fighting is far away in the paddy fields and mountains. It's the peasants who are suffering.'

'Do you hate the Vietnamese?'

Her father looked taken aback. 'Of course not. Your mother was Vietnamese. But we French have made the country what it is today. Us alone. And only we can rule it properly. Now I must be off. I have a late meeting with Mark Jenson.'

'He's nice, isn't he?'

Her father frowned. 'Best not to get too close to him, Nicole.'

'Why not? He's just a silk trader.'

Her father didn't reply.

'I'll start tomorrow at the shop, if that's all right. Give it a bit of a clean.'

He patted her hand and left.

It was almost night and when darkness came it would be virtually instantaneous. Nicole gazed out at the trees and could just about hear the song of the night birds above Lisa's clattering in the kitchen. She pulled her light wool wrap around her and felt as if she was poised on the edge between two different worlds; one all human activity, where it was sometimes hard to fit in, and one nature's own province. And there the rules were different. As she watched the orange sky turn the water in the ponds bright yellow, she became aware of something unfamiliar inside her. It was a tingling undercurrent of excitement that had everything to do with Mark. She didn't know why her father had warned her off, but decided to ignore it. There was a rustle of leaves as the wind got up again, followed by a soughing in the branches of the pipal tree and the creaking of its trunk. When complete darkness wrapped around her, she imagined Mark sitting there too.

6

The next day, Nicole's first at the silk shop, Sylvie helped her wrap a black piece of fabric, a *khan dong*, round her long hair, forming a tube. They agreed it was better if Nicole wore Vietnamese clothing when she was there, and so she had on a peacock blue *áo dài* over black silk trousers.

Nicole took a bow, and laughed when she looked at her reflection. She was excited not only to be starting at the shop but also because, at last, she'd be seeing Mark again.

'Now I don't look French at all,' she said and wondered what he'd think when he saw her dressed like this.

'Only at the shop. You can be French at home if you want, though of course you never will be.'

'Neither of us will be, Sylvie.'

'No. You're right.'

A little later Nicole was sitting by the fountain opposite the Métropole. A typical city morning, the light breeze carried the damp smells of the leafy trees surrounding the lakes. Soon it would heat up and, beneath the harsh sunlight, the streets would be bleached of colour. But she was early so she watched the birds peck at the gravel and the flow of glittering water as it fell.

Although she loved the moving reflections on the green water of Hoàn Kiếm Lake above anywhere else in Hanoi, this spot was her favourite place at the start of the day before the traffic built up. While she waited she thought about her father. You never knew who Papa was dealing with, nor why, but after his comment about Mark she had felt curious about why the two men were meeting. If Mark was only a silk trader surely it would be Sylvie he'd be dealing with now? Her father had been developing relations with the Americans for some time and she felt certain it had started when he had joined Sylvie in New York for a few weeks. And she knew he had assisted the Americans in their efforts to aid the Vietnamese in their fight against the Japanese because she'd overheard the phone calls when she was a child.

As she was thinking, she caught sight of Mark. He stood with his back to her outside the hotel, hands in his pockets, talking to someone. Arms hanging loosely by her sides, she waited, and her heart leapt when he turned and strode across.

'I almost didn't recognize you dressed like that,' he said.

She grinned, delighted by his obvious pleasure at seeing her. Where she could see the colour of his face and forearms, it was clear his tan was deepening, and when he smiled she saw how white his teeth were, and that his hair, darker at the roots, had been lightened by the sun.

'Coffee?' he said.

As they walked, the sun on the pavements shone silver. She listened to the rhythm of his footsteps and kept pace with him, aware of his closeness and the restless energy he seemed to have.

'I'm taking over our family's oldest silk shop. It's my first day there today.' Suddenly shy, she mumbled, 'Hope I can actually do it.'

He stopped walking and gave her a broad smile, then held her upper arms for a moment as if to pass his own confidence through to her. 'You're the girl who wants to travel the world, right?'

She nodded.

'You choose your life, Nicole. At least to some extent.'

Something about the persistence of his gaze unsettled her. How could she resist a man with eyes as blue as his and a smile so irresistible that it lit up his whole face? It affected her so much that she could actually feel it physically. She stiffened and wondered what he thought of her dark, shallow-set eyes and lack of height.

He let her go and put an arm round her shoulders. 'Come on.'

At the cafe, she waited in the queue with him while he ordered. The place looked brighter, more cheerful than usual, though everything seemed beautiful when she was with him. As they went to sit at a window table, she laughed at herself for being fanciful. When she noticed Mark studying her face, she looked away.

'Tell me to shut up, but I can't help think there's something wrong.'

Nicole sighed. 'I didn't think it showed.'

'So?'

She hesitated and gave him a quick glance, but his closeness brought her buried feelings to the surface. 'It's nothing. I'm just still smarting over the fact that all I've got is the old silk shop whereas Sylvie has been given the entire business.' She paused and listened to the clink of coffee cups and the conversations happening around her, then glanced out at the street. Even though she liked him, how far could you trust a stranger with your heart?

There was a short silence.

'So I'm not going to be a buyer after all.'

He smiled. 'Give it time. Where is this silk shop, anyway?'

'In the ancient quarter. I've decided to make the best of it. I look Vietnamese enough. I love silk. The smell of it. The feel of it. I'm good with silk.' She smiled. 'Or rather, silk is good with me.'

'Have you any special plans for the shop?'

She laughed. 'First, I'm going to stock up with disinfectant and a mop. The place looks as if it needs a good clean. After that I'd like to make it so enticing that customers can't resist coming in and buying.'

Mark touched her hand. 'Is there anything else you'd like to do?'

She smiled. 'Well, I loved singing and acting at school.'

'I meant with me. How about swimming? Or a trip out on the lake?'

She twisted her face. 'I'm not so good with boats.'

'I'll row. All you need do is lean back and look beautiful.'

She laughed. 'A tall order.'

'You have no idea, do you?'

'Of what?'

He leant across and touched her cheek. 'You are so beautiful and you just don't know it.'

It was enough to make the heat crawl up her neck and she lowered her eyes in confusion. Was he laughing at her? She hated the thought that she might be nothing more than a diversion to him. A toy. Someone to joke around with but not to take seriously.

The rain looked as if it was on its way back, though sunlight still filtered through the trees in patches; one of those strange days when the darkness and the sunlight fought each other.

'Do you believe I can make a go of the shop? I've done some stupid things. Embarrassed my father. He thinks I can't be trusted. Sylvie has never set fire to a marquee, nor taken off on a bus to Saigon without telling anyone. And I was always in detention at school for talking too much and spilling ink.'

'We all do stupid things when we're young.'

'That makes you sound ancient. How old are you?'

'Thirty-two.'

There was a crash of thunder and she looked up.

'Trust me,' he said. 'It will all work out. Just prove to your father that you can make the shop a success.'

He smoked a Chesterfield and they talked for a little longer. Too soon he scraped back his chair.

She was anxious for it not to be over so she blurted out, 'What are you doing with Papa? It must be something that isn't silk. Are you working for the French?'

His look did not change, but the split-second pause before he answered bothered her.

'Why say that?'

'Because Sylvie's in charge now, so it should be her you're working with, not Father.'

'I shall be, with your father's help. Though none of us want to see the spread of communism across South East Asia, do we?' He reached out a hand to her but she pulled back a little. She felt the intensity of his look was capable of making her so self-conscious that even the sound of her own voice might become strange to her.

'So I'll pick you up tomorrow at six and we'll watch the sun going down over the lake. It'll be fine.'

She wanted to question him further, but he stood up and, with long strides, left the cafe. She bounded after him, only to find that he had paused outside. When she bumped straight into him he gave her the lightest of kisses on the lips, sending a thrill through her entire body. She pushed back the hair from her face and, still spinning from the sensation, wanted more; he must have known it, but he drew back as if thinking better of it.

By the time Nicole had finished her shopping, the air was laced with the smell of drains, although it wasn't too unpleasant as the aroma of freshly baked pastries was stronger. This place was like that. Good and bad mixed up together. Luckily the clouds had passed over and children were running about doing chores for their mothers or playing in the gutters, though goodness knows what they might pick up from the slimy brown water or the clouds of mosquitoes thickening the air.

Nicole stood at the entrance to the shop with the key in her hand. Next to her a crippled man held out a carton of fried greens and ginger-marinated bean curd from where he sat on the pavement. She turned to give him some coins and exchange a few words.

She heard a radio playing Vietnamese music and glanced at the upstairs window of the narrow silk shop opposite. Not as colourful and smaller than theirs, it stocked lengths of inferior fabric for curtains. As the widow of the man who had previously managed the Duval silk shop scowled down at her from behind a partially closed curtain, Nicole caught sight of her teeth. The woman still had hers enamelled in black; obviously a member of the old school who believed white teeth were only suitable for the fangs of dogs. When Nicole lifted her hand in greeting, the curtain whipped across and the woman disappeared.

She heard someone behind her and spun round but it was only a trader selling grilled spring rolls. The smell of charcoal from his stove hung in the air. As she glanced across she noticed a young man staring at her. He had the typically wide face of the Vietnamese, thick eyebrows and dark shallow-set eyes. She nodded at him and slid the key into the lock, but before she could go inside the man had come across.

'You running it now?' he said, showing the gap between his front teeth.

'I am.'

He had spiky black hair, was barefoot and wore dark *áo bà ba*, the typical rural working-men's pyjamas.

'You look better like that,' he said, and touched her sleeve.

She sniffed and glanced down at her clothes. 'Have you been watching me?'

He inclined his head and began rolling a cigarette. 'Maybe.'

As she turned away she sensed he had moved off too. There had been a hint of arrogance about him and it crossed her mind he might be the 'protection' Sylvie had said she would organize. She looked over her shoulder to see him melt into the medley of street hawkers selling sticky rice puddings from their baskets.

Once inside, Nicole explored the poky downstairs rooms of the shop, noting the stained wooden beams, the ancient carvings and the dark tiled floors; most rooms, divided only by decorative wooden trellises, provided no privacy at all. She had not broached the subject yet, but her idea was actually to live here as well as manage the shop. It would be a startling departure and she was anxious about it, but it would give her the independence she craved. A place she could be herself without Sylvie breathing down her neck or her father telling her what to do and how to think.

Upstairs it smelt musty, but she was relieved when close scrutiny revealed that the silk stored there in zinc-lined wooden chests was safe. The trunks had been locked and only she had the keys.

Nicole opened the drawers of an old chest. The last people had left their rubbish behind so she bundled it all into a sack. In the bottom drawer she spotted an old purse covered in dust. She was about to throw that into the sack too but shook it first. Dust flew everywhere, and she began to cough, but another look revealed the purse was made of hand-embroidered silk. A Vietnamese antique, faded and a little threadbare, but still beautifully decorated with a mythical creature. She ran her fingertips over it, knowing she held the past in her hands. She turned the purse over and, as she did, she could almost hear the voice of its original owner. As she held it against her heart, she felt part of something special; the history of silk and the history of the Vietnamese people was her history too, and it had been woven into this little purse.

With a French father, a French cook and a sister who, although mixed-race, looked French, Nicole knew the Vietnamese side of her life had rarely been given any space. Her mother's parents had disowned her when she'd married a Frenchman, and Nicole had not only never met them but had absolutely no idea where they lived. The French had been dominant for so long in Vietnam that Nicole had always assumed she'd let the family down by looking the way she did. She was the only one who spoke the language perfectly and often wished she had her Vietnamese mother to talk to. As far as the rest of the world was concerned, if it hadn't been for Nicole's looks, they'd have thought the Duval family was wholly French.

She cleaned out the top drawer, wrapped the purse in an off-cut from a bale of silk and carefully replaced it.

After a couple of hours of sweeping, swallowing dust and mopping, Nicole brushed herself down. She had eliminated the smell of cats but not a putrid smell rather like rotten vegetation. Next time she'd bring a bunch of *shi* leaves to deodorize the place. She was hot and sticky but it had been worth the effort. As she'd walked from room to room upstairs she'd uncovered some dark wood furniture inlaid with mother-of-pearl, and also a velvet chaise longue.

In a cool dark room at the back overlooking the courtyard, she found an altar of incense and rotten green mangoes. She cleaned it up and opened the window, leaving it ajar for air to circulate, then stood still for a moment. Though Nicole was not sure she believed in God, she could feel the peace from what must have been decades of usage.

The afternoon was closing in. Once the heat built up you longed to feel the cooler evening hours were on their way. She had been thinking of a bubble bath to dissolve the smell of cats when she was startled by a rooster crowing. Her head shot up and she spotted the young man she'd seen before, now staring at her through the window. He loosened the scarf at his neck and she noticed the tip of what looked like a purple birthmark.

She went outside to confront him. 'Why are you here?'

'That creeper at the back could be useful. Better to keep things out of sight.' He tapped his nose.

'I have no idea what you're on about.'

He drew out a packet of matches and, inhaling deeply, lit a cigarette.

'What is your name?'

'You may call me Trần.'

'Well, Trần, if that is your name, I want you to go before I call the police.'

'You will soon be needing me.' He grinned, showing the gap in his teeth again. 'The Vietminh are already here in Hanoi.'

'You know nothing about it. You're just an overgrown buffalo boy!'

He flicked his fringe away from his eyes and bowed before walking to the other side of the street.

Though longing to get back home for her bath, she ducked back inside and kept watch for a little while, looking through the slats of the blind. A convoy of military cars went by, a rare sight in the old quarter, though it seemed more of the French army were arriving in the city now. Across the street a grandmother dragged a protesting child out to a bathtub she'd prepared on the narrow pavement. She dumped the child in the water and began to scrub its thin back. Nicole grinned.

Here in the old quarter, life was lived outside. She liked that. It felt open and honest. A tea boy approached, his bamboo pole balanced across his shoulders; along its length tiny tin cups, pipes and teapots rattled a tune as they swung. The young Vietnamese man, Trần, paused to speak to him. This was her chance. She slid out of the shop, quickly locked the door and slipped away.

Round the corner she passed an old Vietnamese woman who was airing her views for all the world to hear.

'They don't care, the French,' the woman was saying.

Nicole slowed her pace.

'My neighbour says there's been a bomb,' a younger woman said. 'Not far from you. Got it from the doughnut pedlar. Did you hear it?'

'No, but my nephew said everyone round his way was talking about it.'

The other person lowered her voice. Nicole couldn't catch it all but made out that they both believed the Vietminh were closer to Hanoi than anyone suspected, just as the young man had said.

And they'd spoken of a bomb. Again. Her father had told her there had been no bomb, had even shown her the newspaper denying it. She felt suddenly nervous. Even though many were still loyal to the French, she hated not knowing who to trust. Now overhearing this conversation, it worried her to think that the situation might be worse than anyone in her family was willing to admit.

7

As Mark and Nicole passed the large ponds around the banks
of the lake, she pointed out the sea of fragrant pink and white
lotus flowers coating their surface. Climbing out of the rickshaw, her worries about the ancient quarter evaporated and
she suddenly felt so happy that her fear of being in a small boat
faded a little. A blind beggar man, squatting on the bank, took
no notice of them, but after a few minutes of searching they
identified the man in charge of boats, smoking and drinking
coffee at the water's edge beside a wooden jetty. He glanced
pointedly at his watch when Mark made his request, only
agreeing when offered a few extra dollars.

The sun was still warm and as she'd forgotten her hat Mark
lent her his straw boater. He had on a crisp white shirt that
seemed to make his skin glow, and she wore a kingfisher-blue
shirtwaister.

'Maybe high heels weren't such a good idea,' she said and
laughed nervously as the boatman passed her a cushion. She
made herself comfortable. 'I should have worn pumps.'

Mark laughed. 'You're fine.'

Once he'd climbed in, he rolled up his shirtsleeves and took
hold of the oars. The boat slid away from the jetty. As he
rowed, Nicole watched the sun catch the gold hairs on his forearms. His outdoor upbringing had made him muscular and,
remembering how quickly he'd responded to danger when
he'd grabbed Daniel Giraud by the throat, she could see he
would never be destined for an ordinary office job. Nor was he
a man you'd ever want to cross. She wondered if that bothered

her. You'd need to know, she thought, before committing yourself to wanting him as much as she felt she already did. She smiled to herself. As if there was any choice.

When they reached the centre of the lake he stopped rowing and smiled at her. 'Happy?'

She nodded and watched the surface of the lake blur into a mix of pink and gold. 'They don't usually let you on the lake so late in the day.'

'I wanted us to be out here together, even if only for a few minutes. I used to swim to the middle of our lake at sunset when I was a kid.'

'How romantic.'

He grinned. 'Not sure I thought that when I was twelve.'

'So why did you do it?'

'I know I don't always express myself in the way I'd like to, but it was like being in another world. After my mother died I felt locked up inside and it was only on the lake I could feel close to her.'

The lake and air shimmered as the light continued to change from pale yellow to a deep seductive pink. And he was right, the everyday world of Hanoi seemed to have disappeared, its sound muted and distant; now all she heard was the gentle lapping of the water and the sound of evening birds as they swooped and dived. The trees around the lake were dark and shadowy and it might have seemed lonely had she not been with him. She soaked in every detail and her nerves dissolved in the simple peace of this luminous world. Then, feeling in complete harmony with the lake, the trees, the birds and, best of all, with Mark, she felt herself let go.

Despite the mention of his mother he seemed to be in complete control – possession even – of the boat, the lake, and also the evening itself. As he smiled at her, his face, bathed in the fading light of the setting sun, added to the romantic mood of the setting. Then, for some reason, she felt a twinge of apprehension.

'I don't want to leave,' she said. 'But maybe we should head back before the light fails.'

'Don't worry. There's time. Would you take the oars for a moment? I've got my camera and want to just take a shot of you.'

He handed over the oars, then took out his camera from a small bag. Although he seemed perfectly balanced as he stood up, a real surge of anxiety gripped her. The fear of water had never really left her since the awful time when she and Sylvie had taken a boat out alone on the Perfume River.

'You don't need to row. I just want to catch you looking as if you are rowing. Can you lean forward?'

'You think I can't row?' She laughed. 'I can row.'

She made a sudden movement as if to row. It shook the boat and it rocked. Mark lost his footing, sat down abruptly and, in the sudden confusion, she reached out to him and dropped the oar over the edge. She felt embarrassed and stupid.

'Now that's novel,' he said and laughed.

'Sorry!'

With just one oar they could only go round in circles. Mark attempted to summon the boatman, but without success. He stood up again, intending to kneel at the edge, then lean over to try and catch hold of the lost oar, now caught up in a lotus blossom. But still with the camera in one hand, he moved too quickly; the boat rocked, he lost his balance and in a flash tipped over the edge and into the water. For a moment her blood ran cold and she screamed, but it quickly became clear he was safe. As he climbed back in, she began to laugh. She watched him as he shook his head to remove the water from his hair.

'Hey! That's me you're splashing,' she said as he did it again.

His white shirt was soaked and almost transparent and she could see every line of his arms and chest. Her throat felt full and she swallowed; she had never felt a longing so total that it made her heart race and her breath shorten like this. For a few seconds they stared at each other, neither able to speak, it seemed. She pulled her gaze away, suddenly embarrassed by the intimacy.

She spotted that he'd dropped the camera inside the boat, and not in the lake, so she picked it up and took a photo of him dripping with water, smiling as she did so. Then they waited, but as the sun sank into the horizon the boatman still hadn't appeared. She felt safe with Mark but shivered when she remembered the cold darkness of the river the time she had fallen in.

'So?' she said. 'What now?'

He shrugged. 'That water is freezing!'

'Serves you right for showing off!'

She spotted a point of light on the lake then heard the sound of oars being dragged through water. They both twisted round to look. The supposedly blind beggar was rowing out with a spare oar.

The top floor bathroom was shared by the sisters. Painted white and tiled in shiny aquamarine, one side was in perfect order and the other was littered with pins, clips, hairbands and pots of face cream. A large art-deco mirror covered one wall, the floor was tiled in black and white, and if you looked out of the window you gazed down on tropical fronds.

Sylvie had insisted they have two separate bamboo storage cupboards so their belongings wouldn't get muddled, and Nicole rarely bothered to glance in her sister's. This time, while she filled the bathtub, she ran her fingers over the contents of Sylvie's shelves: Super-Rich All Purpose Crème, Cleansing Oil and Skin Lotion – all three Estée Lauder – were on the bottom shelf, with various shampoos and soaps on the shelf above. Among the pretty perfume bottles on the top shelf was Sylvie's favourite, Coeur Joie, a Nina Ricci fragrance. Nicole, shorter than Sylvie, needed to stand on the tips of her toes to reach. She managed to safely slide the bottle forward and, after she removed the stopper, dabbed it behind her ears. But when she slid it back in, she felt something else. She pulled a small box out and opened it. Inside were two bottles of pills, one labelled Benzedrine and the other Dexedrine, both with Sylvie's name on the labels. But why was Sylvie taking pills? As far as Nicole knew, these were both amphetamines. She felt suddenly anxious. Was her sister unwell?

She put them back, then lay in the lovely hot water to soak and think of Mark. The unfamiliar feelings crowded her thoughts. She felt happy and excited at the same time. Most of all she felt thrilled that by taking her out on the lake he had shared something private and special with her. And now, as she soaped her skin, she felt like a woman who was falling in love but who couldn't quite believe it was happening.

She had finished towelling her hair and was absently picking at the paint coming adrift from the door frame, still thinking of Mark, when there was a tap at the door and Sylvie came in.

'What is it?' Nicole said.

Sylvie walked over to the square of darkness at the window. 'Shall I close the shutters? I don't like a black window. Makes me think of death.'

Nicole shrugged, but understood. It was like when you saw the moon reflected in the water and all your life felt upside down. And sometimes she didn't look out at the blackness, for fear the ghosts at the bottom of the garden would hide behind the trees, and the rustles would not be the leaves and the wind at all, but the voices of the dead.

'Afraid the ghosts will get you?' she said.

'There are no ghosts.'

'You're the one who told me about the bodies. Buried by the Japanese, you said.'

'Bodies are not the same as ghosts.'

Nicole laughed and began combing her damp hair. 'You have no imagination.'

'Well, we know that the Japs shot French people at the end of the war. It stands to reason some might be buried here.'

After closing the shutters Sylvie turned her back on the window and seemed to be thinking as she glanced around. She handed Nicole a white towelling gown and shot her a smile. 'Let's go through to your room.'

Nicole had tidied up the piles of books on the floor, but her glass beads hung in random strings from a hook on her dressing table, and a topless red lipstick had been left to dry up in an open drawer. A little pot of powder lay where it had fallen into the handbasin and a few items of clothing lay in a jumble on the floor near her bed.

Sylvie picked up the pot and a cloud of powder flew in her face, making her sneeze.

Nicole grinned.

Sylvie wiped the powder from her face with her fingers. 'Very funny . . . Anyway, I wanted to talk about the shop. We have to think of your future.'

Nicole pulled a face. 'Like marrying a nice Vietnamese man?'

'Papa didn't mean that.'

Nicole studied her sister's face and wanted to tell her about going out on the lake with Mark, but something made her change her mind. 'You always know how to cope with Papa, don't you?' she said instead.

Sylvie blushed slightly and had the grace to smile. 'About the shop. You do realize that if you make a go of it you'll be able to earn a good income? You are serious about it, aren't you?'

'Of course. I've already begun the cleaning.'

'And will you try to finish your studies too?'

Nicole shook her head. 'I don't see how I can if I'm running the shop.'

'True. Better to focus on the shop. Papa will understand that.'

'I'm looking forward to it. But, Sylvie, why are you taking pills? I came across them in the bathroom.'

Sylvie frowned. 'You were nosing in my cupboard?'

'But what are they for? Are you ill?'

Sylvie seemed to hesitate. 'Just headaches and tiredness.'

Nicole nodded. Since seeing Mark again the unfairness of the division of the business no longer seemed to matter so much and she felt for her sister. 'It's not surprising. You're taking on a lot.'

She watched the breeze from the open window lift the muslin curtains, shifting the air in the room. 'What's happening to the house in Huế?' she asked. 'Are we selling?'

'Papa has appointed a submanager to operate the buying there. He'll live in the house.'

'Well, I'm determined to make the shop a success.'

'I'm glad.'

'Do you know about the assassination in the bamboo grove?' Nicole said.

Sylvie nodded. 'And the possibility of more to come. Still, I suppose the Vietminh could shoot somebody here if they had a mind.'

When Nicole couldn't sleep again that night she opened the shutters and braved the ghosts. The moon was full but the garden was surprisingly peaceful, with every leaf and every blade of grass glowing like silver. It smelt woody out there and the air was thick and syrupy. She thought about what the young man had said to her at the shop: *You will soon be needing me.* Surely he'd been lying? Nobody believed they would lose against the Vietminh – the French army far outnumbered the rebels. Everyone said so. But a small voice echoed in her head – what if everyone was wrong? She'd heard her father talking about an underground network in the port of Haiphong. In contrast to the 570 kilometres they'd driven from Huế to Hanoi, Haiphong was less than a hundred kilometres away. What if the Vietminh were already in Hanoi in larger numbers than anyone imagined? *Ân đền oán trả* – An eye for an eye, a tooth for a tooth. What if the world they all lived in was about to change for ever? She shook her head. For all she complained about her father and Sylvie, she didn't want to lose them. And if the worst happened, who would care about the little silk shop or a young mixed-race girl with hopes of success, and maybe even love?

8

A pan was rattling on the stove and, as steam filled the air, Lisa sang at the top of her voice to an old French song on the radio. Nicole gazed at the kitchen window. Several days had passed since their outing on the lake but she hadn't heard from Mark. The hot, wet season was setting in and it wasn't so bright outside; the day looked likely to be miserably humid. But a crusty golden loaf lay on the table and the sight of that always made things better. She picked at the skin round the edges of her nails and watched as the cook stopped singing and began to sway while chopping some red peppers. The lovely scent of their freshness filled the room.

'Are your eyes closed?' Nicole asked.

'You think I'd chop with my eyes shut!'

'Well, there are sometimes strange things floating in the soup.'

Lisa swiped at her with a dishcloth. 'Impudent child!'

Nicole ducked then went back to picking her skin. 'What are we having today?'

'Rabbit. I caught it myself. Anyway, why haven't you opened the shop yet?'

Nicole shrugged. 'I'm having the courtyard painted and the kitchen spring-cleaned. The smell is too strong for the customers.'

There was a rap at the back door. When Lisa went over to open it, Nicole caught sight of an urchin, who handed something over. The cook closed the door.

'It's for you. Who is sending you little notes, my butterfly?'
Lisa passed her an envelope and sat down to roll a cigarette.
Nicole glanced at her name on the front. Straightaway she got up to leave.

'Secret assignation, right?' Lisa said with a laugh.

'Right!' Nicole laughed.

When she reached the hall, she tore open the envelope and first of all glanced at the signature on the notepaper. Mark. Relief flooded through her as she read that he wanted to meet at Les Variétés that afternoon at four. It would be worth her while, he said. Her first response was to whoop out loud, after which she flew upstairs, all the time working out what to wear.

By ten to four Nicole was pacing the pavement outside Les Variétés, Hanoi's oldest theatre and considered rather down-market. So as not to be late or get wet, she had taken the tram rather than walk, but by the time she arrived the drizzle had died down and patches of blue patterned the sky. The theatre was situated on a crossroads and if she stood outside the imposing front door she could see every direction from which Mark might approach.

She'd never been inside, though Papa had taken her and Sylvie to the French musical appreciation society, the Société Philharmonique. But, much to her father's disappointment, it was not the kind of music Nicole liked. After that he'd taken her to see a visiting French theatre company perform Molière at the Municipal Theatre, known by the Vietnamese as the Western Theatre. It was a beautiful building with arches and domes, but as it had only served to increase her longing for excitement, the visit had not been repeated. The place she loved best and went to alone was the beautiful Cinéma Palace, with its wonderful arched entrance, on what the Vietnamese called Trang Tien Road. Her favourite films recently had been *The Red Shoes* and *The Three Musketeers*.

What Papa liked was listening to the French military band playing in a square near to the lake. Luckily they weren't there today, and as she waited for Mark she watched the flower girls from the villages. Daily they brought in flowers loaded up in great panniers either side of skinny little donkeys. You always saw the girls squatting along with the birds at the edge of the road circling the lake. The scent of the flowers was overpowering and as Nicole took a few steps away she collided with a boy on a bicycle loaded with dozens of baskets intended for steaming dumplings. He tried to persuade her to buy, but when she laughed and told him she was French he called her a *métisse* and spat on the ground. She felt upset but was not going to let it spoil her afternoon.

Soon after she heard Mark call her name. She swivelled round. How confident he looked, she thought, with his arms swinging and a spring in his step.

'On time, I see,' he said and gave her a wide smile.

'I was early.'

'Well, you look lovely.' He touched her hair, lifting it slightly away from her face. 'I like your hair loose like this.'

She grinned with pleasure. After several changes she had decided on a red slim-fitting dress, reaching just below the knee, with a flat broad-brimmed straw hat in cream which she now held in her hand. She felt elegant and knew the outfit made her seem older.

As he held out a hand, she felt the thrill of being with him again.

'Shall we?'

Once inside the theatre it took a few moments for her eyes to adjust to the dark. When they did she gazed at an old-fashioned music hall complete with red velvet seats and oil lamps fixed to the walls, though on closer inspection she saw they had been converted to electricity. The smell of grease-paint, sweat and stale perfume filled her with a thrilling new sensation.

She felt her blood pumping faster as they walked down the central aisle, where a man sitting in the front row twisted round and called out to them.

'Hurry along now. Have you brought your sheet music?'

The sound of hammering came from the wings, and as the cleaners swept and polished it was noisy in the large auditorium too. Nicole hesitated. 'Are you talking to me?'

'No, the curate's prostitute! Of course I'm talking to you. I hope your voice is better than your brain appears to be.'

Mark had been watching her with amusement and now he stepped in. 'Jerry, this is Nicole. The girl I told you about. I'm afraid I got her here on false pretences, but she tells me she can sing. Is she too late to audition?'

'Audition!' she gasped, staring at him in disbelief.

'A friend of yours is always welcome, Mark. Come along, dear, tell me what songs you know.'

'Go on,' Mark said, keeping his bright blue eyes on her. 'The worst that can happen is you'll freeze.'

'Or die!' she said and pulled her hand away. What if she made a mess of it? What if she had to face their embarrassed laughter?

'Nicole, this is your chance,' he whispered. 'You have to take it. The theatre company are encouraging popular musical theatre back into Hanoi.'

As the sounds of the world ebbed and flowed, her palms began sweating. Wondering how she'd ever sing, she steadied her nerve, handed Mark her hat and climbed up the three steps to the stage. From the moment she began singing 'I'll Be With You in Apple Blossom Time' unaccompanied, the background noise of the theatre and the din of the distant city faded. Inside the theatre, the bright lights, the rows of seats and the people working blended into one. As her voice soared she felt as light as air; no longer the overlooked younger sister, it was as if she'd discovered another aspect of herself. She felt buoyed up, high on her own ability, and never in her life had she felt more at home. When she finished, the feeling welled up inside her with such force it nearly spilled over in tears.

Jerry began to clap, Mark joined in and also the carpenters who had been tapping away in the wings. Nicole took a bow.

'No need for that just yet,' Jerry said, but his jaw twitched with amusement.

'So does she get a part?' Mark asked.

'I'm sure I can find her something.'

Mark handed Jerry a note. 'Nicole's phone number,' he said.

Then he came up to the stage and, with light glinting in his eyes, he held out his arms. Full of gratitude, she jumped right into them and he swung her round. As he put her down his hands remained on her back for longer than was necessary. She leant in towards him slightly and felt the warmth as his hands slid up a little way. He let go and took a step back, but something had passed between them; she felt it was a moment from which there would be no turning back. He hadn't kissed her yet, not properly, but she felt sure it wouldn't be long.

'Thank you. Thank you so much,' she said.

He smiled. 'Now look, I'm going to be away for a few weeks, but if you don't hear from Jerry in a day or two, come back and remind him.'

She nodded and smiled, not wanting her disappointment to show. Now she would have to live without him, even though it wasn't for long.

'So all you've got to do is figure out how to tell your father.'
'Oh no,' she said, 'I shan't tell him.'

A week later, and with the night of the summer ball at the Métropole Hotel coming up in July, Nicole slipped into Sylvie's room to see if she could find something to give her a clue about her sister's dress. She looked in the large oak wardrobe where Sylvie hung her dresses and blouses in colour-coded order. As she ran her fingertips over the pretty greys and champagne-coloured silks she acknowledged that Sylvie had been telling the truth: the dress wasn't there. Sylvie's clothes were stylish and elegant, however, and while she had the chance, Nicole tried on a couple of her sister's embroidered blouses. She moved this way and that in front of the mirror, but she was far more petite than Sylvie and they swamped her. She peeled them off, took a peek in Sylvie's underwear drawer and found her journal. She leafed through it and a photograph of a dress fell out. This was it. Not the usual classic design her sister favoured – the dress was adorned and a little extreme – but Sylvie was always ahead of the pack when it came to fashion; Nicole decided to make a few alterations to her own outfit.

Later, on her way back from the tailor, she noticed a flutter of leaflets blowing about in the wind. They'd been slipped under the doors of most of the shops. Written by hand with crude pen drawings and all in Vietnamese, she could read enough to see this was propaganda on the part of the Vietminh. They showed smiling peasants carrying arms and food to the battlegrounds, and also carrying the injured on their backs and on makeshift stretchers. She pocketed one with the intention of giving it to her father later.

The old quarter was built in the shape of a triangle and she usually walked home by one familiar route, but now she needed to go back a different way. The dying sun caught the tiled rooftops and they glowed bright orange; it was beautiful in the streets. Ahead of her the street-stall lamps were burning, tarpaulins slung over supporting poles in case it rained, and the evening braziers were lit. Nicole paused for a moment, and succumbed to the tempting aroma of fried chicken. The trader, in his loose shirt and baggy trousers, handed her two pieces wrapped in a leaf-lined bowl. Straight from the wok, it was coated in spice and utterly delicious.

After she'd finished, she wiped the grease from her chin and walked on, swinging her arms in anticipation of trying on her dress, soon to be modelled on Sylvie's.

Embellished with silk roses attached at the hem and neckline, Sylvie's dress was of pearl-grey chiffon over satin. The photograph had also shown a rose-patterned drape. In an attempt to emulate her sister, the tailor was going to add a swathe of flowering chiffon attached to the shoulder seam over a similar long dress with a plunging neckline in a lime green satin. He would also sew roses along the hem. The dress would cling in all the right places, and she had hopes of impressing Mark.

She was feeling cheerful as she walked down the less familiar street until she spotted something that stopped her in her tracks. It wasn't the woman's black face or the way she was dressed, even if her dress, pulled tight over rounded, well-formed buttocks and slit up the side, was a little too provocative even for Nicole's tastes. It was the person walking beside the woman, with an arm round her waist. As Nicole stared in horror, her father bent over to kiss the woman's semi-bared breast. Then he pulled the woman close to him and kissed her full on the lips. Nicole gasped and turned away. Horrible, horrible sight. She marched off, heels clicking. Of course her father must have been with other women since their mother died, but a woman who looked like a prostitute?

9

Nicole and O-Lan stood admiring the newly restocked shelves and, as the sun painted the floor with bands of light, O-Lan offered to make a silky egg coffee, a condensed milk coffee with an egg in it. Though egg coffee sounded awful, it was probably the most delicious thing Nicole had ever tasted. Thick and creamy with no eggy taste at all, the coffee was like caramel cream with added caffeine, and it was something Nicole was becoming addicted to.

As she waited for the coffee she thought about her father. A battle north of Hanoi had resulted in many French injuries. Her father had been called away to visit the site and, although the image of him kissing that woman kept coming back to her, she hadn't actually seen him since she'd witnessed that. At least with the painting now completed, the shop was open and she could concentrate on her customers instead of worrying about what he was doing.

O-Lan was in the little kitchen at the back of the shop brewing the coffee, and as Nicole slipped through the dark rooms to the brighter sunshine of the courtyard, the aroma of sweet hot milk drifted out.

A few minutes later O-Lan came out carrying two mugs. 'Here we are.'

Nicole passed the paper bag of tiny cakes she'd bought from Yvette's father, Yves, and O-Lan picked out two.

They sat on the low wall around the well in companionable silence, enjoying the warmth. A trace of mint laced the air and a dusty yellow haze hung over the surrounding rooftops. The start of the day, when many of the inhabitants of the ancient quarter were still lost in their dreams, was special.

As they sat, O-Lan began to sing a haunting Vietnamese song, unlike anything Nicole had heard before. O-Lan had a most unusual singing voice and Nicole was impressed.

'What is that?' she asked when the girl had finished.

'Vietnamese folk music. There are many kinds. Do you like it?'

'It's different from French singing. Could you teach me?'

'Of course.'

'If you have time, shall we have a go now? I don't have to open up yet.'

They went to the room above the shop where they stood as far from the open window as they could. It took a while for Nicole to get the hang of the sharp brittle sounds, and she was worried people might laugh. But, without her knowing, some of the locals had gathered outside to lean against the wall and listen. She only realized they were there when, at the end of the session, a round of applause reached them from the street.

The next day Jerry phoned her at the shop to say she had been given a part in his show at Les Variétés. At first a feeling of euphoria washed through her, but then she realized she would have to tell her father and Sylvie about her role in the show. She'd never be able to get to rehearsals without them noticing her absence. She glanced up at clouds of whipped cream melting into patches of blue, though in the near distance a heavier sky indicated rain. With her eye on some delicious-looking caramelized corn on the other side of the street, she closed the shop early and went to see if O-Lan might join her. Across the street the man who roasted corn attempted to light a cigarette with his hands cupping the flame. The wind gusted and he tried again. A bent old woman passed by, her papery skin deeply wrinkled. She smiled at the man and Nicole saw only gums; no teeth at all. A group of young girls came out of a shop, clutching their sides and giggling, each one tiny and exquisite – impossible to imagine the old lady might have once looked like them.

Nicole found no sign of O-Lan at the till inside her shop, so passed through a pair of carved wooden swing doors and walked into the next room, calling her name. A table, standing in the middle, was decorated with a single lotus blossom arranged in a tiny vase. Stone ornaments and earthenware sat on the side tables and a huge brass four-bladed fan, fixed to the ceiling, slowly spun round. The sheer silk drapes at the windows gently stirred the air.

Hearing an unusual sound, Nicole walked outside to the courtyard, where swathes of orange flowering creeper hung over O-Lan's house, the timbered cladding lost beneath it. The moment she stepped out to touch it, rain began to fall. Fast. She glanced at the dark clouds blocking out the sun and took a step back, then stopped to gaze at the solid sheet of water splashing from the overhanging eaves.

Above the rain she heard another sound, like a cat mewing, but she felt certain this was human. In a side room at the back, attached to a kitchen, she discovered O-Lan's mother, Kim-Ly; a tiny Vietnamese woman wearing traditional *áo dài* and with her hair scraped back in a bun. The woman, slumped in a chair and ghostly white, looked as if she'd passed on. Nicole felt for a pulse, then let go of the woman's papery-veined hand: still alive, thank goodness, but with a weak, fluttering pulse. But what to do? She knew Kim-Ly had problems with sugar in her blood. Too much was not good, but too little meant she could fall unconscious. She tried to wake the woman but with no success, so went into the kitchen where she found a jar of honey on the counter beside a small bronze Buddha. She hadn't thought of O-Lan being a Buddhist, but of course she was, like many Vietnamese. You only had to look at the temples everywhere.

Nicole had watched O-Lan trying to spoon something sweet into her mother before and so began trying to slip the honey in, little by little. At first nothing happened, and it dribbled down her chin, but then Kim-Ly swallowed, and after a few more swallows she gradually came back to consciousness.

'O-Lan?' she said.

'O-Lan is coming. I need to keep you moving. Lean on me.'

Nicole managed to get her out of the chair, but the woman stumbled and cried out for her daughter. Unsure if it was right to help her walk, or if the woman should be lying on the bed, Nicole tried walking her first, but ended up half carrying her through to a chaise longue in the room behind the shop. By now some of the colour had returned to her cheeks and Nicole felt it might be safe to let her rest. While she waited for O-Lan, Nicole chattered on – an attempt to keep Kim-Ly awake – then gave her some more honey. But how much was enough? She had no idea.

Kim-Ly seemed tired and much more frail than usual and after about half an hour she fell asleep. Nicole had to choose whether it was best to fetch the herbalist in the next street or whether she should call the Duval family doctor. There was no phone at O-Lan's, so either way she'd have to leave. Mobilized by anxiety, she got up and walked over to the door to see if O-Lan was anywhere near.

Between the shops and the peeling, painted gates of the temples, men wearing conical bamboo hats stood in knots eating boiled peanuts, out of the rain, but the women remained selling tea and cabbage-noodle soup from the pavement stalls. She spotted O-Lan a little way down the street, sheltering from the rain in a doorway. She was talking with the young Vietnamese man. Trần – wasn't that his name?

When he saw her he touched O-Lan on the arm, then pointed to Nicole, who was now signalling frantically. They both ran over, dodging the traders and the downpour, then came into the shop, Nicole explaining what had happened and what she'd done.

O-Lan ran through to her mother and felt her pulse and her forehead. 'She's all right.'

Nicole felt enormously relieved. 'Thank goodness. I wasn't sure what to do next.'

'I cannot thank you enough.'

'Should she see a doctor?'

'I will take her to the hospital tomorrow. She needs rest now.'

Nicole was puzzled when the young man pulled up a chair and began stroking the woman's hair.

'Trần is my cousin,' O-Lan explained.

'Well, I'm glad your mother is better. Let me know if I can help.'

'Stay to eat. I'll show you upstairs.'

Nicole smiled. 'I wouldn't want to intrude,' she said, but she knew it was an honour to be invited into the innermost centre of a Vietnamese home.

While Trần stayed with Kim-Ly, O-Lan led Nicole upstairs and showed her the family's ancestral altar, then took her through several interconnecting rooms divided by carved fretwork screens. They stood at the top of the outside staircase, similar to her own. Now the rain had subsided, a million floral scents filled the air. Nicole breathed deeply, wanting to preserve the magic of the moment.

'I hope you like *bánh xèo*,' O-Lan said.

'I've never even heard of it.'

'It is a kind of crispy pancake. We serve it with *rau sống*.'

'And that is?'

'It includes banana flower and guava leaves.'

'Sounds delicious.'

Nicole decided she would hand her father the leaflet she'd found and tell him about the show when she got home that evening. But when he still hadn't arrived back, a part of her felt relieved. How could she behave normally after seeing him with that woman? Even looking him in the face felt like too much. When Lisa went outside to relax with a glass of wine and a cigarette, Nicole joined her in the garden.

'I ate *bánh xèo* today,' she said.

'Really?'

Nicole nodded.

'Did you enjoy it?'

'Yes.'

Lisa grimaced. 'I can't stomach Vietnamese food.'

In the garden, wild flowers dotted the edges of the lawn and flying creatures clustered round sweet-scented bushes. The trees waved their branches and the yellow sun on the leaves shone gold, throwing the depths into deeper shadow.

'Isn't it lovely out here? Do you remember, Lisa, how I was always falling off the swing hanging from the pipal tree in Huế?'

Lisa smiled and her eyes lit up as she watched a dark-winged bird take flight and then land on one of the top branches of the pipal tree.

'And the time I tore my party dress?' Nicole added.

'Yes, and when we had to get the doctor after you broke your ankle.'

'You sat up all night with me.'

Lisa sighed. 'Such a tomboy. You were always grazing or bruising yourself.'

'Lisa, what if the Vietminh were to win and we had to leave?'

'Don't you listen to your father? The Vietminh can never win against the French army.'

'I suppose you're right.' She paused as a feeling of loss seemed to come out of nowhere. 'I know so little of my mother.'

'You should ask your father about her. She was a good woman and I loved her.'

'He won't talk about her.'

'You're like her, you know.'

Nicole smiled. 'Am I really?'

'In so many ways. She was full of life, just like you. Sylvie's not like her at all.'

'The Vietnamese say that if you don't know who your ancestors are, you're little better than a thief.'

Lisa laughed. 'What ridiculous ideas they have.'

10

A third hairpin sprang from her fingers and skimmed across the floor. Nicole swooped down, scraping a nail on the floorboard as she picked it up. Damn! A broken nail. It was now early July and a typical hot wet summer with daily rain and numbing humidity but at least the streets were dressed in the bright red of flamboyant blossoms. She had, at last, told her father about the show and, after some persuasion, he'd grudgingly given his permission; but when she'd handed him the Vietminh leaflet she'd found in the street, he'd just torn it up.

She hadn't seen Mark for nearly four weeks, and was now so excited she felt all fingers and thumbs. Exactly what she didn't need. She'd have to fix the nail later; first she needed to sort out her hair. She perched on the edge of a stool, her skin grow-ing increasingly hot as her frustration mounted. Great. Now she'd have a red face, a broken nail and hair behaving badly. If only it wasn't so thick and straight. Just a little curl or a wave like Sylvie's would do. With each grip that slid out, she attempted to fix it in again, until, defeated, she flung the pins down. Instead she brushed vigorously to bring out the shine, applied a little rouge to her cheeks and rubbed her lips together to smooth out the pale pink lipstick.

She went on to the landing to scrutinize her appearance in the full-length mirror. Never too confident of what suited her, she frowned. Were the red roses she'd had sewn on to her lime-green dress a bit garish? And that pink lipstick! She rubbed it off.

A knock at the door.

'Are you ready? The car is here,' Sylvie said as she came in.

Nicole stared, struggling not to gasp in surprise.

Sylvie stood in her simple pearl-grey silk chiffon oozing perfection, as if she'd stepped out of the pages of French *Vogue*. No roses on her dress, no flowery drape. She rubbed her hands together. 'Well? All set?'

'But –'

'What?' Sylvie said, pretending innocence.

'Your dress. I thought . . .'

Sylvie laughed.

Nicole felt the pressure building behind her eyes. She must not cry. But compared with her sister's understated elegance, she felt stupid and overdressed. 'Why are you trying to ruin my life?'

Sylvie flicked a stray hair from her eyes. 'Don't be melodramatic. It was only a joke. You look all right.'

Nicole sprawled in her armchair, digging her broken nail into her palm. Her sister had chosen her words for maximum damage. Who wanted to look 'all right'?

'So? Are you coming?'

'No.'

'Do come. They're going to take photos and I want you to be in them too.'

'You want me to look hideous beside you?'

Sylvie threw back her head and laughed again. 'You're being ridiculous. I told you: it was a joke.'

Nicole glanced up. Sylvie was still smiling. She can stand for hours, Nicole thought, waiting for me to make a fool of myself.

'You always blamed me. Didn't you?'

'For what?' said Sylvie.

'You know.'

'I was a child, Nicole. A five-year-old little girl who'd lost her mum.'

'Just go,' Nicole said without raising her voice.

'You don't look all that bad. I could do your hair?'

Nicole didn't reply.

Sylvie turned on her heels and closed the door quietly as she left.

Nicole's mood plummeted. It wasn't only jealousy; more that Sylvie's triumph brought to the surface the old buried feelings of insecurity. She glanced out of her bedroom window as the velvet sky became shot through with silver. It was supposed to have been such a glorious night.

She thought of the day she and Mark had gone out in the boat. The memory made her smile and gave her the push she needed to do something to save the night. It was her own fault for trying to copy Sylvie, but she could not let that defeat her now. She picked up a pair of nail scissors and began to alter her dress. Although she did her best, it was difficult working with silk, and in a moment of inattention she sliced through the fabric of the dress, making a hole. She tore the rose off and flung it at the wall. She felt angry with Sylvie and furious with herself for letting it matter. It hurt far more than a damaged dress ought to hurt; it struck at the truth of who they both were.

She heard a knock at the door.

'Go away,' she shouted, and threw herself back in her chair, thinking it was Sylvie again.

'Aren't you going, *chérie*?'

Nicole turned to see Lisa standing in the doorway. When the cook came across and hugged her, Nicole attempted to choke back the tears.

'Dry your eyes. You're coming with me.'

'I can't wear this,' Nicole said, her voice shaking.

'No, you can't. We are going to find you something far

better. It's time you understood you don't have to look French to be beautiful.'

Though Nicole smiled, she wasn't convinced.

An hour later Nicole paused at the entrance to the ballroom, gazing at the glittering chandeliers and panels of mirrors. Dozens of expensive scents mingled with that of white roses interwoven with trailing ivy round all the columns. Smart waiters balancing trays of champagne nipped here and there among the crowd, and the orchestra at the opposite end had struck up a tango. At first, feeling destined to imitate one of the marble statues in the gardens, Nicole couldn't move. But, as the music soared, she felt a rush of excitement. She pulled her shoulders back and, moving slowly, glided in.

She had arrived late and the ball was in full swing. Now, transfixed by the women dazzling in shimmering fabrics decorated with sequins, pearls and rhinestones, it seemed as if the spell of luxury had wiped away the troubles of the past. It was all colour and light, and in this delicious moment, with the fragrance of roses permeating the air, the best of their French colonial world shone for all to see. Nicole felt it would be the night of her life, after all.

Earlier, after dragging Nicole out of her bedroom, Lisa had pulled from her own wardrobe the most beautiful dress Nicole had ever seen.

'It was your mother's,' Lisa said, then paused. 'Chanel.'

Nicole whistled. 'Are you sure?'

Lisa nodded. 'I think it will fit you.'

'Why have you kept it?'

'Your father brought it back from Paris before you were born. She only wore it once. After she died he didn't want any memories, but told me to pick one of your mother's things to remember her by. I picked the dress. He sold all her beautiful

73

gold jewellery or I would have chosen a necklace. I had the dress altered recently, brought up to date. I'd thought of giving it to you for Christmas.'

The gown did fit perfectly and Nicole had been astonished to see herself looking so glamorous. Made of scarlet grosgrain silk and red chiffon, it had a sleeveless, tight-fitting bodice, fastening down the front with hooks and eyes, a high neckline and a skirt of red silk chiffon, falling from pleats at the waist. Nicole could hardly believe her good fortune as she twirled around. There was nothing old-fashioned about the dress, just timeless simplicity.

'Look at how it complements your skin,' Lisa said. 'See how lovely you are? Now you need red lipstick and black eyeliner. I'm going to pin up your hair Chinese style with a single red rose from that awful dress you were wearing.'

A pair of high-heeled shoes and Nicole was all set, wearing a classic French dress but looking stunningly oriental.

As she stood inside the entrance to the ballroom, the orchestra stopped playing. She could hear the clink of champagne glasses, a steady hum of voices punctuated by ripples of laughter and the odd jubilant shout.

She looked towards the floor-to-ceiling windows lining the entire courtyard side of the room. The drapes had been left open and dozens of torches lit the gardens, their glitter reflecting in the central ponds and increasing Nicole's expectation of enchantment. She spotted Mark wearing a black dinner suit, talking to another man. His shoulders seemed broader than ever and although his hair looked as if it had been trimmed, a curl still fell over his right eye. She found herself wanting to rush over and flick it way. He threw back his head and laughed at whatever his companion had said, and Nicole felt suddenly shy and faltered. Had she imagined that he liked her? But at that moment he spotted her and stopped laughing. They stared at each other and then he seemed to collect himself, clapped the other man on the back and walked towards her.

Happy that for once it was her turn to shine, she waited, her heart fluttering just a bit.

'Let me look at you,' he said as he came close and held out both hands. 'You are absolutely stunning.'

'Am I?' She took his hands and felt her spirits soar as she looked into his shining eyes and saw the affection and admiration there. She hadn't imagined it.

'I was worried you weren't coming.'

She could hardly speak. 'I had trouble with my dress.'

He kissed her on both cheeks and she closed her eyes, wanting to savour every moment.

'Dance?' he said. 'The orchestra are tuning up.'

As he took her arm with a palm resting under her elbow, Nicole spotted Sylvie over at the other side of the ballroom, laughing with a blond officer dressed in white and gold. She witnessed Sylvie's surprise, and didn't try to hide her triumph.

'Well, the little duckling has turned into a swan,' Sylvie said, smiling widely as she walked across. 'Hasn't she, Mark?'

'She always was a swan,' Nicole heard him say, though she didn't think Sylvie had caught it.

At that moment a photographer from the local newspaper came up and snapped the three of them. Sylvie posed for the man, giving him a perfect smile, then drew Nicole aside to whisper.

'You look lovely. I'm sorry about earlier. I didn't mean to upset you. Please forgive me.'

'It doesn't matter,' Nicole said and meant it. 'I shouldn't have been such an idiot.'

She slipped her fingers into Mark's large warm hand. With his other hand firmly on the small of her back, he guided her to the centre of the room. When they began to move Nicole felt light-headed and pressed herself against him. The solidity of his body so close for more than just a brief hug released a tension inside her she hadn't known she had been holding. He whirled her round in a Viennese Waltz and, barely aware of the other dancers, she spun across the floor. The faces blurred – even Sylvie disappeared – until the room emptied of everything but him. When her feet began to perform the steps without her needing to think about them, she acknowledged that those dull ballroom dancing classes had been worthwhile after all. She felt thrilled to feel so free, and couldn't believe the wonder of it. When the music stopped after three dances in a row, his eyes lingered on her face as he blew the fringe from her eyes.

'Your hair has come loose.'

As he ran his fingers down the nape of her neck, she noticed him smile. He'd used the opportunity to repin her hair to touch her and, knowing that, she grinned, so aware of his fingertips that she felt she might melt. He turned her round and held her away from him.

'Thirsty?'

She was. It was smoky too and she felt weightless from dancing, though maybe more from his proximity than anything else. He said he'd fetch champagne and asked her to wait at the side of the room, where she replayed every moment of the dance in her mind to fix it for ever. One of the French girls who had previously called her names walked by with her mother. Nicole smiled but they blanked her. She didn't care. This was her best impression of being a well-brought-up French girl so far.

Mark was gone for longer than expected, so she decided to find him. As she glanced around, a passing waiter handed her a glass of champagne and, after drinking it in one long gulp, she went to look in the lounges.

In the first lounge, cigar smoke mingled with the intoxicating smell of brandy from the glasses of a few elderly men in armchairs. She tried the other lounges and bars, then headed back into the ballroom where the crowd had dispersed a little. She made her way through the people standing about in knots and spotted Mark opening a side door at the other end of the hall. As he went through it she started to go after him, but was distracted by her old school friend Francine, who took hold of her hand and wanted to gossip about inconsequential things. Although Nicole kept glancing at the door, Mark didn't come back out and by the time she managed to shake Francine off several minutes had passed.

Finally she made her way to the door, opened it and found herself in a chilly corridor with no carpet. She followed it round, expecting to find perhaps a discreet way through to the gaming rooms. Instead, the corridor twisted and eventually came to an end at a place where there was only one door. She pulled it open. A steep stone staircase led downwards. She hesitated and, although it seemed odd, she began to make her way down because Mark must have definitely come this way.

A metal handrail provided a degree of safety, and as she reached the concrete floor at the bottom, it became clear she must now be underground and in a wine cellar. She continued along the passage until, hearing the murmur of voices, she came to a halt. The voices faded. She continued past several alcoves, two of which opened into vaulted rooms storing barrels and racks of wine. This far below she could no longer hear the orchestra clearly, and only the sound of her own footsteps echoed around the cavernous place.

Curious about what might be at the end of the passage, she eventually reached a row of shelves that had been swung back but not quite properly closed afterwards. She frowned but pulled them open and saw what looked like a metal door with a small central peephole. There was the sound of scraping chairs and a muted cry. Her palms began to feel a little sweaty. Maybe this was not such a great idea. Upstairs was light and laughter; she should have waited there for Mark. The cry came again. In the cold of the corridor she began to shiver. Why had she ever thought it a good idea to come down here?

She took a step back. The skin at the back of her neck began to prickle and she wiped her clammy hands on her dress. She wanted to retrace her steps but something stopped her. And even though she didn't want to, she felt compelled to look through the peephole. Time slowed right down the moment she saw a young Vietnamese tied to a chair. Although she couldn't see the gap between his front teeth, she recognized O-Lan's cousin, Trần. Her throat tightened and she struggled to hold on to herself. She made a fist and jammed it into her mouth.

She couldn't hear what he said, but from the fear in his eyes and the frantic way he shook his head from side to side, she felt certain somebody was threatening him. She felt sick but could not stop watching. A man stepped forward out of the shadows. She blinked rapidly and her legs almost gave way when she saw it was her own father. As he moved about the room, in and out of her field of vision, she smelt something vaguely rotten – mice or maybe rats – then heard a hollow groaning noise and looked around in panic. She glanced up at the narrow pipes of plumbing attached to the ceiling, then twisted back towards her father. His bearing conveyed something she had never seen before and in his right hand he held a pistol. Desperate to erase the sight, she squeezed her eyes shut to blot it out.

It couldn't be real.

With every muscle tense, she forced herself to look again. A jolt ran through her as she saw him take aim. Everything went completely still. She heard a scream within her own head as he pulled the trigger. It was over in seconds. She shuddered as she saw the boy's eyes widen. He thrashed his arms, his muscles slackened and then his head fell forward where it rested at an unnatural angle, his thick fringe flapping like a bird's broken wing. Blood began to ooze from the corner of his mouth, followed by gurgling. But she couldn't have heard that, could she? Had her mind filled in the sound? A dark stain was spreading in the centre of his chest. He was O-Lan's cousin. Her new friend's cousin. She pictured the gentle way he had stroked Kim-Ly's hair. O-Lan and her mother loved him, but now his life had been taken by her own father.

She tried to make out her father's voice among the noises in the room but he had disappeared from her view. The words 'puppet master' came back to her. Why was her father involved in this? The shock of what she had seen had set off a chain reaction. Though her brain was screaming at her to run, she could not move her legs. He was her father. He had killed a man. As soon as she heard the scraping sound of movement inside the room, Nicole forced herself to step back into the shadows of the nearest wine cellar. There she doubled up, wrapping her arms round her middle.

The door opened, bringing with it the smell of blood. Her father was the first to emerge, followed by two men: one dressed in a waiter's uniform, but looking more like a policeman, and the other the blond man Sylvie had been talking to earlier. They exchanged a word or two with her father, then disappeared from sight. Nicole saw no blood on her father's clothing. Had he changed? She rocked back and forth, wanting Lisa. She heard footsteps and looked up. Another man had stepped out: Daniel Giraud's father. A thick-set, unpleasant-looking man with pale watery eyes, thinning grey hair, heavy brows and large liverish lips: Nicole knew he was a man who hated the Vietnamese.

But who was going to dispose of the body? She was way out of her depth and her alarm at the thought of seeing the poor dead man again meant she had to get away quickly. No matter why it had been done, and aware she shouldn't even have been there, it was clear nobody could know she had seen the killing. But when Sylvie emerged from the room, Nicole gasped. Her sister's skin was ghostly white and she seemed close to tears; Mark was with her too, looking equally shocked.

'Oh my God,' Sylvie whispered. 'I feel sick.'

Neither of them had seen Nicole hiding in the shadows but they were both visible to her and she could see Sylvie trembling.

'Why did he want us to be there?'

'So that you'd know what you're getting into, I suspect.' Mark took both Sylvie's hands in his and rubbed them. 'Grief, your hands are cold. I thought it would be an interrogation. Nothing more. I had no idea. I hope this proves we're doing the right thing.'

'It was terrible. Terrible.'

'Maybe now you understand the American view of French methods?'

Sylvie slumped against the wall, withdrew her hands from his and covered her face with them.

'And that's why we must finance an alternative Vietnamese party to challenge the Vietminh.'

Sylvie dropped her hands. 'Without the knowledge of the French?'

'Exactly.'

'But what about my father? He knows. Doesn't that undermine his position with the government?'

Nicole watched as Sylvie's tears began to fall. Dreadful to have witnessed what happened through a peephole, but to have actually been in the room must have been worse. She watched Mark hold her sister by one shoulder and use his other hand to tip up her chin and wipe the wetness from her cheeks. Then he moved and, now with his back to Nicole, he blocked her view of Sylvie. Nicole couldn't see his face or Sylvie's, but she did see Mark bend forward very slightly and appear to be kissing Sylvie. Then he gave her a hug.

'Let's get out of here,' he said.

Sylvie nodded and they walked away, Mark supporting her. As they went along the corridor to the stairs, the sweet smell of blood thickened the air and Nicole felt the certainties of her life crumbling.

II

The sun was up, its huge expanding light swallowing every-thing. Nicole stared at the window until the muscles round her eyes ached from the effort of focusing on one spot. The night before, utterly appalled by what she'd seen, she had man-aged to slip away from the ball without anyone spotting her leave. Most of the night she'd remained in disbelief, curled up tightly, feeling as if she was suffocating. A high-pitched, keen-ing slid from her mouth. All she could think of was blood. She made fists and pressed them into her eyes. The whole world swam. Red. Bright red. She stopped pressing, waited for her eyes to focus, then climbed out of bed and, to force the internal pain away, slammed her fist against the wall.

Even though it was hot and wet outside, she had to get out of the house.

She splashed her face, threw on the first clothes she laid her hands on and slipped down to the kitchen. Lisa, her back to the door, was stirring something on the stove, but hearing Nicole, she turned round. Not knowing how to behave, Nicole shifted her weight, her arms hanging limply by her sides. She shouldn't have come down to the kitchen; Lisa would see that she was made of paper.

'Heavens, child,' Lisa said. 'You look terrible. There's coffee on the stove. Just pour it yourself.'

Nicole picked up a coffee cup and walked over, but when she tried to pour from the jug, her hand shook so much she spilled coffee on to the stove. Hearing the sound of it sizzling, Lisa came over.

'What a mess. Sit down and I'll bring some.'

Nicole shook her head. 'I'll go out. I can find a cafe.'

'You stay right here. You're as white as a sheet. Your father would never forgive me if I allowed you out looking like that.'

Nicole looked at Lisa longingly. More than anything she wanted to be wrapped in the cook's arms and to tell her what she'd seen, but the wrongness of it silenced her. She lowered her eyes, knowing her silence could not be temporary; she would never be able to speak of what had happened.

The fragrance of coffee filled the room as Lisa ground more beans and made a fresh pot. She brought it across, poured two mugs and came to sit beside Nicole.

'Now you tell me what has been going on to make you look that way. Did you drink too much champagne? Is that it?'

Nicole took a sip of the hot coffee, not caring that it burned her throat, then wiped her mouth with the back of her hand.

'I don't know, you young girls. What you need is a good square meal. Maybe some nice poached eggs.'

'I couldn't eat.'

'A croissant?'

Nicole scraped back her chair as she sprang to her feet.

'Sorry . . . I've got to . . .' She stumbled over her words and, fearing she might dissolve, blinked repeatedly. 'I've got to go,' she said, then slipped past Lisa, turned on her heels and fled.

Outside the house she lengthened her stride, and as she began to run her blood pumped faster. Her skull felt too tight but it didn't stop her. When running she did not think of blood.

By the time it began to rain in earnest Rue Paul Bert was crowded, but she kept her head down and dodged the people. Outside their own Maison Duval on the corner, she spotted her father standing under the roof edge that extended right over the pavement. He waved her across but she ducked her head. She couldn't even look at him. This was the second time he had truly shocked her. It was bad enough seeing him kiss the black woman's semi-bared breast in the street. This was worse. Far worse.

As she passed the Cercle Nautique, the rowing club built on the water's edge, she paused, panting to regain control. During a break in the rain, an entertainment troupe went by. The bands of musicians and actors were often seen on the roads going in and out of Hanoi. Though there were rumours about what they were up to – some thought them messengers for the Vietminh – Nicole usually loved the spectacle. Today nothing distracted her. She kept seeing what had happened. The seconds it took to kill a man. She remembered the fear in his eyes as he'd begged for his life – and that terrible knowing look. Was it always like that when death came? The awful feeling of helpless inevitability?

Once into the Vietnamese quarter, and forced to weave her way around the teashops on the pavements, she slowed down, her hair now damp with sweat and rainwater. Even so, she collided with a transient sandal maker who cursed her as his basket of goods tipped over.

Eventually she stood still to allow a rickshaw pulled by a man on foot to pass.

She had an intense headache; the humidity in July was so brutally relentless. Why had Sylvie been there? Why had her father shot a man in cold blood? She hardly dared think how betrayed she felt by seeing Mark kiss her sister. Why had she ever thought he'd be interested in her when he could have Sylvie? She imagined them laughing at her. Poor old needy Nicole. Wasn't it obvious he would always prefer her clever and more beautiful sister?

She turned into the next street where she saw Yvette come running out of the bakery, a large basket of iced buns hanging over one arm. With her black plait swinging, she waved, beaming with delight at unexpectedly seeing Nicole. She was such a sunny little girl that, despite her pain, Nicole smiled back. At least Yvette was the apple of *her* father's eye. Yves was a good man. Nicole lifted a hand to wave back, then carried on walking until she reached her shop.

It was a day of extremely heavy rain and very few customers but it was well into the evening by the time Nicole made her way home.

When Sylvie came into her room to say dinner was served, Nicole floundered. Her sister wore a grey silk suit and a little white hat with a short black veil covering part of her face. She had clearly spent the day working too, and Nicole could tell they would not say a word about the killing. A man had died and it would be as if nothing had happened, and yet Sylvie had been shocked at what she had seen in the cellar too. Nicole had to know more: why had her father been the one to pull the trigger and what was Sylvie getting into? She longed to confide in her sister.

A yearning for the old familiar days surged through her, but she shook it off. 'I –'

'What?'

Nicole paused and they stared at each other.

'I saw you.'

The horror of the night erupted, but something told Nicole to keep her mouth shut about the shooting.

'What?'

Nicole thought quickly. Don't mention the gun. Don't mention the blood. 'Why did you let Mark kiss you?' she said instead.

Sylvie looked astonished.

'I was in the passage. I saw you with Mark.'

Sylvie gazed at her feet before looking up and staring at her sister. She seemed unnaturally calm and gave Nicole a tight smile.

'I hope that was all you saw.'

Nicole didn't reply.

Sylvie looked at her pointedly.

'I saw you, that's all. He was my friend, Sylvie. Haven't you got enough?'

'I've known Mark for some time, Nicole. I don't know what else to say.'

'Don't you?'

Sylvie gestured at the door. 'I only came in to say dinner is served. Shall I say you'd like a tray? As far as Mark and I are concerned, you need to grow up. Is that why you left the ball without telling anyone you were going? I'm sorry if what you saw upset you.'

'You know it upsets me, Sylvie, don't pretend innocence.'

As Sylvie turned to leave, Nicole struggled with her resentment; failing, she picked up a paperback and hurled it at Sylvie. Her sister ducked as it thudded to the floor.

Nicole gazed at the upturned book, its pages fluttering in the breeze from the open window. There was silence for a moment while Sylvie glanced in the mirror, pushed a curl of hair from her forehead and pursed her lips to spread the lipstick.

'I think you talked Father out of giving me a fair share in the business.'

When Sylvie spoke again it was without looking at Nicole. 'Not this again. It wasn't me. He thought it better if one of us had sole control.'

'Nothing to do with you being perfect?'

'He did it for the sake of the business. Now dry your eyes. And, by the way, I need you to cut me eight metres of the cream silk shot with gold. No rush, but you never know when I might need it.'

After Sylvie had gone Nicole sprawled face down on the bed, buried her head in the pillow and chewed the skin round her thumbnail until she tasted blood. Always longing to be a proper French daughter, she'd thought being left out of the family business was bad enough. Now her pain was far more primal than that. Her sister and Mark had been present at a murder. What did that make them? What did it make her to have witnessed it? How could her father slaughter a man as if he was an animal? And as she thought that, a strange feeling scooped out her middle, leaving her hollow. Apart from Lisa, who could she trust?

2

Moon in the Water

Late July to October 1952

12

In the days that followed, Nicole avoided both her sister and her father, except for the briefest of interactions. With no idea why Sylvie and her father had been in the cell, she longed to confront them over the murder, but the instinct of self-preservation stopped her and she kept silent, gradually locking it at the back of her mind. In her darkening world, she wondered what might happen to the memory of a thing you'd rather not have seen. Could it be suppressed? Wouldn't it remain hidden only until the time came when it began to smell, like the rotten thing it was? And what if she had no control? She clasped a hand over her mouth, as if to prevent the truth from spilling, but nothing could prevent it from haunting her dreams.

They seemed puzzled by her behaviour and Sylvie even popped into Nicole's bedroom early one morning, dressed for work, with a sombre look in her eyes.

'I wanted a word,' Sylvie said as she leant with her back against the door.

Nicole sensed something different in her sister's voice, perhaps even a hint of remorse, but she refused to meet Sylvie's eyes and went to gaze out of the window instead. She didn't want Sylvie in her room. Feeling cornered, she watched a lizard run up the trunk of a tree.

'I wanted to put you in the picture about that conversation you overheard.'

Nicole spun round.

'I thought it best you hear it from me.'

Nicole stared at Sylvie, who hesitated for a moment, as if

weighing her words. 'Look, the Americans are financing an alternative Vietnamese party, non-communist, to fight the Vietminh. People's lives could be in danger, that's why it has to be secret. Can I rely on you?'

'Why don't the Americans just support the French?'

'I suppose they think we've had our day.'

'But you don't think that?'

'Of course not.' Sylvie straightened up. 'But an alternative to the Vietminh can only make us stronger.'

'Is Papa involved?'

'That's what I wanted to say. He is. But the government can't know about the new party or its army yet. It would damage his position to say the least.'

Nicole narrowed her eyes. 'So Mark isn't a silk merchant? You, Mark, Papa. You're in this together?'

'For the good of France. You know that's what Papa cares about.'

Nicole shook her head.

She went straight to the shop and decided to lose herself by working long hours. By the end of the day, with stinging eyes and muscles aching with the effort of lifting heavy bales of silk, she felt a little better. The next day she painted the shop a gorgeous shade of greenish blue, soft, like a duck's egg.

Over the following days she collected lotus flowers to display and worked to make the upstairs flat habitable, polishing the furniture with beeswax and washing the tiled floor over and over with lemon-scented soap. She spent hours sewing off-cuts of silk together to make shimmery curtains, cushions and a matching bedspread. She learnt how to construct tasselled lampshades and devised a way to make beautiful feathered birds out of silk, which she hung in the shop front. After that she began running up shawls and scarves to sell.

As the young Vietnamese girls flocked to the shop to buy them, the silk shop became the centre of her life; she felt safe there, and it was where she intended to carve out her place in the world.

One evening she bumped into O-Lan outside. Her mind tumbled over itself. What on earth could she say to her friend? How would she hide the fact that she knew O-Lan's cousin was dead?

'Hello,' O-Lan said. 'I'm sorry I haven't seen you lately, but I've been occupied with my mother.'

Nicole shifted her weight and struggled to keep the anxiety from her voice. 'No. I . . . I've been busy too.'

'Would you like to sing? My mother is sleeping so I have the chance.'

Nicole hesitated. 'I'm not sure. I'm tired.'

'Please. It will wake you up. It always wakes me up at the end of the day.'

Nicole gave in and the two of them went upstairs, where O-Lan gazed at the changes.

'This room is beautiful,' she said. 'You have a real talent.'

They started to sing but O-Lan looked terribly low and Nicole was gripped by a dreadful feeling of guilt. Neither girl was in good form, and they soon took a break. Nicole opened a bottle of ginger beer and passed it to O-Lan.

'Let's sit on the sofa,' she said, trying to sound relaxed and normal.

O-Lan was quiet and stared at the bottle in her hands. Oh God, Nicole thought, she's going to tell me her cousin Trần is dead. She felt an acidic taste on her tongue. Did lies actually have a flavour? She thought of something else to say. 'How is your mother?'

'Getting worse.'

So that was it. Though it felt unkind to feel relieved, she was. 'Has she seen a doctor?'

'He does not seem to be able to help much.'

Nicole held out a hand to her friend. 'If there's anything I can do.'

She thought about her part in the musical at Les Variétés and was glad the rehearsals took her mind off things in the evenings, even if it did intensify the feeling of being a *métisse*. The night before she had worn a shirtwaister in sherbet pink, with a full skirt falling a fraction below mid-calf, cinched at the waist with a black leather belt. It made her feel glamorous but had only served to increase the growing split within her. With her day-time hours being so thoroughly Vietnamese, she felt as if she was pulling further away from her French family. It frightened her. If she split apart from them, what would be left? She longed to discuss her problems with O-Lan, but she'd have to leave out the shooting, and that was at the centre of everything.

'Your singing has improved,' O-Lan said.

O-Lan was right. With practice, she'd mastered voice control, and that gave her added power. With a wide grin on his face, Jerry had even begun to say he thought she'd make a passable impression on the audience.

'Shall we have another go at it?' Nicole said.

O-Lan stood and gave her a sweet smile.

This is good, Nicole thought. If I can hold on to the positive things in my life, perhaps the awful images from the night of the shooting will eventually fade. She paused in her thoughts. What about Mark? She would just have to try to reconcile herself to what she now knew about him.

On a slow day in the shop Nicole decided to rearrange the stock in order of colour categories, starting with the cooler blues and greens and working her way through to the oranges, reds and magentas. The colours spoke to her. Blue and lilac for their days in Huê. Red for her anger and yellow for the warmth of the garden in summer. She liked to lose herself in the silks, wrap herself up in them and pretend to be one of the emperor's women; the time, long gone, when life must have been so simple. As she stroked the silk, the feel of it comforted her.

She had been wondering about visiting the village where the silk was woven from threads produced by families who lived there. Though much of the Duval silk still came from near to Huế, it would be great to find a local provider too. She knew all about the different qualities and thicknesses of silk and how the thread mattered, varying from so fine it was almost invisible to thick and inferior, which was used for the lesser fabrics bought for everyday.

Just as she was mulling this over, a voice interrupted her thoughts. 'So, you are still here?'

She spun round then felt the blood drain from her face as she stared at the gap between his front teeth. Surely he was the young Vietnamese man, O-Lan's cousin Trần, who'd been killed in the hotel cellar?

'You can't be . . . I thought you were –'

'Dead? You thought I was dead?'

'I . . . I mean, I . . .' Profoundly shocked, Nicole swallowed rapidly.

'So you know about the shooting?'

She rubbed the back of her neck. 'I don't know anything.'

She hadn't meant to use such a haughty tone of voice and regretted it the moment he moved a couple of paces closer. She stepped back beside the desk and cast around for what to say. He came right up and, placing his hands on her shoulders, stood too close. As he wasn't much taller than her their eyes were on a level. She had no option but to look at him, though his eyes bored right into hers. How was she to hold his gaze without giving herself away?

He snorted. 'Really?'

'Yes,' she said as sharply as she dared, though all she could see in her mind's eye was the dead man. She tried hard to hold eye contact, but the stinging in her eyes meant she couldn't stop blinking.

He narrowed his gaze. 'Something wrong with your eyes?'

She heard the sound of wheels from beyond the shop door, the squeal of brakes, a door opening and slamming shut again. Her instinct was to escape his grip and run from the shop.

'So?'

He continued to look at her steadily, and when he increased the pressure on her shoulders she felt as if he could see right into her mind. She thought quickly. 'I hadn't seen you around, and one of the neighbours must have said you'd gone back to your village.'

'Is that so?'

Her palms began to sweat. She nodded but knew it had sounded lame.

He gave her a sarcastic sort of a smile. 'And which neighbour would that have been?'

'I don't remember. Maybe it was your cousin O-Lan.'

He grabbed her left arm and twisted it behind her back. His body, pressed too tightly against hers, felt taut and raw; she could smell peppered onions and vinegar on his breath.

She clenched her jaw, trying to stop herself from crying out. 'Please don't hurt me. I don't know anything.'

'And yet you looked so shocked to see me.'

He let her go. She cleared her throat, but her body felt too stiff, the muscles tense. She tried to read his eyes, and thought carefully before she spoke again. Saying the wrong thing now might cost her dearly.

'Why are you here?' she finally said.

He hung his head for a moment but when he looked up again his eyes were blazing. He slammed the desk with the palm of his left hand. 'We thought my brother had gone back to the silk village where we are all from, but nobody had seen him there. His motorbike is still here with a full tank of petrol. He keeps it in a shed at the back of O-Lan's shop and we couldn't understand why he'd left it behind.'

'You have a brother?'

'His body was found by the river. I've just had to tell O-Lan. The animals were devouring his corpse, but it was clear he had been shot in the chest. He looked like me. People used to call us the twins, though he was taller. You're telling me you know nothing about it?'

She looked at the floor and then up at Trần. 'I –'

'The French shot him in the chest.'

'I'm very sorry for your loss, but how do you know it was the French?'

He frowned. 'Who else? My brother had a police record for nationalist agitation, so *they* would hardly have shot him, would they?'

'He must have committed a crime. Was he in the Maison Centrale?'

His frown lines deepened. 'You mean Hoa Lo.'

'Is that what you call the prison?'

He nodded. 'Hell's Hole.'

'I know what it means.'

'My brother was not there, as far as we know.'

Nicole took a deep breath and saw, behind the menace, a look of pain. 'I'm so sorry, but I don't understand why you think I'd know anything about it.'

'Your reaction when you saw me.'

'I've explained that. It was only surprise.' She paused. 'What are you going to do now?'

'Find out who killed him.'

She lowered her eyes to the counter. 'Of course.'

He shook his head. 'He was a good man. We think it might have been in retaliation for the murder of a French official, something he did not do.'

She searched for a way to change the subject. 'Why are the Vietminh challenging us again? I thought the fighting would be over by now.'

'This is war. It will never be over until we win. Your entire economy is built on the export of *our* raw materials.'

'But what about the *mission civilisatrice*? The French mean to increase the wealth of the country.'

The man spat on the floor. 'To the glory of France!'

Nicole knew that was not entirely fair. The French had tried to educate people as well and develop the country in other ways.

'You know what happened when the Japanese came?' he said.

'A bit.'

'They tolerated you French, while we starved.'

He had hissed the last few words and alarm rose up in her again. She shook her head and thought about backing towards the door. She had heard stories about how the Japanese had requisitioned the stocks of rice, and how a terrible famine had ensued. She'd heard that Vietnamese corpses had been piled up in the streets of Hanoi, and left to rot, but hadn't known if it was true.

Nicole bit her lip. 'You call me French. I'm half Vietnamese. And anyway, when they lost the war, the Japanese shot French people.'

She glanced at the door as he rolled a cigarette and then took out a packet of matches. If she could just keep him talking.

'We had our own country to ourselves, but you French came back with the help of your allies. The destruction was terrible here in the ancient quarter and the Cité Universitaire area.'

He stopped speaking and gazed at the floor. In the silence, Nicole thought hard. There was no doubt he believed everything he was saying, but her father wouldn't have shot Trần's brother for no reason.

He lit the cigarette. 'Tell me. Why is your family in Hanoi now?'

She shrugged and started to fold some silk she'd left on the counter.

'Your father has an important position. I think you might be able to help me,' he said, then drew deeply on his cigarette.

She frowned, uncertain where this was leading.

'This city will be under siege before long. And you could help us.'

'Why would I?'

'You said it. You're half Vietnamese, aren't you?'

When he looked into her eyes, she noted they were as dark as her own.

'Don't you want to know more? I can show you things. Come with me tomorrow after you close up. I'll meet you on the corner.'

She nodded slowly, pretending to think it over. 'How do you know I won't tell my father?'

He narrowed his eyes and smiled. 'Something tells me you will not, little *métisse*.'

That evening she left the shop late, hoping to avoid seeing O-Lan. Trần wasn't dead but his brother was; of course, he had been O-Lan's cousin too.

Back home she had hoped to slip up to her bedroom so she could deal with her mixed feelings alone, but her father met her in the hall.

'Ah, there you are, *chérie*,' he said, brisk but friendly, holding out a hand.

She had no choice but to follow him through to their main sitting room, where she found Sylvie smiling up at Mark, who was standing a short distance away behind the curved art-deco sofa. Sylvie reached out a hand to Mark. The fact that Mark did not take her sister's hand was neither here nor there. The gesture alone was enough.

'As you know, Mark has been doing a bit of business with Sylvie,' her father said. 'A pretty substantial order for silk as it happens.'

Nerves jangling at hearing her father's lie, Nicole sat as far away as she could, on a stiff-backed chair beside the hearth. The room was overflowing with Sylvie's favourite yellow roses and their sickly-sweet scent made Nicole feel nauseous. She glanced at Mark and he gave her the same wide smile that once would have lit up her day. She turned away without responding, but felt as if her heart had been torn apart; it filled her with a sense of absolute futility and she couldn't look at him again. Instead she forced herself to focus on the mantelpiece where a collection of blue-and-white fifteenth-century Vietnamese pottery was displayed.

The room, like many of the others, had a strong Indochinese feel. The floor was laid with glazed tiles decorated with the fleur-de-lis motif, covered only in the centre by an antique Vietnamese rug. The lamps had been lit, lending the room a cosy feel, although Nicole felt anything but cosy. She gazed out now at the darkening sky beyond the two large windows. The monsoon was not over and the rain had started up again. She listened to it pouring from the eaves and splashing on to the verandah below and longed to run outside to stand beneath the downpour so that the water might wash her pain away.

'I wanted you all here,' their father said, 'because rumours are circulating. Whatever you might hear, there is absolutely no evidence the Vietminh are getting any closer to Hanoi. There is no threat from them. I want to reassure you all.'

Sylvie smiled. 'So life goes on as usual.'

'Indeed it does.'

Nicole noticed Mark nodding vigorously. He caught her eye and attempted a smile again but she twisted her head away. The unpalatable truth remained: they had all been in that cell beneath the hotel; they had all been involved in Trần's brother's murder.

For a few moments, Nicole wished things could go back to the way they had been. She had always loved her sister, despite their problems, but the image of Sylvie with Mark came racing back and she felt herself stiffen. Sylvie had the looks, she had the business – and now, it seemed, she had the man.

'I've heard the city will be under siege,' she said to break the silence and to halt the rumpus going on inside her.

'Where did you hear that, Nicole?' her father said.

She shrugged.

'It's nonsense,' Sylvie said. 'Didn't you hear Papa?'

'I wasn't speaking to you,' Nicole said.

'Oh, for goodness' sake, don't be so childish.'

Ignoring the extent to which her sister's words grated, Nicole turned to her father. 'How bad was the famine here during the world war?'

'For the French, not too bad at all.'

'For the Vietnamese, I meant.'

Her father stuck out his chin. 'Terrible, I'm afraid.'

'They say the corpses were piled up in the streets.'

'Yes.'

'So don't you think they might have a reason to hold a grudge against us?'

'The world war is long over, *chérie*. We have to look to the future and build a stronger and better French Indochina.'

Nicole raised her brows but didn't say anything more. She looked at her father's hands – the hands of a murderer – and didn't know how she could ever love him again. And yet in a baffling way she did still love him. She reminded herself that trust was different from love. So what about Mark? Why had he been so loving and friendly to her when all the time it was Sylvie he really wanted? She had asked nothing of him and he had promised her nothing, yet she was sure there had been the makings of something. She had felt it. He had felt it. There had seemed to have been a million possibilities but now nothing. It didn't make sense.

She thought of the murder again and tried to make excuses: he hadn't known what was going to happen; he was an unwilling witness; he'd been forced to be present. But every time she got to the point where she pictured him kissing her sister, she couldn't stop seeing the young man's head rolling forward with his fringe flopping down, and she couldn't stop hearing the ghastly tormenting gurgle repeating inside her own head. Mark with her sister and the young man's head, for ever linked.

How could she ever care for him now? As the hurt came back in a wave, her body was ablaze and she felt her eyes burn. She would not cry in front of any of them. She got to her feet, then stepped stiffly across the room, accidentally knocking a glass vase of yellow roses to the floor. She heard it shatter but did not stop. In the hall she gasped for air and wrapped her arms across her middle. She heard raised voices in the room behind her and then Mark came out to the hall.

'Nicole, what is it? Why are you so upset?'

She felt too choked to speak, or even look at him, and kept her face turned away. He reached out and touched her arm.

She shrugged him off and managed to find her voice. 'Don't touch me.'

'Have I done something?'

She faced him now. 'You tell me.'

'Well, I think I must have. Won't you tell me what it is? Or is this something to do with your mother? It's her birthday soon, isn't it?'

'My mother?'

'Sylvie told me more about her death. I'm so sorry.' He paused and seemed to be choosing his words. She noticed the sadness in his eyes as he put his hands in his pockets and shook his head. 'Of course, you know my mother died too. It affected my whole life. So, you see, I do understand.'

'You understand nothing.' She stared at him as he shifted uneasily beneath her angry gaze. 'Your mother did not die while giving birth to you. Whereas my mother *did* die giving birth . . . to me. And that's something I have never been allowed to forget.'

'Nicole.' He held out a hand to her, but she took a step away and then escaped upstairs.

13

Nicole couldn't get the night of the ball out of her head. It came back in flashes, waking her from her sleep: the man's head, his fringe, the gurgle – a sound like no other – and that awful slump of his body. Over and over. It was bad enough that the high night-time temperatures of August meant sleep evaded her anyway. But without the release of sleep, how was she to find a way to put it behind her? She waved her arms to fend it off but she wanted to scream: *Not again. Please not again.* In fact, she must have fallen asleep and screamed out loud because she woke herself up. Sylvie came into her room looking worried, her pale lips pressed tightly together.

Nicole flinched as her sister sat on the bed.

'Are you all right?' Sylvie asked, putting an arm loosely round Nicole's shoulder. 'It's the middle of the night. You look as if you've seen a ghost.'

'You don't look too great yourself.'

Nicole stared at her sister's hands. She had nice hands, long fingers, delicate nails, like a musician. Nicole hid her own hands under the bedcovers. But she couldn't hide the fear or the dread. And the worst, above all, was the creeping doubt. The way it slid inside you until suddenly it hung around you, fully formed, an albatross that would weigh down your shoulders and steal your peace of mind for ever.

Who could she trust?

She looked at her sister's face. 'How do you survive this life?'

Sylvie gave her a sympathetic smile. 'Not as easily as you might think.'

'What do you mean?'

'I mean you aren't the only one to have bad dreams. I have my own nightmares. My own troubles.'

Nicole noticed her sister's hands were shaking slightly. 'Tell me about them,' she said, longing for the silent understanding some sisters seemed to enjoy.

Sylvie sat motionless for a moment. 'There's nothing to say. I'm just being morbid.'

But she had spoken mechanically and Nicole groaned as the awful images came to life again. Was that why Sylvie was feeling morbid? Did she see the same awful thing when she closed her eyes at night?

'Would you like some warm milk with a dash of brandy?'

Nicole was touched by the act of kindness but there was one thing she had to ask. 'Are you seeing Mark now?'

'You know I am.'

The next morning, as the first sharp rays of daylight pierced the darkness, Nicole climbed out of bed, quiet as a mouse, placing both feet carefully on the floor to avoid the loose floorboard under her rug. She pushed open the window then leant on the railings that curled and twisted around the back of the house. Despite her sadness she watched the birds fly about the place, and the early sunlight sparkling on the ponds, and breathed in deeply. Already warm, it would be a humid day, but at least the rain seemed to be holding off. She pulled on loose cotton trousers and a matching top, then went down to the kitchen.

Lisa was up, of course. Always up before the rest of them. 'Hello,' she said, 'I was wondering what you'd like for supper?'

'So early?'

'I have to get to market. Coffee?'

Nicole took the mug of scalding coffee, wrapping her hands round it for comfort. 'I might not be here for supper.'

As Lisa opened the back door, the sound of birdsong filled the kitchen. Nicole poked her head out to look. The sun shone and the garden, in all its different shades of green, seemed to be in continuous motion. The leaves rustled in the breeze, the branches creaked as they swayed and the flowers that had survived the rain were bright and cheerful. No one could brood for ever and, bursting with renewed life, the garden gladdened her. Sylvie was with Mark. She just had to put it behind her.

Lisa pulled up a chair, brushing her greying hair from her eyes. 'I hope you're going somewhere nice. You look rather pale.'

'Just a nightmare.'

'Not the one about drowning in the river?'

'No.'

Lisa frowned. 'Darling girl, is something the matter? You haven't looked yourself lately.'

Nicole shook her head. She couldn't tell Lisa. It wouldn't be fair. Anyway, wasn't it time she left the horror of that night behind? She tried to think of something cheerful instead.

'Tell you what,' she said as she sat down, 'I'd love an apple tart for dessert. Will you save me some if I don't make supper in time?'

Lisa grinned and reached out a hand. 'There will be a Nicole-sized piece in the larder. With whipped cream?'

Nicole felt the warmth of Lisa's hand, and squeezed. 'Yes please.'

The kitchen went silent.

Nicole sniffed. 'Isn't that burnt cheese?'

Lisa jumped up. 'Oh lordy! The Camembert for breakfast . . .'

Nicole grinned. The smell always brought back one of

Nicole's favourite things – baking Camembert with Lisa in the kitchen in Huế. 'You should have told me. I'd have helped you make it.'

'Burn it more like,' Lisa said as she flapped about.

Nicole raised her eyebrows. 'I rather think you've managed that on your own.'

When Nicole was little, Lisa would first score the fat round cheese, popping in some tips of rosemary before slipping it into the oven. Then she'd cut up the bread into bite-sized pieces. Nicole would wait patiently, her excitement building, until the point came when she was allowed to strip two woody sprigs of rosemary and thread the pieces of bread on to them. She'd drizzle on olive oil and sprinkle on salt, then Lisa would put them in the oven with the Camembert. They'd eat at the kitchen table with the window open, so they could smell the Perfume River, just the two of them. The taste when you dipped the squares of bread into the oozing Camembert! Divine. Baked Camembert, rosemary and the salty river: her favourite smell still.

She reached out to touch Lisa's hand again. 'I love you.'

'Get off with you, girl.'

Nicole felt weary from constantly fending off the gnats infesting the shop. Despite the large ceiling fan moving the air, it remained humid. On days like this Nicole felt so listless she hardly knew what to do with herself. She burned a stick of incense, wishfully thinking it might freshen the air.

Beyond the shop window a woman trader she knew signalled with a cake in her hands. Nicole couldn't resist sugar and went out.

As she ate the cake she thought about Trần. She had decided she couldn't meet him under any circumstances, and yet she couldn't help but wonder what he wanted to show her. She knew it wasn't a good idea; she needed to forget, and going with him would only bring it all back. She definitely wouldn't go. It'd be a big mistake. There. Decision made. So why at closing time was she slipping on a silk jacket and heading out in the opposite direction from home?

He was a little late but when he arrived he held out a hand. 'I knew you'd come.'

She shook his hand. 'You knew more than I did.'

He laughed. 'Must be my charm.'

He seemed in a friendly frame of mind, but she remained watchful as they walked through crowded streets, dodging women packing up their goods in lidded baskets and shaking their heads when traders offered crispy doughnuts and tiny cups of orange tea. She was curious. It was as simple as that. Yet when they reached the alleys where, but for a few shadowy figures, they were alone, her anxiety caught up with her. She hadn't felt he might be planning to hurt her, but if he had wanted to, they seemed to be heading where darkness would conceal it. She stopped walking.

Intimidated by the increasing gloom, she tried for a breezy tone of voice. 'Actually, I've changed my mind.'

He took hold of her by the elbow. 'Too late now.'

She heard someone coming down the street behind them and spun round, but it was only an old Vietnamese man scurrying along with an uneven step. The man turned off.

'Why are there no people here?'

He didn't reply.

'I said —'

He interrupted. 'I heard you.'

She glanced around.

'Just come with me.'

'I want to go home.'

'When the time is right.'

She tried to pull away. 'I want to go now.'

He stopped walking and looked at her. 'I shall not hurt you.'

Her neck muscles tensed as it sank home that a man with his political convictions was a dangerous companion for a girl from a French family. Certain sections of the ancient quarter, known to be hotbeds of Vietnamese unrest, concealed many dissenters. Why had she thought she could trust him?

'I shall not hurt you,' he said again, and this time something warm in his voice reassured her. 'Don't be afraid. You will get home safely. All in good time.'

They passed under the light from an upstairs window and she glanced at him. Her feelings towards him were an odd combination of curiosity and nervousness, but when he gave her a wide smile she saw honesty in his eyes and felt better.

'You can have confidence in me, Nicole.'

'What is your full name?'

'As you know, my family name is Trần. That will suffice for now.'

As they walked on she felt rather thrilled to be out at night in a part of town she didn't know. She heard voices as they turned into a narrow street where every shop window glowed with red and yellow lanterns. She sniffed. A sickly-sweet smell laced the air.

'Opium,' he said.

She frowned.

'As you see, beneath the social glitter of French Hanoi there is an underbelly.'

'I had heard.'

'The French encourage it through a state monopoly of the opium trade.'

They passed a spot where a few Vietnamese men stood outside eyeing up the scantily dressed Vietnamese girls, their bodies draped around French officers in white uniform. Nicole hung back lest one of the French might recognize her, but the group left the pavement and entered the building.

'Are they going dancing?'

He grimaced. 'Not exactly.'

'You're not taking me dancing, are you?'

'I don't dance.'

She looked at his serious face. 'I can believe that. Don't you do anything for fun?'

He didn't say anything, but she registered that he had almost smiled.

The street led to another with even seedier bars, and an increasingly overpowering smell of opium.

'Come,' he said as he came to a halt at the entrance of one.

She hesitated as all her father's horror stories of girls being taken came rushing back. She'd believed it had been an invention, his way of controlling her: now she wasn't so sure.

They went in and Trần led her down narrow stairs and along a corridor to the back where he pushed open a heavy door. She gasped at the heady smell in the room, which was clouded with blue smoke, silent but for soft music playing in the background.

'It's a *fumerie*,' he said.

At first she could barely see in the dimly lit room, but once her eyes adjusted she noticed little pools of diffused light radiating from oil lamps dotted about. The clientele, mainly Vietnamese, lay on slatted wooden daybeds, covered in matting, with a leather roll under their heads. Their dull and torpid eyes revealed everything. Nicole watched a bare-footed Vietnamese girl sitting in a semi-squat at the side of one of the recumbent figures. The paraphernalia of addiction lay on a low table beside her: long black opium pipes, a bamboo pot and a silver-handled needle. She picked up the needle and twisted it with a spinning movement, working the resin close to the heat of an oil lamp.

Trần nodded at another woman who appeared to be in charge and she pointed at an archway. Aware of her vulnerability, Nicole clutched hold of his arm.

'Can't we leave?'

'This is only part of what I want you to see.'

Nerves on edge, she walked on.

Beyond the archway, a wide corridor stretched ahead, carpeted in ruby red, with large cubicles lining either side, heavy brocade curtains separating each one, and stinking of synthetic perfume, a smell that seemed to have impregnated the walls. Nicole held her nose and glanced around. One of the curtains was only half closed and she averted her eyes, not wanting to see what might be inside. The place was dark, not merely from a lack of abundant lighting; she could feel the dread and darkness in her bones.

'Please,' she whispered as she drew back. 'No more.'

'Don't chicken out now.'

She shook her head.

'It won't take long.'

They moved on to where the smell altered. Now it was alcohol. She took another step forward and glanced into a cubicle where the curtain remained wide open. A man and a woman appeared to be sleeping on a velvet-covered couch, with a large grey cat sitting on a shelf above them. Was this all? . . . But there were other sounds from the cubicles further along and she knew it was not. She glanced at one, stepped forward, opened up a gap in the curtain and, feeling her flesh crawl, swiftly withdrew.

They continued to pass along the corridor and then she followed him up a narrow staircase and into a small room. He closed the door quietly and smiled. Only a low tasselled lamp lit the room and there was a cloying smell of incense and oil.

With a finger to his lips he signalled she should come over

to where a velvet curtain hung right across the wall. From beyond the curtain she heard laughter and the voices of men speaking in French. Trần signalled again. The floor creaked as she walked across. She froze, paralysed with fear, then when nothing happened, drew a little closer.

'Some like to watch,' he whispered, and pointed to a chink in the curtain.

Nicole looked through the small gap at a large room furnished in dark wood, where a naked young Vietnamese girl lay on a bed covered in silk. Nicole gazed at the girl's deadpan face and wanted to shout at her to run, though truly she knew the girl would have nowhere to go. Three officers seemed to be taking it in turns with another girl while passing round a bottle of brandy. One of the men slapped the girl's behind and, as he bent her over, she was forced to take another man's privates in her mouth. Nicole stifled her disgust, but accidentally pulled the curtain open a touch. She shuddered when the man looked up. She couldn't be certain if he'd seen her because, with closed eyes, his face spasmed and his thick-lipped mouth fell open: the key person who should have been policing the city – Daniel Giraud's father.

She turned away, sickened.

'Seen enough?' Trần whispered, reaching out to her.

She closed her eyes for a moment and lifted a hand to wave him away. 'Let's get out of here.'

He led her back along the corridor, through the opium-infused room and out on to the street again where she gasped for air.

'This is just one of many brothels. There are thousands of people engaged in prostitution. The least salubrious are in Meteorological Street.'

She turned in shock. Worse than this? How could anything be worse? The day had started so well; she had decided to leave the past behind, and for the first time in ages she'd felt hopeful again. Now her nerves were frayed, and she felt angry at the shameful duplicity of the French and their exploitation of the girls.

'There are hundreds of gambling dens too.' He helped her straighten up. 'Are you all right?'

She nodded and concentrated on calming herself down. When she could speak again she said, 'The gambling seems less awful.'

'Except the Vietnamese are great gamblers. From wretched debt there are many suicides. This is what we wish to change.'

'I thought you just wanted to get the French out.'

'That's only the start. We need to re-educate the Vietnamese people too.' He paused for a moment. 'Come, let's get away from here.'

As they walked, the smell of opium still seemed to cling to her clothes and she felt dirtier than she'd ever been. 'Why did you show me this?'

'To help you understand we are not bad people, but working for the common good.'

'But against the French.'

'How can it be any other way? We want to raise our people up, not keep them squashed by poverty. We want to give them hope for the future. We want to control what is ours. Do you not see?'

Chastened by the experience, she nodded.

As they left the streets behind Nicole thought of the river in Huế. She used to see the boats and watch the poor cooking rice in clay pots as they paddled along. Had they been happy with their simple lives? What if the reality was different? What if all along they had been struggling and miserable?

'You need me to get your thoughts in order,' Trần said with eagerness. 'Like I said, the French encourage the use of opium but only so long as it is government opium.'

'That can't be true!'

'I'm afraid it is. The French seized control of cultivation, manufacture and the trade itself. Now it is being smuggled across from China too, and they don't appreciate losing out to a bunch of black-marketeers.'

'Was that why your brother was killed?'

He shrugged.

Nicole hurried back to the comforts of home, thinking about what she'd seen. Had Trần sensed the discontent in her and decided she might be ripe for conversion? Perhaps he'd spotted that her relationship with her family had come loose. Well, he was wrong. Despite her Vietnamese looks, her mother was dead and her father had always maintained the illusion of a predominantly French family. The Vietnamese blood in her family had been buried for too long.

14

The heavy rains and high winds were increasingly dreary and Nicole couldn't wait for September and October when Hanoi's dry season would return with its clear, cool days. That was Nicole's favourite time of year and, at the beginning of September, the show would finally open. Now, during a break in rehearsals, she sat down in her dressing room to try to deal with the uproar going on in her mind. She ached for those girls but felt angry with herself for having gone with Trần; no matter how much she wished, she could not see a way to make things better.

She came to the conclusion that Trần's brother must have been shot because of smuggling opium. It didn't make the shooting right, but at least it was a reason. If opium was government controlled, he shouldn't have broken the law, though she couldn't rid herself of the thought that any opium trade was wrong. Legal or illegal.

She decided to put it to the back of her mind. She couldn't let herself be overwhelmed and wouldn't let him persuade her again. What use would it be if he opened her eyes still further? She'd wandered too far away already.

A knock at the changing-room door startled her and she heard Jerry call her name. She hadn't been singing well so came out of the changing room expecting a dressing-down.

'Are you all right?' he said.

'A bit tired. Sorry I'm not up to scratch today.'

'We all have off-days. Don't worry. The thing is, Simone has been taken ill. With less than a month until we open I need a replacement.'

She stared at him blankly.

'So?' he said. 'Do you think you can do it?'

She felt a wild surge of excitement as she realized he was asking her to take on the main role.

'Can you learn the songs quickly enough?'

She felt herself blush with pleasure. 'I know them.'

'It's settled then.'

She grinned. 'When do I start?'

'Right now. We'll carry on with Act Two.'

She hesitated. 'What about a script?'

He raised his brows. 'I thought you knew the songs?'

'For the lines and cues.'

'Very well, but you'll need to be word perfect quickly.'

Nicole nodded and made her way to the stage.

The musical was French, written by a French-Vietnamese, and was about a Frenchman who falls in love with a Vietnamese girl. Though Nicole's father had married a Vietnamese woman, such intermarriage had become far less common than it had once been, and so the musical had never been performed. Jerry had thought it worth reviving.

Nicole thought about Mark and wished she could tell him her news. He knew nothing of the difficult times she and Sylvie had shared: the tensions, the arguments, the rivalry. Nor could he know that he'd become a trophy that Sylvie had somehow won. As for the murder, she was beginning to believe his innocence. Her anxiety had faded and seeing things more clearly had meant she could sleep again. Mark had not been complicit; he had only been there as a witness – an unwilling witness. That was all. As for Sylvie? Her sister had already taken up far too much space in her mind.

★

She was walking past the Hollywood dance hall one beautiful Sunday afternoon when the music coming from inside forced her to stop and listen. In an attempt to get on with her life she had taken to walking on Sundays when it wasn't raining, sometimes meeting friends, sometimes on her own. Today she walked alone, with her back straight and her shoulders stiff with tension. She glanced at the enormous glass doors, thrown open for air – inside it was blue with smoke – and watched the people going in and out. She was wearing her favourite black dress, cotton, with a full skirt and rounded neck, and would have liked to have gone in to lose herself in the fug. She had even considered the new gamine haircut, now coming into fashion, anything to make her feel like a different person, but she couldn't make the leap. Instead she'd coiled her thick dark hair at the back of her neck.

How long she had been standing there when Mark appeared in the distance, she didn't know. It was all too easy to lose track of time when you felt a bit lost inside yourself. In a state of anxious expectancy she stiffened, then glanced up as a group of birds wheeled across the sky. She had to create the impression she didn't care about him, but couldn't admit how much she needed to prove it to herself.

She heard him call her name.

'Hello, Mark,' she said, twisting back and trying for a light-hearted tone.

'What are you doing here?'

'Passing by.' She smiled and made a fist behind her back, digging her nails into the fleshy part of her hand.

He leant against the wall. 'You're looking very pretty.'

'Am I?'

He wore a dark blue suit that made his eyes seem even brighter, but there was something different about him, something vulnerable that touched her deeply. His eyes looked tired with dark shadows beneath them and she wanted to reach out and comfort him.

'I've missed you,' he said and smiled.

Nicole raised her brows. 'That isn't my fault. Has Sylvie still not told you why you haven't seen me?'

'Told me what?'

She hesitated. It entered her mind that she could just come out with it; tell him she'd seen him kiss Sylvie. Pride stopped her and, though his eyes seemed to be full of questions, she couldn't allow herself to be drawn back to that night. 'It doesn't matter . . . I have the main part in the show now. Simone has been taken ill.'

'I knew you had talent,' he said and smiled warmly.

'Would you come? To the opening performance, I mean.'

She had blurted it out without thinking and stared into his bright blue eyes trying to halt the redness she could feel starting to burn her cheeks. Neither of them spoke but stood completely still, gazing at each other. She saw a flicker of something and felt sure his feelings for her were reflected in his eyes. It seemed as if there was something he wanted to say. She felt tears warm the back of her lids and longed to touch him, but forced herself to remain where she was.

'Would you like to go for a drink?' he said finally.

She didn't reply and the silence grew uncomfortable.

'So?' He held out his hand but she didn't take it.

He was still staring at her, expecting a response. She forced a smile and he took it as acquiescence.

He walked with his hands in his trouser pockets, so close that she bumped against him from time to time. He kicked an empty cigarette packet to the kerb and she longed desperately to feel him close again, but also felt driven to edge away.

'Isn't Hanoi wonderful now?' he was saying. 'I thought that heat would never end.'

'Don't be taken in. It's not over yet.'

They reached a bar with tables set outside on the pavement. 'Will this do?'

She nodded and he pulled out a chair for her. 'I'll have white wine,' she said.

He went inside and a few minutes later came out with a glass of wine for her and a beer for himself, then lit a cigarette and blew the smoke upwards.

'I'd love to come to the show. Maybe it would be nice if your father and Sylvie came too.'

She stole a look at his eyes. 'Why?'

'Don't you want them to see how good you are?'

She shrugged. She wanted to be normal with him, the way they had been before, but what she had seen had changed everything. No matter what he said now, the damage was done and they were awkward with each other. Moreover, now that he seemed so ill at ease, she wondered if his previous nonchalance had been assumed. She hated not being able to read him clearly any more. She too felt artificial, as if she was playing the part of Nicole and not being her.

'What happened, Nicole? Between us?'

She could hardly believe her ears as he continued to gaze at her, a vein pulsing in his temple, his eyes seeming so clear and honest.

'You're seeing Sylvie,' she eventually managed to say, her voice sounding strained.

He frowned. 'Of course. Now and then. Perhaps she never told you that we dated when she was in the States?'

'Perhaps *you* never told me.'

'It was just a few times, nothing serious, and then, when she was ill, I helped her out.'

'Ill? Sylvie was ill? She never said.'

'It was a long time ago. My business with your sister now is silk.'

'I know that's not all it is.' She lowered her voice and was going to tell him about seeing him kiss Sylvie but at the last moment changed her mind. The curtain that had come down between them meant that she couldn't. Just couldn't. It would make her sound so young and childish.

He frowned and reached out for her, taking her hand in his and turning it palm upwards, then tracing the lines with his fingertips. He looked terribly miserable and she wanted to take his face in her hands and kiss away the sadness. But even though his touch electrified her, she pulled her hand back.

'I know about the work you're doing to fund a third army.'

'She told you?'

Nicole nodded and drank her wine in one gulp. 'So you're in intelligence?'

He frowned and said nothing, the two lines between his brows deepening. A delicious fragrance of roses came from a woman passer-by. The scent reminded Nicole of the ball and she felt herself empty of everything but pain. For a moment she felt glued to her chair but she couldn't stand the torment of being so close to him any more and eventually forced herself up.

'Well, I have to go. Nice to see you, Mark,' she said, and with her mind in turmoil she fled.

Just round the corner she leant against a wall and allowed herself to breathe more freely. She closed her eyes, annoyed with herself for still caring so much. But why was he making out he wasn't seeing Sylvie? An intelligence officer would be well trained in deception and she didn't know what to believe. A memory of her sister as a child came back and the tears Nicole had been holding in welled up. They'd been in the garden. Sylvie was showing a friend the latest photos she'd stuck into the family album, while Nicole was on the swing singing to herself.

Apart from the cloud of insects buzzing around flowering bushes and ripe peach trees, it had been quiet. On the opposite side of the Perfume River, Vietnamese children were flying kites, their paper dragons and painted fish soaring above the haze. It was January, dry and pleasant, and cake-baking day in the Duval house, so Lisa had been busy and they had been left to their own devices. A large-billed crow had stirred the air as it landed near the swing, slapping its wings against Nicole's leg. She'd swiped at it, then watched as it screeched – *caa-haa-caa* – and rose to the highest branch of the pipal tree to stand guard with another shiny crow. It had been the most perfect day.

'You look lovely, but have you seen Nicole?' Sylvie's friend had said, laughing loudly as she pointed at a page in the album. 'She looks so ugly.'

Sylvie had laughed too and had then turned to Nicole. 'You don't photograph at all well, do you, Nicole?'

Nicole had jumped off the swing and come to look. She cringed when she saw the worst photo Sylvie could have picked. The dress was a hand-me-down, her hair looked as if it needed washing and she had the most awful toothy grin on her face. Sylvie, meanwhile, looked perfect.

'Why did you put that one in? Weren't there any better ones?'

Sylvie shrugged. 'I didn't think you'd care. You don't usually care what you look like.'

Afterwards Nicole had felt so hurt and angry she hadn't known how to deal with it. The truth was she'd always felt as if there was some invisible line she would always fall short of. She desperately cared about how she looked and constantly worried about how other people saw her. So she had sneaked into Sylvie's room and taken her sister's favourite doll. Then she'd cut off all the doll's hair and drowned her in the Perfume River.

15

The next day Nicole's head hurt like hell when she opened the shop – too much brandy pilfered from her father's cellar the night before – and though she had discovered alcohol did help her forget, it also made her feel more maudlin. She swept the floor, polished the furniture and was about to start on the windows when she spotted Yves with his daughter Yvette walking past on the other side. Yvette grinned and they came on over, narrowly missing a vagrant chicken running between their legs.

'I looked for you earlier,' he said, 'but the shop was closed.'

'Did you need me?'

'I was going to ask if you could keep Yvette with you for a few hours. I'm off to the hospital.'

'Nothing serious?'

'A check-up. It doesn't matter now. She's coming with me.'

Not wanting to miss the chance to spend a day with a child whose straightforward happiness was so infectious, Nicole shook her head.

'Don't be silly. Let her stay here,' she said. 'If we're not too busy I'll teach her how to cut silk.'

'You don't mind?'

'Not at all.'

'Here's the key to the cafe, if you wouldn't mind fetching Trophy.'

Nicole held out a hand to the little girl and after they'd waved Yves off, they collected Trophy and took him through to the back, then began to wash the shop windows. It was a lovely day with the smell of lime in the air, a clear blue sky and a breeze so fresh it didn't matter when more of the water soaked the girls' clothing than went on the glass. And afterwards it was perfect to sit on the step to dry off and watch the world go by.

As the air thickened with the smell of lunch, their attention was drawn to the spot where a small group of dancers was assembling at the painted gates of a temple. Beside them a man wearing a gold outfit sat on the pavement with a drum. As he began to play, the dancers swayed slightly, gradually building up to a spinning movement. Another group of women began to sing. The serenity and sensuousness of the dancers was tantalizing. Enthralled by the scene, Yvette gripped Nicole's hand and squeezed.

'I don't suppose you remember your mama?' Nicole whispered in her ear.

'No.'

Yvette's mother had been a Vietnamese dancer of great beauty, but during the war she had attracted the attention of a Japanese commandant and that had been her downfall. He had become enraptured by the complexity of the siren-like dancer who, at the same time, embodied utter purity, and had requisitioned her to dance only for him. Except it was never only dancing.

They continued to watch until the dance was over.

'Shall we cut some silk now?' Nicole said. 'I've got the biggest shears you've ever seen. What colour shall we have?'

'Cream, please.'

Before they could get on with the lesson a stream of customers came in. One of Nicole's favourite customers was among them, an old, heavily lined woman with only a few teeth remaining who bought silk for her granddaughters. Despite what must have been a hard life, her eyes still sparkled and she always had a smile for Nicole.

When the shop was quiet again, and once Yvette was standing safely on a stool in order to see, Nicole began to unroll the fabric. It was of the highest quality and, shot through with gold, it shimmered as the sun caught the threads. After she had it laid flat on some fine paper she covered it with another sheet of paper.

'What's that for?' asked Yvette.

'If you cut silk between paper the silk behaves like the paper and it's much easier to cut. First we'll cut one metre for you to take home, and then I have to cut and parcel up eight metres for Sylvie. She asked for it ages ago but I just kept forgetting.'

'It's a lot.'

'Isn't it?'

Yvette hesitated before she spoke, but looked up at Nicole with shining eyes. 'When I'm grown up, could I work here with you?'

Nicole was touched and gave the child's thin shoulders a squeeze. Sometimes Yvette felt more like a sister than Sylvie ever did. 'Not with your father in the bakery?'

'Maybe both?' Clearly still thinking about it, Yvette giggled. 'Don't tell him, but I like silk better.'

With heads bent, the girls worked on the task, Nicole explaining how silk helped to retain heat in cold weather and got rid of excess heat in hot weather.

'Silk is strong too,' Nicole said. 'Finer than human hair, yet as strong as an iron wire.'

'I love it,' the child said. 'The way it shines.'

Nicole was enchanted by Yvette's obvious interest and only the shop bell broke their concentration.

'Hello,' Trần said. 'Two little *métisses* working hard, I see.'

Nicole looked up and bristled. 'I wish you wouldn't call me that.'

He laughed. 'Sorry, young French mademoiselle!' With a

wide sweep of his right arm he bowed and she couldn't help but smile. He looked different. In fact, each time she saw him he looked different as he melted in and out of her world. Today he looked like a student.

He held out a hand to help Yvette down from the stool. 'What do you say to some ice cream?'

Yvette's eyes lit up and she glanced at Nicole.

Nicole nodded and he started to leave the shop with Yvette in tow.

'No, leave the child. Get the ice cream and bring it here.'

He looked at her with a slight frown. 'You really don't trust me, do you?'

'Is there any reason I should?'

He shrugged and released Yvette's hand. As he left the shop Nicole noticed the purple birthmark again. Too hot for a neck scarf, it was almost entirely visible. She doubted if he would come back with ice cream, but he did, and the three of them sat on the step to eat it, along with O-Lan. Nicole had mango and passion fruit sorbet and the others had a mix of chocolate and coffee. Afterwards they sang a couple of Vietnamese songs. Trần joined in and Yvette hummed. He was so sweet with Yvette that, despite his extreme views, Nicole couldn't help liking him.

After a while O-Lan went back indoors and Yvette slipped through to the courtyard to release Trophy for a few minutes.

Trần turned to Nicole. 'Have you thought about it?'

'About what?'

'Helping us.'

'You think you can buy my allegiance with ice cream?'

He laughed. 'No, little one, but you do know you are living with a false sense of security? The war of resistance will only grow stronger now we have the peasants on our side.'

'I thought you were one!'

'I am, but I was lucky enough to receive an education paid for by my uncle, and now I am using my brain.'

'Was your brother killed because he really did assassinate that French official? Or was he a smuggler?'

'There is no evidence he assassinated that man and he was no smuggler. But as I said before, we do believe that, as a known agitator, he was killed in revenge for the assassination. For show, if you like.'

'How was he known?'

'There are spies on both sides. We too have to gather information on French military operations, as well as American interventions.'

She pulled a face. 'You must be mad if you think I can help.'

'You have an American friend.'

'I think the word you're looking for is *had*. Anyway, he's only a silk merchant and wouldn't know anything.'

'You believe that?'

Nicole looked away. 'As I said, he is no longer my friend. Not that I'd spy for you anyway.'

'*Bắt cá hai tay*. You cannot run with the hare and hunt with the hounds. There will come a day when you will have to choose whether you are French or Vietnamese.'

She narrowed her eyes and scrutinized his face. 'You seem very sure, but I am both. I can't change that.'

'A matter of time. You must have seen the condition the workers live in? The sanitation? The poverty? Does it not fill you with dismay?'

He said no more as he got up to leave, but it wasn't hard to imagine.

'One of these days I shall open your eyes still further,' he said.

After he left Nicole slipped upstairs and pulled out the little embroidered purse she had found on her first day working at the shop. She hugged it to her chest as she waited for Yvette. Whenever she was sad or low, or even just a bit unsure of herself, having the little purse in her hands always made her feel better. And, right now, Trần confused her. Even with his black hair slicked back and the beginnings of a moustache, there was still something raw and unfinished about him. She couldn't deny that his full lips and burning dark eyes were attractive, and there was something exciting about his youthful idealism. But it was the passion she saw in him that truly inspired, even if it was all nonsense.

16

The day Sylvie came to the shop to pick up the silk, Nicole had left the front door open to air the place while folding off-cuts into little squares to be sold.

'I'm between meetings so I haven't got long,' Sylvie said, looking smart in a simple white shift dress, with a little feathered hat, grey crocodile-skin shoes and wrist-length gloves. She peeled one off to run her fingertips along the counter. 'You're keeping it clean.'

'It has to be clean to cut the silk.'

'Of course.'

Nicole felt drab in comparison to her sister and wished she hadn't worn her oldest Vietnamese work clothes. She carried on folding. 'Is there anything else?'

As Sylvie glanced around, Nicole noticed that her sister was jittery, not her usual cool self. 'I'll need to look at the figures to get the whole picture, but I can see the shop's looking good. In fact, you've made it beautiful.'

Nicole stopped folding and gazed at her sister. 'Thank you.'

'It must mean a lot to you.'

'It means everything.'

'I didn't expect you to take it so seriously.'

They went on to talk about the family's main department store on Rue Paul Bert and how the profits were dwindling. Sylvie had plans, she said, big plans for when the present trouble was over. She seemed so certain it would be over.

'Look, I wish we could start again,' Sylvie said.

'From when?'

'Way back . . . when we were children, I suppose.'

Nicole sighed. If only it were that easy. 'Do you remember when you told everyone I was adopted?'

'Oh dear, I was awful, wasn't I?'

Nicole grinned. 'Only sometimes.'

'It wasn't all me. You left a dead mouse in my bed.'

'You and your friends excluded me.'

'I'm sorry.' Sylvie paused. 'Can't we try a little harder?'

'To do what?'

'To like each other . . .'

There was a brief silence while Nicole thought about it. The truth was that when they were children there had been times when Sylvie had stuck up for her. She'd helped with maths homework too, and had been kind when Nicole woke trembling from the nightmare of drowning in the Perfume River. A sister relationship was complicated, and so heavily rooted in half-remembered childhood events.

'Tell you what, I'm going to the lantern village tomorrow,' Sylvie said. 'There's a festival. Would you like to come too?'

Nicole didn't answer but bent down behind the counter. She came up with a string-tied white paper parcel. 'Here are your eight metres. It's lovely, this cream. The best silk we have. What do you want it for?'

'Just my bottom drawer.'

Nicole didn't raise her eyes. What was really going on? Could her sister be hoping that Mark would propose?

She felt a burst of anger, her heart banging against her ribs, and she only looked up when she was confident that her distress didn't show. But still it felt like a punch to the stomach and she was sick with jealousy. If he and her sister were as close as Sylvie was implying then it really was all over for her.

'So how is Mark?' Nicole said, aiming for nonchalance, but desperate to find out more.

Sylvie tapped her watch repeatedly. 'Oh, busy, you know. Like me. In fact, he's away in Saigon most of the time. So do you want to come to the festival? We could meet at Hoàn Kiếm Lake at four?'

The festival of lanterns was an evening affair, but Sylvie had suggested arriving early so they could watch some of the lanterns being made. Nicole had only agreed to go in order to quiz her sister about Mark, and had decided to invite O-Lan to come along for moral support.

'The lantern makers here came from Hoi An originally,' O-Lan was saying as they left the car and walked into the heart of the village, where lanterns were hanging in readiness for the evening. While some were in the shape of dragons' heads, others resembled fish and a few were simple boxes decorated with streamers. 'The frames are made of aged bamboo,' O-Lan said. 'They soak it in salt water for several days.'

'Why?' Sylvie asked, seeming like her usual calm self again.

'It protects them from worms and moths.'

'The silk is beautiful,' Nicole said, fingering a red lantern recently displayed. In the shape of a mythical beast, the colours looked as if they were on fire.

'All the silk comes from my family's village,' O-Lan said.

Nicole nodded. 'Let's buy one, Sylvie, for the garden at home. We could have a full-moon party.'

'I'm not sure Papa would agree to that, but it would look lovely. These are much bigger than the paper lanterns we have at home.' Sylvie grinned. 'In fact, I think we should buy several. And you could hang one in the shop.'

They went into a shop to watch the owner making one. A strong smell of incense rose from a coil in the corner and Sylvie began to cough. They went back outside, where the scent still lingered but was less overpowering.

'Heavens,' she said, 'how many different herbs were in that?'

'As many as fifteen,' O-Lan said.

'Too many for me. By the way, how's your mother, O-Lan? I heard she was ill.'

Nicole was surprised at this. She couldn't remember telling Sylvie.

'A bit better, thank you.'

As the daylight faded and the November air cooled, the lanterns were lit and, once the night had properly settled, dozens of them punctuated the darkness, making the sky seem even blacker in contrast. The main road was only a dirt track but it was well trodden and not muddy.

The girls walked on and, reaching a crossroads, came to a simple stage, surrounded by smaller lanterns suspended from ropes between the trees. Excited children were running round the stage, calling to each other and dodging the adults busily trying to collar them. Half a dozen dogs joined in too and the atmosphere was buzzing.

As several musicians took to the stage and the sound of drums took over, Nicole swayed to the music; inside, though, she was so full of anxiety she was surprised it didn't show. Three men came on to dance with a huge red and gold silk dragon. The men held it high above them, each one carrying two long sticks which they used to articulate the creature; its monstrous head, bulging eyes and the paper flames pouring from its flaring nostrils were mesmerizing.

The older Vietnamese still believed everything contained a spirit, including lakes, rivers and trees. The festival was a ritual to honour the spirits of light and it was critical that every year they make it as beautiful as possible to ensure the continuing of the sunlight. The belief was, if mankind did the right thing, they could influence the spirits to look on them with benevolence.

Nicole could see the way the dragon symbolized power and prosperity, and turned round to speak to Sylvie, but her sister wasn't there. O-Lan, caught up in the show, carried on watching as Nicole fought her way through to the back of the crowd.

'There you are,' she said when she spotted Sylvie.

'I've bought two dragon heads. Look!' Sylvie held them up. 'Of course, they'll look better with light inside, but aren't they beautiful? And I knocked the man down on the price.'

Nicole ran her fingers over the silk. 'They are exquisite,' she said.

'Here, you carry one.' Sylvie passed a lantern to Nicole and then linked arms with her. 'It's so nice to spend time together, isn't it? We don't do it enough. Shall we find something to eat now?'

'We need to wait for O-Lan.'

'Oh yes, of course, I didn't mean we should go without her.'

'Actually, why don't you wait for O-Lan and I'll run back to the car with the lanterns? If we try to eat while carrying them, they'll only be ruined.'

Before passing her the other lantern Sylvie touched Nicole's arm. 'I know I should have said so before but I am sorry about what happened at the ball.'

'Mark?'

'I meant the dress.'

'Oh.'

'But Mark too. I didn't realize you thought there was anything more than friendship between you.'

Nicole shook her head. 'There wasn't anything more than friendship. Not really.' It wasn't true but she didn't want to give Sylvie the satisfaction of knowing how devastated she really felt.

'Well, I realize now you hoped there might have been. I wish there was something I could say to make it all right.'

Nicole looked into her sister's eyes. Lit by a lantern hanging from a branch just above her head, Sylvie's eyes looked moist and sincere. Instead of asking questions, Nicole felt more confused and worse than ever.

17

Soon after the night of the festival a sparkling day lifted Nicole's spirits, with the heat tempered by a silvery breeze and a comfortable humidity. Like many Hanoians, she loved September. The cool dry weather was still bright and along the streets the trees flaunted their red and yellow leaves. The sky was a more intense blue, and the lakes glittered, greener than in the rainy weather. Large white daisies and yellow sunflowers grew on every scrap of land, but she especially loved the fragrance of milk flowers in the cool of the evening. The tiny white flowers on the tree in their garden also bloomed on a few trees lining the city streets, and there was talk of planting many more when the war with the Vietminh was won. Their blossom infused the air with a bitter-sweet fragrance and, as the wind blew, Nicole thought the fluttering white flowers looked like falling snow.

It made her feel happy and as she walked to the shop she thought of their life in Huế, recalling a day when her father had taken her beyond the usual Huế villages to a distant hamlet of bronze casters. He'd been looking for a birthday present for Sylvie. Nicole racked her brain trying to remember what he'd bought. The next day he'd taken Nicole to a silk village to show her how silk was made.

There she had seen the three stages of silk production for the first time and had fallen in love. The first stage was the cultivation of the mulberry trees. Next came the breeding of the silkworms and the extraction of the thread from the cocoons. The silkworms ate the mulberry leaves and after they had transformed into pupae they were killed by dipping them in boiling water before the adult moths emerged. She'd felt rather sorry for the poor little pupae, bred only to produce a silk that, once the whole cocoon unravelled in the spinning, would come out as one continuous thread. After that they were cooked and eaten. The third stage, and the most exciting, was weaving the threads into cloth.

Nicole glanced at the street stalls she passed. It was market day, and everyone was milling about, picking up produce or gossiping on the corners. Feeling buoyant, she swung her arms as she walked. Everyone loved to haggle and she listened to the laughter and the sound of voices raised in friendly argument. As the day grew hotter she paused to buy a strong tea from the boy with the little teacups hanging from a bamboo pole, thinking about what she would be doing that day. She glanced up and spotted Yvette standing between two parked cars. Perhaps she'd invite the child to spend some time in the silk shop again. Yvette waved and Nicole lifted her hand to wave back.

Without warning, a deafening blast hurled debris twenty metres up in the air, before showering the street as it fell. Instead of waving at Yvette, Nicole's hands flew to cover her ears and she was thrown back into an alleyway. Fear swept through the street: children crying and running for their mothers; people screaming and shouting; men calling out and women standing rooted to the spot in disbelief. Nicole half saw it all happen, half heard it, but as smoke thickened the air, it nevertheless became clear that two cars were still on fire. Her body felt strangely heavy as she stepped out from the alley. Another explosion rocked the street. A ferocious ball of fire erupted, followed by a rumbling, roaring sound. In a state of terror, Nicole closed her eyes against the blinding white light of the after-image.

She began to choke on the ash, but remembering Yvette,

opened her stinging eyes and stared at the burning cars – the exact place where she'd seen the child. In desperation to reach Yvette, she ran over the shards of broken glass and jagged edges of torn metal. Dogs began howling and in the noise and general panic she barely noticed a man lying on the ground, reaching out his arms to plead for help. As she passed more of the injured, Nicole hesitated, but then she saw the little girl. For a moment Nicole could not move. The smoke had cleared just enough to see, but the air around her was stifling and unbearably hot. As the horror hit her in the pit of her stomach she made a strangled sound. *Please not Yvette. Not a child who had never harmed anyone.*

Water began spreading across the street, and collecting in a pool where the road dipped. The little girl lay beside the water with her left leg crushed beneath bricks and mortar, the little puppy, Trophy, whimpering at her side. Nicole glanced around for help. Wild with fear, she began pulling at the rubble covering Yvette's leg, breaking her nails and scratching her arms. As she released the little girl's leg, the blood spread out on top of the pool of water, shining mirror-like.

Though the street was far from silent, the sound of French music playing on a radio could be heard drifting out from inside the bakery. Nicole fell to her knees and lifted the little girl's head to her lap, hardly able to look at her dark eyes, but stroking her face and murmuring her name. With tears refusing to fall, Nicole rocked Yvette, wiping the child's warm blood and the dirt from her cheeks, and attempting to sing her favourite song, the song they had always sung together on a Saturday morning in their kitchen. The blast must have killed her instantly. As Nicole's throat became too choked to continue, she looked up and saw Yves coming towards her, the bones in his face standing out, the flesh drawn so tight he barely looked alive himself.

She glanced down at her dress where it had soaked up blood and noticed a shard of glass embedded in her hand. Now her own blood was trickling between her fingers. Yves came over and lifted Yvette. Everything went silent. He did not speak and neither did Nicole. She gulped, gritted her teeth, pulled out the glass, ripped a piece of her skirt to wrap round her hand, then picked up the puppy and stumbled after Yves into the bakery.

Yves sat down at a table with his daughter in his arms and wept.

Nicole sat opposite in a state of silent shock.

This was nothing like the black-and-white pictures in the newspapers, mainly of French victories in the remote hills and valleys of the north. This blood was red, redder than she could have imagined, and there was so much of it, the flesh torn and battered, the death real. Far too real. Time seemed to have halted, trapping Nicole in a world where a child's life could be taken in a matter of seconds. She felt colder inside than ever before. Gradually, as the sounds of the street filtered through again, she heard voices raised in anger and became aware that something inside her had changed. The police finally arrived and the sound of their sirens rang out. That was what she would remember: a blur of sirens, people sobbing and the sickly smell of blood and burnt sugar in the street.

The police questioned her at the scene, a few simple questions. What had she witnessed? Was there any warning? That sort of thing. So she was surprised when her father summoned her into his office early the next morning, saying that the police wished to speak to her again. She trailed behind him, feeling raw and wearing only her silk dressing gown. She had wept for Yvette throughout the night and Lisa had held her close. But Nicole's sorrow ran deep. She had loved Yvette like a sister.

As her father closed the door she tried to wipe the images from her mind, but all she could think was that nothing could justify the killing of children. Then she saw who was waiting in the smoky office: Inspector Paul Giraud took up too much space in the room as he stood with his back to the wall, legs apart, and with his arms folded in front of him. Nicole felt a knot twist in her stomach as they came face to face. He focused his watery eyes on her. She glanced at her father with raised brows.

'Monsieur Giraud has a few questions he'd like you to answer, Nicole. That's all.' He had spoken kindly and with warmth in his voice.

The combination of grief and exhaustion had left her vulnerable. She took a step forward and gripped the back of an upright chair. 'Papa, I haven't slept at all. Can't it wait?' Her voice shook.

Her father looked at the floor as Giraud came to stand beside her. He smoothed down his hair, so close she felt as if he was about to pounce. She could identify every black nostril hair and smell the tobacco on his breath. Remembering what she'd seen him do, she shuddered.

'If I can have a minute,' Giraud said and carried on smoothing his hair. 'An amicable chat. It has been noticed you have been spending time with a young Vietnamese man.'

His voice was low, not much louder than a murmur. She hated that. It meant she had to strain to hear and that gave him power over her. She gazed at him before replying and something in his eyes told her he had caught sight of her watching him at the brothel. The knot in her stomach grew tighter.

'It's not against the law, is it?'

Her father interrupted with a warning note. 'Nicole.'

'You know you can put your faith in me,' Giraud said, holding out a hand. 'You trust me and I'll trust you, if you get my meaning.'

Nicole shook her head. 'I haven't been *spending time* as you put it.'

With an exaggeratedly patient sigh he continued. 'You were seen eating ice cream with him while sitting on the front step at your shop.'

'Is that a crime?'

'I didn't bring you up to behave like a common native,' her father said, but he hadn't spoken angrily.

'He's a student. I hardly know him,' Nicole said.

'What is his name? Or rather, what is the name he has given you?' Giraud asked.

'I don't know.'

'Come on, Nicole,' her father said. 'We are trying to find the killers of Yvette. I know you care.'

'Of course I care.' She clenched her jaw so tight it hurt but really she wanted to sit down and howl. She closed her eyes. If she could just make Giraud disappear and the questions stop . . .

'Well. Does he have a name?'

She hesitated. But, knowing she had no choice, opened her eyes. 'I only know he's called Trần.'

'They are all called Trần or Nguyễn. Is that all you know? Think, Nicole, anything you can give us might be the clue we need. Anything at all.'

There was a pause as her father smiled at her. 'Monsieur Giraud is not blaming you, Nicole. We know it was nothing to do with you.'

Nicole could no longer hold on to her tears and as they began to drip down her cheeks she brushed them away, furious with herself for crying in front of the odious man.

He pulled a chair out for her and smiled. 'Why not sit, my dear? You'll feel better.'

She did not want to sit but did as she was told, then watched as he turned to her father. 'Édouard, could you arrange for a glass of water, please, or maybe a lemonade.'

He could have rung the bell to request the drink, but her father left the room. As soon as he had gone Giraud's smile faded and he wiped a hand across his brow. Now he raised his voice. 'We have been watching young Trần.'

'You came here just to question me about Trần?'

Giraud shook his head. 'Yvette is our shared interest. But your young man and his conspirators are our prime suspects. You were seen with him one evening. I think we both know when. How do you explain it?'

'Why? What does it matter anyway? He's not my young man, he's just a stu–'

Giraud broke in. 'Time to tell the truth. We can do each other a favour.'

There was silence for a moment.

'So? Tell me about it. You and him.'

'There is no me and him.'

'What were you doing with him? You might think I'm not on your side. But we want the same thing, don't we?'

Nicole swallowed. Trần couldn't have had anything to do with the atrocity. He had been so kind to Yvette. And yet he had said the city would be under siege. Had it been a warning? Not knowing how to feel, she remembered how he'd also said he would open her eyes.

'He told me his brother had been shot by the French.'

'Ah, now we're getting somewhere.'

She shook her head. 'He was nice.'

'Anyone can be nice when they want to be. Even me.' He laughed. 'But you're stepping into a world you don't understand. Now, I help you, you help me. That's how it works. The next time he comes to the shop, I want you to telephone this number. You do have a telephone there?'

'The line was disconnected, but it's all right now.'

'So do we have a deal? You don't need to speak, let it ring three times, put it down and do the same again once more.'

Nicole gave the slightest nod while staring at the floor. The one thing she would not tell him was that O-Lan was Trần's cousin.

Giraud squeezed her shoulder and left his hand resting there. 'That's a good girl. I want us to understand each other.'

Her father came back in with a glass of lemonade.

'Nicole has agreed,' Giraud said, moving away to light a cigarette.

'Are you sure about this, Giraud?' her father said as he handed her the glass and then patted her on the shoulder. 'I don't want you putting my daughter in danger. I'd prefer her not to go back to the shop at all.'

'Don't worry. Give it a few days while the American CIA place their undercover agents in the area. We will all be keeping an eye on Nicole.'

Nicole glared at her father. 'Who told Monsieur Giraud about me talking to Trần?'

'Don't be so quick to fire up, Nicole.'

'In any case, I'm afraid we can't reveal our sources,' added Giraud. 'Thank you for your cooperation.'

'Well, as long as you can ensure her safety. I love both my girls very much.'

Nicole glanced up at her father again and saw that his eyes were moist.

18

For a few days Nicole did not see Trần; nor did she want to. She had thought about it carefully. And the more she thought and tried to remember everything he'd said, the more she began to believe he might have been involved in Yvette's death. The thought horrified her. And it wasn't only a matter of Yvette's death either, as several other innocent people had also lost their lives – the old woman with the black enamelled teeth for one. Many others had been injured, most of whom now stood about the street talking to anyone who'd listen. Many did listen, especially the wizened old women, hair scraped back in buns, whose only joy in life was gossip. The local people could not leave it alone and Nicole, knowing they all blamed the French, was aware of a shift in the atmosphere. Because of the general increase in tension, Nicole made every effort to ensure she wore Vietnamese dress and did not draw attention.

Even though she didn't want to speak to Trần, she knew she had to and, when she didn't see him at the shop, she decided to walk around the lake to think. Once there, she was surprised to see the thin back of the still figure who sat gazing out across the water. She felt a flicker of fear and bit down on her knuckles to stop herself from crying out.

Yet Trần looked so defenceless. Surely he could not have been responsible for Yvette's death? But when he twisted round, the accusation her father and Monsieur Giraud had made came storming back. She felt the heat explode in her head.

'How could you?' she hissed.

There was silence, her accusation hanging between them. The scene in front of her began to pulse, the green of the trees, the silvery lake, his solitary figure. It merged together and she felt dizzy. She couldn't take one step forward. Not one step. She hesitated a moment longer but knew that she would have to speak or run.

After a few moments he sighed. 'I knew you'd think that.'

'They told me it was you.'

'They?'

She stared at the ground, seeing nothing, before returning her gaze to him. 'Giraud and my father. They laid the blame on you.'

'You believed them? You really think that?'

She narrowed her eyes. 'I argued with them. I told them nothing.'

'And?'

'Trần, did you do it?'

'You have to ask?' His eyes hardened and he stood up, taking a few steps towards her.

She held out her hand. 'Don't come any closer.'

'Before you judge, think about it. Why would we kill our own people?'

She shook her head. 'To discredit the French.'

He kicked at the dead leaves lying on the grass. 'Have you considered it might be the other way round?'

There was a short pause.

'On my mother's life, I promise you it was not us. I would not have harmed a hair on the child's head.'

An image of Yvette with her plaits swinging as she ran made Nicole tremble. She folded her arms across her middle and hugged herself, bending over to gaze at her feet. 'I can't bear it. She never harmed anyone.'

'I can't bear it either, Nicole.'

She lifted her head and, thinking over what he'd said, watched the birds flying across the lake. The moment went on and though she wasn't looking at him she knew he had not moved. Eventually she turned back to him. 'How can I believe you when everyone says it was the Vietminh who killed her? How can I trust you?'

And now he did take another step towards her. 'Because you have my word.'

She looked at his face for signs of a lie, really looked at him. Everything about him was taut. He gazed back at her without blinking, defiant and determined. Then his face crumpled as if he too had been holding on to overwhelming sadness and only now could release a little of it. His eyes filled with tears and he looked so vulnerable it tore her apart. Yet still she never would have believed him, had she not seen her own father kill a man in cold blood. If her father could do that, what else might the French be capable of?

'So who?'

'The Americans, perhaps. We know the CIA have been sniffing around. We think they are in league with some key French people who are working to set up a third army in Vietnam.'

'To fight against the Vietminh?'

'Yes, trying to discredit us.'

There was no arguing with that. She walked up to him and, gazing right into his eyes, hoped she could hide the fact that she already knew about the third army. 'They want me to inform on you. Let them know if I see you.'

She watched the tears appear again. Moved by his sincerity, she reached out. He was so young but already looked so frayed at the edges. She hated to see him waste his life in a hopeless cause.

'Trần, why not forget all this? Go back to your studies. The Vietminh will never win against the French.'

He took hold of her hand and squeezed.

She felt a wave of uncertainty and, for a moment, didn't know how to respond. Behind his strong beliefs and eagerness there was also something naive. Was he telling the truth? How could you tell? She reached for his other hand. They stood and she felt the warmth of his skin against hers. She closed her eyes and listened to the wind ripple the water. He coughed and her eyes snapped open. As he smiled, something passed between them, and she felt as if she'd known him for ever. He was like a Vietnamese brother. She couldn't help but feel protective towards him, just as she couldn't help loving her father, even after what he had done.

'You promise never to lie to me?' she said, even though she knew she would always have to lie to him about what had happened in the cellar.

He touched a palm to his heart, and then to hers. After that he took hold of her hand and led her to a secluded area of trees and shrubs. He parted the branches and they crawled through to a small clearing completely covered by the canopy of leaves.

'I never knew this was here,' she said as she attempted to sit, but had to double over under the low hanging branches.

'You have to lie down here. No space to sit,' he said. 'Come.'

He reached out both arms to help her lie on the grass beside him, her head resting on his shoulder. There was the occasional screech of bicycles or the sound of a car. Mainly they listened to the birds and the leaves rustling in the breeze. She raised herself on one elbow and watched the pattern of the dappled sunlight on his honey-coloured skin.

'You are not such a mystery to me as you were,' she said. 'I thought at first you were full of hate.'

He smiled. 'No mystery and no hate. I want what's right for our people.'

'And to be dominated by another country is not right?'

'Exactly.'

'What if you lose? There will be terrible reprisals.'

'There are already reprisals. Think of my brother.'

Nicole shook her head, trying to rid herself of the memory, the fringe, the gurgle, the slump of the man. The look in his eyes just before her father shot him.

There was a long silence before she spoke.

'I used to gaze out on the moonlit Perfume River. During the war, I wasn't supposed to open the windows but I couldn't bear it. I felt I had to be free or I would have died.'

'So you understand how I feel.'

She nodded. 'It frightens me, but I think I do.'

'Then help us.'

'How?'

'Promise you will not speak of this to anyone. It is dangerous.'

She breathed air drenched with the scent of earth and water, and felt roused by his vehemence, but was he blind to the truth? The French could not lose, but still it was exhilarating to feel so connected to the cause of the Vietnamese people. She knew she was betraying her family by feeling that way and, at the back of her mind, she understood she could be in very deep trouble just for being here with him.

'We are opening up tunnels,' he continued. 'Through the shops in the ancient quarter.'

'Underground?'

'We open up the walls between the shops on the ground floor, an archway if you like, wide enough for one of us to pass through quickly. It's a hidden network.'

'Surely the tunnels can be seen?'

'The owners block them from view.'

Nicole frowned. 'You want to make holes in my walls?'

'Yes.'

'But what about the silk? Won't it be stolen?'

'Not if people understand you are with us. I will protect you. I promise.'

'What about my family?'

'Nicole, they are French and our enemy.'

She sat up and bent her head forward to her knees, covering her face with her hands. She didn't want to hear. It was too brutal to think of her father and Sylvie like that and, despite everything, she still loved them.

'I'm sorry. There is no other way.'

There was a long stretch of silence while she thought about what he'd asked her to do.

'If you want to save your family, persuade them to leave for France,' he said as if he knew exactly what she was thinking. 'It's all you can do. The days of French rule are coming to an end.'

Trần still lay on the grass, his hands behind his head. She dropped her hands so that she could support herself as she twisted round to look at him. 'If I join your cause I will lose my family.'

He inclined his head.

'You seem so sure about everything.'

'I am. Thousands of peasants have joined us. They supply food, carry arms and look after the wounded. The Vietminh army are coming closer. Have you seen the number of French tanks in the streets? They are gearing up for a final battle they cannot win.'

'You promise you had nothing to do with Yvette's death?'

'Believe me.' He raised a hand and tilted her chin towards him. 'I won't betray your trust. And, as I said before, the

Americans are trying to organize a third army to fight the Vietminh.'

'The Americans hate us colonials.'

'They hate communism even more.'

'One question,' she said. 'Is the Vietminh really communist?'

'We are nationalists, Nicole. The communist countries of China and Russia have been supporting us, and America is unhappy about that. The West has turned its back.'

Nicole thought about it and felt the divisions were false. Surely there had to be a better way of deciding the fate of a country than through violence and war. 'Why can't we carry on living together?'

'You know why. We're not free. We have our own culture and it's completely different to the French.'

'My father loves this country. He was even married to a Vietnamese woman, my mother.'

'Yet he seeks to maintain French domination.' He paused. 'Nicole, I wish I could say enough to steer you towards the truth, but I have to leave soon for the north. I might be gone for a few weeks but I will be back.'

'And if I choose not to help you?'

'Then we will not see each other again. But remember your true family may not be the one you were born into. My comrades are my family now.'

She gazed at him. He looked so determined but she worried his convictions could only end in sorrow. She wanted to trace the contours of his cheek with her fingertips, the impulse so strong that he shifted slightly as if sensing it.

'But think of this too. If you choose the French, you may not be safe at the silk shop. There may be people ready to hurt you if they suspect you know about the tunnels. And they know you and O-Lan are friends. They'd suspect her of telling you about them. You'd be putting her life at risk too.'

'Is that blackmail?'

'No, it's reality. We need to get *our* country back. Whatever it takes.'

She narrowed her eyes. 'I'll be perfectly safe as long as you tell no one that I know about the tunnels.'

'And what will you do in return?'

'I will not tell the police about them.'

19

As autumn got under way, the streets of Hanoi were carpeted with red eagle tree leaves and before long it was the opening night of the show. Astonished that her life could carry on in the way it did, Nicole thought of Yvette every day. Now, as she made up her face in the tiny dressing room, she also thought of Trần. She began to see her meeting with him as one of those milestones, when you sense everything is about to change; if you allow it to happen, you know you'll never be able to go back. Rather like the night her father had shot Trần's brother and the certainties of her French life became blurred. One thing was clear: whichever side she chose, it would mean losing the other. If she turned her back on her family she'd lose them, and Lisa too. But she couldn't help feeling drawn by the awakening of her Vietnamese side. She had been so touched by Trần's hope for a better future. He'd spoken passionately, but also rationally, and now she had no choice but to question her own allegiances. What if he was right and it had been the French who were responsible for Yvette's death? She shook her head, suspecting the truth would never be known.

Trần had asked to come to the show, but with both Mark and her father likely to be present, she'd managed to dissuade him.

As she put the finishing touches to her make-up as a woman of ill repute, she sniffed the air. Greasepaint! It was something she couldn't explain, but from the moment she'd first held the little Leichner Grease Sticks wrapped in gold foil, her heart had flown. She sighed, slipped into her costume and went to wait in the wings. Her character didn't appear until halfway through the first act, so she was able to peer through a slit in the curtain and watch the audience. Her character was not considered a good woman, but she had a heart of gold; Nicole loved the liberation of being somebody else, if only for an hour or two, especially when she so often felt uncomfortable being herself.

At first she couldn't see them, but as her eyes grew accustomed to the darkness of the auditorium, she made out her father sitting in the third row. She glanced to his left and caught sight of Sylvie sitting with a blond French soldier on her left and Mark on her right. As she watched Sylvie lean towards Mark, Nicole's eyes began to smart. But she held her nerve. Nothing could be allowed to ruin her one chance to excel and, even though she had seriously considered Trần's proposal, impressing Mark and her father still mattered to her.

The chords of her first number began. She stepped out into the bright lights and began to sing. As she gave herself to the song, the world stopped turning. Aware of her voice soaring as it filled the entire auditorium, it was as close to joy as she had ever been. There was the music and nothing else, and the elation felt like a huge relief. At the end of prolonged applause, one glance at her father revealed him beaming with pride. Then, shocked to see Trần standing right under a single wall light at the back of the hall, her heart gave a little jolt. He wouldn't be safe.

After the interval she noticed Mark had left and only her father and Sylvie remained. It was too dark now to see whether Trần was still there at the back. She hoped he'd slipped away. The show progressed with a couple of lighting mishaps and a few prompts, but as first nights went, it was a great success.

Once it was over, Nicole removed most of her make-up, changed, then slipped into the small coffee bar where the performers and their families and friends were congregating. Sylvie came across to her smiling broadly and clapping her hands, accompanied by the blond soldier.

'*Chérie*, you were absolutely wonderful. I was so proud.'

'Thank you.'

'Of course, I always knew you could sing but you sounded like an angel. It was truly astonishing. By the way, this is André,' she said, introducing the soldier.

Nicole raised her brows.

'Just a friend,' Sylvie whispered and gave her a wink.

Her father joined them. 'Wonderful,' he said before kissing her on both cheeks and ruffling her hair.

Nicole glanced about the place. 'And Mark, what happened to him?'

Sylvie had been smiling the whole time, but now her expression changed a little. Was there a touch of nervousness in the way she kept scratching her neck and fiddling with her earrings?

'He had a little bit of business to see to,' Sylvie said.

Nicole couldn't hide her disappointment or her worry. 'Couldn't it wait?'

'It would seem not,' Sylvie said, still looking uncomfortable. 'But never mind. We are so delighted to see you come into your own, aren't we, Papa?'

Their father nodded and linked an arm through Nicole's. 'You are my little star, but I'm afraid André and I must leave you for a moment. There is someone I need to speak to.'

Sylvie turned to Nicole. 'By the way, I'm pleased with you. The accounts you sent over were good.'

Nicole nodded as she watched her father walk across the room.

He hadn't said much but at least he had come. She remembered when she'd been chosen to sing a solo at the Christmas festival at school and Sylvie had taken ill. Her father hadn't been able to come and Nicole couldn't shake off the feeling that Sylvie had pretended to be ill to prevent him from attending.

She watched him stop and clap another man on the back. Giraud. The policeman looked over and smiled at Nicole as if they were conspirators.

'What's he doing here?' she asked Sylvie.

'I have no idea. Probably came to see the show. You were divine. I'm so proud of you. But you mustn't let it go to your head.'

'Thank you, I think.'

'By the way, I hope that little problem over Mark has passed.' Sylvie scrutinized Nicole's face. 'It has passed, hasn't it? Because I never meant to hurt you and now . . . well, he's away a lot but let's just say I'm very happy.'

Nicole felt tense but concealed it behind a fixed smile. She might feel as if she was coming apart at the seams but she had enough dignity to want to conceal it.

'So you'll come back in the car with us?' Sylvie was asking.

Only when Sylvie turned away could Nicole give in to the horrible fear inside her. Even if Mark and Sylvie were together, she still cared about him. But she had no way of knowing if Mark's 'bit of business' had actually been something to do with Trần, and worse, she had no way of knowing if either of them was safe.

20

Nicole moved into the apartment above the shop, hoping that away from her family she might feel more settled. She still couldn't get Mark out of her mind and the days she hadn't spoken to him felt like weeks, and the weeks felt like years. She wasn't ready to join Trần, but she was intrigued by him, and worried for his safety. Her sadness over Yvette's death hadn't dulled, but she busied herself with selling and, as the aroma of beef pho and shrimp noodles drifted through the open windows, she could feel herself becoming more truly Vietnamese with each passing week. It made her feel different. Not better. Not worse. But as if the French shell that had been enclosing her had now begun to crack.

She made it her business to order even more colourful silks than before, but as her customers grew fewer she took refuge in reading everything she could lay her hands on. By night she performed in the show, but when it came to the end of its run, she learnt that because of increased tension in Hanoi people were staying home and there was not to be another. Few spoke of their fear, but Nicole knew some people were already planning to leave for Paris or Saigon. She ignored the possible risks and spent her evenings making silk lampshades and mobiles of butterflies and birds; the soft feel of the silk in her hands comforted her.

She constantly turned over everything Trần had said. He was idealistic and believed in the Vietminh cause, and she had begun to think that he might be right. But the truth was nobody knew how it would turn out for sure. Perhaps the French would hold on to Indochina after all, perhaps they would not. They certainly wouldn't give up without a fight. She went over the night of the show in her mind and the way Mark had disappeared so suddenly; and she worried constantly that something dreadful had happened between the two men.

In the following weeks, living away from her family, Nicole often felt lonely. She had too much time to think, and spent endless hours roaming around the city when the shop was closed and wondering how to view things. How to choose. These had been the questions of her life: she still had no answers.

But as she began to really know the city, she understood how much the city planners had intended to keep the French and Vietnamese sectors separate. Right from the start they had demolished ancient buildings and temples to make way for their new city. Now wide streets dominated in the French areas, with spacious villas and grand government buildings, while in the Vietnamese area, even where the French had rebuilt, they'd retained the narrow tube-like buildings and merely added a French-style facade.

While dodging the bicycles in the ancient quarter, Nicole thought she spotted Trần one day. With a feeling of trepidation she followed him, got lost, and found herself at the entrance to a market she'd forgotten about. Feeling hungry, she poked her head round the open gates hoping there might be somewhere to grab a doughnut and maybe a condensed milk coffee. It was dimly lit and from the initial smell – there had been chilli peppers laid out at the entrance – she thought it might be a spice market.

She ploughed on, but beyond a curtain of dried figs, a strong smell of fish hit the back of her throat. She'd made a mistake. She hated the smell of fish. It clogged up her throat and prevented her from swallowing. Thinking there might be an exit at the other end, she carried on past a queue of women waiting to choose from grotesque live fish still swimming in buckets. She quickened her step but worse was to come and her skin crawled as she passed a stall where flies swarmed around fish laid out on ice.

The rest of the market was mostly devoted to vegetables and fruit, although there was another section where pigs' feet, frogs and snakes seemed to be lumped together. Once she reached the end she found the exit was padlocked, so had to retrace her steps. Eventually she found the way back to her shop but by then she was drenched in sweat, the smell of fish clinging to her hair and to her clothes. She undressed and ran through to the little bathroom where she washed every part of herself.

Fish reminded her of the river in Huế. Some memories of Huế were intensely happy, especially the ones involving Lisa. But along with the strong smell of fish, something else nagged at her, something much older, something insistent. She heard Sylvie's voice in her head and frowned with the effort of trying to remember.

'Go on. You first, then me,' her sister had said.

She remembered Sylvie laughing and laughing, and she remembered the water. It had seemed so big, so endless.

And then she had woken up in hospital. She heard Lisa's voice and the mechanical noise of the trolley clicking, the sound going on and on until she wanted to scream.

She brought herself back to the present with a jolt, but her hands were still shaking at the fragmented memory. She could remember little of that day now but did recall the following weeks, when the sun had been so bright on the water it hurt her eyes, and all the birds were pecking and flying and squabbling as if nothing had happened. It took weeks for her to go near the water again, and ever since then she'd loathed the smell of fish.

Her thoughts moved on to how much everything had changed. When had she really stopped trusting? Had it happened over a series of days? Had she only ever seen what she wanted to see? Believed what had made her feel better? Truth could be bent, switched, altered to suit you, and she felt it had been.

What if there had been clues all along? Clues that would have alerted her to the fact that something bad was going to happen. There had been those boys bullying Yvette, and long before that there had been the move to Hanoi. Had her father been lying when he'd said it was all over for the Vietminh? Had he brought the family here knowing the dangers they might face? It had been bad enough after Trần's brother was shot at the hotel – he would always be dead and there was nothing any of them could do about it – but since Yvette's death, the cracks in Nicole's world had grown even wider. She felt as if she was falling through one and before long might be lost for ever.

Every day she looked in the mirror and could see her face had changed. 'Who are you?' she said each time. 'I don't know you.'

The expression in her eyes had darkened, permanently it seemed. She no longer cared to look more like her sister, and only went home occasionally, mainly to see Lisa.

One morning they were having coffee in the smaller dining room at home, the one overlooking a little pavilion where a table and chairs sat beside the lily pond. Lisa and her father were there and only Sylvie was absent. The news on the radio the night before had spoken of escalating French losses in the north.

'You have to leave Hanoi,' Lisa said. 'You must see.'

But Nicole's father did not answer. At the sound of planes overhead she gazed up at the fluffy white clouds and cherubs flying round the central chandelier. How ridiculous they seemed at a time like this. Then she studied her father. Lisa was right. He should go back to France. Brows permanently furrowed, he didn't look well, and the strain also showed in his pale, pinched face. Whoever won the war, it didn't seem as if life would be settled enough for him as he grew older.

'And you too, Nicole,' Lisa added. 'You're so different. I hardly know you. I'll come with you, if that helps, then I could go to my sister, Alice, in the Languedoc.'

But Nicole wanted to stay and shook her head. 'Where is Sylvie?' she asked.

Her father and Lisa exchanged anxious glances.

'There's no need for anyone to leave,' her father said. 'We will win as we have always done before. Have a little faith.'

'What about the losses last night?' Nicole asked.

'There were losses but the extent of them was exaggerated, as usual.'

'I thought I heard gunfire.'

'The wind carries the sound,' he said.

'And Sylvie?'

'Your sister has taken a little break on her own.'

'Break? Why?'

He twisted his mouth to one side and scratched his chin. 'She was a little under the weather.'

'She's unwell?'

'She's been a bit up and down, that's all.'

'She takes pills, I know that, though she wouldn't really explain what they were for.'

'She doesn't take them now. They didn't suit her constitution.'

'But what is actually wrong with her?'

'Your sister is more delicate than you realize, more delicate than I thought too. Now consider the matter closed. I promise you, there is no chance the Viets will win the war.'

But where Nicole had once believed him, now she did not. At least, not so much. And neither did Lisa.

'You're not well either, Papa. And don't you see, Indochina is changed for ever?'

He was standing by the French windows and had turned his back to her. He didn't say anything.

'You know, many have already gone,' she said. 'Too disheartened to stay. Can't you see?'

Finally he turned round and his face looked sad. 'No, Nicole, I cannot and will not see. I have always loved Hanoi and I will not consider letting it go.'

And yet, no matter what he said, they all knew it had become a more dangerous place.

Lisa sat down and looked close to tears. Nicole crouched down beside her and tried to give comfort, murmuring that everything would be all right. Her father watched them for a moment with no expression on his face. Only when Lisa seemed to recover did Nicole get up and, not wanting to think about it any more, she and the cook went down to the kitchen together.

In the place Nicole had always felt happiest she gazed at the familiar white brick-shaped tiles and the row of copper pots hanging from an iron bar. While she had been waiting for Trần to come back she'd felt as if she had no roots. Not in the French world, nor in the Vietnamese world. Now all she wanted was to be certain of something, and being with Lisa usually made everything feel better, if only temporarily.

She sat herself at the table next to Lisa but still her old ally was looking unusually morose. There was a distinct feeling of something being wrong throughout the entire house. Even the kitchen felt hotter than usual, and stuffy too. The blinds were only half up, and worse, there was no delicious smell of cooking.

'What's going on?' Nicole asked. 'Where's Bettine? And why are the windows and door closed?'

'I forgot to open them. And Bettine has gone.' Lisa shrugged. 'Not that I miss her, except for the extra work, that is. It's impossible to find a replacement.'

'Nothing's quite right for me either.'

'Well, you know the solution.'

'Open the blooming windows and bake some Camembert?'

'And we could make a cherry clafoutis. What do you say?'

As Lisa searched in the cupboards for the ingredients for the pudding, Nicole went to open the windows and the back door. The kitchen felt instantly cooler.

'So what's been happening?' She raised her eyes to the upstairs. 'Here, I mean.'

'Your sister has been unsettled lately. Then last week she went to Hué with Mark.' She pulled a face.

'Don't you like him?'

'I like him. It's not that. When she came back . . . well, let's just say it's clear that all is not well in paradise. I'm not saying I don't feel sorry for her, but –'

'Are you saying Mark doesn't love her?' Nicole couldn't ignore the little flip her heart had made. 'Do you think that's why she's gone away?'

'Well, she has been a bit downhearted.' Lisa paused. 'Look, what do I know?'

'You know more about what's going on than anyone, Lisa. You always have done.'

21

Things had begun to darken. Just occasionally gunfire really could be heard, and the atmosphere in the town had changed. You had to watch where you walked and who you spoke to. Though hens still squatted in the dusty street and cats stretched out to enjoy the sunshine, Hanoi had become a place of shadows. Most of her spare time Nicole would sit on the little wooden sofa upstairs at the shop, trying to find something to do. Other times she gazed into the distance, straining to hear soldiers' voices or the tread of army boots. Trần never phoned though she had hoped he might; of course, he believed the French had all the phones tapped. For him the only means of communication was personal contact and, as he was away in the north, she had no idea what was happening.

Nobody had come to talk to her about the tunnels and it was a few weeks before she saw Trần again. One afternoon when she was about to close the shop, she'd pulled down the shop blinds and was standing at the door with the keys in her hand when she saw him. She noticed straight away how thin he was. He looked terribly exposed as he removed his neck scarf and wiped his face with it. The birthmark on his neck stood out, his head was shaved and, when he held her, she could feel his bones. She stood in the doorway, with her eyes misting up, the relief so intense she forgot there might be someone watching.

'We need to go in,' he said, pulling her inside.

'Of course.' She came to her senses and locked the door.

He reached in his pocket and took something out. To her astonishment he handed her a bar of chocolate.

'Chocolate!? Trần, where have you been? I didn't know if you were alive or dead!'

'I was in Bac Can. It's one of the centres of the resistance. You should see it, Nicole.'

She glanced out at the street. 'Let me close the door, then tell me.'

But he didn't stop talking. She continued to listen but thoughts kept running through her mind. His eyes glittered and he spoke in a rush, telling of the intellectuals who had joined the cause, the actors and actresses, the singers and musicians. He said the Vietminh had stockpiled rice and hidden it in the mountains, reserving it for when it would be most needed. There were factories in caves where they made everything from soap to ammunition.

'After the French bombed Bac Can in 1947 we spread into the mountains. They thought they could wipe us out by capturing our leaders and annihilating the army. It didn't work.'

'So what is happening now?'

'War is happening now,' he said. 'The peasants are with us too. The French will soon be facing a crushing defeat.'

'Why did you not get in touch? I really thought you might be dead.'

'It was too dangerous. The Americans were watching you closely.'

'Mark?'

He nodded. 'You know the CIA are working closely with the French now, exchanging intelligence about our movements? The CIA teach others to lie and deceive. They call it tradecraft. You can't trust him. Close the shop permanently. Come with me, Nicole.'

'I can't fight,' she said and, horrified by the picture he was painting of Mark, she felt her life split in two.

'If you stay, he will manipulate you. You can perform. We have several travelling theatre groups, teaching the people through their shows.'

'Propaganda?'

'You could call it that. I call it educating the masses. There's nothing like music to inspire the peasantry. Why squander your life trying to be someone you are not? Come with us.'

'Was that the only reason you came to the show? To see if I could sing?'

'I believed you could sing. I brought someone with me to prove it to him as well. He is a composer who writes wonderful songs based on traditional tales. The troupes travel the countryside performing to army units and in the villages too. Sometimes they perform plays. Like wandering minstrels but with a message.'

'To inspire hatred of the French.' She shook her head. 'I am half French remember.'

'I've told you. There will be a time when you will have to choose.'

'I can't turn my back on my family. Anyway, it doesn't make sense. The Vietminh wouldn't accept me.'

He shook his head sadly. 'I think you're wrong.'

He held out a hand and they went upstairs so that he might rest. She'd arranged a spray of jasmine in a vase by the bed and the room was sweet with its scent. He took off his boots, then lay down on his back and closed his eyes. She lay down beside him and expected him to fall asleep straight away.

She'd been alone for too long and her body throbbed with the need for physical contact. Though she felt a bit awkward being so close, she was pleased when she felt him reach for her hand. He turned to face her and she gazed at the deep exhaustion lines around his eyes. What happened next was not what she'd expected. Trần put an arm round her and pulled her to him. Then he opened her blouse, loosening each button deliberately slowly and continuing to watch her as he did. Excited by the desire she saw in his eyes, she sat up and removed her chemise, then piece by piece peeled off the rest of her clothes. He reached for her but she insisted he remove all his clothes too. When he had done so they looked at each other. She ran her fingertips over his ribs then, holding his hands, examined his blackened, broken nails and his body covered in scratches and bruises. He leant across and touched the hollow at the base of her neck. She'd thought it might be hurried, but he was gentle, and as she gave him her body, she acknowledged how much she had needed to be held. It was not passionate but the gentle lovemaking of friends.

'This is my first time,' she whispered and felt close to tears.

She traced the outline of the birthmark on his neck. 'We're both marked, aren't we?'

He turned her round and kissed her back. When it was over she stretched out her damp body and lay next to him.

'Comrades,' he said. Then they lay in silence.

Afterwards she made a simple dish of rice and chicken, which he ate ravenously.

'You are so thin,' she said.

'It has been hard.'

'I don't know what to do. If I go with you they will look for me.'

He shook his head. 'If you don't come they will watch you. You'll see how much your precious family care. You can't save everyone.'

'I'm not trying to. And anyway, I've done nothing.'

'You have been seen with me. It's enough. I must go now but I'll be back soon.'

'Don't go.'

'I have to. It isn't safe. I'll come back in one week's time, before you close the shop for the evening. That is my deadline. I hope you will have an answer for me. Either you come or this must be the last time we can meet. In the meantime, you can prove which side you are on by listening to your father and the American. Go home for a few days. See what you can find out about French plans.'

'Mark is not party to French plans.'

Trần laughed. 'Don't be so blind. You believe he'd still be sniffing around here if he wasn't? Be careful, Nicole. They all want to destroy us and will trample over you if you get in their way.'

An hour after he'd gone she regretted having sex with him. She didn't love him, but had felt so alone she'd convinced herself it was the right thing to do. It wasn't that she didn't care. She did care, but not in that way, and now she'd confused everything. 'I don't know where I belong,' she whispered. Picturing herself back in the family home, she knew it was no longer there. As for Trần? He offered her nothing but exile.

Taken by surprise when Mark appeared at the shop door the next day, her heart gave a jolt. He was back to his usual self with that easy-going glamour she had fallen for from the start, and when he smiled at her, she felt the same longing. So that's how it felt. She'd wondered how it would be if she were to be alone with him again and now she knew.

He wandered about the shop whistling, but she sensed something wasn't right.

'Are you looking for silk?' she asked, knowing full well he was not.

He didn't reply.

It was such a humid day that, despite a fan constantly

shifting the air, the atmosphere was still oppressive. Time stretched out as he ran his fingertips over the silk and glanced behind the tall shiny rolls of fabric banked up against the walls.

She'd been holding herself tight but relaxed a little, glad there were, as yet, no tunnels for him to uncover, but at the same time wishing there could be a reason for him to stay. 'Then what is it?' she said.

'I want you to be safe.'

She stared at him, trying to figure out his intentions.

'There has been talk,' he continued. 'Of a Vietnamese man you've been spending time with.'

'What kind of talk?'

With his back to her, he shrugged.

'What kind of talk, Mark?'

He turned to face her. He was big and tall, utterly American, and exuded masculinity. The contrast with Trần couldn't have been sharper. It shook her, that difference.

'Talk that you might be getting into something you will regret,' he said, his eyes so clear she found it impossible to believe he could be anything other than candid. 'Is it true?'

She didn't reply.

'I worry about you, Nicole. Surely you must see that? You would tell me if you'd heard anything of the Vietminh's plans, wouldn't you?'

'I'm just selling silk.'

He raised his brows.

'How is Sylvie?' she said. 'Is she back from her trip? I got the impression from Father she wasn't well.'

'She's back. She just had a few emotional problems.'

He reached out a hand to her but when she didn't take it, he let it drop. And before he spoke again she saw a trace of something sad. 'Nicole, I want you to know that you were right. I am not a silk trader. But I had nothing to do with Yvette's death.'

'Then who?'

'I have my suspicions, but it's not something I can discuss. You must realize that.'

'And whoever it was, there will be no consequences?'

'Probably not.' He paused. 'It's tragic when innocent people suffer but at times like this we are all at risk.'

'Does it never occur to you to ask what you are fighting for?'

They remained silent as she gazed at him, but his eyes gave nothing away.

He shook his head. 'Come home, Nicole. Your family miss you.'

'And do you miss me too?' She swallowed hard. All manner of intense emotions were going on inside her and she felt sure he could see them written on her face.

'I miss you more than you know.'

She waited for him to speak again.

'Nicole, we're at war. I don't sleep. I'm finding it harder to do my job and I'm worried for your safety. And in answer to your question, I am beginning to wonder what we are fighting for.' He paused. 'Please go home. Take my word for it. Close the shop.'

She sighed deeply. Going home now would fit in well with Trần's request, but she felt completely torn. How could she ever pass on information about Mark?

'Look, I'll go back for a while, but I'm not going to close the shop.'

He held out a hand to her again and this time she took it. He pulled her to him as if he was about to embrace her, but even though she wanted to be held, she stiffened and he let her go.

'I'll go home a little later,' she said.

Standing with his feet apart in the way that was so familiar to her, he gazed at her and they both seemed to still. For a few seconds neither of them spoke, then he exhaled slowly. 'Oh, Nicole.'

But what was going on behind those eyes? Had she ever really known him? There was something there that stirred her so deeply she hardly had a word for it, and it made her ache with wanting him. But after Trần's damning accusations she felt uncertain and, needing to defend herself from her own feelings, she tried to conjure the Vietnamese boy's face as a buffer.

'If it's because of Sylvie ...' he said, interrupting her thoughts.

'If what's because of Sylvie?'

'The way you have been.' He paused. 'Your sister and I are not together, Nicole. We never have been, apart from those few times back in the States.'

'But she said –'

'She is not always as honest as you. Whatever her reasons, I've come to realize that she believes there is more between us than there is or ever could be.'

Nicole wanted to believe him so much but she had been hurt and couldn't let herself go.

'I feel so at ease with you, Nicole. Don't you see?'

'I think you'd better leave now,' she said, trying to hide the catch that crept into her voice. Despite the notion that somehow he was the key to finding her real self, she was turning him away. 'I said I'll go home in a little while.'

He stepped away but he looked sad, terribly sad.

After he'd gone, she closed the shop and went upstairs where she pulled down the blinds, drew the curtains, lit a scented candle and then lay on the bed where she had so recently lain with Trần. Hardly able to fathom her own emotions, she felt drained. She was fond of Trần, yet when she saw

Mark her insides twisted into a knot. Even now. In fact, being with Trần had only served to intensify her feelings for Mark. But how could you really tell who was honest? It seemed increasingly impossible.

When she closed her eyes the longing to lie naked and feel Mark's skin against her own consumed her. She had tried to tell herself they'd only ever been friends, but there had always been the hope of so much more, for her at least. She removed her clothes and lay under the sheet.

She thought of Trần: intense and idealistic. She believed much of what he said was true. The Vietnamese had been used and mistreated by the French for decades. The French might pretend altruism, but it had all been about self-interest. Why she cared so much about Mark was harder to fathom. Maybe because he wasn't French and that meant there was something different about him. He could seem detached at times and she knew it was because he'd been wounded by his mother's death, just as she had been. Trần was earnest but it was hard to identify what other feelings might lie beneath the rigidity of his beliefs. All her life she had been paying for her mother's death and Mark brought those buried emotions to the surface in a way that did not frighten her. With him she felt unlocked and calm. Trần was not much more than a boy and she knew that the party, so intrinsic to his identity, would always come before everything else. Before his village, before his family and before her. And she knew that if she went with Trần, what had just passed with Mark might be the last words they ever shared.

She put one hand where she could feel the swell of her breast, and the other between her legs. Maybe one night with Mark would be enough to dispel the attraction. But how would it be? Would they lie together in silence? Would they talk? She imagined his lips so close to her neck she could feel his breath on her skin and a shiver ran down her spine.

She could no longer hear the sounds of the street as her thoughts ran wild. The air seemed to chill as the truth of her situation gradually dawned on her. She had hoped she could keep the two halves of her life separate, without splitting herself in two, but her feelings were far too complicated. She had to accept that she had already crossed the line. Breathing in the scent of jasmine in the silence of the room, she understood that she might be forced to make a choice. A choice she did not want to make: one that might drive her to the very edge of her world. If it happened, not only would she lose part of herself, but also, of the two men who meant the most to her, she must surely betray one. Between bouts of crying and longing, and with her heart thudding and thumping, the devastating truth of that hit home.

22

The familiar smells of tomatoes and mushrooms met Nicole as she let herself into the family home. She closed the door behind her and sniffed, her mouth watering at the prospect of Lisa's slow-cooked chicken chasseur. How long had it been since she'd enjoyed such a meal? Sylvie must have heard her arrive because she came through to the hall and stood hovering in the doorway of the main sitting room. Looking effortlessly chic, she wore a black strapless sheath dress and pointed red shoes. As she took a few steps towards Nicole she held out a hand.

'Leave your case. The housemaid will take it up.'

Nicole stood still and looked at her sister. 'I haven't seen you for ages. Papa said you hadn't been well and you'd gone away for a break.'

'Nonsense. I'm back now and I'm absolutely fine.'

'That's good.' Nicole thought her sister looked thinner than usual, but well enough, and she headed for the staircase. 'I'll just get out of these clothes.'

'Why not come in for a cocktail first?' Sylvie tilted her head towards the sitting room. 'Papa would love to see you.'

'I'll nip up to my old room first.'

Sylvie smiled and rang the bell for the maid. 'Don't be silly. Change afterwards. We've hardly seen anything of you. Papa's in there.'

With a slight sigh of defeat, Nicole put down her case. She walked in front of Sylvie into the sitting room, where her eyes fell first on her father and then on the blond soldier, André.

Why was he here? She looked at her father as he got to his feet and she smiled at him. He shifted from one foot to the other, then took a step towards her, holding out both hands. She allowed him to hold her and enjoyed the momentary warmth between them before twisting back to speak to Sylvie.

Nicole's smile faded as Giraud stepped out from where he had been standing behind the door, gave Sylvie a nod, and then moved into the centre of the room. 'A pleasure to see you,' he said with a cigarette between his lips.

Nicole raised her brows but did not acknowledge him. Branded a liar as a child, she knew when to keep her mouth shut.

'Monsieur Giraud needs to ask you a few questions. Nothing to worry about,' Sylvie said.

Giraud removed the cigarette and coughed into his hand before he spoke. 'We'd like to know if you've had any further dealings with your little friend.'

Now she sneaked a look at him. 'What are you saying?'

He smiled as he walked over to a marble ashtray where he stubbed out his cigarette. 'I think we both know who I'm referring to.'

'Have you asked me to come home just for this, Papa?' Nicole said, playing for time while working out how to respond.

'Of course not. We've missed you.'

She pressed her hands together. It might be better to say something rather than nothing, but what she needed was a small diversion. 'Trần dropped in, but only to say goodbye.'

'We wanted you to let us know if you saw him,' Giraud said with a frown. 'Do you recall?'

'Why does it matter?'

His frown deepened and he scratched the skin just inside his collar. 'Winning comes before everything.'

'Well, I wish you luck,' she said.

'*Chérie*, don't be flippant, you could be in danger,' her father said.

'Papa is right,' Sylvie said. 'None of us want to see you hurt.'

Nicole shook her head and hoped her face looked sincere as she replied. 'I'm sure I'm not in danger.'

Giraud narrowed his eyes and then sucked his teeth, deliberately slowly it seemed. 'We need to know where he is.'

'He didn't say.'

'Nicole?' This from her father, followed by the same from Sylvie.

Nicole turned on her sister. 'What are you, Papa's bloody echo?'

Giraud sighed deeply. Nicole found his exaggerated tolerance annoying and fought to control herself. What did he really want? There was something menacing about his slow approach that made her feel even more vulnerable.

'Really, Papa, he didn't say. He said he was leaving Hanoi and would not be back.'

'You see, Nicole,' Giraud continued and gave her a steady look, 'we have information that he did a lot more than drop by. Have you lost control, developed feelings for this man?'

'I don't know what you mean.'

Giraud stepped towards her and held up a finger. 'Ah, but I think you do. Know that it won't end there. What do you think the difference is between you and them?'

The tone of his voice had lowered and there had been something in the way he'd spoken. Nicole attempted to reply but found that with a knot in her throat she could not.

'Are you going to tell her?' Giraud looked at her father. 'Or shall I?'

Her father gave an imperceptible shake of his head.

'Have you forgotten all this, Nicole?' Giraud waved a hand to indicate the splendour of the room. 'Have you forgotten your French family? I must admit, I'm disappointed. I thought we had an agreement and now this lack of cooperation . . . Believe me, I'm sorry to have to do this, considering your father's position.'

Suddenly very fearful, she backed towards the French windows. Giraud gave her a cold smile and drew out another cigarette. She glanced around the room, regretting wearing her oldest *áo dài*. It made her feel as if she was of less significance than them. Sylvie was standing in front of the door to the hall, her eyes cast down. Nicole barged right past her and tried to turn the handle. It was locked.

She glared at her sister. 'Give me the key.'

Sylvie stood firm. 'I'm sorry. Honestly, I am.'

'Give me the bloody key!' On the edge of panic at the possibility of being trapped, Nicole swivelled round. 'So whose brilliant idea was this? Was it you, Papa?'

Her father looked distressed but didn't reply.

'Monsieur Giraud, I demand you let me go.'

'Sadly, I need more information before I can do that.'

'Was this your idea?'

Giraud glanced away and then back again. 'It was brought to my attention that you might be in danger. We can't have a girl from a French family fraternizing with the Viets. Although, of course, you are virtually one of them.'

'Just a minute, Giraud,' Nicole's father said.

'You know my views, Édouard. The races shouldn't mix. They aren't like us.'

The scornful twitch of his nostrils as he spoke provoked a storm of dislike inside her.

Sylvie stepped forward. 'It was me who called the police and we asked Mark to persuade you to come home. I thought he might succeed where we would fail. We thought you'd be safer here.'

'Who are you to decide what I do?'

'You are clearly involved with an undesirable. I was worried.'

Nicole snorted, horrified that Mark had colluded in bringing her here to be treated like a common criminal.

'You've never had good judgement and you have no sense of propriety. Can't you understand we did it for your own good? Tell her, Papa.'

Her father nodded his agreement. 'It's true your sister has been worried about you. We both have.'

'You don't realize how much we care,' Sylvie added. 'Please calm down. Everything will be all right.'

Nicole stared at her defiantly. 'What did I ever do to you?'

'Enough,' Giraud said, butting in. 'In case you want to change your mind, I will give you one last chance to speak.'

'Or?'

There was a moment's silence before her father spoke. 'I'm sorry, chérie, but you have been placed under house arrest.'

She gasped. 'How long for?'

'Until further notice.'

Nicole thought quickly, remembering Trần would be back in a week's time for her answer. 'And if I remember anything?'

'Then we shall reconsider.'

'Papa?'

Her father shrugged in a hopeless kind of way.

'There is one more thing,' Giraud said. 'A minor detail. You will be confined to your room.'

She squared her shoulders and stared at the three of them: her father still looking distressed, Sylvie with a totally blank expression and something like amusement in Giraud's eyes. Because of them a young man was dead; who knew what else they might be capable of, maybe even Yvette's death. The thought stopped her cold. But if they imagined they'd be able to keep her locked in, they were very wrong. She longed to tell them what she'd seen Giraud doing at the brothel, but they wouldn't believe her, and it would only serve to make things worse. Sick to her stomach, she knew his type: Frenchmen who looked down on the Vietnamese but used the women for sex. Before she could say anything more, Giraud flicked his wrist impatiently and continued.

'It pains me to do this but the door will be locked and an officer will be detailed to watch over you. André here will drop by from time to time. You see, you're so important you have the full attention of the police and the army. You will have no contact with members of the household apart from the cook, who is under strict instructions not to let you out, except to the bathroom.'

Unable to control the flash of temper, Nicole walked up to Sylvie and slapped her hard across the cheek. She stared with satisfaction as a red mark developed on her sister's surprised face. It wasn't going to help her cause, but if they thought she was going to submit meekly . . .! She faced the door fighting the hurt that was tearing at her self-control, then twisted back to Giraud.

'And in case you've forgotten, Monsieur Giraud, even though she may look French, my sister Sylvie is also half Vietnamese,' she said. Then, keeping her voice as level as she could, she added, 'Shall we go?'

Once in her room and hearing the key turn in the lock, her bravado deserted her. How could Mark have done this to her? Trần was right, Mark had manipulated her by making her feel she might not be safe at the shop. He'd forced her hand by using the old attraction between them. Utterly betrayed but trying to hold on, she felt like weeping. Her room was the same as it had always been, except that it felt airless. She thumped her pillow then flung herself face down on the bed, hoping the musky night-time smell might ground her, but the pillow smelt only of lavender. She couldn't bear them to hear her crying, so forced a handkerchief into her mouth to muffle the sound as the tears fell, but the lack of air was suffocating and her scalp began to prickle. She glanced around at all the familiar things she hadn't bothered taking to the shop, her glass beads and the clothes Lisa must have folded. Her palms grew sweaty so she rubbed them on her eiderdown. With a flash of hope she thought of the window and tripped over in her rush. Fresh air – if she could open the window.

She tried the handle. The window was locked.

She glanced up at the sun. Not so high in the sky now.

Her heart began to flutter like a tiny bird, first missing a beat, then adding several extra as her fear began to rise. It went on and on, as if her pulse had lost its way back to a regular rhythm. She placed a palm on her chest and ordered it to come back to normal; the fluttering grew worse and made her dizzy. She surveyed her room, looking from one thing to another, searching, hoping for something to anchor her.

Determined not to cave in, she picked herself up. But the memory came rushing back, clearer than ever before and sucking the air out of everything. Within moments she was eight years old again and drowning. The water wasn't cold. Warm like a bath, Sylvie said. *Let's do it. Let's do it.* They said she'd imagined it. Sylvie full of smiles. *The water is warm. It's warm, Nicole. Why not jump?* Whose idea had it been? Sylvie had told them it was hers. Had Sylvie pushed her in? *Let's swim,* she'd said. *Let's jump.* In a flash, something had gone wrong. Where was Sylvie? In the boat or in the water too? As she heard her sister's words Nicole saw herself jump in, saw herself go under, heard the booming sound of the water. The icy cold. The dark.

Nicole began to shake. She ran to the door and thumped, battering and jolting her body until her fists became bruised and her arms ached.

'Sylvie!' she shouted while the feeling of dread mounted. 'Papa!'

Nobody came.

'You know I can't stand to be confined. Sylvie!' She shouted her sister's name again, then screamed as loud as she could.

'Papa, I'm claustrophobic!'

Sweat poured from her head, plastering the hair to her neck. She tore off her clothes in an attempt to lessen the feeling of confinement. Her head began to explode as images flooded her mind. The water. The sun shining on the surface. She raised an arm as if to fend them off, and then forced herself to listen. But there was no sound. In fact, the house was strangely silent. All she could hear was the blood thundering in her ears. She tried to tell herself it was all in her mind – just her imagination – but when her throat closed and a horrible sensation of choking stopped her breath, she dropped to her knees. She felt herself slipping under, and with all the air squeezed from her lungs they remained constricted. She was at the bottom of the river again, hearing the river roar, its voice thudding and thumping in time with her heart. She doubled over, touching her fore-head to the cool of the floor. And with the cool, a single thought consumed her. Even if her father didn't realize how deep her terror of confinement was, Sylvie knew.

Nicole's hysteria did not subside. Just when she thought she could stand it no longer, Lisa came in and threw a glass of icy water in her face, then held her while she gulped, spluttered and coughed. Finally, paralysed by the shock of it, she calmed.

'Oh my dear, how did it come to this?' Lisa said as she got up to leave.

Nicole clutched at her sleeve, comforted by the smell of cigarettes and cooking clinging to her. 'Please don't leave me, please.'

'I'll stay for a few minutes but they'll be on at me if I stay longer.'

She held Nicole, rocking her back and forth in the silence.

'What on earth has been going on?' the cook eventually asked, holding Nicole at arm's length. 'What has happened to you?'

'I just don't know who to believe any more. I thought I trusted Mark but it's his fault I'm locked up here. He's not who I once thought he was.' Nicole shook her head. 'It hurts, Lisa. It hurts so much.'

She couldn't bear to think about what he'd said about not being in a relationship with Sylvie. How could she possibly believe that now?

'My dear, you will get through this,' Lisa said. 'I promise you will. You know I can't stay but I'll keep checking on you. Bang on the door if it gets bad again.'

Then, after a few minutes more, she left.

Gradually Nicole fought the symptoms of her phobia. At the first sign of it – usually when she woke up and remembered she couldn't get out – she told herself nothing terrible would happen. When that didn't work, she forced herself to ride out the attack, concentrating on her breathing, even when she felt as if she might pass out. Breathe in. Breathe out. Shaky, incomplete breaths but breathing nevertheless. Breathe in. Breathe out.

As the anxiety started to diminish, her breaths grew longer – if not normal, at least more whole. She walked about the room: clockwise, anti-clockwise, right across the middle and back. She touched all her things as if to re-acquaint herself after a long absence, and then gazed through the window where she could see the world was unchanged. The trees blew in the wind and the garden was still occupied by the ghosts of the dead. In the house below, sounds of life continued, and she missed her little silk shop terribly.

Even though she sent pleading notes to her father begging for his or Sylvie's presence, the only person she saw was Lisa who, charged with bathroom duties as well as bringing food, continued to be unhappy seeing her in this state. By the fourth day Nicole was surprised to find she'd learnt how to face the fear a little better, and that had lessened the hold it had on her. She was still reluctant to wash or even dress, but Lisa held her hand and helped her. When she was clean, Lisa plaited her hair. With shaking hands, Nicole passed up the rubber bands to hold the plaits in place. The simple activity didn't stop the fear from rising but she felt better equipped to handle the early signs: the sweating, the trembling, the feeling of being winded.

No note came back, nor any word from her father. Faced with his implacable silence, Nicole paced the room. There had to be a way out. There had to be. Trần would be back in three days' time and she wouldn't be there to meet him. She owed him her presence at least, but she just wasn't ready to leave everything behind; despite what they had done to her, she could not go. She hoped Trần hadn't meant it when he'd said she wouldn't be safe at the shop. It was the only good thing left. She longed to be there now, soothed by the neat rows of brightly coloured silk and enjoying the smell of silk and camphor. She would convince him she'd never say a word about the tunnels, but if that failed, there was always the export side of the business in Huế. Maybe she could go there.

With an ache in her bones she couldn't bear to think that it might have been Mark who had informed Sylvie about Trần's last visit. And Sylvie had told Giraud. But if Mark had been central to this lock-up, was it really out of concern for her safety or because he was a CIA officer and would do anything to arrest the spread of communism? He'd hinted that he wanted to know details of the Vietminh's plans, just as Trần had wanted her to find out about French intentions. Unable to clear her head of the mistrust, she hated what was happening. Why couldn't things go on as they had before? Yet even as she asked herself this question, she knew the answer: the wealth of the French had been made off the backs of the Vietnamese – Trần had taught her that if nothing else. No doubt there were good Frenchmen too, men who didn't abuse their power, men who believed in their purpose, but she would never forget what her father had done in the cell beneath the hotel.

One day when Lisa came in she decided to ask her again about what had happened the day she was born. For Nicole, everything seemed to come back to that. And although Lisa had refused to discuss it before, this time the cook sat down on the bed and said she'd tell her the truth.

'Your mother had a difficult labour with Sylvie and an even more difficult one with you. It went on too long, but that was because it was happening too early.'

'Why? What happened?'

Lisa closed her eyes. 'Your mother was meant to have been away for the weekend, but she returned early and saw something she should not have seen.'

Nicole frowned, not understanding.

'Are you sure you want to know?'

'Of course.'

'Your mother went up to the room she shared with your father and found him in bed,' Lisa paused, 'with somebody else.'

'Oh my God. Who? Who was he with?'

'One of the maids.'

Nicole shook her head. 'I don't believe you.'

Lisa blinked rapidly. 'I'm so sorry.'

'So what happened?'

'Your father bundled the maid out of the house and, after a while, we heard crying from your mother's bedroom, and then screams. I told your father the baby was coming, but he wouldn't believe me and forbade me to go to her. They hadn't been getting on for some time. She was often ill and he thought her a hypochondriac. He judged her terribly but she was genuinely fragile.'

'Didn't he love my mother?'

'He adored her at the beginning, but then I think the consequences of a mixed marriage hit home. Well, he kept repeating that she was just trying to seek attention, yet again. And then it all went quiet and, as the baby wasn't due, I thought maybe he was right.'

'But it wasn't?'

'In the end it seemed unnaturally quiet. I disobeyed him and when I went to see for myself . . .' She paused and stared at Nicole. 'Are you sure you want to hear?'

Nicole nodded.

'*Chérie*, there was blood everywhere. I called the doctor, and I delivered the baby – you, of course. But it was too late for your mother. She had lost too much blood. The doctor arrived and hurried into the room with your father, but by then she was already dead.'

Nicole felt a huge lump form in her throat.

'He was utterly destroyed by guilt.'

Nicole screwed up her eyes and balled a fist into her other palm. 'So he should have been.'

'It changed him. It changed all of us.'

There was a pause but Nicole needed to hear more. 'What

did the doctor say? Could he have saved her if he'd been called at the start?'

'Maybe. He said he'd have taken her straight to hospital, but couldn't guarantee she'd have survived.'

'It wasn't my fault, was it?'

'Not at all. You were an innocent baby. If anyone was to blame . . .'

'It was my father.'

Nicole felt a great whooshing sound in her ears as if she was drowning all over again. If only she had known this before.

'I tried to encourage him to hold you, but he wouldn't even look at you. You were so tiny I feared for your life too. But I think you reminded him of his own guilt too much.'

Nicole couldn't think clearly.

'The house was in complete confusion. Your father vanished for days on end, sometimes taking Sylvie with him. Someone had to see that life went on, so I kept you down in the kitchen with me until you were a few months older. I had a sweetheart myself, but he wouldn't wait.'

'You must have resented me.'

Lisa looked at her. 'You, my love, never. You were so sweet. So funny. I thought of you as mine.'

Nicole blinked away tears. 'But the maid must have known my mother was pregnant.'

Lisa nodded. 'I'm so sorry.'

'You have nothing to be sorry for. But Sylvie has always believed our mother died because of me. She has never let me forget it.'

'Sylvie saw how your father behaved towards you. He wouldn't touch you, and even as you grew older he showed little interest.'

'That's what I always felt.'

'Obviously he eventually had to acknowledge you, but the

harm had been done. Sylvie was convinced your mother's death was your fault and that your father hated you for it. She simply copied him.'

'Why didn't you tell me this before?'

Lisa shook her head. 'It wasn't my place.'

Nicole's head was spinning and she felt such a burst of rage she thumped her fist against the wall.

'I feel sorry for Sylvie,' Lisa added. 'She was only very young when she lost her mother. It hit her hard and affected her whole life.'

That prompted a further outburst from Nicole. 'Sorry for *her*! You know, even as a child she made me feel unwanted.'

'I do know.'

'She was always the queen bee. She'd invite me to join her and her friends on an outing and at the last minute, when I was ready and feeling excited, she'd say she had changed her mind. I always felt excluded.'

'Why did you never try to tell your father?'

Nicole shook her head. 'What would have been the point? He would never have taken my side. Never have even believed me.'

'Well, it's really your father you should be angry with, isn't it?' Lisa put a hand on her arm. 'Let me ask you one thing. Would you rather be you or Sylvie?'

Nicole stared at the cook. 'What kind of a question is that?'

'Haven't you ever stopped to think? Don't you realize what a deeply troubled woman she is?'

But Nicole would not be pacified. 'I don't care. I only know how unhappy she made me.'

'Sometimes I wonder how you'd both have turned out if your mother had lived.'

Nicole had loved her sister, but now she made up her mind: behind Sylvie's angelic looks lay nothing she could ever want to see again. Sick of bearing the blame for her mother's death, and sick of feeling ashamed of being who she was, the pain she'd tried to repress all her life felt as if it might overwhelm her.

'Did my father ever love me?' she asked. Words she'd never before been able to say out loud.

'He tried to. I believe that.'

'Tried.'

'I'm sure that eventually he did love you in his way. When he married he had no way of knowing how things would go between them. He had a position to maintain and his marriage didn't help matters. Of course, your presence was a constant reminder. And now men like Giraud are no friend to your father.'

Until now her family had mattered most to Nicole, or at least finding a way to feel part of it had mattered most. But now the French life and the identity she could never have was gone, and in a way it freed her. She'd always hoped that better things were round the corner; hoped that one day her father and sister would love her as much as she loved them. Now she let go of that hope. Her French world was slipping away, and to know that gave her power. She had lived among them but was not one of them and didn't have to remain trapped in their world any longer. Apart from Lisa, there was nothing left for her here. She had thought she couldn't bear to leave but now, whatever might lie ahead, it would be a relief to go. She would do it for her mother, if nothing else, and she silenced the little voice in her head telling her that Sylvie had only been a young child too.

23

When Nicole woke her cheeks were wet. All she could remember from her dream was a golden pagoda surrounded by bright blue butterflies, and the smell of incense in the air. But then she remembered hearing Trần's voice. With one day left before she was due to meet him, she needed a lucky break.

The image of a maid in bed with her father while her mother was pregnant had tormented her for two days and when Lisa came up with her breakfast tray, Nicole told her she had been terribly sick into her chamber pot all night. In fact, as soon as she felt Lisa would have the boiler stoked up, she'd stuck two fingers down her throat, and then soaked a facecloth in the hot water from her handbasin. Angry and determined, she'd kept on rewarming it and plastering it to her head for half an hour.

Faced with the overpowering smell in the room, Lisa felt her forehead. 'You do seem a bit hot. Why not try to eat something nice now?'

'I couldn't. I need air, Lisa. I'm sure I'd feel better.'

The cook stood with her hands on her hips and frowned. 'I promised your father.'

'Please let me come down to the kitchen. Keep the door locked, just open the pantry window. It's so small, nobody could get out through there. Anyway, I feel much too ill to go anywhere, even if I could.'

While Lisa thought about it, Nicole stared at the floor, willing the cook to give in. She got up and glanced in the mirror. Excellent. Her eyes glittered and her skin looked mottled.

'Oh, Lisa,' she said, and held out a hand to steady herself against the wall. 'I feel so dizzy.'

The cook seemed to decide. 'Well, I've had enough of this shameful state of affairs. You're right. You do need air and maybe something to eat. Here, let me get a wrap for you.'

While Lisa's back was turned, Nicole quickly slid open the drawer of her bedside table and rooted around for her shop keys. Though they had taken her house keys, they hadn't taken those, and at the shop there was another set of house keys. Even if she was caught and brought back, as long as she was able to conceal the house keys, she'd still be able to get out again. She located the keys, and pocketed them along with a nail file.

'Here we are,' Lisa said and handed Nicole a shawl, once belonging to her mother.

Nicole took it. Nobody knew she had found it hidden away in an old trunk of her mother's belongings in one of the stable rooms at the back of the house in Hué. It seemed like a good omen. Her mother would be with her. She took it from Lisa and didn't allow any emotion to show.

'What if someone sees?' Nicole whispered as they paused at the top of the stairs.

'There's only you and me here.'

Nicole looked around. 'But the policeman. Isn't he on guard?'

Lisa grinned and gave her a little push. 'Don't worry about him. He's a lazy sod. Half the time he nips off home.'

Nicole pulled a face. 'Giraud won't be happy.'

'Our Mr Giraud has got bigger fish to fry at the moment.'

'What fish?'

'Let's just say there are some ugly rumours circulating about him.'

★

In the kitchen Nicole faltered at the sight of the familiar red floor and the walls lined with white brick-shaped tiles, and wished she didn't have to trick the woman who'd been such a good and loyal friend. Nicole glanced at the row of copper pots hanging from the bar attached to the ceiling, but avoided looking at the arch leading through to the glass doors of the conservatory. She had missed this so much.

'I'm sorry to have to lock you in,' Lisa was saying. 'But I'm hoping to tempt you with a lovely *soupe au vin blanc* I've got on the go.'

'I feel too sick to eat.'

'You make yourself comfortable near the window and I'll brew you up a nice tisane instead. Any particular flavour?'

'I couldn't drink a thing.'

'Well, I'll keep you company, shall I?' Lisa settled her ample body on the chair next to Nicole's. 'Things have been pretty strange around here this last week, I can tell you.'

Nicole pretended disinterest but knew Lisa loved a gossip. She also knew one of the conservatory windows had a faulty catch.

'Mighty strange.' Lisa gave her a mischievous smile. 'You'll never guess what I overheard yesterday.'

Nicole shook her head. 'I don't suppose I will.'

'Two of those army types were here and I heard them talking in the hall about Giraud. He's been found in a compromising situation.'

'How?'

'He's been siphoning American money to fund the movement and maintenance of North African prostitutes for the French army.'

Nicole thought about it and wondered if the black woman she'd seen her father with was one of them.

'I heard them say the women are from Constantine, the Ouled-Naïl tribe. Beautiful, I'm told.'

Nicole didn't speak.

'The army reckon to be heading north using civilian pilots and planes too. American ones. And between you and me, I heard they were expecting to send fifty thousand troops. What do you make of that!'

A shaft of light fell across the cook's face, showing up the wrinkles round her eyes and the skin beginning to loosen at the base of her cheeks. When had she become so much older? It felt wrong to cause Lisa more sorrow and Nicole felt ashamed. Startled by the strength of her own feeling, she paused. Perhaps, after all, she should not go? Lisa deserved better than this, but when Nicole thought of what her father had done – what choice did she have?

She shook her head. 'Lisa, I feel terrible. Maybe I will have that tisane. Anything fresh from the garden would do.'

'Sorry, *chérie*. Here's me chattering on and you at death's door. Wait while I get my scissors and nip out the back. I know just the thing.' She looked a bit embarrassed. 'You know I'll have to lock the door.'

While Lisa was gathering herbs, Nicole tiptoed into the conservatory after her, making sure the cook was on the other side of the garden before identifying the window with the faulty catch. She heard a sound and, ready to panic, glanced round with a guilty start, but it was just someone in the next-door garden. She turned back to the window, knowing exactly how to loosen it with her nail file. She did so quickly, then crouched down to undo the bolt at the bottom. She eased it open, giving thanks for French windows. Then, as the panic was replaced by a burst of energy, she slipped out and made for the wall at the back of the garden. Recalling how many times Lisa had shielded her, she halted for a moment. Deeply sorry for the trouble it would cause Lisa, she felt distraught to think they might never see each other again. Then she thought of

Mark. Despite everything, she did not dare consider how she'd feel if she were never to see him again. But as for her father – after what Lisa had told her, how could she allow herself to care? She shinned up the wall and scrambled over the top, the feeling of relief spilling over as she escaped.

24

The shop was the first place they'd look for her, so Nicole quelled the bubbling sense of euphoria at being free, and got on with what she had to do. She glanced around at all the things she'd made and done. It was hard being in her shop again and knowing she had to leave it behind. Despite an intense feeling of loss, she worked rapidly, picking up the house keys, binding up her hair, and then changing into Vietnamese dress. In the little bathroom at the back she quickly splashed her face while holding on to her nerve.

At the last minute she dashed upstairs and pulled out the antique purse; her little emblem of the past. It made her feel connected. Should she take it in her bundle? She hesitated for only a moment and then slipped it in. While she had the purse with her the ancestors would keep her safe. On an impulse she also slid in the only photograph she had of Mark. She longed to stay in the shop and wait for Trần there, but it wasn't safe.

It would be tricky to spend the day waiting, but she knew the back alleys leading to the lake and, more importantly, the hidden spot where she had lain with Trần beneath the trees and bushes. She'd wait there and come back through the alleys later.

So she spent the day hiding by the lake and, in the late afternoon, at the time the shops would be shutting up, she covered her head with a scarf and came back to find Trần. Fewer people were about than usual – a warning sign that the street might be under surveillance – so she slid into a dark alley opposite her shop. Frightened that Trần might have been caught, she poked her head out to look, but when a couple of

French officers passed by she ducked back into the shadows. She had no idea how long she'd have to wait. An old lady peered up the alley as she passed and Nicole stepped further back, concealing herself in a doorway.

When she saw O-Lan come out of her own shop, Nicole held back for a moment but couldn't restrain herself. As she watched her friend peer through the window of the silk shop, she pulled the scarf further over her face and slipped across.

O-Lan turned round, smiling when she saw Nicole. 'Where have you been? The shop has been closed for a week. I've missed you. Were you ill?'

Nicole shook her head, took O-Lan by the arm and drew her across the street. 'Can we talk in the alley?'

'Why don't we go inside your shop?'

'I can't.'

They quickly crossed the street and passed into the shadows.

O-Lan held Nicole's arm. 'What's going on?'

Nicole couldn't keep the eagerness from her voice. 'I'm going north with Trần.'

O-Lan's face fell.

'Why do you look like that? I thought you'd be pleased.'

'Trần is passionate, idealistic and –'

'A good man,' Nicole interrupted.

'Yes, but . . .'

There was a pause.

O-Lan clasped her hands together and Nicole was taken aback by the look of solemnity in her friend's eyes. 'The party is everything to him. He will sacrifice you if you get in the way.'

Nicole shook her head. 'He'd never do that.'

'You are too trusting.'

'But I thought you sympathized with the Vietminh?'

'I never said that.' O-Lan's tone was dismissive, her eyes full of reproach.

'So whose side are you on?'

'Nicole, I haven't taken sides. I love my family. And I don't care whether they are with the Vietminh or supporting the French.'

'But wouldn't you hide Trần if he was on the run?'

O-Lan looked upset. 'I hope it will never come to that. Please, Nicole, do not go. Look at your lovely shop. It is the prettiest in the whole of Silk Street. What will happen to it?'

'I've thought of that.'

O-Lan gripped her hand. 'And? Are you not tempted to stay?'

Nicole felt a twinge of regret. 'It's not that I want to leave.'

'Please don't then.' O-Lan paused and reached out to her. 'And what about your father and Sylvie? I know you've had problems but you love them. They are not your enemy.'

'If not them, then who?' Nicole shook her head. 'Lisa told me what happened when I was born and I can't forgive them. I don't belong with them. Even if I stayed, for my shop, I'd still have to deal with Sylvie, and I'd have to see my father and Mark – I just can't.'

'So you're running away?'

Nicole shook her head. 'No. I'm going to help a worthy cause.'

O-Lan shot her a disappointed look, tears shining in her eyes. 'You are wrong. You persuade yourself, Nicole, but it's not the truth. You don't even know who the enemy is. It's not good enough.'

'Come on, don't be so down.' Nicole smiled at her friend. 'I don't want to fall out with you.'

O-Lan stared at Nicole and didn't smile back.

'Well, there it is,' Nicole said. 'You'd better go back inside. Trần will be here any moment now.'

O-Lan took both Nicole's hands in her own. 'Be safe, Nicole, and if you ever need me I will be here.'

Nicole's eyes were damp and she felt uncertain as O-Lan walked away. Was her friend right? She had spoken so vehemently and it was frightening to think it might never be safe to return. But then she pictured her father in bed with another woman while her mother had been so vulnerable. Haunted by the image, the pain of it came rushing back, strengthening her resolve.

Suddenly someone had a hand over her mouth.

Certain it was one of Giraud's men, Nicole froze. She heard a low chuckle and spun round, relief flooding through her when she saw it was Trần. His eyes were sparkling and he seemed very excited. They grinned at each other and she nearly laughed out loud. His eyes grew wide as he motioned for her to follow him but not speak. She'd already guessed not to walk beside him. Once they were away from the shop, he whispered the plan. They would walk to where they'd mount one of the buses used only by the Vietnamese.

An hour later they were squashed together on a bus heading out along the Red River Delta, where steam rose in waves from the surface of the water and the smell of rotting fish swept in through the open window. Nicole tried to close it but, rusted and jammed, there was no chance. She tried to think of anything but fish and, as the roar of the few cars faded, she felt a shiver run through her. As the landscape became more distinctly rural, she gazed out at the sampans and junks moving past riverbanks flanked by plum trees. A dozen or so geese flew by in formation, their slow measured honking a contrast to the harsh squawking seabirds.

Further on, and away from the river, the bus trundled past shabby hamlets where naked children played in the dust. She fell into a doze until, eventually, they came to a halt at a jumble of huts protected by a bamboo hedge. How peaceful, she thought, until a shrill bird's cry broke the silence.

'We are here,' Trần said as he rose from his seat. He smiled and she noticed that streak of childlike enthusiasm again. He lowered his voice and brought his mouth to her ear. 'And your name must be Vietnamese. You must now be Linh.'

She grinned. 'Spring. I like it.'

She followed him off the bus, then looked about at the houses, not much more than huts or shacks, with pointed roofs of plaited bamboo. A few people trudged down the paths, dressed in brown or dull green, their shoulder poles clicking as they transported vegetables and rice from one place to another. Swallows flew above, swooping and diving endlessly.

'This way,' he said and pointed to a small track between two huts. As he did so she felt as if he were pointing towards the future.

This was a fresh beginning, just as her new name suggested. She had high hopes of finally feeling she belonged, and at the same time it would be a chance to prove herself.

They skirted one-roomed huts built on stilts, where the smoke from cooking fires hung in the air. They dodged crowing roosters and chickens who, standing their ground, barely noticed them, though the various dogs on chains set off a terrible racket, barking and straining to get free. Despite that, Nicole thought again how unexpectedly peaceful it was. Naked babies slept on mats, young children ran about between the tethered goats and vegetable plots, while the older ones, sitting on the compacted earth, played stones or shot at birds with catapults. One or two stood up to call out to Trần, but watched Nicole with hungry eyes.

It felt unfamiliar and for a moment she had a little flicker of regret, feeling the absence of something, but it was quickly dispelled.

The village was a labyrinth. Washing hung from lines of string suspended across the courtyards, and the plots were packed with fruit trees and pumpkins. She glanced into the few huts not built on stilts, noticing the earth floor and glassless windows.

'They must get cold,' she said and glanced at Trần. He had stopped to speak to an old man with parched skin, who seemed burdened by something as he spoke.

Trần bowed then shook the man's hand and turned back to her. 'It is cold at night.'

Nicole noticed a menacing eye painted on one of the huts.

'What's that?' she asked.

'It's an American idea.'

'I don't get it.'

'They know the villagers are scared of vampires and ghosts, so they get the French to paint an eye on a hut facing the home of a suspected terrorist.'

'I still don't get it.'

'The villagers think it's the eye of their ancestors, and will no longer support or hide the suspect. But we have our ways and means. This is a war of resistance.'

They went a little further out, trekking along a narrow path between luminous rice fields where herons pecked and boys lay asleep on the backs of water buffalos. After a short distance they seemed to head back in a semicircle to a different part of the village, where a kite hovered high in the sky. Trần paused and, shading his eyes, looked up at it, then carried on walking, only stopping when they reached a large two-storey house, adjacent to an orchard on the edge of the village.

'Is this your home?' she asked.

'No, but it used to be my uncle's.'

'Used to be?'

Trần frowned. 'It was his ancestral home. It has been requisitioned by the party. He was a landowner.'

'What does that mean?'

'It means he was given a fair trial.'

'Why?'

'He owned three fields and was a silk merchant.'

'Is that all?'

Trần nodded.

'So what happened?'

He shook his head. 'He was turned out. That man you saw me talking to, he's my uncle.'

She couldn't keep the shock from her voice. 'The one who helped you receive an education?'

'Change the subject,' he said and walked up to the door. 'Come, this is where we'll stay until we get our orders. I have told them you're Vietnamese.'

'They don't know I'm half French?'

'No and let us keep it that way.'

'Where will they send us?'

'We are both to join a travelling troupe of performers. While you are in the show I shall be charged with talking to the villagers.'

'To persuade them to join the resistance?'

'That is right.'

The next day Nicole watched a stick-thin woman with a split-bamboo trap catching fish and shrimp in a small stream running beside the village. Nicole had barely slept, and the hard wooden bench she'd been given for a bed hadn't helped.

'What else do they eat?' she asked Trần.

'Fish, vegetables and rice. That's it. Boiled, steamed, pounded into cakes. Always rice.'

The daily life of the women seemed to concentrate on taking care of the children, feeding the animals, trying to catch fish and cooking. It was clear there was a definite hierarchy at play between the sexes; the women also had to fetch and carry water and do all the other domestic chores too.

'Life is not easy,' Trần said. 'A drought will destroy the crops, a flood the same. They help each other. We all play our part.'

'I see.'

'No running hot and cold water here, Nicole.'

She frowned, feeling a bit insulted. She had not expected there would be. He led her to a hut where she was told to follow the lead of a woman who was chopping mulberry leaves to feed the silkworms. Another woman was removing cocoons and plunging them into boiling hot water.

As Nicole began work, they looked at her sideways but did not speak. Nicole felt ill at ease and shifted from one foot to the other.

'It's to kill the larvae, isn't it?' she whispered to her companion, hoping to show her knowledge. 'The water.'

The woman nodded. 'If we do not they will turn into moths. And moths would chew through the threads to get out of the cocoon.'

In another room Nicole spotted two women pulling the thread from the cocoons and spinning it into hanks ready to be woven into cloth. As she chopped the bunch of leaves, she thought back to the evening before. She'd been sitting next to Trần, while trying to keep up with the conversation in the hut. About eight of them had been huddled together, sitting cross-legged on the floor and smoking some foul-scented root. With a convincing accent her Vietnamese was good, but it wasn't her first language. She had only been half listening while watching the flickering shadows cast by the flames of small wicks soaked in shallow bowls of oil. Trần had prodded her in the ribs.

'Pay attention,' he'd muttered.

'Sorry.'

'Smile at the leader. Look grateful. We are being put to work in the silk sheds until we get our orders.'

She had been surprised they weren't immediately to set off for the north, but Trần said it was a test and she should simply obey and look pleased to do so.

Now as she chopped the mulberry leaves she lost concentration again and sliced the tip of her finger. Without thinking, she swore in French. The woman looked at her suspiciously and told her to find a rag to wrap round the wound.

It was only later on in the evening, after a supper of a surprisingly good shrimp soup served with soya bean loaf, that the full weight of what she had done sank in. The group had convened by the time she returned from the raised squatter toilet, the stink of it still clinging to her clothes. Although there was room for everyone it felt damp, crowded and intimidating. What she wouldn't have done for a *café sua*, the Vietnamese name she must remember to use for a *café au lait*. The chilly atmosphere in the room grew colder as the leader began firing questions at Trần, speaking so rapidly she only managed to pick up some of the words. She heard her name mentioned twice, while at the same time the leader glanced her way. Trần, looking mortified, spoke more slowly but stuck up for her, explaining she was indeed half French but that she wholeheartedly believed in the cause.

Another man spoke up and Nicole cringed at the hatred in his voice. 'She's a spy.'

Everyone apart from Trần and the leader nodded.

'Get rid of her,' one muttered.

'Agreed.'

'We don't need a *métisse* here.'

A man with unusually heavy brows and a narrow

sun-darkened face withdrew a knife from a pouch at his waist and wiped it on his trousers. He grinned at Nicole. She shuddered and glanced at Trần, who was now gazing at the floor. The leader ignored the men and, speaking a little less rapidly, addressed Nicole directly.

'You can trust her,' Trần butted in as he glanced up. 'I vouch for her.'

'Let her speak. What do you have to say for yourself?'

As everything Trần had ever said about the resistance ran through her mind, she clutched at the fleeting phrases. 'I believe in land reform,' she said. 'I believe the rich should be made to pay for what they have done. I want to help free the country from slavery. The French have enforced inhuman laws. They have drowned uprisings in rivers of blood. They have robbed us of our raw materials.'

The leader glanced at Trần. 'You say she gave you information?'

Trần nodded.

A tense silence spread across the room as the leader leant back and returned his gaze to Nicole. Sweating profusely and feeling the patches spreading beneath her arms, she hardly knew where to look. Even though she had just been to the toilet she desperately needed to go again. One or two of the men muttered, but the leader held up a hand for silence. He rolled a cigarette very slowly, flattening out a paper, shredding the tobacco, then laying it in a neat line on the paper, the frown lines on his forehead deepening. Nicole wanted to shout at him to hurry, but the moments kept dragging. At last he slipped it between his lips, but still did not light it.

'So what was it?' he said, tilting his head and speaking out of the side of his mouth.

Suddenly feeling cold, her mind refused to work. What was what? What did he mean?

He slammed the table with the palms of his hands. 'This information. What was it?'

It was on her lips but, close to tears, she faltered. She steadied herself and the words came out rapidly. 'The French are sending fifty thousand troops north, including American planes.'

He nodded. 'You are a singer?'

She continued to make a huge effort to control herself. He must not know how scared she was. 'Yes.'

'You know Vietnamese songs?'

'My mother was Vietnamese.'

With a sinking feeling in her stomach, Nicole felt certain she was about to come unstuck. All eyes were on the leader as he bowed his head.

'If you want to stay, you will sing for us. Stand up.'

She got to her feet, her mind a complete blank. This felt like a terrible mistake. She risked a glance in Trần's direction but his face was passive and he avoided her eyes. She tensed. What would she do if she couldn't think of the right song? A tune came back to her, a line from her show, and then another, but the rest of the words were missing. From there she frantically ran through more songs in her head. Would she be judged on her choice of song as well? Or would it be the quality of her singing? Certainly they would expect her to come up with something typically Vietnamese, something they would all be likely to know, but her mind kept giving her French songs. Why couldn't she recall the songs she'd learnt with O-Lan?

She felt as if her throat would implode, but at last a tune sprang into her mind; a lullaby about an autumn wind and the coming of the winter, one of the songs she'd sung with O-Lan recently, so most of the words came back. Ignoring the feeling of dread that threatened to consume her, she began. And, as the haunting rhythm of the song filled the room, she closed her eyes and pictured herself at home in the garden with leaves floating on the breeze. She managed to convey the peace and melancholy of autumn and, when she opened her eyes, she saw all the men were listening. When she had finished nobody spoke.

After a moment, the leader nodded. 'She stays. Is everyone agreed?'

They all agreed, with the exception of the man with the knife, who looked disappointed and left the room muttering.

The leader finally lit his cigarette, slowly blowing the smoke out as he turned to her. 'You are not lying about the troops. We have heard this too. But you will be watched. Put one foot wrong . . .'

He got up and walked away, but turned back at the door. As he did so he smiled, then went out, leaving a trail of smoke behind. It had not been a warm smile.

The following day, while they waited to hear when they'd be leaving, Nicole and Trần sat in the privacy of the walled court-yard behind the house. She watched a chameleon race up the wall and, feeling a little out of place, she reached for his hand. He refused to take it.

'We cannot be seen to be close. We are comrades now.'

She blinked in confusion. 'What about affection or friendship?'

'Cannot come into it.'

Nicole picked up a pebble and threw it at a tree. She had not expected to experience such tedium or for Trần to be so cold.

'Once we have won the war,' he said, 'things will change. I will have status within the party and will be free to marry.'

'Strange idea of a proposal.'

He grinned. 'Not romantic enough for you?'

She shrugged. She liked him but marriage had not been on

her mind, and certainly not to him. The thought of Mark's photo in her purse popped into her head.

'Now remember, show an attitude of humility. Be vigilant. Respect age, knowledge and social rank. Remember too, with strangers, it's best to always say *ong* or "grandfather".'

'I know what it means,' she said, irritated by the patronizing way he'd spoken.

She glanced at the orchids growing on the trunk of the nearby tree and listened to the birds. It would be all right. Everything would be all right. It had to be. She didn't tell him she was beginning to feel homesick.

'When you meet anyone, bow slightly and smile. If they ask how you are, say *"Tôi khỏe. Cám ơn. Còn bạn."* And nothing more. Whatever you do, keep a civil tongue. Nobody will reveal their true feelings so you must not either.'

'And as a woman I must be modest.' He didn't seem to notice the sarcasm in her voice.

'Exactly.'

A jasmine hedge ran all along one side of the courtyard and the sweet scent made her sneeze. She leant against him, the morning sun sparkled between the gaps in the clouds and she felt a little better. Dozing in the warmth, it seemed her best option was to surrender to whatever lay ahead.

'What about the man with the knife?' she asked.

'Duong? Don't worry about him.'

Her mood lightened further when one of the village women brought out a pot of rice and a fresh green papaya salad with pickled vegetables.

'It's a good sign. If they're feeding us now it means we'll be leaving soon,' he said. 'We may not eat again for several days.'

'Will the journey be hard?'

'It will. You'll get used to doing without luxury.'

Not without a pang, Nicole thought back over the journey her family had made from Huế to Hanoi. That had been a turning point too, just like this. It had seemed like a tough journey at the time, but compared with what might lie ahead, she now knew it had been nothing at all.

3
Mists and Clouds

November 1952 to September 1953

25

Northern Vietnam

The journey north during early November was not as arduous as Nicole had expected; rather, she enjoyed the sense of freedom, and loved the evenings when the countryside, softened by the gold of the setting sun, cast a spell that made anything seem possible. These were the months when it was good to walk. They walked at night when they could, ducking bats flying haphazardly between low trees. When they glimpsed a black bear in the blue light of the moon, Nicole froze. Trần's wide-eyed look warned her not to move. The bear passed by. When they tried to sleep during the day, it was snub-nosed monkeys who woke them, pulling their hair and sniffing their bags in the hope of finding food.

It might only be an interlude before the hard work began but, determined to make the most of it, she was content to sleep rough, thrilled by the wilderness, and took each day as it came. There were moments when they drew too close to French troops and the sharp feeling of danger coursed through her blood, but being out in the open with the wind, the rain and the birds for company created a kind of exhilaration that fizzed and bubbled inside her. She felt as if she was starting to discover something new about herself, and she was relieved that Trần wasn't expecting to have sex again.

The early days with the theatre troupe passed quickly. She felt strange at first, but followed Trần's instructions and managed not to give herself away. She had learnt to watch for signs, little facial giveaways and the like, and was good at spotting what people were thinking. She hoped none of them could see into *her* mind. Hospitable and ready to share, they tried to engage her, but she kept to herself, sang her songs well and made sure she never uttered a word of French. She made one particular girlfriend, a musician called Phuong, and they'd usually smoke together at the end of a show before striking the stage and moving on.

The show was a form of Chèo, previously a satire showing vignettes of everyday life and performed by peasants in a village square; a simple drama with songs that suited Nicole, who found all her work with O-Lan was paying off brilliantly. Traditionally the action had shown people dealing with ethical quandaries and religious issues, but now the narratives were more frequently modern Vietminh versions, riddled with the theme of self-sacrifice. Intended to reinforce the spirits of the rural supporters and persuade drifters to join the resistance, the stories showed men and women heroically defending their country against the French.

The songs were performed accompanied by traditional instruments: zithers, lutes, fiddles and bamboo xylophones. And the drums beat to the eight-rhythm structure of the military.

At first Nicole felt roused by the music and content with her new world. And so the days turned into weeks, and the weeks into months and, as time went on, she was surprised to realize that she'd been in the show for almost six months. One afternoon after a long trek through marshy land, she was sitting on a log in a quiet spot in the shade, thinking. Lately the paltry food supplies and dire personal arrangements had become worse than before. Now they were having to sleep in draughty barns and rat-infested hovels, her thoughts more often turned to the little luxuries of the past. An empty stomach didn't help. Perpetually hungry, she also felt hot and sticky and, as she scratched the multiple bites on her legs, the memory of their French villa became more appealing. She tried to remember the details of each room but the images were hazy. She racked her brain trying to recall, but only her old bedroom, the upstairs bathroom and the kitchen came into focus.

She would have liked nothing better than a bath in the little bathroom she had shared with Sylvie. She smiled at the memory and even missed her sister as she thought of the way one section of the bathroom had been tidy, and the other littered with her pins, clips and pots of face cream with the lids left unscrewed. She pictured the large art-deco mirror covering one wall – the way it steamed up when you had a bath – and how, if you looked out of the window, you gazed down on tropical fronds. It seemed so long ago; how innocent she had been.

Now, lonelier than ever before, she questioned herself. Had it been a mistake to come north with Trần? Had she been wrong about Mark? Maybe he really had been looking out for her when he encouraged her to go home. She had acted on impulse, but perhaps if she'd demanded the truth about the house arrest and the shooting, things might have been different. She checked to make sure nobody was watching, then ran her fingertips over the photo of Mark before stuffing it back inside her purse. She looked at it every day, and always smiled at the memory of him falling into the lake. But she had grown up in a family who did not tell each other the truth, and so, instead of standing her ground, she had run away. O-Lan had been right about that.

Though Trần had insisted he would be working in league with the troupe, in fact he went away for weeks on end. When he did turn up, he paid her less attention than before, and the warmth in his eyes was gone. It upset her more than she cared to acknowledge; not because she wanted him, but because it left her feeling even more adrift. She knew certain members of the troupe were messengers for the Vietminh – she couldn't be sure which ones – but in every village they passed through, they spied out who was on the side of the nationalists, and who was not. Harsh reprisals were becoming increasingly frequent.

The troupe performed in masks or painted their faces in red and white, which meant there was little chance of any French recognizing her. By day she wore traditional Vietnamese dress, which also acted as a disguise, and while of course she worried about being found by French army officers, at times she wished she could be, if only to be able to speak French again. But it was also true that in the months she'd been with the troupe she'd seen things she wished she had not: things that had shattered any remaining belief that Indochina should still be French. And the longer she spent with the troupe, the more Vietnamese she felt.

She got up from the log, stretched and went to get made up in the wagon she shared with three others. They'd already finished and she'd need to hurry.

She loved painting her face, and only had her lips left to outline when the spell was broken by a new performer appearing at her side. She glanced in the mirror and froze when she saw his reflection. With growing unease she recognized Duong, the man who had relished showing her his knife all those months ago. He nodded, so she stood and, recalling Trần's words about respecting her elders, gave him a scrupulously polite bow before leaving the wagon, heavy in mind and body.

That evening the show went on as usual. Nobody said anything to her but she had the impression they all knew why the man was there and nobody was telling. She could see him observing her throughout the show and it saddened her that, despite all the months she had travelled and performed with them, the troupe still considered her an outsider.

The next day she came across some members gossiping. The talk ceased once they spotted her and a chilly silence followed. The little knot quickly broke up, though one remained: her musician friend, Phuong, who was now in the process of restringing her instrument. Nicole tried to question her, but she shook her head and lowered her eyes. Nicole had the impression she'd wanted to speak, but could not. When you didn't know who you could trust, it made you vulnerable and a careless word could mean disaster. If she wanted to find out what was going on, she would have to confront the man with the knife.

As she scanned the area, she longed for Trần to be there and on her side, in the way he had once been. But Trần wasn't there and she would have to tackle this on her own. She soon found the man sitting beneath a gnarled tree next to one of the cara-vans. She stood tall and made eye contact with him. It would have been safer to take it slowly, but the words spilled out.

'What are you doing here?'

He tapped the side of his nose and lit a cigarette. 'It's been a long time.'

'Where's Trần?'

The man didn't speak, but blew the smoke out through his nostrils.

'Is he all right?'

He stuck out his chin and rubbed it. 'I think you and I need a little time to get to know each other.'

'And Trần?'

'Are you a virgin?' He narrowed his eyes and grinned.

Nicole was not going to allow him to intimidate her. 'What's that got to do with anything?'

'Why are you so interested in the boy?'

'He's a comrade.'

'Good answer.' He coughed on the smoke. 'But there's a bit more to it.'

She steeled herself not to react. The Vietnamese rarely showed their feelings, and she knew he was trying to provoke her.

She shrugged. 'I am loyal to the cause.'

'We shall soon see,' he said, then got to his feet and strode off.

The underlying threat in his manner unnerved her and for the next few days she watched him. He had some kind of power, but with no idea what it was, or how he was planning to use it, she felt defenceless. The other troupe members were wary of him too, and it seemed none could risk taking her side. The feeling of unease grew and when she could not sleep for the heavy, oppressive air, she went outside to listen to the cacophony of night-time sounds rising from the jungle. Imagined dangers loomed disproportionately at night, so how could she tell if it was just her own fear or if the man really posed a threat?

The next day, a small village nestling in a valley where they had stayed for one night was torched by the French. She had watched helplessly from higher up the mountain as the last curls of smoke broke up in the wind. Even women and children had been slaughtered and those who survived were now destitute. When she asked who would bury the dead she was shocked to be told they would not be buried; such outrages reminded the peasants of what the French were capable.

As she was thinking about it, she caught sight of the man. She had not sought him out this time, but there he was sitting beneath a battery-driven lamp swinging from a branch. He pulled out a cut-throat razor, like the one her father used, and began whittling a stick, the blade gleaming in the light from the lamp.

'Can't leave me alone, can you?' he said and winked at her. 'I can help you out there. You're available, aren't you, like all French women? Don't think I haven't had the experience.'

It frightened her more than his previous behaviour had done. She noticed his thick wrists and heavy shoulders. She'd stand no chance.

The next day was foggy and cold. Their wagons passed through a village where they had to swerve to avoid a blanket of black flies feeding on the corpse of a woman who'd been thrown in a ditch. The woman wore the typical black costume of the female Vietminh and had been chucked away as if her life was nothing at all. Nicole forced herself to keep looking out of the back of the wagon and spotted a little girl partly concealed by the woman's body. She was painfully thin, no more than five years old, and though her clothes were also black, around her neck was a bright blue scarf. At the sight of the child's brown eyes, wide open and utterly blank, Nicole immediately thought of Yvette. With tears in her eyes, Nicole turned away. She could do nothing for them.

A short while later, as the trail of caravans snaked along the mountainside, the road became little more than a ledge, so Nicole followed one of the wagons on foot. It wouldn't take much for a wagon to tip over the precipice, and she felt safer walking. Soon after, Duong brushed alongside her and she caught sight of a satchel on his back. She had been waiting for him to make the first move, and wasn't surprised when he grasped her by the elbow and began to draw her aside.

'Please,' she said. 'You're hurting me.'

He laughed.

'Where is Trần? Is he hurt?'

'Not that again. Tell me, are you truly loyal?'

'Of course, surely you must believe me? The party demands obedience and I am obedient.'

'Just words. But you can rest easy. I have been instructed to take you to Trần.'

She stopped walking, tripping herself up on her boots. 'I don't believe you. I want to stay with the others.'

He gave her a blank stare. 'Believe me or not. You will soon see. When the road descends shortly it will fork. We shall linger at the back of the caravans and veer off to the left, while the rest will go right.'

Her breath deepened. She must not show her fear. 'What about my things? They're in the wagon.'

'You won't need them. You can only take what you have on your back now. Flatten yourself against the side of the mountain and let everyone pass.'

'And if I won't?'

He glanced down the edge of the precipice and sucked his teeth. 'Mighty long way down.'

Nicole did not know what to think. Nobody could survive a fall like that. If this was to be a death sentence, the few members of the troupe who might have noticed her with the man would simply claim they'd seen nothing. She could feel her chest rising and falling, and hoped he couldn't see the early signs of panic. At the likely outcome, her mind went into free fall, but she had no choice. She'd have to do what he wanted.

26

Nicole and Duong walked from the highlands, where wild rhododendrons in the north-west gave way to the lower hills. There, monkeys, bats and flying squirrels leapt through the air while giant ferns reached for the sky. Where the dwarf bamboo sprouted up they had to watch out for yellow marsh water. If she hadn't felt so scared it would have been beautiful.

She was hungry too and, beneath what seemed like perpetual clouds, they ate dry biscuits and drank only the smallest amount of water. Hour after hour, she suspected he might be about to attack her and as they lay beneath a canopy of white blossom she longed to be wandering free in the streets of Hanoi. She could not think ahead, but kept one eye on the trio of vultures following their progress and the other eye on him, hoping all the time that the awful birds would not soon be swooping for their prey.

At least it wasn't too hot; it could only have been about twenty-five degrees. When they eventually padded over a deep carpet of lush grass on the edge of a clearing and reached bamboo fencing, they had been walking for nearly a week. Luckily the monsoon rains were a little way off or the whole week would have been hell. Her heart lifted as a silver pheasant rose from the undergrowth, its long white tail as elegant as any bird she'd seen. It looked as if they'd reached the outskirts of a village so at least there might be a chance of a bowl of rice and some kind of bed for the night. But as they drew closer and none of the usual signs of village life appeared, she began to work out that this was no ordinary village. Closer still, she saw guards with rifles placed at intervals. The place was eerily silent. She stopped walking and the man prodded her in the back.

'Re-education camp,' he said.

Nicole had heard of these dreadful places, but had never believed the rumours. Now it looked like they might have been true all along. They were allowed entrance by the guards and, as she drew closer, the bleak appearance of the camp sent a chill right through her. From her months with the troupe she knew re-education was used as a means of revenge, repression and indoctrination. Thousands had been imprisoned with neither charge nor trial. And here the thin grey prisoners' faces betrayed the awful truth. This was where French soldiers and wealthy Vietnamese mandarin families were brainwashed into obedience: men, women and children too. Forced to show gratitude for the harsh treatment meted out to them, they were also made to plead guilty to their so-called crimes. Most looked barely alive.

'Those who do not comply are sent to a reprisal camp,' the man said and smiled, clearly enjoying her unease. 'Much worse.'

Nicole's throat tightened. Was he going to leave her here? As he walked her through the camp, she tried to catch the eye of a shackled Frenchwoman, but the empty eyes conveyed a loss more terrible than the loss of mere physical freedom.

'Why am I here?'

'I told you. I am taking you to Trần.'

She gasped. 'Surely he's not a prisoner?'

The man laughed and pointed to the other side of a clearing where a Vietminh was inspecting a line of gaunt French prisoners.

'He is *cán-bộ*. In charge of re-education.'

Her scalp pricked with apprehension. 'A political cadre?'

She watched as Trần called out one of the men from the line. The man held out a hand in front of himself as if to guide his steps, but he stumbled, and by the look of his blackened face, it seemed as if he might have been blinded. Trần stepped forward and she hoped he was going to help the man; instead he handed a rifle to a woman standing in the line. Nicole watched as Trần spoke to the woman and then pointed at the man. The woman shook her head. He pulled a small boy from the line who couldn't have been more than five or six. The woman screamed and, hearing her voice, the man shouted out.

Nicole took a step forward but her companion pulled her back.

The reality of what happened next came crashing down on her. She searched for some clue in Trần's face, watching in horror as he snatched the rifle back and called a guard who brought out two small bamboo cages. Nicole's temples began to throb as one of the cages was put over the woman's head and secured with rope. A plank of wood was attached to either side of the cage, pressing down on her shoulders. They did exactly the same to the young child. Nicole lost all sense of accurate time. It seemed to be taking so long, yet at the same time it was already over. Sickened by the naked fear in the child's wide eyes as he was led away, she took in the weeping woman and the blind man on his knees, pleading in French.

'Why?'

'The father has refused to become a new man. He is a reactionary who has violated camp rules.'

'But why punish his wife and children?'

The man shrugged.

'What's going to happen to them?'

'They will be made to stand in the river for twenty-four hours.'

She couldn't keep the shock from her voice. 'The water is freezing. They'll drown.'

The man shrugged again. 'Come. Let us join Trần.'

Nicole folded her arms around herself, hardly believing Trần could have ordered this. The memory of nearly drowning in the Perfume River came back sharply. The terrible pressure, the booming sound of the river. Feeling as if her legs were made of stone, she forced herself to move. Now, more than at any other time, she wished she could simply return to her old life. When she reached Trần she could not keep the dismay from her voice. 'I don't understand. Why hurt the child?'

He flicked a lock of hair away and wiped the moisture from his brow. 'You saw those cages?'

She nodded.

'Those cages belong to the French. They have used them for decades. On men, women and children. Now let them get a taste of their own medicine.'

She stared at him, trying to find the man she had known. How had he become so cruel? He returned her gaze and she remembered his gentleness with Yvette, but she could also see that his eyes, once so passionate about the cause, now seemed pitiless.

'What?' he said.

She shook her head slowly.

'Remember, Nicole. I said there would come a time when you would have to choose.'

Her jaw stiffened. 'I thought I had chosen.'

'It is a choice that has to be reaffirmed.'

'I've been with the theatre troupe for six months. If you don't believe me now, you never will.'

'We shall see.'

Devastated by what she had seen, she knew she was on shaky ground, but decided the only way was to brave it out.

She threw back her shoulders and spoke in a calm voice. 'I am true to the cause, Trần.'

He beckoned a group of his Vietnamese guards to come over. 'We have many hundreds of French hostages now and gaining more every day. You can be useful to us.'

'Doing what?'

The men gathered round and nodded to each other.

'You will soon see.'

'Tell me now, Trần.'

'Very well. You are to join the *Bordel Mobile de Campagne.*'

'A mobile field brothel? You aren't serious.' She almost laughed.

'We need information. You are French.'

He smiled, and she reeled at the look in his eyes.

'You mean it?'

He glanced at the other men and one or two of them smirked. 'I think it's amusing, especially as it was your own father who, not so long ago, brought over hundreds of black girls from Africa to service the French.'

'Not my father.'

'Defending him now?'

She recalled seeing her father with one of those black women and blinked away the image. Lisa had mentioned Giraud's involvement too. Is that what her father had been doing? Procuring prostitutes with Giraud?

'It is the truth,' Trần said and smiled again.

'I won't do it.'

'It has been decided. Now come. I will show you where you are to sleep. Tomorrow you will be cleaned up and taken to where you will volunteer for your task. Here is the clothing you will wear when you reach the French post. And remember, we shall know if you betray us.'

★

For the first part of the night Nicole could not prevent her thoughts from churning. How naive to have thought she could keep the two halves of her life separate. Of course she'd had to choose. Of course. But horrified by Trần's behaviour, she now felt that she'd picked the wrong side. It was as if the war had let loose a slew of monsters, and she couldn't be sure if the brothel was a test or a trick. They were sending her into French-held territory, where she might divulge information about Vietnamese locations to save her own skin, and yet she was a wanted person, and that meant the French must surely imprison her. Trần had to know that.

She tensed as she listened to the sounds of snoring rising from the tent next to hers, though it wasn't much of a cover, simply tarpaulin flung over four or five bamboo stakes. She crawled out of her tent, then glanced about, her breathing shallow. Lit only by a weak moon in an overcast sky, mist slid between the tents. Even the guards on duty had fallen asleep, but when she saw a dark figure her heart almost stopped.

An owl hooted. She jumped. The man came closer and she saw it was Trần. He stepped forward, put a finger to his lips and motioned to her to follow him as he crept round the bamboo fence behind the tents, testing for a stake that had not been firmly hammered into the ground. Every step seemed deafening, the leaves and twigs echoing as they crunched underfoot. Though she saw no one else awake as they stalked the perimeter, her imagination ran wild as she thought she saw and heard things that were not really there.

He found the loose spikes he had been searching for and lifted them clear of the earth, then ran his fingertips across her lips. 'Go now, Nicole. Tomorrow they will look for you. You must get far away and quickly.'

The loose spikes gave her little space, but maybe enough to push through on her belly. Did he really mean to let her go?

What if it was a trap? The thought stuck. She'd have her back to him. He had a gun. Surely he wasn't about to risk his own reputation?

'Hurry,' he said and gave her a little push. 'Crouch down. Steal through.'

He would say he'd shot her while she was trying to escape. At any moment she'd hear the shot.

'Why did that man bring me here?' she hissed.

'The party suspect betrayal by mixed-race members. Now there are reprisals. You are not safe with the troupe. I had to get you away. Take this.' He handed her a compass and her hands were shaking as she took it. 'Head south. There are some French clothes in this bag.'

She took the bag, and his voice, already low, dropped further. 'Make haste. Do not stop. Do not sleep.'

She thought of her antique purse with the photograph of Mark inside it. 'I need to get my purse.'

'No time.'

'Why are you doing this?'

He stepped away. 'I care for you, Nicole, very much. I always have. I will come for you when it is over.'

Over the following days Nicole moved as quickly as she was able, creeping over perilous land, often losing her footing and sliding into steep wet ditches. Cold and wet, she learnt to scramble out and grew better at picking her way through jungle and swamp. She found ways to sneak across mountain streams, and begged for food in the tiny villages where some of the people were friendly.

Each time the sound of her footsteps set off a troupe of howling monkeys she paused in fear. She never knew who might be following, nor who she might encounter, but worked out that her only chance was to make it back to Hanoi. If it was a chance at all. Never had home seemed more appealing, and when she found herself longing to see it again, the image of it comforted her. As she walked she thought of Lisa, who had always been so solidly on her side.

A memory came back of the time they'd lived in Huế and she'd been in the garden with Lisa. It had been early and as the sun came up she'd watched it paint the edges of the trees with a frill of pink light. The breeze filtered through the garden and she'd felt uplifted. A little bit of heaven that didn't happen every day.

'Here I can still feel the voice of God in the sound of the wind,' Lisa had said, 'and his spirit in the endless sky.'

Nicole had joined in. 'Here I can still smell the fragrance of lotus blossom and imagine the lotus ponds and the little frogs leaping and splashing.'

Lisa hugged her. 'How poetic we are today. Let's take a little walk and then I'll give you the most beautiful French plait of any girl in your class.'

The memory faded and now Nicole thought about Trần. It was not a comforting thought at all. Had his behaviour been a masquerade? Yet those people he punished? No deception there. She had to force herself to stop thinking and concentrate on getting home.

Home. She thought of it all the time, and even when her eyelids were bitten and so swollen with dirt she could barely see, she stumbled on. Her waterlogged boots fell apart and the sores on her legs became infected, yet despite the savage pain she continued to walk. Winded by fear each time she heard signs of life, she took refuge inside bamboo thickets or behind liana-cloaked trees, only stopping to rest when she could go no further.

One day while gazing down at the little dykes and paddy fields she noticed woodsmoke and saw the roofs of a ruined village still smouldering. She crossed a stream and, closer up, spotted a French soldier dragging a woman from where she'd been hiding. Horrible, horrible sight. Still in her nightclothes, the woman had long chestnut hair, lighter than was usual, and must once have been pretty. She stumbled and fell backwards to the ground, then reached out her thin arms, pleading and begging as the soldier pulled her to her feet again. Nicole closed her eyes, unable to witness what was coming. But when she heard the woman's scream, she forced herself to look. The screaming stopped quickly. The woman's face had grown rigid. She must have known what the soldier was going to do and was not about to give him the pleasure of her fear. She repeatedly spat in his face as he pushed her against a hut, lifted her nightdress and raped her. Then he shot her in the head. Blood. So much blood. Heartsick, Nicole doubled over. The woman had been somebody's wife, somebody's daughter, somebody's mother. How could men do it? She felt the rage crushing her chest and at that moment she hated men. All men. She wanted to slit their throats, and worse, in revenge for what had taken place.

She waited until long after the soldier had gone then, forcing herself not to buckle, she dragged the woman's body into a hut and covered her with whatever sacking she could find. Afterwards she scavenged the abandoned vegetables plots, scratching with her fingernails for any remaining root vegetables in the red earth. At the back of one hut she found a large pot full of rainwater. She drank and ate, looking out at the dusky blue horizon, then rested for an hour.

Gradually, over the coming days and weeks, she identified with the wildness of the landscape, and felt herself growing braver. No longer frightened at being alone, she discovered that, of course, nature was incredibly powerful, but she too was strong, in a way she'd never understood before.

Sometimes she stopped to marvel at the carpets of purple flowers stretching in every direction. Once, when the mists came and thunderclouds exploded, she sheltered under bushes and, sitting with her knees drawn up, attempted to sleep. But even there, hidden away and enveloped by a rain-lashed wall of blue-green jungle, she couldn't block out the sound of thunder. She was desperately hungry and there could be no respite.

One morning, perched at the top of a jagged limestone cliff, she watched a drift of enormous dragonflies. Except for that one storm, the weather had been relatively dry, but it meant that the midday glare was intolerable and the light too sharp. She closed her eyes for a second or two and dreamt of toast and eggs. With the taste on her lips, she opened her eyes again and, shading them with her hands, looked down over the valley. A troop of Vietminh soldiers was creeping past. She would have been right in their line of sight, but crouched down behind the bushes from where she watched, they couldn't see her. The soldiers wore helmets wrapped in black net, laced with palm leaf; circles of wire on their backs swathed in foliage completed the camouflage. They exactly matched the green of the surrounding vegetation. Nicole felt sorry for any French planes circling above, with no way to spot these columns of men.

She kept very still until the Vietminh had passed then felt dizzy with relief.

When hills rose to the right of marshy land stretching as far as the eye could see, she wasn't sure what to do. Should she attempt to wade through or take the long way round? She had to keep going, and eventually decided to risk the stepping stones through the marsh. A little further on she watched the Vietminh blow deep holes in the roads and dykes, so when the French finally caught up they'd have to spend all their time and energy repairing the damage before they could move their heavy vehicles forward.

Soon after that, she witnessed a Vietnamese mortar attack on an unsuspecting French garrison and she felt utterly divided. Her life as a Vietminh supporter had come to an abrupt end, and she couldn't allow them to find her. But neither did she believe in French rule either. Within an hour the devastation was total and she had no choice but to watch from afar as the French survivors shuffled past with raised hands, guarded by a double column of Vietminh. One thing was certain: her father had underestimated their strength. Everywhere she had been people were turning against the French in their thousands, and she was aware that from the moment the Vietminh had reclassified themselves as communists, their support was growing all the faster.

Intellectuals like Trần had joined the cause early on but now she'd seen peasants acting as a support network, ferrying the injured to makeshift hospitals and trekking across stark mountain terrain to deliver food and weapons. Many had died for their country and Nicole knew many more would do so. She truly recognized now that it was *their* country. Neither side was free from blame when it came to clandestine operations, but she had a better understanding of why it had to be that way.

She had no plan for what she would do when she reached home, and no idea if her family would even accept her. Going back was a huge risk. She'd be branded a traitor to the French – which of course she was – but it was a risk she had to take. There was nowhere else to go. The police knew she'd escaped house arrest and would have long suspected she had joined the enemy. She prayed they wouldn't imprison her, and hoped that her father might persuade Giraud to deport her to France. She thought of going to Huế but it was much too far on foot.

To take her mind off the fear, Nicole thought about her life in Huế. She'd learnt to do that. When you have to keep going, no matter what, you don't dwell on what frightens you, even if it shadows you. To prevent it crushing your spirit, you have to think of something else. Something good.

For as long as she could remember, while they'd been living in Huế, they'd spent summers in the hilltops of Dalat, with cool breezes blowing in the trees and bright hydrangeas everywhere. The house they used to rent was in a dusty, tree-lined boulevard and belonged to the owner of the area's largest rubber plantation. The whole place was overgrown with camellia, hydrangea, chrysanthemum and roses of all colours. While their father went hunting – deer, wild boar, black bear, panthers, tigers and even elephants – she and Sylvie lived in a blissful outdoor world, with days so long she'd thought they would go on for ever.

She closed her eyes and in a flash was back there on the day Lisa had taken them to a waterfall where they gazed at gentle cascades of white water. It wasn't noisy as the falls didn't drop vertically but took a slow diagonal path, the water flowing along several rivulets.

Lisa pointed down at one of the natural platforms. 'Shall we sit there? They're smooth enough.'

After they climbed down they made themselves comfortable, and Lisa unpacked the picnic. They took off their shoes and dangled their feet in the water.

'Come on, Lisa,' Sylvie said. 'It's not too cold.'

'This is the most peaceful of the waterfalls,' Lisa said.

She was right. The peace was infectious. Nothing went wrong that day. Nicole, feeling the sun on her skin and breathing in sparkling air, had fallen in love with the spot and Sylvie seemed happy too.

'Why is it called Tiger Waterfall?' Nicole asked.

'It's named after a cave they believe was once a tiger den.'

When she spotted a large monkey with a golden face and fluffy white beard staring at her, she sat still, feeling amazed.

'It's a red-shanked langur,' Sylvie whispered. 'Look at its bright red stockings.'

Nicole saw at once. The reddish-maroon fur ran from its knees to its ankles. As quickly as it had appeared, the monkey vanished.

But one summer, their last at Dalat, war had come and the Japanese arrived. Those days had not gone on for ever after all. They'd left for Hué the moment the war had broken out and when it ended Sylvie had been sent to America, because their father had wanted her to make contact with Americans sympathetic to the French cause. She'd stayed with a cousin of their father's in New York, while Nicole had remained in Hué. Nicole recalled a sense of emptiness without her sister, and a horrible feeling nothing was going to turn out well. A bit like now, she thought. You could never imagine how the world you knew and loved could be so suddenly and so unexpectedly broken.

At the end of one day as the sun dropped in the sky, and still using her compass, she reached the Red River, close to a French defence tower. It looked as if it had been erected to guard an area of land the French were in the process of clearing. She took in the piles of wild bamboo and the heaps of rubble, then crept back to where she'd spotted a stream. She splashed her face and, where there was enough cover, quickly changed into the French dress she'd been given. She brushed herself down and straightened her back. Then, though every muscle was aching and her feet were in agony, she walked into the outpost. There she told the guard she had been captured by the Vietminh and held in a re-education camp, but had escaped. He looked doubtful at first, but when she told him stories of her life in Hanoi, and how it had been at the camp too, she managed to convince him. The state of her legs and feet helped. She had been hoping for food, but all he offered was a cup of water, which she gulped down, and a filthy black Gauloise Troupe cigarette, which she refused.

The next morning she was piled on to a truck with French soldiers heading for Hanoi. Most were kind, though some looked at her warily, but their mood was low as they talked about the advance in the communist penetration. They spoke of villages abandoned by people who knew an attack on nearby French camps was imminent. They talked about their own control of the air while, increasingly, the Viets, masters of camouflage, were controlling the land.

As Nicole dozed on the journey their voices faded in and out, but she was jolted awake when the truck came to a shuddering halt at some kind of depot in the French quarter. As she climbed out she saw a line of officials and a group of people being shepherded into a queue. In the confusion of their arrival, she slipped behind a stationary van and swiftly crossed the road. With a quick backwards glance, she disappeared down a side street adjoining a familiar avenue, not far from her home. She could not go straight back to the house, as first she needed to retrieve the keys hidden at the shop. And dressed as she was, she could only enter the Vietnamese quarter under cover of darkness. So again she concealed herself in the same clearing beneath the trees where she had once lain hidden with Trần. She longed to be clean and pictured the aquamarine bathroom she had shared with Sylvie, imagining filling the bath with warm scented water and letting it wash away the last few months. Layer by layer, each awful thing would be gone.

Being back there made her think. She had abandoned her

family; had pushed them to the back of her mind for more than six months. She couldn't help feeling deeply ashamed and it made her want to weep for what had been lost. She thought of her mother, and what her father had done. People made mistakes. It was still wrong, but considering everything she had seen since leaving home, what her father had done seemed less shocking than before. She thought of Sylvie too and a fist closed round her heart. Despite learning that under the right set of circumstances anyone could inflict terrible suffering on another, she found she could not forgive her sister for helping Giraud to place her under house arrest.

With no boots, socks or a coat, the damp Hanoi air seeped through her thin cotton dress and yet, exhausted by a journey that had taken almost a month, she fell into a dreamless sleep for a couple of hours. Hearing gunfire, she woke suddenly. Surely the war hadn't reached Hanoi already? Silence followed. She listened carefully. Wondering. Frightened.

27

Under cover of twilight, Nicole summoned the courage to retrieve the key from the shop and, despite feeling conspicuous, managed to slip back to the house by sticking to the shadows. She passed the lake, leaving the glittering water behind her. After a last glance back, she twisted the key in the lock and stepped over the threshold, crying with relief at being in the safety of her old home. The hall was in darkness, and she tripped on something discarded on the floor. She listened to the tick of the hall clock, then felt around for the light switch. It clicked but no light came on. She leant against the door and, after waiting for her eyes to adjust to the gloom, groped her way to the sitting room by the faint moonlight shining down from the cupola. The light switch there didn't work either, so she tiptoed to the kitchen. It seemed as if her family must have left quickly. Alert to danger, she felt a rush of heat. What if they hadn't been able to leave? What if the Vietminh had taken possession? She struggled not to allow her imagination to spin out of control, but in her absence anything could have happened to her father, Sylvie and Lisa.

The house smelt damp and felt cold, as if uninhabited for weeks, or possibly months, and that shocked her. She listened to the creaks and groans of the place and pictured Papa snoring and Sylvie lying perfectly, beautifully asleep. The images faded. It might be the enemy who lay asleep upstairs, even as she shivered down below. But no, if anyone was living here, the house would not be so icy.

In the darkness she fumbled her way around the kitchen to

the dresser, feeling for the top drawer on the left, where Lisa had been in the habit of accumulating an assortment of bits that might come in handy: candles for power cuts, matches for oil lamps, a nail file, a pair of extra-sharp scissors, postage stamps, envelopes. She pulled the drawer open and fished for candles and matches, eventually locating them. The first matches were damp. It took six or seven attempts before she finally succeeded in striking one, then watched as the darkness bunched back against the light.

In the flickering glow she glanced around at the shadowy ceiling and dark corners. She pulled open a shutter and stepped back in alarm. The window had been completely boarded up. She went back to the drawer to find and light more candles, then dripped wax into the coffee cups abandoned on the table. She rammed the candles in, using one to find her way to the pantry to search for food. The sound of scratching mice meant there'd be nothing fresh to eat, but Lisa kept a store of pickled vegetables and jams, plus a few tins of beans. At the thought of the cook, Nicole could hardly keep standing for fear of what might have happened to her old ally.

She yelped as hot wax dripped on to her hand, so covered her hand with her sleeve as she searched for an empty wine bottle. Once found, and the candle successfully jammed into the bottle, she twisted the lid from a glass storage jar and devoured the pickled courgette, vinegar dripping down her chin to her chest. The cold tap in the sink was still in working order, so she filled a mug and drank the rusty-coloured water. She would have liked a baguette with butter and jam but, of course, there was none, and she couldn't make coffee on a cold range.

Her feet were raw and hurting badly, so she pulled Lisa's old blanket from the chair by the window and, wrapping it round her, picked her way towards the back stairs, wanting to head up to the sitting room.

At the sound of footsteps in the hall above, the muscles in her neck and shoulders went rigid. Thoughts raced through her mind – memories, fragments, words – as she pulled the blanket round her and tried to concentrate on keeping silent. As the footsteps halted, her heart was clamouring so much she felt as if it might burst from her chest. She listened as the door at the top of the stairs opened. Was it Giraud now coming down the stairs? The dark corners of her mind caved in on her as she prepared herself to meet her old adversary.

The hall clock chimed. Then silence.

The silhouette of a man appeared in the doorway. Lit from behind by the moonlight, his face remained in darkness. He took a step towards her.

The armour, built during her escape from the north, fell away, and with fear ringing in her ears, she waited.

The man did not move again. Silence for a moment, then the sound of a car's tyres outside. Nothing more.

At the precise moment her candle revealed the glint of a gun in his hand, she spoke. 'Who are you?'

He cleared his throat. Such an ordinary sound, but all the more terrifying because of that. Surely she hadn't come this far for it to end now?

'Nicole, is that you?' he said.

'Mark?'

As he came forward she dropped the bottle. She heard it smash on the floor, her legs gave way, and a moment later she was barely aware of being carried upstairs to her father's old bedroom.

As the hours passed, Mark took care of her, bathing her feet and legs and treating her cuts with disinfectant. He was infinitely gentle, albeit a little distant, bringing food and water and changing her sweat-drenched sheets. He brought her a commode and even took care of that. As she drifted, she was too tired and too ill to feel embarrassed. She lay in a bed that smelt of lavender, with him sitting in a chair beside her. When she was able to sit up and ask what had happened, he said he didn't know. He'd had to go to America and when he'd come back, the day before she herself had arrived, the house had been empty. He explained that before he left he'd heard she had run away with a Vietnamese man. Sylvie had told him.

'That was exactly what I worried might happen,' he said.

'What? That I'd run away with another man?'

He didn't meet her eyes. 'This isn't a joke, Nicole. God knows what you thought you were doing or what you got yourself into while you were with him. He's a terrorist.'

'Does anyone know you're here?' she asked, ignoring his comment because the same could be applied to Mark. Nobody knew what he'd been doing and she was well aware of the ongoing atrocities on both sides.

'No,' he said. 'I've been using the back door via the garden. I've kept everything as it was. All the windows are boarded on the outside and I don't open the shutters or curtains.'

'How did you get into the house?'

'Sylvie had given me a key.'

'Nobody else has a key?'

'Not that I know.'

She gulped back a sob. 'What has happened to my family?'

'I'm trying to find out. It may be that Sylvie and your father simply packed up and left.'

She stared up at his bright blue eyes, hoping he wasn't concealing anything. 'I wish I could know for sure. I let my father down. I wanted to get back at them.'

He sighed. 'It's been hard for everyone. Nobody knows what's right any more.'

She nodded and the silence that followed seemed to spill over, making further talk redundant.

'I'd like to have a bath,' she eventually said and, feeling utterly soiled, examined her broken nails and dirt-ingrained hands. 'I must smell terrible.'

He smiled. 'Pretty ripe, but there's no fuel for the boiler so no hot water.'

'Oh. I had hoped.'

'I'll see what I can do.'

Deeply touched by his kindness, it brought tears to her eyes.

While he was gone she drifted again, but plagued by dreadful dreams, she was shaking by the time he returned. He dropped the box he'd been carrying, came over and took her in his arms, then stroked her back while she cried.

'Why are you here?' she asked when she stopped crying. 'I mean, back in Hanoi?'

'I still have a job to do.'

A long pause followed during which he stared at the floor. When he looked up again she saw his face had changed and he was smiling.

'I have something for you.'

'In the box?'

'Yes. A portable gas cylinder and burner. It won't make the water piping hot, but at least it will take the chill off. I'll get it ready.'

She caught hold of his arm. 'You were never going to propose to Sylvie, were you?'

'No,' he said without a moment's hesitation. 'I told you before. Sylvie and I were not together.'

'She asked me to cut eight metres of cream silk. She never really explained what it was for but I always thought she intended it for her wedding dress.'

During the following week, Mark only left the house at night, leaving her alone in a strange candlelit world. She didn't ask where he went, knowing he probably wouldn't be at liberty to say. By day he kept her company, reading to her and ensuring she was comfortable.

One morning she woke to find him sitting beside her bed with a tray balanced on his knee.

She blinked herself awake. 'Oh my lord! Coffee?'

He nodded. 'I used the last of the gas. And there's fresh baguette with butter and jam.'

'How did you know I've been dreaming of it?'

'Talking in your sleep.'

'Do you watch me sleep?'

He looked embarrassed. 'No, but I do come in sometimes to make sure you're still breathing.'

'Just like a baby.'

He laughed but she'd seen his eyes darken. 'We must do nothing to arouse Giraud's suspicion. You do understand, don't you? He will consider you a danger to the French.'

'I'm not a terrorist.'

'You never knew their plans?'

'I was just a singer.'

'I can't tell you how much I hope that's true.'

He had been watching her sleep. The thought of it comforted her and she wished she could see the sun's winter rays fall on his face. In the gloom of the house he looked pale. She reached out and turned his face towards her.

'You have stubble,' she said.

He covered her hand with his own. 'So, coffee?'

She noticed two mugs and two plates. 'Are you having breakfast with me?'

He nodded.

'Well, get under the eiderdown.' She patted the space beside her. 'The house is freezing.'

He removed his shoes and did as she asked.

They ate in companionable silence. Nicole, having regained her appetite, ate ravenously, dripping butter and jam on to the sheet.

'What a mess you are,' he said and, one hand resting on her thigh, wiped her mouth with a tea towel. He was so close she could feel his warm breath on her cheeks, but then he withdrew.

'Right,' he said. 'A bit of shut-eye for me now and then I'll be off again.'

She stared into her empty coffee cup, the sudden loneliness biting painfully. 'Do you think you might help me back to my old room? I'm longing for some natural light. The windows aren't boarded up on that floor.'

'I'll need to find some sheets. The beds up there have been stripped.'

'I'll feel better surrounded by my old things.'

Once the bed had been made up, he helped her up the stairs. At the sight of her room bathed in flawless light and looking so lovely, she couldn't control her tears.

'Don't you like it? I tidied up a bit.'

She shook her head, unable to communicate the flood of mixed feelings.

'Well, into bed with you. I've put a candle beside the bed for when it gets dark. But make sure you keep the curtains and blackout blinds closed so the light can't be seen.'

'Might someone notice if my curtains are open by day but closed at night?'

'I think the pipal tree will pretty much block the view. Don't open any window overlooking the street at the front.'

'Will you be back?'

'Not for a bit.'

She reached for his hand. 'Please don't go.'

'Nicole, believe me, I don't want to leave, but I have no

choice. I'll bring you some food to last and, as long as you're okay to reach the bathroom unaided, you'll manage. But please take into account how ill you've been. Rest is what you need, so stay up here and keep quiet. We want the place to seem abandoned. Like I said, it's okay to open the window a little but only when it's dark.'

After he had gone she lay back on the bed and thought of how she had never told anyone what she'd seen on the night of the ball; not Sylvie, not Trần, not Mark. It weighed heavily on her mind while he wasn't there. She knew the near starvation of her journey south and the months of hardship with the theatre troupe had weakened her, but unable to lie still for long, she walked up and down on the landing to regain some strength in her legs, then carefully wandered around the house. In the gloom she explored the rooms and, thinking of her family, ran her palms over their few remaining belongings, as if she might conjure their presence through contact with the things they had loved: Sylvie's beautiful screens, her father's oak desk, Lisa's old chair. She was surprised the furniture hadn't been packed up and shipped back to France, but perhaps Sylvie was intending to come back after all. So many memories haunted the rooms. Would she ever see any of them again? She went into the little aquamarine bathroom she had often dreamt about while she'd been away and opened Sylvie's cabinet. One jar of face cream and a bottle of perfume inside. No pills. She picked the glass bottle up, sniffed it, and felt so lonely that tears began to form.

Back in her room, she knelt beside her old bookcase and ran her fingers over the spines of all her favourite books. She pulled one out and sniffed, did the same with three more, and finally fished out her all-time favourite childhood book: *Little Women*. It reminded her of their old life in Huế, where she'd first read it, and all the memories attached to their old home came racing back. She flicked the pages and was surprised to see an envelope fall out. Had she left an unfinished letter in there? But no, this one was sealed. She slid a finger under the flap and tore open the envelope, then unfolded a single sheet of paper.

Chérie,

I don't know where you have been or whether you will ever read this, though I know you are the only one who'll ever be likely to look in that particular book. So if you are reading this now, it means you are alive and have come home. See, I do notice what you do. I always have. More than you know.

We waited for you as long as we felt able, but times have changed in Hanoi and eventually we could wait no longer. Papa made sure he had fulfilled his obligations to the government, but it's hard to know who to trust and he made the difficult decision to leave without telling many.

I have accompanied Papa to Paris to help settle him in. He hasn't been at all well since he had his stroke. (Perhaps you don't even know about that?) We managed to sell Maison Duval on Paul Bert, though only for a fraction of its true worth. Still, it was enough to purchase a small apartment in the Marais area of Paris, Rue des Archives. Papa still has some stocks and shares so he will be fine, if not wealthy. I know it is not the most salubrious of districts, but Papa needs the money to live.

After you left he was distraught and blamed himself. He spent three months sending out people to try and find you. I don't say this to worry you, but he was so frightened by what you might have done, he decided the only thing to do was to leave before things got worse. Had we left it longer, and with his poor health, it might have become impossible to go. We left in quite a hurry. Giraud was sniffing around on a daily basis and I no longer trusted him. However, I don't believe the scaremongering about the war either, and I shall return either to wind up our affairs and pack up the rest of our belongings or to continue running what we have left.

Papa wrote to you when we arrived in Paris. Did you receive that letter? In the meantime, if you ever do read this, look after the silk shop in the ancient quarter if you can. A local girl has been *running it while you've been away. Your old neighbour, O-Lan. I'm not sure where her sympathies lie, but there was nobody else to do it. I don't think she'd cheat us. Her own shop was flooded and her goods have all been destroyed. You can keep her on or dismiss her as you wish. It may be a few months before I get back.*

By the way, Lisa has gone to live with her sister, Alice Brochard, in the Languedoc.

Now I want you to do me a favour. The decision to go was made as soon as we'd sold our store and, though I wanted to explain, I didn't see Mark before I left. He had gone to America but promised he'd return to Hanoi as soon as he could. If you see him please would you tell him that I will be coming back.

Thank you, chérie. I hope you are safe. You may not believe it but I do worry about you.

Your sister, Sylvie

Nicole read the letter twice before slipping it back inside the book. She wanted to forget she'd ever seen it but even as she stuffed the book back on the shelf, knew she could not. She was intensely relieved her father and Lisa were safe, but how did she feel about Sylvie?

That night she left her window open a fraction, enough for a hint of damp air to drift in. Hearing the footsteps of people passing by, she wondered who they were in a vague sort of a way, the faceless ones who had remained. Maybe soldiers on their way to war? Meanwhile, her sister's letter played on her mind. Would Sylvie really return to Hanoi?

In the pale grey light of dawn Nicole dared to peer out before closing the window for the day. Everywhere was quiet. In a way, she feared the silence and longed to hear music or the laughter of her family. When happy times came back to her, she cried; but worse by far than her sorrow over bygone times was the thought of what she'd seen Trần do at the camp.

Assaulted by the memory, she crawled into bed, but it was impossible to close her eyes without it all coming back. Though he had helped her escape, she felt frightened that he was no longer such a sweet, impassioned man. As the simple pleasures of a warm kitchen were denied her, she curled up against the wall for comfort. How she wished she had not gone with Trần, had not seen what she'd seen. She kept picturing his dark eyes as he sent the woman and child to their certain deaths.

When she heard banging at the front door that night, she lay awake in fear, her thoughts spinning. The same thing happened a couple more times during the next day.

The second night it happened, she lay in bed and focused on her breathing, forcing herself not to give in to her fear. One palm on her ribs, the other on her belly, she encouraged her breath to settle. She must not panic, but if this was Giraud still coming after her, she would not be safe while Mark was away. As the minutes ticked by she trembled; if only Mark would come back. He'd divert the policeman. When the banging on the door stopped and no other alarming sounds followed, she listened to the pipes, the creaks, the scurrying in the attic and, despite her fear, must have fallen asleep.

But, suddenly, startlingly, she was wide awake once more.

'Nicole?'

She heard her name again.

'Nicole?'

As she recognized his voice a feeling of warmth surged through her. Her instinct was to leap out of bed, but she felt so stiff and cramped that she couldn't move. She shook her head and at last the tears fell.

Mark crouched down beside her bed. 'Come on.'

She gulped and sat up. With her face close to his, she comforted herself with the sweet, salty smell of him.

'Will you stay with me now?' she said after the tears had gone.

'Of course,' he said. He stroked her forehead and turned to pull up a chair.

It was impossible to hide her need. 'I mean in my bed. Can you hold me? Please, Mark.'

Still trembling, she told him about the thumping on the front door. He stroked her face and the feel of his hands on her skin made her want him so much more. What an awful moment to be this close, with him looking after her as if she was a baby.

'I . . .' she began.

'I'm here now,' he said as he climbed in with her.

She rested her head on his shoulder and she longed to tell him she loved him. Loved him. Loved him. And that she always had. The sadness was that she could not. He had been kind to her. Just kind.

But then he pulled away so that he could look at her. 'You feel so fragile, I'm scared that the slightest puff of wind might blow you away.'

'I'll be all right. It's just that when I close my eyes, everything comes racing back.'

'I know.'

'And then I get really scared.'

'I wish I could be here all the time.'

He stroked her cheek and the tenderness in his eyes as he smiled made her spirits gallop. 'Even frail as you are, you're very lovely.'

Then he cupped her face in his hands and kissed her. She closed her eyes and, savouring the taste of salt on his lips, gave herself fully to this long-awaited moment.

28

Nicole asked Mark to sit with her. He had done no more than kiss her the night before and she was starting to feel as if she'd imagined it. Self-conscious about her dry, cracked lips, she licked them as he pulled up a chair. The window was only slightly ajar but in the hush of the room it was enough to hear the rustle of leaves outside. A very green tree, the pipal was extremely large, maybe even a hundred feet tall, with a pale trunk about ten feet wide and branches exploding outwards from the centre. It had always been Nicole's favourite. Best of all was when her father had constructed a rope ladder up to a little platform where she and Sylvie had spied on the world below. It had seemed so high at the time, though it was probably only two or three metres up in reality. She shook her head; she could not let nostalgia cloud her thinking.

'Shall I get your blanket?' Mark asked and began to rise.

She waved him down and then began, attempting a neutral tone as she spoke. 'While you were away I found a letter hidden in one of my books.'

There was a short silence.

'I didn't know what it was at first.' She looked away, couldn't bear to see what might be in his eyes when she spoke again. 'It was from Sylvie.'

He seemed to hesitate and she glanced at him. 'That's wonderful,' he said, but she couldn't read his expression. She carried on to say that her sister was safe in Paris. And that Lisa was living with her sister, Alice Brochard, in the Languedoc.

She'd been working up to telling him that Sylvie was

coming back, but dipped her head and, hiding behind her hair, held her tongue. After a moment she looked up and smiled.

'Sylvie said that they managed to sell the department store. They've returned to live in France on the proceeds. She said they waited for me.'

She held out a hand to him. This was it. The lie that might change everything and ensure Sylvie was out of the picture, or at least in Mark's mind. 'She is engaged to someone in France, Pierre somebody or other.'

He glanced down at the floor for a moment. She felt a knot tighten in her stomach. Mark had brought her back to life, saved her, and Sylvie was safe in France. She couldn't really be coming back – it would be madness – and he denied ever having been with Sylvie anyway, so it was hardly a crime.

'She said she'd met the man in Hanoi and he'd proposed. A life in France must have seemed like the safest option.'

'Perhaps it's for the best.'

The silence hung between them. Nicole wondered if he was thinking of Sylvie and couldn't quite work out why she'd lied.

'Penny for them?' he said.

'It's nothing.' But she didn't want her sister to end up like the ghosts in the garden, not there, yet always present. She felt a rush of guilt, then thought of how he'd looked after her so lovingly and that brought tears to her eyes. He genuinely cared for her so why shouldn't she do everything she could to keep it that way?

'What about the remaining shops?' he was saying quite calmly, not seeming at all upset by what she'd said about Sylvie's engagement.

She studied his face. Perhaps he had told her the truth about his relationship with Sylvie then? Her sister had got herself caught up in a fantasy about Mark and then couldn't bear to have to back down.

'As the shop in the old quarter is yours, it might be an idea for you to move back there. People know you're a *métisse*, yes, and I realize it's going to be risky anywhere you are, but at least there you can melt away into the crowds more easily.'

'You may be right. Mark, you've done so much for me. And I am truly grateful.'

There was a long stretch of silence before he spoke again.

'I'm afraid there is something else. I found out Giraud knows I'm living here,' he said. 'We are not on the best of terms since I reported him for using American cash to fund African prostitutes.'

'So it was true. Lisa said as much. Do you think it was him at the door?'

'It may have been. Even if it wasn't, I don't think it will be long before he comes sniffing around.'

'I love my little shop, but I don't feel strong enough to move yet.'

'And I don't want you to overdo things. You might find it takes some time to recover from everything you've been through.'

She nodded but didn't tell him how unwell she still sometimes felt. 'A friend is taking care of the shop. O-Lan.'

'Look, I'll keep an eye on you there, and I have a Vietnamese man I trust. I'll get him to check on you too.' He put an arm round her shoulder and stroked her cheek. 'Come on, my brave little one. We'll leave it for a few days longer.'

A day later, while he was sleeping, she made it down to the kitchen and went straight to a small cupboard under the pastry shelf in the pantry. She opened the wire door and found a bottle of Bénédictine and brandy liqueur. It was Lisa's favourite and only Nicole knew the cook kept a secret bottle in what looked like a cheese safe.

In the evening she rooted around in the bathroom cabinet. Perfect! A few drops left in a bottle of Coeur Joie. She had no perfume of her own and sprayed a little of the scent on her neck and between her breasts. She slipped on a silk robe held loosely together by a ribbon tied at the top, then found a pair of tweezers and shaped her brows. After that she smothered her lips in Vaseline. Though in need of a cut to get rid of her split ends, she brushed her hair until it shone, pinched her cheeks and then slipped downstairs where she checked the shutters were closed and the curtains drawn. After that, she carried through the cheese and bread he'd bought and lit some candles to make the comfortable corner of the sitting room cosier. She considered lighting a fire, but abandoned the idea. The smoke from the chimney would give them away.

When she heard him enter the hall, she lay down on the sofa with her eyes closed and, apart from his footsteps, there was silence when he entered the room. Even with her eyes closed she could sense him staring at her. She opened her eyes.

'You look so beautiful,' he said.

She sat up, smiled and showed him the bottle. 'I found us something special to drink.'

He grinned at her and came to sit close by while she poured them both a generous glassful.

'Would you like something to eat?'

He shook his head. 'I'm not hungry. Maybe later.'

'Wouldn't it be nice to play some music?'

'No electricity. And anyway –'

'I know.'

They sat in silence and she poured them both another glass of the liqueur.

'Mark, what is it you're doing here?'

'Here, in this room?'

She laughed. 'You know what I mean.'

'I'm currently charged with getting the CIA out of Hanoi and the entire north, should the Vietminh win. But my orders may change.'

'You think they might?'

'If they do, and I have to leave suddenly, it's another reason you might be better off in the Vietnamese quarter.' He pushed the hair from her brow and studied her face. 'You look different; your face has changed.'

'I'm too thin, but at least I have cheekbones now.' She grinned. 'Sort of. Starvation diet will do it every time!'

'That's not even funny.'

They drank a few more glasses until the bottle was drained. For Nicole, unused to alcohol as she now was, it went straight to her head.

He leant against her. 'You smell –'

She laughed. 'I smell?'

'Delicious.'

She felt his breath on her neck and as she leant back he stroked the soft skin at her temples. She felt her pulse racing but maintained control.

He pulled away suddenly and searched her eyes. 'What about your Vietnamese boyfriend?'

She gazed back at him, horrified. 'Trần? He's not my boyfriend.'

'Sylvie told me you were living with him in the north.'

'Of course I wasn't.' She paused. 'You thought that? He's never been my boyfriend.'

He shook his head and gave her a half-defensive, half-warm smile.

'But it's why you've sometimes been a bit distant, isn't it?' she said.

'Not only that. Nicole, you spent six months with known

terrorists who've committed terrible atrocities. It makes me very sad but we can't dodge that issue.'

'You were sad!' She felt a burst of anger and got to her feet. 'What about me? And what about the French and American atrocities? I know I made a dreadful mistake going north with Trần. But don't you have any idea how much I wanted to be with you?'

He shook his head. 'I thought so at first, then everything suddenly changed after the ball.'

'Yes, I know. I didn't want it to but it did.'

They stared at each other.

'Then after you helped them put me under house arrest, what else could I do but go?' At the memory of that she took a step back and shook her head.

'No!' He sprang up. 'You can't think that. I swear I didn't know the house arrest was going to happen.'

'No?'

'No!'

Then he came to her and held her so tightly she thought she might break. She tried to resist and struggled to free herself from his grip, but when his lips brushed her neck just behind her ear, she felt as if her skin had unpeeled. He began to kiss her and she arched her back, feeling so much a part of him that her inner self unrolled and lay bare before him. The sensation of being known was so intense her legs began to tremble.

'I'm sorry,' she said.

'Me too. We have wasted too much time,' he whispered. 'Are you sure you want this?'

'Oh God,' she murmured and felt the heat of his hand on her breast. 'Dance with me, Mark, like we did before.'

They moved together while she whispered the words of a song. After a few minutes they stood still and she pressed against him with only the robe between her breasts and his shirt. She felt him shudder, then he held her away and touched his fingertips into the hollows of her throat. She gasped and he began to undo the ribbon at her neck, looking deep into her eyes with a silent question. She nodded and he quickly finished the job. When the garment slipped from her shoulders it fell to the floor and she stood before him, physically naked, just as moments before she had felt emotionally naked.

He stared at her, then cupped her breasts with his hands. When he bent his head to take a nipple in his mouth, she unzipped his trousers and pulled him to the floor. She lay back and parted her legs as he removed his shirt and trousers. He wore no underwear.

He sank back on his haunches and they gazed at each other. She tilted her head back; now that her body was coming back to life, she gave herself to the sensation. He leant forward and caressed both breasts before his mouth slid to her stomach. She held the back of his head and groaned as his lips moved to her inner thighs, and finally reached the damp curls between her legs. Then she could take no more and pressed her hands beneath his armpits and pulled him up to her.

'Now,' she said and gave a shudder as he entered her. They began to move in rhythm. It was hard, fast and wild, the tension between them far too strong for the first time to be a gentle release. Then he cried out and she did too.

Sometime after that they lay flat on the floor, side by side, both slippery with sweat, and with a sensation of peace unfolding around them. She could never have anticipated how incredible this would make her feel. This had been nothing like her one time with Trần. Mark had made her feel truly wanted.

He propped himself up on one elbow and pushed the strands of her hair away from her eyes. 'So,' he said and grinned.

She gave a sigh of pleasure before reaching up and tracing the contours of his face. 'Again?'

As France's hold on the country stuttered, their time together was all they had, the danger of war adding to the tension and ensuring the release of sex was even sweeter. She felt sure the more they could be together, the deeper their bond would become. Often they studied each other silently. The way he narrowed his eyes and smiled and the way he sometimes looked so mischievous when they made love, made her think he could see inside her head.

She was lying alone late one afternoon trying to sleep when she heard the buzz of a bluebottle in her room. She covered her head with a pillow. Nicole had no fear of spiders or snakes, but the sound of a large fly continually buzzing drove her to distraction. Even beneath the pillow she could still hear its annoying whine. After a few more minutes she threw the pillow on to the floor and sang to herself to drown out the noise. Still the buzzing went on and she soon realized it was actually in duplicate; there were two little demons in her room. Low in the sky, the afternoon sun had cast a golden glow around the room, so she climbed out of bed, wearing just her pants, and opened her bedroom door, hoping the insects might find their way out. She watched, wafting the air to encourage them, but they declined to leave. She began to stalk them and, picking up the pillow again, made a leap, smashing it against the wall. The annoying drone continued. In fact, the more irritable she became the louder the buzzing. She whacked the pillow against the wall again but missed the flies.

After ten minutes of hurling herself around as she chased after them she stood in the middle of her room, sweat dripping from her. The light was fading. Then she spotted both flies together on the door frame. This was her opportunity, so she closed her eyes and threw herself, pillow in hand, at the spot. She opened her eyes just as the pillow burst, bits of fluff rising like a snowstorm in the air and then a rain of white feathers curtaining the doorway. As they cleared she saw Mark standing there, picking feathers from his hair, his forehead and the shoulders of his shirt. She stepped back and looked at him in horror.

He coughed and blew the feathers from his lips. 'Whoa. What have I done to merit this?'

'I didn't see you. I was chasing flies.'

'As one usually does wearing just –' He pointed at her.

'You think *I* look funny?' She began to laugh.

'You will pay,' he said and picked her up as if she was a feather herself and threw her over his shoulder.

'Put me down.'

He ignored her.

'Where are you taking me, you horrible man?'

'Horrible? I think you're forgetting I'm the injured party here.'

On the floor below he pushed open the door of the bedroom he was using and she gasped when she saw what he had done. Hanging upside down over his shoulder, she could see dozens of night candles dotted around the room, the little pin-points of light sparkling and glittering as if they were stars. She felt as if her heart might burst. In the midst of war he had created a shimmering fairyland. For her.

'Well, at least you've saved me the bother of undressing you,' he said and put her down. 'So what do you think?'

She gazed at the room and her eyes filled up. 'I love it.'

'Happy birthday, my darling. I know I'm useless at expressing how I feel in words, but –' She didn't let him finish but ran at him and hugged him so hard he had to pull away.

'I must light candles more often,' he said.

She tugged at his jacket and he slid his arms out, then he removed the rest of his clothes, feathers still floating around, until he stood before her, naked.

'Look at you,' she said.

He smiled and spread his arms wide. 'Look at us.'

'So much has happened, in one year.'

'Good and bad.'

'Well, this is good,' she said and she blew a feather from his chest, feeling happier than she'd ever felt in her life.

Like the ghosts who inhabited the garden, when Mark wasn't there Nicole also became a shadow in their strangely boarded-up world. One evening at dusk she needed to get out so much that she wandered around the neighbourhood with a headscarf hiding her hair and face. A cool wind swept down the street as a man and a woman walked past her. It made her feel uncomfortable so she dropped her gaze and mumbled good evening, then went back indoors.

When she told Mark what she'd done, he again expressed his reservations about her staying on at the villa. All things considered, she felt he might be right. Even if she didn't open the shop, she could more easily get out and melt into her surroundings there.

As she was making her preparations to return it occurred to her that she'd missed a period. But the days with the troupe had caused havoc with her cycle and she didn't think too much of it. She washed and dried her Vietnamese clothes and practised putting her hair up in a roll of cloth. Her *áo dài* was far too big for her now but she used safety pins to make the trousers fit. That would have to suffice.

She moved back to the shop the next evening and Mark went with her. They made up her old bed with clean sheets, a feather duvet and a silk throw she'd brought from the villa. In the morning, she woke to find he'd already left, and lay listening to the sounds of the street vendors setting up their stalls and smelt the familiar aroma of pork patties and fish sautéed in dill. She sensed an ease slip back into her. Her shoulders felt less rigid, the knot in her stomach releasing, the guilt over lying about Sylvie diminishing a little bit. She heard the sound of the shop door opening. It must be O-Lan. Nicole was in two minds about how much to tell her friend, but went downstairs to greet her.

O-Lan jumped when she heard the footsteps and spun round, wide-eyed.

'I didn't think I'd ever see you again,' she said.

It was so lovely to see O-Lan's friendly face, Nicole had to swallow hard to overcome the emotion. She hadn't realized how much she'd missed her. O-Lan was as pretty as ever, but there were dark circles under her eyes. As the two gazed at each other, a multitude of mixed emotions collided. What was she going to tell her friend about Trần?

O-Lan stared.

'Come here,' Nicole said.

While they held each other, several minutes passed. Nicole could feel her friend's heart banging against her own, and neither of them seemed willing to let the other go.

Eventually O-Lan drew away. 'Let me look at you,' she said.

'I'm fine. Really I am. How is your mother?'

O-Lan sighed deeply. 'Not getting any better. Sleeps most of the time, in the room above the shop.'

'I'm so sorry about your shop. What happened?'

'A water main burst under our house. You were lucky the water didn't get in here too.'

O-Lan sat down on the sofa and Nicole could see how alone with her unhappiness her friend seemed to be. She sat down beside her and held her close. 'I'm here now,' she said.

'I kept peering through your window to make sure the water hadn't got in, and when your sister asked me to look after your shop, it seemed an ideal solution. I couldn't afford to buy more stock for my shop, so here I am.'

'I can't thank you enough.'

'But shall I go now you're back?'

Nicole only hesitated for a moment. 'No, please stay. I'm still not completely recovered. I'll continue to pay you.'

O-Lan frowned. 'You are so thin. I thought you might have been ill.'

Nicole decided to play down how bad it had been. 'A little.'

'And Trần? We've had no word except for a message saying not to expect him until the war is over.'

Nicole felt relieved to hear it but picked up the worry on her friend's face. She shook her head.

'Is he alive?'

'As far as I know.'

'Did you part on bad terms?'

Nicole glanced away. 'It's complicated.'

'He's not a bad man, Nicole.'

'War changes people,' said Nicole, looking at her feet. She didn't want to say too much, though it was hard to know what was too much and what was not enough. 'I think I need a wash and another rest.'

O-Lan dipped her head. 'Of course.'

Nicole walked towards the bathroom but twisted back. 'Oh, one more thing. Mark will be staying here at night.'

O-Lan's mouth hadn't fallen open but it may as well have. 'You are seeing him again?'

'Sort of. But he wants to keep an eye on me too.'

'You need that?'

'I think I might.'

*

Over the following days Nicole watched O-Lan. They had been best friends, but who knew what might have happened while Nicole had been away with the theatre troupe. Yet, apart from looking tired, O-Lan didn't seem changed at all, just the same open girl she always had been. After a week Nicole decided she could still put her faith in her. Also, as she was feeling so washed out herself, her friend's presence meant she could rest when she needed to, and if Giraud or one of his men should come prying, she could quickly leave by the outside staircase to the courtyard, and escape through the back alley.

The days passed peacefully enough and Nicole began to heal. She couldn't believe how good it felt to feast her eyes on the gorgeous colours of her beloved silks. So what if they weren't selling much? O-Lan was accustomed to shopping frugally and they pooled their provisions and their money.

Nicole had been devastated when forced to leave her antique purse behind, the one with the photo of Mark inside it. Now she came up with the idea of making copies of the purse from memory, and selling them in the shop. So after they closed the shop at the end of the day, while chatting amicably, they sewed little bags. Mark rarely arrived before O-Lan went home, and if he was still there when she arrived in the morning, he slipped away by the outside staircase.

One morning she and Mark lay in bed, legs tangled in the sheets and fingers laced together. It was later than usual but Mark showed no sign of wanting to leave.

'Are you staying for breakfast today?' she said. 'I'm starving.'

'What would you like?'

'Well, we have coffee, condensed milk, bread, butter and not much else.'

'Sounds like a feast. I'll go,' he said. He unlaced his fingers but didn't move anything else.

She poked him in the ribs and he untangled his legs.

'But you're so warm,' he said.

'Out! And put something on. The size of you. You'll terrify O-Lan if she arrives early.'

He grinned as he climbed out of bed then posed in a stance exactly like the statue of David.

She laughed and threw a shawl at him. 'Here, cover yourself, you vain American!'

He wrapped it round his middle and headed for the kitchen. While he was gone she thought about how happy they were. He hadn't told her he loved her but she was certain that he did, and now that she rarely thought of Sylvie, it seemed like nothing could come between them again. She closed her eyes and daydreamed about their future. America maybe, when this was all over, or even Saigon.

When he came upstairs again, carrying a little silver tray, she sat up to see what he'd brought. She stared in wonder when she saw that he'd cut two pieces of toast into the shape of hearts and placed them, already dripping with butter and jam, beside a lotus blossom on a small plate.

'What have I done to deserve this?'

'Just being the sweetest, loveliest girl I've ever known.'

'Aren't you forgetting something?' She lowered her eyes and fluttered her lashes.

'That too!' he said and kissed her on the cheek. 'Toast first and then we'll see.'

When she missed her second period, Nicole felt a little thrill. Could it be possible? She didn't speak of it at first, wanting to keep the warm feeling to herself until she felt certain.

The day she ventured out with a scarf over her head, she

noticed far fewer French in the streets around the shop. She went to see Yves at his bakery; she was shocked by how pale and thin he looked. He kissed her on both cheeks but didn't ask where she'd been. He told her he would be packing up soon and returning to France. Like so many others, he'd sold the shop for a pittance but there was nothing left for him in Hanoi.

Not a single policeman passed by on foot, though a couple of tanks thundered through, sending stalls and people flying. Nicole felt more certain France would eventually lose the war and told herself Giraud would not matter then. The danger to Mark was what worried her most, but his Vietnamese was fluent and he was good at appearing and disappearing without being noticed.

She felt stronger wandering her favourite streets. Nobody took any notice of her and anyone who'd seen her with Trần in the past would assume she was on the side of the Vietminh. The truth was she wasn't on anyone's side. Not any more. But the Vietnamese part of town afforded the only place she might still feel at home. She rarely served in the shop, but enjoyed spending time with O-Lan. The two grew even closer, until Nicole felt as if O-Lan was her real sister.

'I've brought you a book about Vietnam,' O-Lan said one day. 'I imagine you've only learnt French history.'

Nicole thanked her and looked forward to curling up with the book.

On the way upstairs she flicked through the pages and, once comfortable in bed, began to read about the emperors and how they'd lived in the forbidden purple city in Huế. In a paradise of golden palaces, the emperor held banquets for special occasions and lived a fabulous life with concubines, ladies-in-waiting, maidservants of royal birth, eunuchs and even female courtiers. And when an emperor died his tomb was no less opulent, though the poor were as poor as they were under the French.

Nicole lost herself in the world of concubines, many of whom were high-ranking mandarins' daughters. The drawings of them were gorgeous and she loved the flow of the old-fashioned *áo dài* outfits they wore. They gave her an idea for what she might make with some of her remaining silk supplies.

She read of nine ranks of concubine, depending on their father's position, but was shocked to learn that once settled in the imperial city a concubine could never set eyes on her family again. She was trained to be soft-voiced and obedient, gratifying the emperor's sexual needs, combing his hair, dressing him, polishing his nails and so on. It made fascinating reading, but she ached for these women who could never leave their gilded prison.

She closed the book and settled down to sleep. Mark did not come by every day, but as each week passed she felt a little safer than the one before. Now, at night, the world wrapped its arms round her and for the first time in a very long while she slept free from fear.

29

By the third missed period Nicole was certain. Her breasts tingled whenever Mark touched them, they looked swollen too, and the area around her nipples had darkened. On the evening she prepared to tell him, he had been absent for a few days and her heightened feelings of restlessness and sheer excitement meant she could not sit still. She hadn't known she could fall in love so deeply, but now that she had he meant everything to her and she could not imagine a life without him. She was upstairs with one red lantern lit, perching on the edge of a chair, when he arrived in just his shirtsleeves, jacket slung over one shoulder, looking unshaven but utterly irresistible as he stood gazing at her. When she didn't speak, the two frown lines appeared between his brows, and she noticed a kind of rough texture to his skin. She'd seen it before when he was tired and it wasn't unattractive. She never found it unattractive. But it wasn't that.

'You have a moustache,' she said. 'It's quite changed you.'

He twisted his mouth to one side. 'Oh yes, I'd forgotten. I'll shave it off.'

His eyes sparkled as he held up a bottle of Sauvignon.

'From one of the few stores still stocking decent wine,' he said.

'Well, come here.'

When he came across and kissed her, she wrinkled her nose at the unfamiliar feel of the moustache, then ran her fingers through his hair. 'It's growing, and it's darker.'

'I've had to dye it.'

She was a bit taken aback. 'Why?'

He tilted his head to one side and shrugged. 'You know. The job.'

She studied him as he sat down opposite her and poured them both a glass of wine. He did look different from time to time and she quite enjoyed the thrill of wondering who he might be when he came to see her. This time there was such a gentle look in his eyes, quite at odds with the slightly alarming appearance caused by the addition of a moustache. She'd seen it right from the start, that vulnerability, but hadn't known where it sprang from.

He took a sip. 'Not bad, is it?'

'So now you're a connoisseur?'

He laughed.

'Mark, there's something I need to tell you.'

He glanced across. 'Oh?'

She undid the buttons of her shirt to partly reveal her breasts. 'Notice anything?'

'Not sure.' He grinned. 'You do look rather wonderful. But then, you always do, and if you don't cover yourself up, we won't even get to drink the wine!'

'Well, thank you. But can't you guess?'

He shook his head.

'We're going to have a baby. I'm pregnant.'

He came straight over to her but she had seen the blood drain from his face at the word baby. He knelt beside her and reached out to touch her breasts.

'They feel awfully full,' she said, but he still looked shocked and, feeling a bit upset, she shuffled back in the chair.

He stood and rubbed his jaw.

'Mark?'

He looked down at her and shook his head. 'You'll be so much more at risk now. What are we going to do when I'm away?'

She smiled. 'If that's all you're worried about, I'll be fine.'

'But I thought we used –'

'Not the first time.'

'You're sure about this? It isn't that I'm not thrilled, it's . . .'

'What? It's what?'

There was a short silence. He didn't look thrilled. The smile had not completely left her own face, but now her happiness really began to ebb away and her eyes began to smart. She watched him struggle with his feelings as he crouched down in front of her again. He took hold of her hands and cradled them in his own, but remained silent. She felt a twinge of conscience as she gazed into those bright blue eyes; she had rushed him into this, seduced him, really. She placed her palms on either side of his head and longed to nestle him between her breasts. As he looked up at her, she read the worry in his eyes.

'You've been so ill,' he said. 'And pregnancy can be very demanding. Are you well enough?'

'I'm not as strong as I used to be, but I'll be fine.'

'And you definitely want the baby?'

Upset by his response, she swept a lock of hair from her face. 'Of course, I'm a Catholic. Anyway, abortion is illegal. And . . . I love you.'

'Oh, my darling girl.'

They remained silent for a few moments. She wanted him to be as excited and happy as she was, but all she could see was how worried it had made him.

'Anything could happen when I'm not around to look after you. And what if something happens to me? I don't usually speak of it but, Nicole, my job is dangerous.'

'I can look after myself.'

'If something happens I may not be here for you or the baby. Oh God, this is my fault. I wanted you so much that first time . . . the only thing on my mind was to make love to you. But we should have waited. I should have waited. I'm so sorry.'

'Don't be sorry. I'm glad. We are having a baby together. Our child, Mark. A human being we have made together.'

He stood, inhaled sharply then let the breath out slowly. 'Nicole . . .'

'What is it?'

'I want to be glad too. I really do. At any other time this would be a miracle . . . but we are at war, the city might be under siege at any time. My job takes me away and I may not be able to get you out. And don't forget Trần might show up again.'

She bit her lip. 'I hadn't really thought. I was too busy watching out for Giraud.'

'You're not showing yet but in a few weeks' time you will.'

'Can't we go to America?'

He shook his head. 'I can't leave yet. It will get very sticky here before I can. I don't like it, but my orders are changing.' He paused and his eyes darkened. 'The more people I have to pretend to be, the harder it gets. Look, Nicole, it's you who keeps me level. You bring me back to who I really am.'

'And I think of you as making me solid.'

'Solid and level – can't be bad, can it? But a baby? Now? I remember how I felt without my mother. It made me so unsure of who I was.'

She hesitated but the words were already on her lips. 'Couldn't we be married?'

'I would like nothing better than to set up home with you. But, my darling, we can't be official, you're still wanted by the police.' He shook his head. 'And I still have a job to do. I shall be involved in covert operations in Russia soon. A potentially dangerous search for ruthless people harbouring Vietminh leaders.'

'To you? You mean dangerous to you?'

He nodded.

'Mark, what about when the baby comes?'

He wiped a hand across his brow but didn't speak.

She felt a knot settle in her throat.

'I don't want to leave you alone. When is the baby due?'

'Next February. It's the best time of year to have a baby, not too hot, not too humid.'

'Well, that's something positive, isn't it?' He pulled her up and drew her across to the sofa where they could sit together. She leant against him and couldn't stop the tears from falling. He lifted her head up by tilting her chin and kissed them away.

'When the war is over . . . it'll be different. I promise. And I am glad. Really glad. It's the most wonderful news in the world, and we will find a way.'

They didn't speak again for several minutes. Nicole had no idea what he was thinking, but she was thinking about her sister.

'Did you ever love my sister, Mark?'

'No. She fascinated me when we were in America – clever, beautiful and with the knack of making you feel the way she wanted you to feel. And so sure of herself. But underneath she was needy. Very needy. We only dated a few times but I felt as if she wanted to own me, so I backed off.'

'Then she was sick.'

'She took too many sleeping pills. I didn't know if it was intentional or accidental, but after that I couldn't just abandon her. She wasn't in her own country surrounded by people who loved her. But let's not talk about your sister. Let's at least enjoy the time we do have together.'

He wrapped his arms round her and she felt comforted and aroused at the same time. He made her feel safe in a way she had never felt before and she didn't want it to end. The only thing she wanted to end was the war, but would it ever? She sighed and, snuggling even closer to him, breathed in the mix of cigarettes and the salty smell of his skin.

For the next couple of months Nicole's pregnancy showed very little. The *áo dài* covered the small bump and she wore a loose shawl round her shoulders which also helped disguise her growing belly. Feeling indolent, she spent much of her time reading upstairs and trying not to think of what she'd do if one day Mark didn't come back. But the anxiety reared up in dreams from which she woke in dizzying fear. One day she went in search of Yves, but was sad to see the little bakery had already been boarded up.

She cooked simple Vietnamese meals in the little kitchen at the back of the shop, developing an overwhelming desire for steamed spinach, which she shared with O-Lan and her mother, and crispy brown rice from the bottom of the burnt pan which she did not share. One day she decided she wanted to make the best of the small courtyard garden at the back of the shop. Mark rolled up his sleeves and helped by reaching the high creepers, while she cut back the jasmine and the scented roses, repeatedly scratching her arms.

As he made his way down from the stepladder carrying a huge bunch of greenery she watched him and could almost imagine there was no war. They were a normal couple making a home together and preparing for their first child.

'I might learn to knit,' she said and smiled at him.

He smiled back. 'I didn't have you down as the knitting type.'

'I thought that was why you loved me.'

The skin around his eyes crinkled with laughter. 'I don't recall saying that I did.'

He did love her. She knew it. Even if he didn't say it. 'So how much *didn't* you say you loved me?'

'Acres, tons, mountains.'

'As high as the sky is what Lisa used to say.'

'Well, there you have it.'

'Anyway, even if I can't knit, at least I can cook.'

'If you like burnt rice.'

'Oh, that's not fair!'

He dumped his armful of cuttings, bent towards her, then kissed her hard on the lips. At that moment she felt the depth of his love.

'Shall we forget the gardening?' he said.

After they'd made love, they continued to lie in bed watching as the light gradually faded. When it was dark she lit the oil lamp at the side of the bed and asked him about his family.

'There's not a lot to tell,' he said. 'My mother was Russian, as you know. White Russian.'

'And that's how you speak the language?'

'Yes. She managed to get out of Russia in the nick of time, but she'd lost everything and never really got over it.'

'How did she die? Do you mind me asking?'

He shook his head. 'It wasn't long after my twelfth birthday.' He paused. 'I'm afraid she took her own life soon after the new baby died . . . and I found her.'

'Oh God! How awful for you. I'm so sorry.'

'She tried so hard to be rational but she never was. In truth, she was a passionate Russian and fond of the grand gesture.'

'Her suicide was a gesture?'

'No. Not that. But at other times of emotional crisis. She liked to storm out of rooms. My father loved her but he never understood her.'

'She had lost both her parents. She must have felt broken inside when the baby died.'

'Yes. And after she'd gone it was so hard. My father

disappeared into his shell, and I felt cut loose. Rootless. Didn't know who the hell I was. Perhaps that's why I do the job I do. I can be anyone.'

She took his hand and ran it over her belly. 'I hope we'll be able to make up for it a little bit.'

'I'm going to ensure our little one will never go through anything like that.'

'We are going to be happy. This baby will make everything come right. You'll see.'

'I do care, Nicole. Very much. I hope you understand.' He kissed her on the nape of her neck and behind her ears, then kissed her breasts until she was defenceless. After that he put an ear against her stomach.

'What are you listening for?' she whispered.

'Intelligent conversation.'

She hit him on the head with a cushion. 'I'm tired,' she said. 'Do you feel like cooking?'

He laughed. 'I could probably manage some burnt rice.'

30

Nicole opened all the windows. She had grown to love the ancient quarter: the wonderful aroma of fried shallots and minced onions, the narrow alleys, the open markets and the din of the traders tempting you with their food. It always made her feel better, though her growing size was a problem they would have to think about. Under a vivid blue sky, the streets were infused with the smell of caramel and dumplings, and she couldn't have felt happier. When O-Lan struggled back from shopping with two bags bursting with produce, she was intrigued.

'What have you got?' Nicole asked, following O-Lan as she carried them through to the kitchen.

'I am going to teach you to cook Vietnamese style – properly, I mean. Your steamed spinach is wearing a bit thin, not to mention what it's doing to my mother's digestive system. Think of this as a late lunch.'

Nicole smiled. 'Where do we begin?'

'By emptying the bags.'

Nicole pulled the lettuce out first, red and green, then a huge bunch of coriander, plus some celery and another green leaf. Nicole sniffed. 'Lemony.'

'Look in the other bag.'

Nicole opened the bag. 'Fresh white noodles. So what are we making?'

'*Bun cha*. But you've missed the important ingredient. The pork. We'll cut up the leaves, make the broth and grill the pork outside over charcoal.'

They worked together in companionable silence. Nicole chopped while O-Lan made the broth.

After they began grilling, a gorgeous, sweet aroma of pork filled the air. Nicole's mouth watered as O-Lan finally slid the meat into the broth.

'All done. Let's eat,' O-Lan said as she placed three bowls in front of Nicole, noodles, meat and broth, and chopped leaves.

Nicole copied O-Lan, who took some of the leaves, then a few noodles, and dipped the mix into the broth, picking up a slice of pork as she did so.

'It's delicious,' Nicole said as she slipped a second attempt at the mix into her mouth. 'Thank you for this. Exactly what I needed. I'll make it for you next time.'

Nicole stood silently listening upstairs as late-afternoon sunshine slanted through partly closed curtains; below her there were French voices in the shop. If anyone should come asking questions, she had asked O-Lan to say she didn't know where the owner of the shop was. Her friend was good to her word and after a few minutes the men left. Nicole peered through the gap in the curtains to watch them walk away. Her confidence dissolved when she saw Giraud was among them.

O-Lan came up the stairs. 'Did you hear?'

Nicole nodded.

'What if they arrest me for harbouring you? I have my mother to think of.'

'They won't arrest you.' Nicole checked that they had really gone then reached up to close the curtains fully. As she did so, O-Lan stared at her stomach, noticing her swollen belly for the first time.

'Oh God, no. What have you done? You aren't even married.'

'Don't be so old-fashioned. Aren't you pleased for me?'

'Since when is it old-fashioned to want a father for a child? Is it Trần's?'

'No, we were only ever together once, long before we even left to go to the north.'

'Mark's?'

'Yes.'

'But don't you see, you'll never get away with a child who doesn't look Vietnamese here. Not when –'

The air suddenly felt heavy as if there was nothing left in it.

'Please don't tell anyone.'

'Of course I won't, but if the French come sniffing around again, I'll have to think of my mother.'

Nicole nodded.

'We may need to get you away from here, perhaps to France where your baby will not be out of place.' She had spoken in a hushed tone and paused to stand up, push the curtains aside and look out of the open window.

'What's the matter?'

O-Lan turned back to look at her. 'When the Vietminh win, your baby will really not be safe here.'

Nicole wondered if there might be a better chance for her child if they went to live in Huế. She thought about their old home and the colours of the Perfume River. She remembered her cycle rides along the bank under the trees, and the blossom falling into the river. Her baby could have a happy childhood.

'I was wondering about going to Huế,' she said.

O-Lan shook her head. 'Not when the Vietminh win. You may not even be safe yourself.'

'*When* the Vietminh win?'

O-Lan nodded. 'They will. You know they will. Everything will change.'

Nicole batted away the gnats floating around their heads. 'Have you heard something?'

O-Lan nodded and leant closer to whisper. 'A letter from Trần. He says the Vietminh are gaining ground. He asked me to keep an eye open for you until he returns.'

'So he is coming back?'

'Yes, but not for a while. Do not worry yet. But you will have to leave sooner or later. Do you have money?'

'Not much. Only what's in the shop's account. Oh, and the value of the goods in my shop. But Mark will help.'

After they'd talked for a while longer, O-Lan left. It was the time of day when the shrill noises of the day faded and the world seemed to slip into slow-motion before true darkness fell. Nicole went downstairs again and, to pass the time, pounded some rice with a pestle and mortar. It satisfied her need to be active and she'd use the flour to bake rice cakes in the outdoor oven in the courtyard.

She thought again about trying to learn to knit. Her baby would need clothes to wear. She knew Lisa had wrapped up all their old baby clothes and stored them in a zinc-lined chest at the house. Some of them would have survived – perhaps she could go back and look for them.

She changed into her nightgown and went to sit on a bench in the courtyard. She glanced up at the dark, bruised sky, fading to pink where it met the rooftops. A slight breeze brought in the evening scents she loved. Not only roses and jasmine, but cigarettes and a leafy, earthy smell too. Mark had promised he would be back that evening. She didn't want to think of Giraud or Trần; didn't want anything to disturb her peace. Later, she chopped and then fried onions, garlic and peppers, and when they were soft added the mixture to the rice flour to form patties. As the smell of charcoal filled the air she lined them up on the grill, and when done, she put them in a bowl for Mark. Suppertime came and went. When the evening grew a little cooler and it began to drizzle she ran upstairs to fetch a shawl. She intended to go back outside to watch the stars, if the clouds allowed it, but she didn't have the chance to go back down. As she was wrapping the shawl about her shoulders she heard a sound and spun round.

'Mark! I'm so glad to see you.' She smiled at him. 'But where have you been? I cooked.'

'You don't own me, Nicole.'

She frowned. 'I never thought I did, but I was worried. Giraud was here today.'

'Really?'

The look he gave her was like a slap in the face. 'Don't you believe me?'

He narrowed his eyes but didn't speak.

She smelt the alcohol on him and felt uncertain. 'I was frightened, Mark, and when you were late . . .'

'You're safe enough here. The man has been watching the door, hasn't he?'

'And Giraud?'

He sighed. 'Forget Giraud.'

'Why? Has something happened?' Suddenly tired, she sat on the sofa.

He didn't answer but took out an envelope from his shirt pocket, then pulled up a chair and sat down facing her, legs spread wide.

Nicole was conscious of some shouting in the streets, but thought it distant. Nothing to worry about. She heard the sound of the rain starting up, gently drumming on the roof tiles. Unable to fully read Mark's eyes, she detected something unfamiliar. Beneath the smell of alcohol and cigarettes, something had changed. He didn't usually sit on a chair facing her in such a way, scrutinizing her face.

270

'We've had an up-and-down relationship, haven't we, Nicole?'

Feeling her mouth drying a little, she licked her lips.

'Don't you want to know who the letter is from?'

She gazed at him. 'Of course.'

He took a cigarette out of a pack, lit it with a match then threw the match into a metal wastepaper bin.

'Mark!'

'It'll burn out.' He leant back in his chair.

She watched him carefully. This was a different Mark and she didn't like it.

He cleared his throat. 'Why did you lie about Sylvie?'

She wiped a hand across her forehead. It was dreadfully hot. 'You've had too much to drink!'

He stared at her and she could see the confusion in his eyes. 'I have two pieces of news. Firstly, I now have the complete address of your old cook's sister. I thought if the worst happened you could go to her.'

'Oh, that's wonderful. I –'

He cut her short. 'And this is a letter from *your* sister.'

She screwed up her brows. 'But I thought the post was halted.'

'Halted, yes. Finished, no.' She watched as he struggled to find more words. When he spoke, his voice was low. 'Maybe you should have thought of that.'

His words struck her to the quick. She picked up a beautiful striped red and silver silk cushion to hug against her chest. 'I don't know what you mean,' she said, but her voice seemed to stick in her throat.

A vein in his neck was pulsing. He narrowed his eyes and continued to stare at her. 'I know you've always had problems with your sister. Sylvie told me.'

Nicole gasped. 'It was the other way round. She was the one who had problems with me.'

271

'She told me you'd say that. Told me how much she'd tried to make you happy.'

'She was lying. It wasn't like that. She tried to drown me.'

He shook his head. 'I don't know what to believe any more. But I do know that *you* lied to me. Don't you understand? *You* deceived me. That's what's so cutting.'

'Mark, please.'

'Everything is always about your sister, isn't it?' He got to his feet and walked over to the window, where he looked down at the street. There was a long silence before he turned back to look at her again.

She felt a flash of anger. 'Well, if it's Sylvie you want, why don't you go and get her?'

'For Christ sake, woman, you know I didn't mean it like that. I don't want Sylvie. But I feel I've been manipulated. By you. Why did you feel you had to lie?'

'Isn't it obvious? Because I thought you still had feelings for Sylvie.'

'You didn't believe me when I said there was nothing between me and your sister. I tried to convince you of the strength of my feelings for you.'

Nicole chewed the inside of her cheek until she tasted blood.

'But all along it was *you* who *I* couldn't trust. I trusted you, Nicole. There's so little trust left in the world, but I completely trusted you.'

'You *can* trust me.'

'No. There have been too many lies in my life, too many double lives, too many different versions of me. I felt that with you I was my better self, my true self, and now I see that it was based on a lie.'

'You were obsessed with my sister.'

'You're the one who's obsessed with her. It's not a good thing, Nicole. For whatever reason, you believe you live in her

272

shadow. But you don't need to. You're beautiful, generous and loving, and all I ever wanted.'

He came over, and now he was close to her, his face twisted. She looked up at his eyes and a tear slid down her cheek. 'We've been happy, Mark. You know we have.'

He smoothed the hair from her eyes but didn't speak. They stared at each other for what felt like minutes. The room went still and the silence swallowed her. She didn't move, didn't even blink. She couldn't bear to think that this might end now. What did Giraud matter? What did anything matter?

'I'm sorry I lied about Sylvie's letter,' she said. 'Really sorry. Let's eat now.' She got to her feet and held out her hands to him. He didn't take them.

'Mark. Please.'

Something awful was snapping at her heels and she felt so lonely it physically hurt. She closed her eyes but everything seemed to blend together as she heard him move about. She felt cut-off, disconnected. After a few minutes she managed to speak.

'What did Sylvie write about?'

'She's coming back. She told you she would be back in that letter she left for you, didn't she?'

'You lied to me too. Pretending to be a silk merchant!'

'That was different.' There was a pause as he came round to face her. 'I need time to think.'

She stared at his bleak face, then pushed him away and ran across to her bed, where she curled up facing the wall with her back to him. She listened to his footsteps fade as he went down the stairs. After a few moments all she could hear was the rain on the roof. She remained motionless as the lonely darkness of the night closed in, the rain pounding harder and harder, and the smell of sweet sticky rice drifting in from a nearby house.

Then she wept, drenching her pillow and feeling more turmoil than she'd ever felt before. She put her hands on her belly, hoping for comfort. All night long, as the wind and rain continued to batter the windows, the roof and the street below, she felt the loss of him.

At dawn, she thought about her sister. When was Sylvie coming? When had she sent the letter? Had Mark written back? Had he told her about the baby? Her sister had painted such a distorted picture of their childhood relationship, could Mark really believe what Sylvie had said? By the time O-Lan called out, Nicole was feeling dreadful.

Her belly hurt and, fearing for her baby, she slipped her feet into her slippers then attempted to reach the bathroom downstairs. O-Lan tiptoed up to help Nicole down the stairs and through to the back.

'You look unwell. Shall I bring you some scented tea?'

Nicole perched on the edge of the small bath while she calmed herself. After that she splashed her face and washed her hair using a shampoo with the fragrance of wild roses. She wanted her child with a fierceness she could never have imagined. The baby was the only thread of light in this terrible mess.

O-Lan brought the tea, which she drank in one big gulp.

'What has happened?'

'Mark has gone.'

O-Lan sighed. 'Will he come back?'

'I don't know.'

As Nicole battled with conflicting emotions, the hurt deepened and she began to sob. She had an independent spirit and had never wanted to lose herself in loving him, but he'd helped her to feel whole and she'd been able to be herself. For the first time in her life she'd felt completely accepted, and that had helped to heal the old division within her.

O-Lan came over and put an arm round her.

But Nicole's nerves were frayed and her mind was dark. If Mark didn't come back, how would she cope alone with a baby who didn't even look Vietnamese? The future beckoned and she felt terrified by what she saw.

31

A week later, Nicole lay upstairs asleep on the sofa in the afternoon. She stirred in her sleep and, sensing someone in the room, opened her eyes to find she was looking right into Mark's intense blue gaze.

'How long have you been there?'

'Can you forgive me?' he said. 'For being such an idiot.'

Despite the look of anguish in his eyes, pride made her turn away. She couldn't bear for him to see the effect his absence had had on her. Her mind was full of the things she wanted to say but could not, and the room seemed to vibrate with unspoken words and feelings. She felt tight inside and, as a way of avoiding the intensity, focused on the lamp light gilding the floor.

'I think you should go.'

'If it's really what you want. Is it?'

He had made her laugh, he had made her cry, and now here he was, apologetic and the very soul of remorse. What was she doing sending him away?

'I needed time to clear my mind.' He lowered his head. 'I am so sorry.'

She turned to face him and thought for a moment. 'Look at me, Mark.'

He raised his head.

'You look tired.'

'I've spent the last seven nights struggling to sleep – worried about you, us, the baby. There's so much to say and yet I never seem to say it. It burns inside me. I –'

She interrupted. 'What I need is the money to leave for France.'

He looked as if he'd been slapped and there was a long silence.

'I will help,' he said eventually, 'of course, but I want to bring up our baby with you. I love you, Nicole.'

She gazed at the floor while her heart somersaulted. Then something happened inside her, like a wire wrapped tightly round her had suddenly loosened its grip. She hadn't known if he would come back. Still loving him with a feral intensity, she could no more turn him away than stop living. As he dropped to his knees beside her, she leant forward and allowed him to wrap his arms round her.

'You are wonderful, Nicole. Never doubt it. And we'll face every difficulty together.'

She nodded. 'What you said before, about me having problems with Sylvie. It wasn't true. I always loved her, but she –'

'I know. Listen, I told you I had Lisa's address. Well, I found a phone number too and managed to call her. She told me the whole truth about what happened when you were born.'

Nicole smiled. 'Is she all right?'

He nodded and glanced at the floor before continuing. 'Look . . . there is one thing I still have to say. I was working undercover with Sylvie.'

'But I already knew that. The third army, remember?'

'I just wondered if that might have been why you came to the wrong conclusion about my relationship with her.'

Nicole shook her head. 'She made sure I came to that conclusion.'

'And I was working with your father.'

'I realized that too but I never knew why.'

'He was made head of the anti-terrorism unit.'

Trying to understand, but feeling puzzled, she frowned and searched his face.

Mark held her gaze. 'I assumed you must have guessed.'

'I knew that officially he was working for the government, but that's all.'

'A front. His reputation was excellent and he was a skilled negotiator. I didn't enjoy the subterfuge of posing as a silk merchant, especially with you, but having a job where you need more than one passport can be like that.'

'So what about my sister? You did kiss her. I saw you, the night of the ball, down in the wine cellar.'

He looked shocked. 'You saw? Is that why everything changed?'

She nodded. 'Partly.' Was this the time to speak of the shooting? The time at last for honesty?

'But there was nothing to see. It was just a peck on the cheek. I was only trying to comfort her and that evening –'

She felt dizzy as the smell of blood came back to her. 'I know what happened.'

He looked baffled and the lines between his brows deepened. 'She told you?'

'No, she only told me you were raising funds to support a third party in Vietnam.' She paused. 'I saw my father shoot Trần's brother.'

He puffed out his cheeks then blew out his breath. 'Dear God, I had no idea. But how?'

'I came looking for you. The peephole hadn't been blacked out.'

'That evening was too much for Sylvie. She was emotionally taut, brittle, and I could see the shock in her.'

'It was horrible, truly horrible.'

He nodded. 'It was. But there's something else I want to say. Whatever you think you saw, it wasn't a real kiss. And even in

America, whatever she may have led you to believe, we were never intimate.'

Nicole was so relieved she felt instantly better.

'But your sister! Some time after the ball, she vanished for a few days to frighten us – your father and me, I mean.'

'Emotional blackmail?'

'I think your father put it about that she had needed a break. She knew it wasn't going anywhere between us, but Sylvie is a lot more troubled than people realize. By the time your father cottoned on, he'd already given her the business. When you told me she wasn't coming back, to be honest, I only felt relief. She'd been a complete headache to work with.'

Nicole shook her head. How had she known so little about her own sister?

The room was now in darkness, but she could tell he was genuine. They remained quiet for a few minutes and she listened to his breathing, only faintly hearing the sounds in the street. His rhythm changed and she became acutely aware that he was holding back a sob. It cut right through her. The father of her child.

'Oh, Mark.'

His tears shook her. She leant towards him and he held her in the dark. She smelt his hair, and felt the warmth of his body. 'I thought I might have lost you,' he whispered.

'It's all right,' she said. 'It will be all right.'

These were extraordinary times. People changed. Behaved out of character. The danger brought out the shadows inside them as well as the courage, and she knew only too well that sometimes people had to do things they didn't want to do.

'I promise, I will never do anything to hurt you again,' he said.

'I'm sorry too. I should have trusted you and told you the truth. I lied because I loved you and I was scared you might want Sylvie and not me. I was frightened I'd lose you.'

'What fools we are,' he said. 'You will never lose me.'

She felt herself relax. Hearing the sound of children laughing outside, she got to her feet to glance out of the window before turning on another lamp. Mark's face was lit on one side by the glow and she looked at the dips and hollows. He was so dear to her now.

'Have you heard anything of Giraud?' she asked.

'He has his hands full. His son Daniel died running from a sniper while in a village just north of Hanoi.'

At the mention of death she shivered. 'How awful. I'm sorry to hear that.'

'Giraud is a wreck. Drinking heavily. Plus he's trying to cope with the influx of refugees coming in from the outlying districts. Not doing too well.'

She nodded. 'I thought the streets were busy.'

'It's the higher-ranking Vietnamese who supported the French. They think their days are numbered and are looking for ways to get to Saigon.'

'Maybe we could go there?'

'Maybe. Are you hungry?'

They went down to the outdoor kitchen and as Mark sliced and began to fry some onions, Nicole thought about what he'd said. People were so complicated. Never wholly good or wholly bad. Look at Trần, or even Giraud, now half mad with grief.

'We might be in danger if Trần comes back here,' she said. 'He isn't a bad man, not really, but now I'm showing . . .'

Mark twisted round to look at her. 'Have you heard something?'

'O-Lan had a letter from him. She was the one who suggested I should go to France.'

'Can you trust her?'

'I'm sure of it. She says he won't be back for a while yet.' But although Nicole had defended Trần, she had seen how cruel he could be and the thought of seeing him scared her.

'I have to go away, but when I get back we'll think about getting you to France. How does that sound?'

She felt the tears springing up. 'Please don't go again.'

He came across and held her in his arms. 'I must. You know I must. This is war. Now that the Vietminh have gained so much ground here, the plan is to set up operations down south. I'll have to be in Saigon and, as I said before, eventually Russia.'

She pulled away and held him at arm's length. 'I hate the thought of Russia. Will you be safe?'

'I can't pretend it's not dangerous. The Russians are supporting the Vietminh, providing weapons and so on. We need to know what else they're doing. And who they're hiding.'

She hung her head and tried to brush the tears away.

'Don't worry, if you decide against France I have friends in America who'll help.' He tilted her head up and kissed her damp cheeks. 'I won't be too long this time, although I may be gone for months later on. But we'll have sorted something out for you long before then.'

She looked into his eyes and prayed it would all happen as he said.

'But if you need to leave suddenly, before I've organized a place for you, then go to France and leave an address at the American embassy in Paris. Or better still, go to Lisa. She's in Narbonne, Rue des Arts, near the canal.' He pulled out a scrap of paper. 'This is the address. I'll wire you some money.'

'I need to go back to the house to see if I can find the baby clothes that Lisa packed away.'

'Well, do it soon and then stay put here until I'm back. Shouldn't be gone more than a week or two.'

She recalled the way she'd found the courage to make that

terrible journey south completely alone, even though it had almost killed her. The next journey might be to France, and Lisa, and maybe sooner rather than later. She hoped it wouldn't be without Mark.

'Whatever happens, I will never abandon you. Don't ever forget. Not for as long as I live.'

And there it was, the spectre of death again.

Nicole loved Vietnam with all her being; it was where she'd been born and where she'd lived all of her life. It would be hard to leave a place so deeply imprinted in her blood. She loved Mark too, and hated the thought of leaving without even knowing where he was. But even as she thought that, a far worse fear uncurled inside her. She would find a way to push through the dark days ahead and it didn't really matter where he was going. What mattered was that he returned to her.

'Come back safe, Mark,' she said and reached for him again. 'Just come back.'

4

The Smell of Fish

October 1953 to May 1954

32

After dressing in clean French clothing, Nicole slid the hooks of some pretty pearl earrings through her lobes. With the rain over, the fresh weather had arrived, but had not as yet reached the pinnacle of heat. Outside, the street was swarming after the recent downpour, as if everybody had rushed out for air, and now bicycles, *cyclos* and pedestrians narrowly missed each other.

She was out testing the water to see if it was safe to return to their villa in the French quarter to look for baby clothes. She passed a pagoda, busy with people carrying suitcases, and was able to melt in with the crowd. But as she reached the crossroads at the end of Silk Street, she saw the area was crawling with French officers, so returned quickly to the shop without looking back.

By late afternoon things seemed back to normal. In the street outside the shop, Nicole stood holding a large canvas bag with wide straps and leather buckles. As she waited to hail a *cyclo* to take her home, she glanced back at the window where the silk lay folded in rows of magenta, yellow, emerald and sky blue. So bright. Like a sweet shop, she thought. There had been good times at her little shop, despite everything, but now she had to think ahead. At any other time she might have been able to bring up her child in the Vietnamese quarter, but with the Vietminh and Trần possibly drawing closer, she had to accept the danger she was in. Huế might not be any safer, and she'd seen for herself what the camps were like. She put the bag down on the kerb then with both hands eased her backache, pressing hard into the points of pain.

As the sky turned indigo she surveyed the street and, raising a hand, shaded her eyes from the low sunlight. A couple of men stood in a shadowy alley opposite smoking and relaxing; next door a mother was bathing her child in a tub on the pavement and an old woman was gathering up her possessions ready to pack them away in a wide basket for the next day. A few shops were already shuttered and others were following. The toothless man who sold boiled peanuts had left. As a young woman passed by, Nicole caught a trace of musky perfume. From a window nearby, the monotonous sound of singing reached her, and for a moment or two Nicole sang along. As she watched a lone *cyclo* approaching from between the line of distant trees, a wave of sadness swept through her and she had to accept how much she would miss all this if she was forced to leave. And yet, against her better judgement, she still harboured the hope that things might turn out all right.

Drunk on the aroma of charcoal and ginger, Nicole felt dreamy and particularly languid. Even the thought of Sylvie's return didn't bother her. Something to do with her pregnancy, she thought, as she closed her eyes to absorb the atmosphere. Mark loved her and that was all that mattered. She opened her eyes as the *cyclo* came closer, bent down to pick up her bag, saw one of the straps had unbuckled and spent a moment doing it up again. She didn't notice the two men slip across from the alleyway opposite, but when she looked up she saw they were now a metre away.

The *cyclo* pulled to a stop and a passenger stepped out. She gasped as Giraud straightened up and turned his watery eyes on her. She twisted round in panic but saw the men now stood either side of her, hemming her in.

Giraud cleared his throat. 'Nicole Duval. You are under arrest. You will be taken to the Maison Centrale where you will remain until you are tried.'

She attempted to maintain eye contact with him. 'For what? Tried for what?'

He laughed and puffed out his chest. The laugh had been scornful, revealing his world-weary state of mind. 'You broke your house arrest and, far worse, you are a traitor to France.'

'How long have you known I was here?'

'Let's just say you have been under surveillance.'

Terror-stricken, she blinked rapidly, glancing around for a means of escape. When she saw there was none she noticed the self-satisfied look on his face. 'Why now? Can't you see I'm expecting a baby? I'm five months pregnant.'

He grinned and she saw his teeth were stained. 'I always thought you a Viet whore.'

'This baby is nothing to do with the Vietminh.'

'Tell it to the judge.'

She squared her shoulders as they clipped the handcuffs round her wrists. She was not going to cry in front of this odious man, but as fear crept through her, everything she'd ever heard about Hoa Lo prison came racing back to her. As she climbed into the *cyclo* with him she was visibly shaking.

For the first twenty-four hours she kept her spirits up, even though the rumours about the formidable Maison Centrale had not been exaggerated. It reeked of rancid fat by night and rotten fish by day. With only a small round porthole for light and the daytime air hot and humid, she felt suffocated. A hundred times her heart began to race. She had to fight the brawling going on in her mind, and when not in a state of panic, the tedium drove her crazy. If only she had gone to France when O-Lan had first suggested it.

She was held in a cage, her wrists loosely chained to the wall and her ankles shackled to a fixed metal bar on the floor on a level with her concrete bunk. The French guards brought in a tin can of water at the start of the day, though they delighted in spilling it. Everyone else in the women's wing was Vietnamese. She tried to speak to the skeletal glassy-eyed person held in the next cage, but the woman spat on the ground and turned her head away.

It wasn't her first experience of appalling colonial brutality but it had never been this personal before. By the second day in the stagnant cell her back ached and she longed to move to ease the pain. Her bladder stretched to bursting with the effort of trying to maintain control, but with the frequency of pregnancy she couldn't always reach the bucket in time. She was forced to relieve herself where she lay. Her throat was so dry she feared the dehydration would harm her baby.

Why did this have to happen now while Mark was away? If he had been there she felt sure he'd have found some way to get her out, on health grounds if nothing else. Thoughts of his touch comforted her a little, but with growing terror she knew that if he didn't get back to Hanoi soon she'd be tried and executed and her baby would die with her. In a state of utter dread she called out to the guards until her face was streaming with tears. By the time her skin had become hot and clammy and her vision had blurred, a kinder guard brought her an extra jarful of water. She gulped it down. Frightened that the morbid conditions might hurt her baby, she steeled herself to think of better times, and when twists of doubt took hold, she pleaded with God to be saved.

But if it wasn't her fears tormenting her, it was the thought of food. The prisoners were fed one small bowl of thin brown-rice gruel twice a day. She began imagining her favourite food. Poached eggs floating on a spinach soup, grilled corn and delicious patisseries. Most of all she craved a café au lait made with condensed milk.

When night fell the urban chill took over from the heat of

day and the cats started screeching and fighting until the small hours. Damp seeped into her bones and she twisted and turned on the cold concrete in an effort to find some way to rest that did not hurt. Every time she thought she had achieved it, if only for five minutes, she could not sleep for the sound of scuttling creatures and the harsh glare from a warden's lamp.

After five days, she was taken to a small airless room and told she would be questioned. The minutes ticked by as she waited with her hands still cuffed. Her skin itched, especially at the top of her back, where she couldn't reach to scratch. The minutes turned into hours. The itch became intolerable. To try to distract herself, she stared up at the small square of daylight at the window, and tried to imagine what was going on out there, but the more her skin itched the more she wanted to scratch. It went on until, completely maddened, she called for a guard.

The guard did not come; instead Giraud walked in, with a smug look on his face. Paralysed with fear, she watched as he sat on a stool, fat legs spread open with his crotch on display. He said little while he smoked a Gauloise Bleue. The stink of it in the confines of the room made her feel sick. She bowed her head to escape the smell, and the heavy curtain of her hair concealed her face. She felt safer when he couldn't see the disgust in her eyes, and she couldn't see what was in his.

'So,' he said finally. His voice was unusually grating as if he had swallowed gravel and some of it still clung to his throat. 'What can you tell us?'

'I don't know anything.' She lifted her head and stared at the window again. But now the light appeared to throb, swelling and shrinking so much it seemed to make the room hum.

He moved his stool closer and bent towards her, then put a hand out to hold her by the chin. She squirmed beneath his grip but, compelled to look at him, she couldn't avoid seeing his dark nostril hair, nor could she turn from his odour, stale with the smell of yesterday's alcohol. The sense of his own importance shone in his eyes. She shuddered and a feeling of dread welled up inside her. She had pitied him for the loss of his son but he was utterly pitiless.

'You know nothing? After so long on the road with the Vietminh?' He tilted his head to the side as if to suggest total disbelief and then let go of her.

'They didn't trust me.'

He smiled. 'And what if I was to say the right information could secure your release?'

She shook her head. 'I went to a re-education camp, but I don't even know where it was. I never knew where we were.'

'What did you see, when you never knew where you were?' He smiled again.

She couldn't bear the way he looked at her as if she was stupid and she stared at the window again. 'I saw the mistreatment of women and children. Much as you are doing to me.'

'You will look at me,' he said. 'That is not a request.'

She turned away from the window and faced him but, recalling the awful spasm on his face that night at the brothel, recoiled.

He did not withdraw his gaze and laughed a bitter, mirthless laugh.

'I saw what you did,' she said quietly.

He did not speak, and though she struggled to hide her fear, she felt it in the pit of her stomach. She glanced about her. The air in the room had now completely filled with smoke and she began to cough.

'Perhaps a little air,' he said as he walked over and reached up to release the window catch.

The fresh air blew in and she felt wild with the sweetness of it. Just air, but such a precious link to the outside world. As he

290

leant against the wall, she tried to see him for what he was – a jaded, pathetic man with thick black brows – but nevertheless the fear of him slid deeper within her.

He gave her a haughty look. 'Whatever you think you may have seen, you are clearly unreliable. Nobody will believe anything you say and nobody trusts you. I have made certain.'

'I also saw the result of what the Vietminh did to those who refused to support them. I saw burnt-out villages and shallow graves, and I saw people with nothing to eat. I saw the results of French bombing too. I saw rape and I saw murder.'

With three strides he was standing over her. Her flesh crawled at his proximity and there was no way she could conceal her revulsion. He lifted the bulk of her hair from the nape of her neck and bent over to hiss in her ear. 'Such a pretty neck.'

She cringed at his touch.

'What? An upstanding Frenchman not good enough for you?' He allowed her hair to fall, twisting it round in his hand and pulling her head backwards. 'Admit the child you are carrying is the result of your sexual "relationship" with a Vietminh.'

He was hurting her but she managed to speak. 'Of course it is not. What do you take me for?'

'You want me to say?' he said.

His sarcasm had not escaped her, but he went to the door and called the guard to take her away.

During the remainder of the day, feeling hotter and hotter, she called for air, but her cries remained unheard. It was a long day. She yearned for comfort, but as flies thickened the air in the evening, she scratched the bites on her ankles and neck and began to believe she'd never even reach her trial. Still no sign of a visit from Mark, and with deepening anxiety she realized he had to be out of the country. With nothing to distract her, the past reached out and sucked her right in. She thought of her father, and she thought of Sylvie and how it had been between them. Even though she had told Mark how sorry she was, the lie about Sylvie's letter lay heavily on her mind. Every wrong thing lay heavily.

By the second week she felt so ill she could barely lift her head from the floor. Nobody knew she was here. Mark was gone. O-Lan would have no idea she was in the prison; even if she guessed, she'd have no power to do anything. There was nobody to get her out. Nobody. Without possibility of escape, despair took hold, eating into her heart and mind, so black and cruel she wept until there were no tears left. It wasn't even her own life she cared about any more, it was her unborn baby's. When she began to feel a terrible gnawing cramp in her stomach, she called for the guard, terrified she was already losing the baby. Her voice came out as a croak and nobody heard. Night came and was no relief. Light came and the hours were long. Days passed and she had no idea how many. As the sweat poured from her head, her eyes stung so much she couldn't stop herself from rubbing them; they became so swollen she could hardly see. She scratched her skin where it itched and bled. She sucked the blood from under her nails and began to feel delirious. Hideous spectres and phantoms took over her mind, spinning her further from reality. Deep underwater and drowning, her sister's face loomed before her. But this time Nicole wanted it to happen; longed for the dark waters to take her and her child, where they'd be safe and out of this hell for ever.

But she didn't die and one night, maybe two weeks in, she watched a full moon light up the world beyond the small window and in a few moments of lucidity racked her brain, desperate to think of something she might tell Giraud. She knew the names of some of the actors, but they had been kind to her. Then she recalled the man with the knife. She'd heard his name. Duong. It was only his given name but it would have to suffice. In the morning she'd ask to see Giraud, at least tell him that, and maybe the name of the village she'd first gone to with Trần – but would it be enough to secure her release? She paused in her thoughts. If she gave Giraud the name of the village, the French might torch the whole place. Could she bear to be responsible for the deaths of women and children, innocent farmers, the elderly? Even if it saved her own skin, how would she ever live with herself? She thought of her baby. Could she do it to save her child?

33

Nicole glanced up as one of the kinder women guards came in. She smiled and unlocked the cage, then briskly removed the shackles and chains. But when Nicole stood up her legs felt too weak to bear her weight, her knees gave way and the woman was forced to hold her up. Feeling raw with fear, she shot the woman a puzzled look.

'What's happening? I must speak with Giraud.'

The woman put a finger to her lips. 'No talking.'

She led Nicole through to the yard. With the assistance of another female guard she used a hose, a brush and some carbolic soap then scrubbed her red. Where her legs and wrists had been bitten by insects her stinging skin became almost intolerable, but at least she'd be clean again. She held on to that. Then a searing pain ripped across the small of her back. Her heart lurched: the baby wasn't due until February so she shouldn't be feeling this now.

She doubled up. 'Oh God! The baby.'

The women guards exchanged looks and one fetched her a glass of water while the other gave her a stool to sit on.

Dazzled by the sunlight, Nicole shaded her eyes with her hand and squinted as she took the glass. The pain in her back passed but she'd felt so constricted it took a full minute before she could even drink, let alone stretch or breathe properly. When she had finished the water, one of the women handed her a pair of elasticated trousers and a smock.

'I must speak to Giraud,' Nicole said as they helped her climb into the trousers. 'I have information.'

The woman shook her head before taking her through the prison and out of the front gate to the pavement beyond the high stone wall. Nicole felt terrified that this might be the day of her trial. If it was, it would be too late for anyone to help her. Next to the prison the equally daunting Palais de Justice towered, just the sight of it enough to make any unfortunate prisoner quake. Nicole closed her eyes and allowed the outside world to wash over her. Everything smelt so clean and, as the beautiful sound of people living their lives filtered through, she opened her eyes on streets that seemed to glow in the sunlight. She glanced up for a moment, longing to lose herself in the empty blue sky. She heard children laughing and turned her head to watch. She wanted to run over and hug them; tell them to live every precious moment. When she saw lovers passing by, as if in a movie, she pictured herself walking there with Mark and, aching with a loss too vast to bear, she wanted to cling to life. To feel. To love. To bring up her child. She felt that she'd tell Giraud anything. But she'd made her decision – it had taken her half the night to reach it – and she would only give him the name of the man with the knife. Her conscience would allow no more.

She heard a taxi draw up and turned to look. She stepped back in shock when her sister climbed out.

'Get in, Nicole. Quickly, before they change their minds.'

Her knees buckled but Sylvie grabbed her and bundled her into the back of the car.

'I'm taking you home,' Sylvie said.

There was a moment's dizzy silence while Nicole tried to take it in.

'I'm sorry it took so long,' Sylvie said. 'I tried to get you out straight away. I've been so worried.'

'I'm frightened I'm losing the baby.'

Sylvie reached out a hand. 'I've already called a doctor to come to the house.'

'I don't understand,' Nicole said. 'How did you get me out?'

Sylvie smiled. 'Giraud likes me and I also reminded him of certain information confirming the use of American cash to fund the African prostitutes.'

Feeling hot and dizzy, Nicole was barely listening. 'I think I'm going to be sick.'

'Shall we stop the car?'

The wave of nausea passed and Nicole shook her head.

'But not just that. Planting evidence too. The French High Commissioner has ordered a clean-up. Giraud is corrupt. We can easily prove a personal vendetta against you.' Sylvie put an arm round Nicole. 'Are you all right? They didn't hurt you?'

Nicole leant her head against her sister's shoulder and her tears began to fall. 'They didn't.'

'Don't cry. It's over now.'

All Nicole could do was nod, the emotion of the moment too overwhelming for words.

'Now we just have to make sure the baby is safe.'

Nicole began to cry again. 'I don't think it is. Something terrible has happened.'

'I'm going to wind down the window. I think you need fresh air.'

With the window down, Nicole gazed in wonder at the golden buildings, at the trees rustling in the wind and at the elegant pavement cafes. They passed the Opera House, the Métropole Hotel, the villas overlooking the lake, the Louis Finot Museum. How beautiful Hanoi was. But where was Mark? He'd said maybe two weeks and she'd been in the prison for longer than that.

That evening Nicole inspected herself in the mirror, touched her transparent skin, ran her fingers over her cheeks, pulled at the dehydrated skin of her lips and picked up a comb to untangle her hair. Lifeless and dry, some fell out in small clumps. She scratched her bitten legs and pulled on some loose trousers to cover them, embarrassed that Mark might see her looking like this.

Sylvie came into the room. 'Now let's get you properly dressed, shall we?'

'I am properly dressed,' Nicole said, but when she glanced down at her clothes, she saw her trousers were inside out.

'Never mind.'

'I don't know what I could have been thinking,' she said.

'You're very weak. It doesn't matter.'

Why did she say that? Of course it mattered. It mattered that her relief at being free was tempered by guilt. It mattered that Mark wasn't there. It mattered that some things you couldn't undo, despite how hard you might wish otherwise. And it mattered that she had lied about Sylvie's letter. Everything mattered. Every bloody thing.

'Look, I bought you some lovely maternity clothes,' Sylvie said, holding out an embroidered silk smock in her favourite shade of grey.

Nicole glanced at it and then up at her sister, surprised by the tender look on her face.

As Sylvie helped her change, Nicole watched her sister's eyes. Neither of them said a word but they both listened as a fierce rain started up, hitting the windowpanes and splashing on the paving as it fell in a sheet from the eaves.

'Just tell me the father of your baby isn't your Vietminh boyfriend.'

Nicole stared at Sylvie. 'The baby is Mark's.'

Sylvie looked at the floor for a few seconds before looking up again. Nicole had never been sure what kind of face Sylvie was wearing, nor how to interpret what she saw. This time her sister's face showed no emotion.

'I see,' was all she said.

★

The next day Nicole was lying on the sofa in the sitting room when Sylvie showed Mark in. Sylvie smiled at them both then left the room, closing the door carefully behind her. Nicole struggled to get to her feet but Mark held up a hand to stop her.

'Stay put,' he said and came straight across and knelt on the floor. As he took her hand, a lump grew in her throat and she could say nothing.

'Oh my love, I've only just heard what happened. A friend at the embassy got wind of it and I managed to cadge a flight on one of those old French rust buckets.'

He wrapped his arms round her and she leant against him, the side of her cheek pressed against his, and they stayed that way for a few minutes. She sighed deeply, her relief at his presence so profound she still couldn't find her voice. She never wanted him to stop holding her like this.

'Sorry, I haven't shaved,' he said.

She didn't care. He was there and that was all that mattered.

'I could kill Giraud for what he's done to you. Are you all right?' He glanced at her stomach. 'Is the baby –?'

'I wasn't sure yesterday. I had a terrible pain . . .' She paused. 'I was so frightened.'

He stroked her hair then pulled himself up to sit beside her. Leaning against him, she felt the thump of his heart against the palm of her hand.

He moved and held her at arm's length for a moment in order to study her face. 'Have you seen a doctor?'

'Yesterday. He's coming again tomorrow.'

'What did he say?'

'He didn't really say anything about the baby except that he could hear a heartbeat.'

'Well, that has to be good news. And you, what did he say about you?'

'He took some blood and said he'd be back.'

'Do you want to talk about what happened?'

She shook her head. She didn't even want to think about it.

Mark stayed with her all afternoon and by the evening she was feeling a little better. But Sylvie seemed agitated and kept coming into the sitting room with odd questions as if she couldn't quite leave them alone. Did they want tea? Were they hungry? Did they want the window open? In the end Mark suggested that maybe Sylvie could prepare a light supper for her sister, as Nicole ought to sleep.

That night Mark and Nicole lay together in one of the spare rooms. He touched her face gently and then kissed her on the lips.

'I don't want to do anything you can't cope with,' he said.

She smiled. 'I'll be fine.'

They made love gently and Nicole allowed the feelings to wash over her. He was an infinitely caring lover and she felt as if she was being rocked in the arms of the softest wave. When they had finished she lay close to him and listened as his chest rose and fell.

'Are you okay?' he said.

'Better than before. But what happens next? How long can you stay?'

'I leave in the morning.'

'I don't think I can bear it.'

'I have to go. One of our agents has disappeared. We think he is somewhere in Moscow and I have to find him.'

'But isn't that terribly dangerous? What if they capture you?' She felt his sigh go through her own body. 'Mark?'

'I won't lie to you. It is dangerous, but I know what I'm doing. It's you I'm worried about and as soon as you are well enough, we need to get you safely out of here.'

'I'll be all right here with Sylvie.'

'She's acting oddly, don't you think?'

'Well, she has only just found out that you're the father of my baby.'

'I'll write,' he said, 'as often as I can. And you must write to me at the embassy in Saigon. If they can, they'll forward letters, though probably not to Russia.'

After he left the next morning Nicole tried to remain happy but she missed him terribly. And although he'd tried to reassure her, she couldn't help feeling anxious. The doctor arrived and confirmed her blood pressure was still a little high and her pulse a fraction too fast. He told her to keep her feet up as much as possible and prescribed iron supplements, good food and gentle exercise.

Sylvie seemed less agitated and gave her the space she needed to recover from the prison ordeal, also preparing her meals and bathing her sores. But despite her relief at being free, and her joy at seeing Mark again, images of the prison cell continued to storm her mind. Although her incarceration had been relatively short – just over two weeks – it had shaken what little remained of her French sympathies. And though she'd told Mark everything was fine with the baby, secretly she was worried by niggling pains. An inconsolable feeling of loss gripped her as she was forced to face up to her own vulnerability and that of her child.

She did little but rest and eat, and felt lucky that she could at least sleep. Her sleep was like a drug, blanking out the fearful thoughts that led her into the darker places of her mind. During her waking hours she still feared the baby might not live because of what she'd been through. But one day as she lay in bed, staring at the ceiling, she felt a small kick. She pulled up her nightdress and spotted a little bump appear on her rounded belly. Then another kick and another small bump. She laughed with the joy of it and tried to speak with the little one by gently pushing back the bumps as they appeared. A feeling of hope zipped through her and with it the sense of something going right at last. The baby was stronger than she'd thought possible. This little person would save her and she would save him. Or her.

It went on to rain all day and a pool of water started to collect in a dip on the kitchen floor. Nicole watched as Sylvie fetched a mop and dragged it over the tiles to absorb the water. When she'd finished she gazed at Nicole.

'Sit down. I have something to say.'

The light in the room had faded. Nicole had no idea if evening had come or if clouds had suddenly blackened the sky. It felt so gloomy she went across to glance out of the window, her body still slow and aching. Just clouds it seemed. She turned on a lamp and then struggled to settle herself in a chair.

She saw her sister's look grow more serious.

'I want you to know that Mark explained what happened,' Sylvie said. 'He told me everything.'

Nicole felt anxious and rubbed her fingers back and forth across her forehead. She had known this moment was bound to come.

'Your letter?'

Sylvie nodded and gave her a tired smile.

Nicole shifted in her seat. What could she say? 'I'm sorry I lied about it. You must be angry.'

Sylvie didn't reply for a moment, just narrowed her eyes.

'Sylvie?'

'A bit. Well, wouldn't you be angry?'

'Yes, I suppose I would.'

There was a long silence as Nicole put herself in her sister's shoes. Of course her sister was angry, but other than that she had no idea what Sylvie was feeling.

'There's something disturbing about this time of day,' Sylvie said eventually, rubbing her hands together. 'Don't you think?'

Nicole didn't speak.

'Still day. Not quite night. It's the transition, I think. You don't know where you are with it. I've never liked it.'

Nicole watched her sister. 'I'm so grateful that you got me out of that terrible place.'

Sylvie scratched her neck. 'Papa would have expected no less. All I want is for you to fully recover.'

'And the baby?'

'Of course.'

Nicole nodded, relieved Sylvie was taking it so well.

Sylvie smiled. 'Now you need to regain your strength. The less excitement the better. As soon as you feel well we will take a daily walk. Giraud won't be a danger now, especially as most of his old colleagues are gone and the new force has far bigger fish to fry than you.'

Nicole decided her sister must have mellowed.

'No more worry,' Sylvie said. 'And don't think about your little friend, Trần, either. I've employed an armed guard to protect the house at night.'

'Is he here now?'

Sylvie smiled. 'Rest assured, your Vietminh past won't be able to touch you. You will give birth here in the house. Now concentrate on getting better. For the sake of my little niece or nephew.'

Nicole gazed at her sister. 'Why are you doing this for me?'

'You're family. Now I must go out for bread and milk. Tomorrow I have a business to get back on its feet.'

'You still believe the French will win?'

'Of course.'

Nicole frowned. Her sister seemed so sure of herself. 'Don't you think we'd be better off cutting our losses and returning to France?'

'And what would we live on if we did? Anyway, you shouldn't travel in your present condition. Wait until the baby's born. Then we'll see. Don't worry about anything. All the downstairs windows have bars.'

While Sylvie was out picking up their supplies, Nicole chose Lisa's favourite chair by the conservatory door, where she once used to keep an eye on her vegetable plot. The dark clouds had shifted now and, sitting alone in Lisa's chair, Nicole tried to imagine her there. What would their old cook have advised her to do? The night before, her longing for Mark had been intense and she'd lain awake until exhaustion finally closed her eyes. She thought of her father too. Her entire childhood might have been different had her father not allowed Sylvie to believe his lie about their mother's death. If she and her sister were ever to truly trust each other, the time for secrets was over. If she was going to give birth here, she and Sylvie would need to talk about the past, no matter how hard it might be.

As soon as she heard her sister come back, Nicole called up the stairs. 'Have you got a minute?' She began to bite the loose skin at the edges of her thumbnail.

Sylvie came down, fetched a glass of water and sat at the table. Nicole stayed where she was, leaning against the kitchen sink, comforted by the warm glow of their kitchen bathed in low evening sunlight.

'What is it?' Sylvie said. 'Gosh, it's nice to catch the last of the sun, though it'll be dark any moment.'

Before she began, Nicole took a moment, resolutely keeping her eyes on Sylvie. 'I saw Papa shoot Trần's brother at the ball.'

Sylvie did not lose eye contact either, though she looked startled and her eyes widened. 'You saw that?'

'I was in the corridor.'

Sylvie shook her head. 'All this time you've kept it to yourself?'

Nicole wasn't sure if her sister was worried because she'd witnessed it or was nervous she might have told somebody. The silence between them went on too long and, though Sylvie's face was composed, she began to tap her foot.

'Are you sure you kept it to yourself? You didn't tell Trần?'

'Of course not.'

Sylvie frowned. 'Why not?'

'You said it yourself. You're family. He'd have looked for revenge.'

Sylvie gulped down her water. 'I'd have been out of your way.'

'Sylvie!' Nicole gasped, and sat down opposite her sister. 'How can you even think something like that?'

Sylvie leant back in the chair and stared at the ceiling. 'We're different, you and I.'

Nicole thought about it. Perhaps they were. As children Sylvie had been the quiet one, whereas Nicole had been accustomed to having her fingers slapped, usually after dipping them into Lisa's homemade plum jam or nipping into the larder to pilfer a slice of cake. She'd always been in trouble for racing up the stairs or shouting down from the top, for sliding down the banisters or falling into ponds, and later, on the terrible day when they'd taken the boat out without permission. Despite Sylvie's denials, Nicole had known it had been her sister's idea. That the whole thing had been Sylvie's fault. Any further than that she never dared recall, wanting only to turn her back on feelings that still retained the power to shake her. Once you come close to drowning, it never lets you go.

Sylvie coughed and Nicole came back to the present with a jolt. 'What I want to know is why Trần's brother was killed.'

'We didn't know beforehand,' Sylvie said.

'We?'

'Mark and I.' Her sister straightened up but still seemed all nerves. 'Jesus, I could do with a cigarette.'

Nicole couldn't help smiling. 'You don't smoke.'

'No, but I wish I did. Listen. It's all water under the bridge now. No need to go over old ground.'

But Nicole, propelled by the need to know more, continued. 'All this time I have wondered why Papa had to kill him there.'

Sylvie sighed. 'It was a secret interrogation cell with another exit through the grounds. He was a Vietminh and suspected of the assassination of a French officer.'

'He hadn't been tried.'

Sylvie got to her feet. 'Inciting rebellion against the French. Wasn't that enough? An example had to be made.'

'And you didn't know it was going to happen?'

Sylvie shook her head but there was a pallor to her skin that hadn't been there before.

'Why did our father have to pull the trigger?'

'It was his job. I suppose he had no choice. He'd been a businessman with links to everyone and he was well placed to find out anything going on. But he had married a Vietnamese. That was a black mark and because of it the French government used him.'

Nicole felt the blood pumping through her veins and, even though it was almost dark now, got up to open the door for air.

Sylvie took the cap off a fresh bottle of milk. 'You should drink a litre of this a day,' she said.

Nicole nodded. She still wanted to talk to Sylvie about what had happened the day she was born, but felt it would have to wait until they'd built up more trust. In the meantime she'd write to her father telling him that Lisa had revealed the truth. Perhaps that was the best place to start unravelling such a sensitive issue.

She stretched to shake off the tight feeling in her muscles, then moved around a bit, keeping her eyes on her sister. 'Maybe we need to talk about Mark.'

Sylvie didn't speak but something flickered on her face.

'Sylvie?'

'There's nothing to say.'

Nicole thought about it. 'You liked him, right? In America?'

Her sister bowed her head for a moment then looked Nicole in the face. 'Yes, but when he arrived in Hanoi . . .'

'Did you believe he loved you?'

'I don't want to talk about it.'

'But, Sylvie –'

'I said I don't want to talk about this.' Sylvie slammed the milk bottle down with such force the bottle cracked and milk started leaking all over the table. 'Now look what you've made me do!'

Perhaps Mark had been right when he said her sister was far more troubled than people knew. 'Did you believe he loved you?' she asked again.

Sylvie glanced at Nicole while she was mopping up the milk. 'Just leave it. All that matters now is that we prepare for the baby.'

Nicole went upstairs, her head spinning.

On her way to her room she passed the long mirror on the landing and stared at her deeply rounded belly and full blue-veined breasts. At least her hair had stopped falling out when she brushed it, and she no longer had to pick strands out of the washbasin. Her face was softer too; it was as if she was seeing herself with new eyes and, for the first time, she was astonished to see real beauty in her Vietnamese looks.

Before lying down on her bed she wrote to Mark, telling him what the doctor had said and that the baby was now moving around. When she had finished she could have sworn she smelt a trace of Camembert baking. In a flash she was back with Lisa in their kitchen in Huế and it felt so real she had to smile. Tomorrow she'd write to Lisa too. The past was a powerful place and she so wanted her child to have happy memories to look back on. Memories rooted in a life full of love. Her own childhood had been so mixed, and there were moments when she could hardly think beyond remembering how difficult it had sometimes been.

34

When Nicole thought about the future it was still with a sense of unease. Whatever Sylvie said to the contrary, there was little doubt in Nicole's mind that sooner or later the Vietminh would come. They had thousands of people on their side, thousands and thousands of people who believed their cause was just, and while it saddened her to realize the old days were gone for ever, she had seen enough to know they had right on their side.

Once she was a little stronger she walked early in the day to steer clear of people. She avoided reading the newspapers, where she knew French victories would be proclaimed, while their losses would go unreported, especially where the battles raged around the Red River Delta. She'd seen how people ignored what had happened during the terrible battle of Hòa Binh in 1952. The French commanders had refused to see how their losses there had foretold the future, but Nicole had known the Vietminh first-hand. They were single-minded and their focus would see them through. She couldn't help but admire that, even in the face of the mighty French army, they would never give up, and though their rhetoric was extreme, their passion couldn't be denied. Yet, despite their just cause, she knew many more people would suffer for it during what lay ahead.

On the day a letter arrived from Mark she had been trying not to obsess about him, though she worried constantly about where he was and if he was safe. If anything happened to him now she just couldn't bear it. She went upstairs to her room to open the letter in private and was pleased to read that he hadn't yet left for – and there he left a blank. She knew what it meant, though of course he couldn't write it down. At least he was still in Saigon and not in Russia. He had received her letter and said that he longed to put a hand on her stomach and feel the baby kick. He also suggested they liquidate their remaining assets in preparation for leaving soon after the baby was born. While Nicole was overjoyed to hear from him, she choked back tears at the thought of what he might have to face in Russia.

Images of grey communist buildings and ruthless men filled her mind. He'd said he would have to discover the where-abouts of a missing agent. That the man might well have defected. What would happen to Mark if he was captured? She was weighed down by the dense shadow of the war within Vietnam; death was everywhere, even if she could not see it. Nobody knew for certain how much of the land the Vietminh had already taken, nor how deeply involved the Russians were. For Mark's sake, she hoped it was minimal.

35

The winter months passed rapidly and Nicole had been excited to receive two letters from Lisa. Her old friend sounded settled in her new life and Nicole was relieved to hear it, but as February approached she was feeling increasingly worried about Mark. She had not seen him since just after her release from prison and hadn't received a reply to her last two letters either, which had to mean he was now in Russia.

One afternoon Sylvie had her head buried in a book on childbirth, and Nicole was sitting on the sofa attempting to knit the baby a blanket, but kept on dropping stitches. Mark had been right about that; she was hopeless at knitting. She couldn't get him out of her mind and constantly thought about where he might be and what he was doing. Already beginning to think of the future, she wondered if supplies of silk were readily available in the villages around Saigon. If he could work out of Saigon when the war was over, that might be the way ahead for her. She had never been south herself but her father had said it was a teeming city with none of the serene charm of Hanoi. She'd also heard that, while the use of opium was only moderately widespread in Hanoi, in the Cholon area of Saigon it was everywhere. The city was corrupt, but it was the place where many were fleeing.

She glanced up at Sylvie. 'What if something happens to Mark?'

'He can take care of himself.'

'I don't want my baby to grow up fatherless.'

Sylvie put her book aside. 'We both grew up without a

mother, so of course I understand. You weren't the only one who felt different, you know. All my friends had mothers and then suddenly I didn't any more. They turned their backs on me.'

'At least you had her for five years.'

'But because you never had her you didn't know the difference. I felt as if you could have punched me in the stomach and your fist would go right through. There was a big hole inside me.'

There was a long silence as Nicole thought about how awful it must have been for Sylvie to lose her adored mother at the age of five. It would be more than enough to alter a small child's life and instil a deep-seated insecurity.

'I understand. I felt there was a hole in me too,' she said in a small voice.

Sylvie came over, knelt beside her and took her hand. 'Well, we have each other now.'

Nicole nodded and Sylvie straightened up again.

There was something else Nicole had been thinking about. 'What's happening with my shop, Sylvie?'

'People don't have much to spend. O-Lan is still there but we're struggling to make a living from it. But we have other businesses and I feel confident, if carefully managed, we can retain our assets rather than having to sell.'

Nicole wasn't sure. 'You do remember what Mark said in his letter about the liquidation of our assets?'

Sylvie gave a short, scornful laugh.

'You don't want to believe everything he says, Nicole. We have standards to maintain and when we win the war we'll need everything we've got.' She rubbed her hands as she walked back and forth, almost muttering to herself. Her eyes were darting here and there, and then she lowered her voice. 'We have to be careful not to be overheard.'

Nicole frowned. 'By who?'

Sylvie didn't seem to hear her and carried on talking to herself. 'It will all be fine. Yes, absolutely fine. Everything all right. Just as before. Exactly as before.'

Then she turned to Nicole as if suddenly remembering she was there. 'We will remain here. Don't worry. It's all under control. There's nothing to worry about. We'll have a lovely time when the baby comes. I wish it would hurry up.'

'You can't dictate when a baby will be born.'

'You're right, nature will take its course.'

'You seem unsettled, Sylvie. Is something wrong?'

Sylvie sighed deeply. 'Nothing at all. Now, I've found Lisa's old recipe for your favourite lemon cake. Shall we give it a go?'

'After the baby comes I think we should go straight to France. French people and Vietnamese too. So many have already left for Saigon.'

'Cowards. In any case, the government has forbidden further departures.'

'You think that will stop them?'

Sylvie shrugged. 'Now, I know you like the cake –'

Nicole felt a sudden twinge and doubled over.

'Are you all right? You look a bit odd.'

'I feel rather more than odd,' Nicole gasped.

But the twinge passed and they headed down towards the kitchen, Nicole pressing a palm against the wall to steady herself.

'These steps are treacherous,' she said.

'You used to race up and down.'

'I used not to be pregnant.'

The kitchen was clean but not the place it used to be: the hustle and bustle, the delicious aromas, the radio turned up too loud with Lisa singing along – all that was gone. Nicole sighed and opened the door of the conservatory for the smell of damp earth and trees to drift in. It was a lovely February day and really quite cool. She thought fondly of Yvette and of the Saturday mornings when the little girl, followed by her dog, Trophy, would bring their treats. Though so much of the past had gone, Nicole felt sure the baby would bring them fresh hope for the future.

Sylvie pulled out one of Lisa's old recipe books from a drawer beneath the table. She flicked it open. 'It's written entirely by hand. I left a scrap of paper to mark the place. But goodness, her spelling is awful.'

'She wasn't an educated woman.'

'Here it is. We need eggs and flour. And lemons. Can you get the sugar from the larder?'

Nicole found an opened bag of sugar in the larder. It had to be kept in an airtight canister or ants would take up residence. She checked to make sure the ants hadn't got in, but another strong twinge made her gasp and she accidentally tipped the sugar over herself.

'I think the baby is coming.'

Sylvie looked up from Lisa's book. 'You're sure?'

Nicole felt prickly. 'No. I haven't done this before, remember?'

'I'll fetch the midwife. I'll only be half an hour. At least she can have a look at you.' Sylvie closed the book. 'We'll do this another time.'

'What if it comes while you're gone? Can't you phone?'

'The line is off.'

'Again?'

Sylvie nodded. 'The whole area.'

'I want you to stay.' Nicole was sobbing now. 'Look at me. About to have a baby and covered in sugar.'

Sylvie gave a short laugh. 'I'm no use at that sort of thing.'

'I need the downstairs bathroom to get all this sugar off.'

'Very well, I'll help you get comfortable and then go.'

Nicole reached out a hand. 'Please don't leave me.'

'Come on, Nicole. Just up to the ground floor. Women give birth all the time, don't they? You'll be absolutely fine.'

'You wouldn't say that if it was you. Think of what happened to our mother.'

Sylvie looked at Nicole pointedly. 'Ah, but it isn't me, is it?'

'But I don't know what to do,' Nicole wailed.

'Instinct will kick in, won't it?'

As they made their way up the stairs, Nicole hoped her sister was right. Instinct might be all they had. She washed the sugar off in the bathroom and then went into the sitting room, where Sylvie organized some cushions on the sofa. 'There. Will you be comfortable?'

Nicole nodded and sat down. Then a truly awful pain twisted her insides. 'I can't do this without Mark. You have to stay. Please.'

Sylvie agreed to stay after all and almost immediately the pains ceased and Nicole felt fine. False alarm, she thought. Wasn't there a name for it? They had both read that childbirth book, but it was old-fashioned and the information had been veiled in odd little euphemisms. She struggled to her feet and Sylvie helped her walk about.

'It might be a false alarm, but maybe I should go for the midwife now?' Sylvie said.

Nicole felt small and tearful. It felt like it was happening but not happening at the same time. What if the woman came too late? What if something happened to the baby? She began to panic. 'I really don't want to be on my own.'

Sylvie nodded. 'All right. We'll do this together.'

Nicole smiled through her tears.

It was just as well Sylvie stayed because a few minutes later the waters broke and a ferocious new pain stabbed at Nicole's stomach. She wrapped her arms round her middle in surprise. It had not been a false alarm and now she knew with absolute certainty that this was it. She searched for reassuring thoughts, trying not to think about what had happened to her own mother. Sylvie was right. Women did this all the time, often out in the fields. She was stronger now, wasn't she? She could manage.

Another contraction seized her lower back and she cried out.

'Let's get you to bed.'

Nicole shook her head. 'I can't. This sofa will have to do.'

'I'll get towels.'

While her sister was gone Nicole tried to focus on her breathing to help with the pains. But with each contraction it felt as if her insides were being pulled and squeezed beyond endurance. Why hadn't anyone said it would hurt like this?

She kept her eyes shut and counted to ten. She did it again, hoping to count away the pain. She tried to tell herself she could cope without Mark, and of course, she could. But she longed for him to be there in the next room, or at least within calling distance, while their child came into the world. She consoled herself by picturing him holding her hand and stroking her back, could feel him inside her head, talking, encouraging, willing her on. As she imagined being swept up in his arms, something new kicked in, something that made her feel alive, and so full of energy she felt the urge to whoop out loud. She, Nicole Duval, was about to become a mother.

Sylvie came back in. 'You look better. You were awfully pale before.'

'I think it's going to be okay.'

But the pain came back in a wave. Sylvie sat beside her and held her hand.

'Remember to breathe, Nicole.'

Sylvie's presence helped. A few minutes later Nicole was dying for water, but before she could ask, her sister had brought her a glassful.

'You seem to know what I need before I even say it.'

Sylvie smiled.

Nicole wanted to be fearless but for the next few contractions she felt as if she was drowning all over again. She had not foreseen any of this. Her pulse seemed to be going too fast and she was scared.

'Don't fight it,' Sylvie was saying. 'Go with the pain. Let the wave pass.'

It felt like being trapped with no way out and for a few minutes she howled with pain. When she stopped, a short silence fell over them during which Nicole felt strangely distanced from herself, as if she was somewhere on the outside looking in.

'You can do it,' Sylvie said. 'One day this will just be a memory. Keep going.'

Nicole felt the baby's head pressing. 'I need to push.'

'Then push. It's your body telling you.'

Nicole groaned but was relieved Sylvie's earlier agitation had been replaced by sympathy and understanding. She felt her sister was right there with her and, judging by Sylvie's red face, they really did seem to be doing this together. It went on and on. Nicole grew more and more tired with every push, but Sylvie encouraged her to take breaths in between. In one of the quiet moments, Nicole drifted away. She wanted to see the moon, look at the stars, feel the earth beneath her feet. She wanted to sing songs with Lisa, cut silk. Anything. Anything other than this. Then she felt a terrible burning and stinging as if she was being ripped apart.

'Oh my God. It's close. This baby is killing me.'

'I think now's the time to pant.'

Sylvie smiled so calmly it touched Nicole.

Something changed in her again. Though bruised and exhausted, her fear evaporated. Sylvie was right. Childbirth was something she had been born to do, and this was her moment. Hers and her baby's. She was not going to let her child down.

Just a few minutes later the baby was born. With tears in her eyes Sylvie held up the grey, blood-streaked wriggling baby. 'It's a girl, Nicole. A lovely little girl.'

There was a loud screech from the baby and Nicole broke down and wept as exhaustion and relief collided.

Sylvie patted her hand and passed her a handkerchief. 'Come on. You've got a little girl waiting for you here.'

Nicole smiled and wiped her wet cheeks. 'I have, haven't I?'

'You did really well. I'm so proud I could burst. Shall I clean her up?'

'Not yet. I want to feel her against my skin.'

Sylvie wiped the baby down as she lay her against Nicole's chest. With a soaring sense of relief and overwhelming happiness, Nicole gazed at her newborn child. Who could have told her it would feel like this? 'Is she real?' she asked.

Sylvie nodded, seemingly as full of feeling as Nicole was.

The baby had now turned pink, with fair hair, wrinkled hands, tiny nails and downy cheeks. She opened her eyes and Nicole saw they were blue. Bright blue. Nothing could ever match a moment like this and she felt certain the memory would last a lifetime. She looked up at her sister. 'Thank you.'

Sylvie was trying to hold back tears. 'I wouldn't have missed it for the world. Just look at her. I never thought she'd be so beautiful or that you'd be so brave.'

'I couldn't have done it without you.'

'You'd have coped.'

The baby was sucking at air and both sisters were crying now.

Sylvie wiped her eyes and recovered first. 'I'll help put her to the breast.'

The baby continued to suck at air for a bit longer, but eventually latched on.

'She knows what to do,' Nicole said in bemusement.

'And now that we have an addition to our little family,' Sylvie said, 'I'll see if there's a way to get hold of Mark.'

While Sylvie was gone, the room dissolved around Nicole. She stared at the wrinkled red face of her daughter and felt such a surge of emotion it overwhelmed her. She felt worn out, but this tiny dot was her own little baby, and such a toughie, surviving her mother's imprisonment and her father's absence. Nicole kissed the child's perfect cheeks.

A little later she delivered the afterbirth alone.

But how lovely it had been to have Sylvie with her for the baby's birth. It had been a hugely poignant experience; she'd never felt so close to her sister before. She'd wanted to discuss the baby's name with Mark, but she knew he might not be able to come soon.

Sylvie appeared a short while later and asked to hold the baby.

'She's so sweet,' she said and smiled as she gazed at the tiny thing. 'I'm so proud of you both. Have you thought of a name for our little angel?'

'Celeste.'

'What a beautiful name. Celeste Duval. Doesn't that sound wonderful?'

'Did you get hold of Mark?'

'I sent a telegram to the American embassy in Saigon. It's our best way of reaching him. He has to know he's a father, doesn't he?'

★

Over the coming days Nicole concentrated on her baby. When the milk came in, her breasts felt swollen and tender, but it wasn't long before she and Celeste settled into a rhythm. Nicole kissed her nose, her chubby fingers and her warm tummy, and feeling the child's skin against her own she felt something inside her shift. It was a paradox, but now she had so much to lose, she felt stronger, more herself, and was surprised by it. When the baby cried she walked her around the house, and the simple soothing act calmed Nicole too. It was a joy to draw courage and strength from nurturing her child, and cradling her baby delighted her. Her exhaustion passed quickly and before long she felt happy and alert.

So that Celeste could enjoy a little sunlight, a pram Sylvie had borrowed was kept in the conservatory. A few days following the birth, Nicole nestled her under her white coverlet and wheeled the pram through the garden and out of the side gate.

The day was beautiful with a huge blue sky and birds singing in all the trees. White blossom was everywhere and you could easily be forgiven for forgetting it was a time of war. Complete strangers stopped to look at the baby, all of them remarking on her fabulous blue eyes and reddish-coloured hair. Nicole was falling into motherhood as if she had been made for it and, feeling an immense amount of pride, loved to show her daughter off. She still found it hard to believe this beautiful blue-eyed child had sprung from her.

But gradually the state of dreamy contentment came to an end. Severed from the one person who had sustained her, she felt terribly alone. And without Lisa or her father either, their old family home had become too large. In what almost seemed like a moment of inattention, everything had changed. There was still no news of Mark and she began to feel sick inside. If the embassy hadn't been able to get hold of him, it probably meant he had no idea that the baby had already been born. Nicole understood the implications of bringing a child into such an uncertain world and was frightened by the dark days that might lie ahead. She sat on the sofa, closed her eyes and dreamt of leaning her head against Mark's shoulder as he stroked her hair. She pictured him with a wide smile on his face while tenderly cradling the baby. She so wanted her family to be whole and for a moment the image was so clear it felt as if he was really there.

When she opened her eyes she felt unbearably sad that he wasn't and she ached with love for the two people who meant everything to her. In a moment of total stillness she thought about how much she hated the war and the awful helpless knowledge it brought with it. How could it be that the lives of people you loved might be wiped out in an instant? People with warm blood in their veins, people who breathed and laughed and loved. People who did not deserve to die. It seemed impossible to her that she might never see Mark again. The whole world seemed to be standing to attention as the truth of it sank in. She glanced up and saw Sylvie hovering in the doorway watching, her face completely devoid of expression.

36

As spring continued, Nicole played with Celeste in the garden, making the most of the breezes and drier air. She was genuinely happy being with her beautiful daughter, loved waking to Celeste's early smiles and even looked forward to holding her when she was disturbed by shrill night-time cries. Sylvie seemed quieter than before, but spent much of her time pacing up and down, rubbing her hands together and talking to herself. One night Nicole was surprised to hear Sylvie wandering the house and the back door opening and closing. After she had left Celeste finally asleep, she followed Sylvie out to the garden, treading quietly so as not to startle her sister. The garden was alive with night-time scratchings and snappings and, despite the darkness, there was enough moon to light Sylvie's pale nightdress. Nicole blinked rapidly: Sylvie seemed as if she was one of the ghosts who lived out there.

A tune from the past came into her head and she hummed it softly. 'Do you remember it, Sylvie?' she said.

For a moment or two her sister joined in but then stopped suddenly.

'What's wrong?' Nicole said in a gentle voice.

Without a glance in Nicole's direction, her sister said nothing.

'Sylvie?'

Sylvie twisted round but had an odd look in her eyes. 'Nothing's wrong.'

'But, Sylvie, you're barefoot and outside in the garden at three in the morning. Aren't you cold?'

Sylvie glanced at her feet. 'Oh. I didn't realize.'

Then she carried on standing silently in an attitude of vacancy and Nicole couldn't prevent the thought that her sister seemed tired of life.

She put her arm round Sylvie. 'Come on. Hot chocolate for you.'

Sylvie gave her a thin smile but Nicole saw tears in her eyes. She didn't want to leap to conclusions but feared something inside her sister was wearing very thin.

The next day, neither of them mentioned their night-time encounter – it was as if it had not happened.

A few days later she and Sylvie were in the garden again. Nicole still hadn't heard from Mark and his absence was becoming a source of real anguish. While she longed for news, any news, she also lived in terror of receiving a telegram saying he was dead or missing.

Despite Sylvie's previous protestations of confidence in their business, the larger of their two silk shops in the ancient quarter had been up for sale for several weeks and the lack of a purchaser had been a concern. Now Sylvie told Nicole she'd managed to sell to a Vietnamese woman hoping to turn it into a restaurant. Sylvie thought the woman a fool.

'If we don't sell everything else soon we'll never find buyers,' Nicole said. 'And we'll need the money. Maybe we could set up a silk import business in France? We could do it together. All the top designers want to source quality silk.'

Sylvie was walking up and down on the lawn. 'Don't be defeatist. No need to think of France. We will still win the war. You'll see.'

Sylvie had replied a little uneasily, Nicole thought, and her insistence that everything would be fine lacked conviction. Although there were rumours that a showdown was planned at Dien Bien Phu, her sister more or less maintained the usual French attitude of entitlement. The truth was nobody knew how things were going. Misinformation and rumour were rife; who was winning and who was losing depended on which paper you were reading.

'So our store on Rue Paul Bert is gone and now the large silk shop too. There's only my little one left and our two houses,' Nicole said.

'We still have the export business. We could run it together in Huế once Celeste is a bit older.'

'I'd love to.' She paused. 'Though, to be honest, I'm not sure if we'll stay in Vietnam.'

'You and Celeste?'

'Mark and me, I meant, though Celeste too, of course.'

Sylvie's face had fallen a little. 'Oh.'

'And if the Vietminh win, they'll ban anyone from owning anything. The state will take it all.'

'Over my dead body.'

'That's exactly what I'm worried about.'

'Shall we go in?' Sylvie said, ignoring her comment and seeming to want to change the subject.

'Shouldn't we leave now while we still can?'

'And leave everything for the Vietminh to take? I don't want to go, and anyway, things will still go our way. But if it's what you want, you go.'

'Sylvie, you know I can't leave you here alone. I'll wait a bit longer. Maybe Mark will be in touch soon.'

Sylvie just grunted and they went indoors together.

A couple of weeks later Nicole's milk was drying up and she sat at the kitchen table in tears, with Celeste on her lap, red-faced and screaming. Sylvie was staring at the window and muttering as if in another world.

'I haven't got enough to feed her,' Nicole wailed as Celeste's screams reached fever pitch.

Sylvie turned away from the window. 'Sorry?'

'I haven't got enough milk. Look at her.'

Sylvie seemed to wake up. 'I can fix that. No need to worry. I'll do the bottles. I've already got three and the milk powder too. No, this is fine. Great, in fact. Great.'

'Why have you already got them?'

'Always be prepared. That's my motto.'

Nicole stood up while cradling the baby with her free arm, hoping the gentle rocking movement might calm her daughter. Maybe it was the worry over Mark that had dried up the milk. As she was thinking this, Sylvie was clattering about boiling water and mixing powder in a jug.

'Here we are,' she said at last. 'All done. Now let me.' She held out her arms for Celeste, then sat at the table holding the baby and began to bottle feed her.

'If she's going to be bottle fed, I can eat garlic again.' Nicole added some chopped garlic to the stew, then she picked up the newspaper but couldn't concentrate on it. A moment later she flung it down and came over to plant a kiss on the baby's cheek.

'I'll feed her,' she said and reached out for her baby.

'No, she's fine. Look, her eyelashes are fluttering.' Sylvie got to her feet and danced around the kitchen, rocking Celeste as she did so. 'She's fast asleep. Go and have a lie-down. I'll look after her.'

'Very well. If you're sure?'

'I love this little girl,' Sylvie said, and she kissed the baby on the nose. 'You are my little beauty, aren't you?'

'Is the phone line fixed?' Nicole asked.

Sylvie stopped dancing. 'It was, but now there's something wrong again. There's such a lot of sabotage just now.'

Nicole sighed. It was true. The electricity frequently failed too and they never knew why. It was a dark, unsettled time and horrible to feel so cut off. The post office had been bombed, so the lack of mail was hardly surprising. She smiled as she watched her sister kiss Celeste's fat little cheeks.

'Shoo!' Sylvie said. 'Go and lie down.'

'I'm going.'

'I'll give her a bath too.'

Nicole tried to bury her fears about Mark by continuing to mentally plan the silk business she would develop if they lived abroad. When Celeste was a little older she would begin again. If Vietnam was no longer possible it might be something she could do in either France or America. She knew about silk and, after all, there were other silk-producing countries. When she thought about Sylvie she hoped her sister might one day have a child of her own. Looking after the baby seemed to be good for her. When she wasn't with Celeste, she seemed jumpy and distracted, and didn't always hear what was said, and that worried Nicole.

She still hadn't told Sylvie the truth about the day of her own birth and felt rather cowardly for avoiding it. She couldn't put it off for much longer, but it was such a sensitive subject. She worried that if it went badly, it might shatter the hard-won peace between them, and that wouldn't be good for Celeste. A resentment so deep couldn't be handled casually.

A day or so later they were both in the little dining room reading while Celeste was sleeping. Nicole had decided that now was the moment to tell Sylvie the truth, but kept losing her nerve. Playing for time, she glanced up at the ceiling. 'God, how I hate those flying cherubs,' she said.

'I rather like them,' Sylvie said. Seeming to spot something in Nicole's face, she tried to be encouraging. 'We mustn't give up, Nicole. We must keep believing.'

'If you think believing will be enough to win, I reckon the Vietminh believe a lot harder than we do.'

'Was that why you ran away to join them? You thought they were stronger?'

'It was less of a running to join them than a running away –'

Sylvie interrupted. 'From us? You were running away from us? I'm sorry, if I'd known the house arrest was going to have that result . . . I only wanted to protect you.'

'Control me, more like! But it wasn't that – at least, not only that.'

'Then?'

'Lisa told me the truth about what happened to our mother the day I was born.'

Sylvie frowned. 'But we already knew.'

Nicole got up and walked across to look out of the window at the thatched pavilion. The wicker chairs looked faded and there was no longer a glass table beside the lily pond. In fact, the pond looked thoroughly neglected.

She twisted back to look at Sylvie. 'It was a lie. Our mother didn't die because of me. Not directly. She died because of our father.'

Sylvie gave her a puzzled look but didn't speak.

'Our mother found him in bed with one of the maids that day. She'd come home early from some trip.'

'Stop!' Sylvie covered her ears with her hands. 'Why would you say that? I don't want to hear it.'

'It's the truth. And later that day our "perfect" father refused to believe she was in labour. He heard her crying and screaming and forbade anyone to go to her. He said she was seeking attention. In the end Lisa disobeyed him and found mother bleeding to death. She called the doctor, but it was too late.'

Sylvie was white as a sheet and absolutely motionless.

'The shock of seeing him in her bed with another woman caused the labour to start prematurely.'

Eyes downcast, Sylvie was still not moving.

'Say something, Sylvie.'

At last, Sylvie looked up. 'He wouldn't. It's a terrible, wicked lie.'

Nicole shook her head but, seeing her sister so stricken, began to wish she hadn't brought the subject up at all. Sylvie was knitting her fingers together, twisting her hands repeatedly, and Nicole felt sorry for her.

They avoided each other for the rest of the day, but in the evening Sylvie came into Nicole's room with red eyes and a pinched look on her face.

'Now you have Mark, you don't need me, do you?'

'Of course I still need you.'

Sylvie stood frozen to the spot then gave Nicole a strange smile. 'It's not true, is it, what you said about Father?'

Nicole sighed. 'It is true.'

With an air of defeat, Sylvie sat down. 'You are never to speak of it again. Is that understood?'

Then she folded her arms on Nicole's dressing table and, resting her face on her arms, began to sob.

As the days passed by Nicole was becoming more and more certain something had happened to Mark. The thought that he might already be dead caused a knot in her stomach and sent her rushing to the bathroom to be sick. By April, the general situation looked as if it was changing and not for the better. With tension in Hanoi so high, Nicole felt sure they must prepare to evacuate even if, in the end, it wasn't necessary. She was halfway through preparing a bag for herself and Celeste, in case they needed to leave quickly, and had tried to persuade Sylvie to do the same. The responsibility was daunting but she'd do anything to provide her child with a safe and happy life. If it had to be in France without Mark, or Sylvie, then so be it.

One afternoon she took Celeste into her father's study and thought about him. Even after all this time the air still seemed to retain the smell of him, though the trace of alcohol and cigars was stale. She sat down in his leather chair and longed to be able to go back and change things. With a sigh of regret over her past relationship with her father, she got to her feet. Just then she heard the rattle of keys in the front door and went into the hall, where she saw Sylvie looking white-faced. Nicole stopped in her tracks. Sylvie sat down on the hall chair with her head in her hands. Then she looked up and, twisting her hands in her lap, told Nicole she'd heard some bad news. The French-held garrison in the valley of Dien Bien Phu was large and strategically important; Sylvie, like everyone else, had believed the Vietminh could never take it, but she'd just heard that the French army had made tactical errors.

Sylvie got to her feet and paced back and forth in the green light of the hall. 'Oh God. Oh God. What is going to happen to us?'

'What kind of errors?'

'Terrible errors.'

'Tell me.'

'Calamitous losses and the chance of a Vietminh win growing imminent. Assistance from China is boosting the Vietminh war effort; the only hope will be if America send further aid.'

'Who told you?' Nicole asked.

'André left a message at the office.'

Nicole sucked in her cheeks as she considered this. 'What does he think we should do?'

'He didn't say. But it looks like the Vietminh fighting spirit means they may succeed where we have failed.'

'It's exactly what I've always said. So does that mean it's actually over?'

Sylvie sighed before she replied and when she spoke her voice seemed brittle. 'Not yet. We may be losing through over-estimating our strength and underestimating theirs. As I said, with more American aid it could change for the better. We can still win.'

'You still believe that?' Nicole hugged her daughter to her.

'Yes. Yes. Of course. But I wish Papa was here. He'd know what to do.'

'Maybe.'

Sylvie's eyes hardened. 'I want to go back. Just to go back. Why is that so hard?'

'Back where?' Nicole asked, realizing that her sister was lost somewhere in her own interior reality. 'You're not making any sense.'

'Before all this. Before.' Sylvie stood wringing her hands and looking half mad with fear. Then she seemed to snap out of it. 'But we've got to do the best we can for Celeste, haven't we? With sandy hair and blue eyes, she'll never survive if the Vietminh win.'

'I need to decide the best way to get her out in a hurry. Saigon maybe? What do you think?'

As Sylvie was about to reply, the lights went out.

Nicole spun round. What did it mean? Were the Vietminh in the city? Had they blown up the electricity generators?

'Here, take Celeste, I'll go down to the basement.'

She imagined the entire city in darkness and men and women in black sneaking through the streets. The houses either side of them were empty now and there would be nobody they could trust. She held on to her nerve and looked for the torch they always kept in the hall. When she reached the electricity cupboard, she found a fuse had blown. That was all. She sorted it out and, as the light came on again, she glanced at the old brick wall where the phone cable should enter the house. Something didn't look right. She pulled away a board that had been resting against the wall and concealing the cable. The trouble with the phone didn't seem to be at the exchange at all. Nicole made a mental note to get hold of an engineer in the morning. The line looked as if it had been accidentally disconnected.

37

For some time after Sylvie's prediction of impending doom, nothing seemed to come of it. There was a brief lull and all the talk in the papers insisted morale had improved. Despite fierce fighting and heavy casualties, French troops could still gain an advantage, they said. The headlines continually demanded aid, and more American intervention, which had eventually come.

But it was hard to get hold of accurate information and the atmosphere in the streets had grown tense. Nicole longed for the oblivion of sleep but couldn't drop off for worrying about Mark. She tried talking herself out of it but as each night went on too long she felt that her heart might break. When she looked in the mirror in the mornings the purple shadows under her eyes revealed the strain. Despite attacks and counter-attacks, French successes were few. Bad news followed bad news and panic hit Hanoi. Nicole hated waiting, hated the terrible feeling of not being able to do anything and having no control over what lay ahead. And during one impossible night she decided to wait no longer. Whatever Sylvie said, it was long past the time to go.

She decided to look through her father's filing cabinet for anything they might need to take with them. At first there seemed to be nothing useful, but then she noticed an unmarked file. She opened the file and found two envelopes addressed to her, plus three of her own letters to Mark that hadn't been posted. Though reeling from the physical pain in her chest, she managed to hold herself together. Both envelopes addressed to her had already been opened. She withdrew a wad of dollars and a single sheet of white paper, dated 6 February, just after Celeste was born. In this letter Mark told her how overjoyed he was about the baby and how much he longed to see them both. She could hear his voice. Actually hear it. Almost overcome with emotion, she read on – he told her he wanted her to keep safe, and he suggested it was time to sell up. She drew out the second letter, dated 5 March. Here he told her he couldn't wait until they could be together again but didn't understand why she'd stopped writing. He hoped it was because she'd already left for France, but insisted that if she hadn't already left, she should wait no longer and go ahead without him immediately. There was no point delaying. He repeated that Lisa was living in Narbonne and had scribbled the address again.

Nicole felt as if she might pass out with the relief of knowing he was still alive – or had been, at least, in March.

He went on to say that as he was constantly on the move he was unable to leave an address but that she was to let him know where she was via the embassy. At the end he told her that he loved her and begged her not to forget that. She held the letter to her heart: as if she could ever forget.

But it could only be the briefest moment of joy because an instant later the truth hit her. When the intensity ebbed away she was left with a feeling of shock and a growing knot of anger in her throat. How could her sister have been so cruel? She slammed her palm against her forehead and tried to think clearly. After a moment she went up to her room, hid her passport and Celeste's birth certificate under a loose floorboard, along with the money, and covered the board with her rug.

Determined to confront Sylvie over the letters the moment her sister came home, she paced back and forth. She had so wanted the reconciliation with Sylvie to be real, especially after her sister had been so wonderful at the birth, but was furious with herself for having believed things would ever change. Now she must save herself and her daughter. Nothing else mattered.

She tried to find out Mark's whereabouts through the old CIA office, calling on the few clerical officers who remained on the second floor of the Métropole. Nobody could tell her anything and they hadn't any news of Mark. She gathered what she could to sell at an impromptu market that had sprung up in the heart of town; the more money she could raise, the better chance they'd have. Everyone was selling anything portable so she took the black mother-of-pearl tray they used to keep in the hall. It sold for peanuts. After that she success-fully sold their collection of blue and white fifteenth-century Vietnamese pottery. Then she piled silk lampshades, jewellery and whatever else she could lay her hands on into the pram with Celeste before wheeling it to the market. She did it with-out nostalgia; only at a time of peace could there be the luxury of time and space for looking back.

When Sylvie returned that evening she barged into Nicole's room looking as if she'd run up all the stairs from the kitchen in the basement.

'What have you been doing? Everything's gone.'

Nicole was lying on her bed trying to read, the baby asleep at her side. She stared at Sylvie, closed the book and sat up. 'Don't wake Celeste.'

Sylvie frowned and seemed to find it difficult to keep still.

'Why are you so jumpy? Can't you see it's what the whole of Hanoi is doing? I told you we should liquidate everything while we had a chance. Mark said it too.' Nicole rose to her feet, but carefully, so as not to disturb Celeste, then drew herself up to her full height. 'Why did you hide his letters, and mine to him?'

Sylvie took a step back but didn't speak. To her astonishment,

Nicole noticed her sister's trembling lips and eyes so wide they looked as if they belonged to somebody else.

'Sylvie?'

Her sister looked as if she was about to launch an attack, but instead staggered back and seemed to deflate. She sat on the edge of the bed, looking pale and drawn.

Nicole tried to control her temper but what Sylvie had done was unforgiveable. 'For heaven's sake, Sylvie. You know how much I was longing to hear from Mark. How terrified I was that he was already dead. How could you do that to me?'

When Sylvie didn't speak, Nicole wanted to shake her. Instead she folded her arms and waited.

'I felt left out,' Sylvie whispered.

'*You* felt left out? I've felt left out all my life. You and Papa made sure of that.'

Sylvie looked up. 'I know . . .'

The moment went on as they stared at each other. Closeted together with Sylvie like this, Nicole became more aware of her sister's unravelling.

'I shouldn't have done it. I shouldn't have done any of it.'

Sylvie began to weep and beneath her sobs the semi-coherent words struck at Nicole's heart. What else had her sister done?

Sylvie wiped her eyes with her sleeve. 'After Mark came to see you, I felt awful. You didn't need me. Nobody needed me.'

'You weren't left out. You must know how good you've been with Celeste.'

'I felt I'd lost everything. Our business, our old life . . . Mark.' She paused, her eyes filled again, then she bent over, holding her head in her hands.

'You wanted to destroy my relationship with Mark?' Nicole said with a break in her voice.

Sylvie shook her head as she looked up. 'I don't know what's happening. Sometimes I feel like I'm disintegrating. As if little bits of me are breaking off. I was frightened I was going to lose you and Celeste too. You said it yourself, you and Mark might have gone to live in America.'

As the tears rolled down Sylvie's pinched cheeks, she looked vulnerable and so touched by sadness that Nicole couldn't hold on to her anger.

'Oh, Sylvie. Why did you do it?'

Sylvie shook her head from side to side.

'It didn't have to be like this. You wouldn't have lost me or Celeste. She adores you. We would always have been in your life.'

'Do you think so?'

'Of course. You're her only aunt. You were there when she was born. That means something. Think how much she chuckles when she's with you. But now, Sylvie, how can I ever put my faith in you? You must see what you've done.'

Sylvie gave a small nod. 'I feel so alone. I always have. And the world is so dangerous now. I feel it coming in on me and I'm frightened.'

'But you're not alone. You were never alone. Now come on, dry your eyes. We have to plan what to do.'

'I'm sorry, Nicole. I sometimes feel as if I don't know what I'm doing. Like there's someone else inside me.'

Nicole held out her arms. Sylvie stood up and, as they hugged each other, Nicole felt her sister's heart thumping and her chest heaving with sobs. It seemed as if Sylvie's heart might break. Struck by her sister's remorse, Nicole wanted to believe her and it was clear Sylvie was struggling, but the fragile trust between them had been damaged. She wanted to leave right away with Celeste and wait for Mark in France, but how could she abandon Sylvie in this state? They'd have to leave together. And, even if she wanted to, how could she choose between her sister and the man she loved?

*

While Sylvie left to try to get them a passage out of Hanoi, Nicole went to the Cercle Sportif, the sporting and social club that had always been such a pillar of their French colonial society. There were often soldiers at the pool and it was the best place to pick up the real news while they were off guard. With the baby in the pram, she walked there. The temperature was rising and soon Hanoi would be sweltering. Consumed by anxiety, Nicole glanced up to check the sky; there was always a chance of rain or drizzle at any time. A few heavy black clouds lurked in the north, but with a bit of luck they wouldn't reach the city. Far worse than the clouds was the increase in the number of planes circling overhead.

Nicole asked the attendant to keep an eye on the baby while she swam a couple of lengths. Afterwards she lay in the weak sunshine to dry off, watching the army officers whoop and splash as if there was nothing to worry about. When they got out one of them looked at her with narrowed eyes and offered her a cigarette.

'Thanks, but no.'

'Your baby? Or are you a nanny?'

'My baby.'

'You don't wear a wedding ring.'

'I don't,' she said, feeling defensive.

'Would you like to come to my place for a drink?' he said with an eager look. 'You can bring the baby.'

She looked at him: one of those empty, facile men who think they're doing you a favour with their interest. 'No thanks.'

'Well, do you mind if I sit with you?'

She shrugged. 'I'll be heading home in a few minutes.'

He pulled up a chair and threw himself into it. 'Lord, but I'm tired!'

She sized him up. 'How's it going at Dien Bien Phu?'

He drew on his cigarette and blew the smoke out slowly. 'I've come back for treatment. Had an infected injury.'

'So what's it like out there?'

'The enemy have thousands of peasants who drag supplies and machinery through impossible mountain ranges. Things aren't going our way. I'd say it's only a matter of days.'

'We're going to lose the war?' she asked.

He sighed deeply and reached out a hand to touch her arm. Nicole flinched.

'Good God, girl!' he said, and touched her ringless finger. 'You surely can't be fussy. I could get you a flight to Saigon for your trouble.'

'I'd rather pay.'

He laughed. 'You mean it, don't you?'

She nodded. 'I'll need two.'

'Well, I admire your spirit, but the price is high.' He told her how much and scribbled his name on a scrap of paper. 'If you decide you want them, call at the Métropole early tomorrow morning with the money. I'll have tickets for you on the midday flight.'

'Thank you.'

Though she had expected it, she felt sick at the knowledge that the French were now facing certain defeat. She believed the Vietnamese had the right to govern themselves, but would have preferred a graceful acceptance by the French and a dignified retreat, followed by a peaceful handover of power, like the British in India. She knew things hadn't gone well during the partition and many blamed the British, but why such a long drawn-out battle here? And a war that had been so hungry for rape and murder. Or were all wars like that? Once civilizing restraints were no longer in place, anything seemed to be fair game, no matter how cruel.

As she imagined how it would feel to leave the country she

loved, she thought of her journey after escaping the camp – how she'd travelled down through the tiny hamlets in the north on her own, how in the open she'd been forced to cross narrow bridges over mountain streams and how she'd scratched around for food and shelter in abandoned villages. Though she had been frightened most of the time, she'd seen the rural beauty of the north in a way she could never have imagined, and the trees, so many trees in a million shades of green.

She thought of Huế. It was still her favourite place in the world. She so wanted to give her daughter the kind of experiences she'd had when they'd lived by the river. Apart from one, of course. She thought of the way she used to watch the water and sky turn purple at night and smiled at the memory of spying on the robed monks chanting at their tiered octagonal temple overlooking the Perfume River. They never noticed her there – or if they did, they never let on.

The officer by her side stood up. 'Anyway, I have to leave. Nice to meet you.'

Nicole prepared to leave too, and a little later she wheeled the pram round the lake, sniffing air smelling of water and flowers. She glanced around at the broad French streets and tree-lined boulevards and felt shaken by how much she had grown to love Hanoi's gentle serenity. She went to the bank and found that Sylvie had already closed her shop's business account.

It was time to feed Celeste, who was now wide awake and beginning to cry. Nicole put a palm to the baby's forehead. She felt too hot. Once they reached the house the clouds had blackened and the beginning of a storm was rolling over, setting off the hundreds of city dogs, whose howls would continue to echo long after the storm was spent. At home, the house was silent. Nicole prised up the floorboard, gathered together the cash, her passport and Celeste's birth certificate, and added them to her purse with the money from selling off the family belongings. She stuffed some nappies and some of Celeste's clothes into an already half-packed carpet bag and left it in the hall while she waited for Sylvie.

Luckily the storm passed quickly. At teatime, after Celeste had been changed – the little girl didn't seem to be hungry – Nicole wheeled the pram out through the conservatory to a sheltered spot under an old apple tree, hoping the fresh early-evening air might help her daughter feel better. The sun had come out and it was a little bit brighter.

She aired Celeste's comfort blanket. When they left, her baby would need it.

The garden, no longer cared for, was tangled and over-grown, apart from the area around the washing line. After she'd pinned up the blanket she checked the back of the baby's neck. Still a bit too hot and, though her daughter was asleep, it was a restless kind of sleep. She touched the child's burning cheeks and took off the coverlet. She'd take her inside and cool her down with a wet flannel in a moment. First she needed to see if anything remained in Lisa's old vegetable patch. Even if they flew to Saigon the next morning, they still needed to eat tonight. Food was scarce and they'd had to make do with end-less lentils, the odd scrawny chicken and what root vegetables they could still dig up. She knelt in the damp earth and con-centrated on poking about with a trowel, only realizing someone had entered the garden when she heard a cough.

Still kneeling, she twisted round and saw movement on the had other side of the garden where she'd left the pram. Sylvie had picked up Celeste and was gently rocking her with one arm. Her sister's friend, André, stood at her side. What was he doing here?

'She's not very well. I've only just got her off to sleep,' Nicole said as she got to her feet. 'Can you put her back down?'

Sylvie took a step forward. 'Do you want to go inside?'

Nicole was taken aback by the solemn look on her face and spotted a small suitcase on the ground between her sister's feet.

'There's no easy way to say this,' Sylvie said, and Nicole noticed her eyes looked red.

'What?'

Visibly, Sylvie drew in her breath and held it for a moment before she spoke. She glanced at André. 'Something terrible has happened. Our army is now in retreat. The French garrison at Dien Bien Phu is about to fall.'

'I heard that at the pool. Do you know any more?'

Sylvie shook her head. 'Only that Giap, the Vietminh general in command, has surrounded French positions using a huge network of trenches and tunnels.'

Nicole stared at her sister.

Sylvie gulped. 'They are overpowering us, Nicole. I didn't think it would happen so suddenly. I thought we had time. But they have as good as won.'

'I'll get our things.'

Still rocking the baby, Sylvie seemed less agitated than she had been for days. 'No. You don't understand. I've only secured one ticket. I have a taxi taking me to an American armoured vehicle, travelling in a convoy tonight to the port at Haiphong. From there I've arranged a berth on a naval liner, hopefully leaving in two or three days for France.'

'One ticket?'

'It's only me who is leaving. It was virtually impossible to get even one ticket for the convoy. They're taking out officials and army only.'

'I don't understand. You mean you're leaving me and the baby behind?'

Sylvie shook her head. 'I know it sounds crazy but I thought

Celeste could come with me. I don't need an extra ticket for a baby.'

Nicole's brow creased. 'You're serious?'

Sylvie nodded. 'Think about it. Look at her colouring. Bright blue eyes and sandy hair – you know she'll never survive once the Vietminh arrive.'

Nicole gazed at her baby. Her sister couldn't believe this was the right thing to do. 'But I've arranged flights to Saigon.'

'Who with?'

'A soldier I met at the pool.'

Sylvie snorted. 'And you believed him? Nicole, you must decide now. I have to go. The taxi won't wait.'

'I don't know. I don't know.' Nicole felt her heart pumping. 'Celeste isn't well, Sylvie. She has a fever.'

'This is the best way for her. You look Vietnamese. You'll get by. She would not. You said so yourself.'

'But I didn't mean –'

As Sylvie tightened the blanket around Celeste, her hand was shaking.

'You said you wanted a way to get Celeste out of here. That's what I'm offering to do. But there's no time to lose. Please, Nicole. Let her go. It's now or not at all.'

As Nicole stole a look at André, he picked up Sylvie's case. She felt her chest constrict. 'You can't separate us like this. You're my sister.'

'Did you think of that when you lied about my letter and slept with Mark?'

Nicole stared in disbelief. 'You want to take my child because of that?'

'Truly, no. I really could only get one ticket.'

'Come on, Sylvie. Why don't we all go in our car? It would be better, wouldn't it?'

Sylvie shook her head slowly. The feather in her hat, perched on the side of her head, shivered in the breeze. 'No petrol. None for private vehicles anyway. This is the only way.'

Nicole thought quickly. Maybe Sylvie was right. She had no way of getting out of here except for the flight to Saigon. What if the officer had been lying about the tickets? She'd be completely stranded and then what would happen to Celeste?

Sylvie turned to André. 'Give her the envelope.'

He passed it to Nicole.

'The house in Huéis in your name now. You could go there, lie low for a while and then follow on when things calm down. I'll be at our father's flat in Paris. I've made this house over to the army, though much good it will do them. I wanted to sell up, but there wasn't time. Now it's worth nothing.'

André stepped forward. 'Best let the baby go, mademoiselle. The Vietminh would never allow her to live. You wouldn't be safe either if she was with you.'

Nicole was in tears now. She had to decide whether to trust some unknown officer to get her an aeroplane ticket or trust her sister with her daughter. Both were a risk, but she had to put her daughter's safety first. Sylvie was going now. Who knew what might be happening by the morning. There might not even be any flights left to Saigon. She made a snap decision and came across to smother her daughter with kisses. She could hardly bear to do it but Sylvie was right.

'I promise I will take care of her.'

Nicole looked into her sister's eyes and nodded, then stroked her daughter's cheek, feeling the softness of her skin. After a moment she managed to speak. 'There's a bag of her things in the hall.'

Sylvie turned on her heels, followed by André.

Nicole stared after her, feeling numb. 'Remember she's not well,' she called out with a break in her voice. She listened to the spaces between her own words. Was she insane to let this happen? The question went right through her but was left unanswered.

She glanced around the garden. How could it look so normal when it was possible she might never see her daughter again? We should have gone before, she thought. She'd known it was foolish to wait yet she'd stayed for Sylvie's sake. 'We should have gone before,' she whispered, 'we should have gone.' Mark had told her to go but she had listened to Sylvie instead. Her throat was completely choked and she couldn't swallow, but a cool breeze on her skin and another rumble of thunder galvanized her into action.

She straightened up and ran after them.

When she reached the hall she saw they'd left the front door open. She took in the scene instantly and flew out of the house, just in time to see André closing the taxi door on Sylvie and getting in himself. Sylvie and the baby were sitting in the back and Nicole could clearly see her little girl's bright blue eyes fill with tears.

As the car pulled away, she followed blindly, stumbling past anyone who got in her way. By the time they were too far off, she was forced to stop and gasp for breath. Her sister had been acting oddly for weeks, and at times had seemed almost unbalanced. Would she be able to look after Celeste properly? People were staring as Nicole gulped and spluttered. Everything in the street became blurred; people, cars, rickshaws folded into one heaving mass. Then, as night fell suddenly in the way it did, she sat on the ground and howled.

38

For a few minutes after she'd stopped crying, Nicole's chest was so constricted she couldn't breathe. Didn't believe she'd ever breathe again. She clutched herself and rocked in silence where she sat on the pavement. Nobody stopped. She got to her feet and looked at the street full of people without seeing any of them. Eventually she managed to make it back home where, leaning against their front door, she ached with the need to hold Celeste's warm little body in her arms. She gazed up at the dark clouds staining the sky in patches of purple then glanced across the street where she caught sight of a couple walking rapidly past on the opposite side. They both carried cases and, from the way the man was lagging behind and the harsh way the woman spoke to him, Nicole suspected the woman would have been running, had she been on her own. Nicole took a step towards them. What if she threw herself at their feet and begged them to help her find the convoy? Then she remembered Sylvie hadn't mentioned where in Hanoi the convoy was leaving from. She held her throat. There was no air.

After a moment she felt for the door handle and let herself back into the house. She gazed at the four walls of the hall, at the glass cupola, at the floor, and finally at the phone, now reconnected and sitting on the hall table next to the drawing-room door. She wiped her face and forced herself to think rationally. She rang the police. They told her they had more important issues to deal with, like looting on the streets and losing the war.

'But my daughter's been taken to Haiphong,' she pleaded.

'By your sister, you said.'

'Yes. But I need to go too.'

'And she went with your permission?'

'Well, yes. But my daughter isn't well.'

'Then it's a family matter.'

'Can't you help me get to Haiphong? At least tell me where the convoy is leaving from.'

'We don't give out that information.'

She slammed the phone down, then sat on the stairs with her head in her hands while every cell of her body screamed with the loss. Who could help her follow them to Haiphong at night? There had to be someone. She stood and walked back and forth, clinging to the hope Sylvie might change her mind and return.

In the silence she heard the squeak of a rusty bicycle chain, some mother calling to her child and a siren in the distance. The prolonged hooting of an owl brought her back with a jolt. Other people were on the move so why wasn't she? She switched on the radio and listened to the news. It was true. The French had as good as lost the war. They still held Hanoi and Haiphong and the road between the two cities, but it wouldn't be long before the Vietminh would be scouring the streets. The news was followed by a recording of the Marseillaise. She remembered the times she had heard it in Huế when she was a child and then, thinking of Huế, recalled how the silvery sky used to hang so low over the icy-blue river you felt you could touch it. During a very long night her memories went on and on, but there were gaps too, whole stretches of time she couldn't remember at all. She bit the skin round her nails until it bled, and as the light from the cupola signalled the change, she watched the first crack of dawn appear.

With daylight, she felt more convinced that there must be a

way to get to Haiphong. There was no point thinking of flying to Saigon now, and she was glad she hadn't paid for the tickets. She'd use the money she'd raised to follow Sylvie. She'd take the car. There had to be somebody with petrol to sell. The railway would be out of the question, even if there were trains running. Everyone knew the line would be mined.

When it was light enough to see, she went into the garden and found the envelope Sylvie had given her on the grass, now a little damp with dew. She sat down on the grass feeling hot and a little bit sick, wiped her hand across her forehead and pushed the damp hair from her eyes. She ripped open the envelope and saw it was true. She owned the house in Huế, though what use would that be without her baby?

As the tears began to spill again, her darkest fears surfaced and something collapsed inside her. Mark might be dead and now her little girl was gone too. She missed them both so much the pain was physical, but now she blamed herself for not thinking it through properly. She had been so surprised and shocked by the suddenness of what had happened that she hadn't truly considered Sylvie's shaky mental state, but now she couldn't silence the whispers in her head. Her sister was ill.

39

Trapped in indecision, Nicole watched as the sun inched across the sky. If only Mark were there. But his last letter had been dated March and now it was May. Surely if he was alive he would have written again? She was certain of it. She clung to the hope that maybe he had and Sylvie had hidden that letter too. She gazed at the herbs and flowers grown wild in the garden and listened to the birds as they flew in and out of the trees. She went indoors and picked up a knitted matinee jacket discarded on the floor, held it to her nose and smelt the sweet scent of her baby. Every moment she'd spent with Celeste catapulted into sharp relief.

When an idea finally came to her she dug out her old Vietnamese clothes and, feeling sticky, struggled into them. She took a taxi – quicker than a *cyclo* – and felt even hotter sitting in the back of the stuffy cab. She wiped her forehead with her skirt, then wound the window down and the smell of dust and summer drifted in. Sylvie had been acting strangely lately and she couldn't picture what might be in her sister's mind. What if Sylvie had been lying? What if she had no intention of going to their father's flat?

When the taxi dropped her close to the silk shop, she paid and ran over to unlock the door. She felt fragile and, needing to steady herself, held on to the door frame for support. A drink of water. That would help. She hadn't eaten either. Not that she felt like it.

O-Lan must have been gazing out of her window, because she came out straight away.

'I heard you'd had the baby. Is everything all right? I haven't seen you for months . . .' She paused and held out a hand. 'You look terrible.'

Nicole shivered. 'I just need water.'

'Coffee. I'll make you some.'

'I have to get to Haiphong.' Nicole's teeth began to chatter. She heard them clicking in her head, as if they belonged in someone else's mouth.

'You can't go in that state.'

'I'll be all right.' Nicole's eyes watered but with no time for tears she brushed them away. 'I let her take my baby, O-Lan. But Celeste's not well and neither is my sister. I have to go after them.'

O-Lan looked at her strangely. 'Have you not heard the news? Dien Bien Phu has fallen. The French are retreating. There are thousands dead and thousands wounded too. They'll be trying to bring back the walking wounded so the roads will be chaos. Easier to get to Saigon.'

'No. Sylvie went to Haiphong. She has a berth on a liner leaving for France. I have some money but I need more if I'm going to follow her.'

'The US are evacuating French and Americans for free, I heard. At least to Saigon. But first you need rest.'

Nicole shook her head. 'I wouldn't ask if I wasn't desperate but it's the only way I can think of to get to Haiphong. Could I take your cousin's motorbike?'

O-Lan smiled. 'It still has petrol. If it's the only way, then you must take it.'

'You're sure? You may never get it back. I'll send the money for it when I can.'

O-Lan shook her head. 'It doesn't matter.'

'I'm sorry I didn't bring Celeste to see you. I was scared Trần might be here.' Nicole closed her eyes for a moment and felt her head spin. She couldn't be ill again now.

O-Lan felt her forehead and the back of her neck. 'You're burning up. You're coming to my house.'

Nicole leant against O-Lan as she helped her inside.

'What about your mother? Won't she mind?'

'She died, Nicole.'

Nicole stepped away and gazed at her friend. 'I'm so sorry.'

O-Lan shrugged. 'She's with the ancestors now. But if he comes, Trần will look for you at your shop or here. As soon as you can, you must leave.'

Nicole bent over slightly and put a palm on the wall to support herself. Her head felt so heavy that everything went out of focus and her legs turned to jelly. 'I'm so sorry –'

Over the next few hours the fever worsened. O-Lan said it was an illness that had been going round and, though horrible while it lasted, it was usually short-lived. As it raged, the hollow feeling inside Nicole derailed her. Her thoughts revolved around her child, but she had to accept she wasn't in any shape to ride a motorbike.

All day she felt ice-cold, and that night she started to be sick. As O-Lan brought her a bowl and held her head, Nicole worried that Celeste was suffering from the same sickness. Sylvie wouldn't hurt the child, but her daughter was so small and so vulnerable. Would her sister know what to do? The thought of her baby dying without her mother left Nicole shaking uncontrollably and, as the hours passed, she felt she was shrivelling inside.

'I'll get her a blanket,' she heard O-Lan say as she turned to somebody outside the room. 'She's still shivering, though her temperature is high. Can you make her a warm drink, please.'

Nicole heard a man speak but didn't see who it was. She mourned the loss of her daughter but an absence of feeling was what she craved now. She couldn't cope with anything more. On hearing vague noises coming up from the street, she sensed something abnormal was going on, but felt too tired to ask what.

By the next morning she had emerged from the depths of the fever; though still feeling insubstantial, she lay awake, her eyes growing accustomed to the gloom. She heard a noise on the small landing outside her room and, fearful of what was beyond the door, she stiffened. She picked up the peppery smell before she saw him and felt a jolt of fear pass through her.

Trần was in the room and walking towards her with a glass of water.

'I will open the shutters,' he said as he put the glass beside her.

'No. Please. The light hurts my eyes.' It was true, but more than anything, she didn't want to look at him and her heart was knocking at the thought of being confined together in such a small room.

When he was close she sneaked a look. The devastating fall-out of war had marked him and his once proud demeanour had changed. In fact, he looked defeated, or at the very least, disillusioned.

She struggled to sit up and picked up the glass. 'How long have you been here?'

'Since last night.'

Nicole sipped the water. 'She told you I was here?'

'She didn't want to.'

She felt that her sickness embarrassed him, saw it in the way he continually adjusted his scarf while remaining silent. His eyes kept sliding to her face for a moment and then he'd look away. Not once did he really see her.

She finished the water. 'Where's O-Lan?'

'Selling your stock for you. She asked me to watch over you.'

'So now you're my guardian angel?'

'I have something of yours.' He reached into a small satchel and drew out Nicole's antique purse.

'Oh,' she said with a smile. 'You found it in the tent.'

'I rescued it.' He smiled. 'So you see, I am your guardian angel.'

'Thank you,' she said, but didn't dare look to see if the photo of Mark was still inside.

Now he looked at her properly for the first time. She saw his eyes change and hoped that he had mellowed.

'I risked everything to help you escape.'

'And I was grateful.'

His head was shaking. 'You don't understand. The *métisse* among the party are no longer welcome.'

As she watched him, he fidgeted constantly and cleared his throat more than once. She hoped O-Lan would be back soon.

'I shall have a position in the new state,' he said at last. 'You don't look French. When you're well we can be married.'

Nicole gasped and looked at him in alarm. This wasn't what she'd been expecting. 'You said *métisse* were not welcome.'

She scarcely remembered what had once connected them. The light had gone from his eyes and it seemed as if the passion had drained from his heart. A man whose revolutionary fervour had dried up. Had he become what he had really always been; not a visionary at all, but rather a practical man, who, like so many others, had been too young to know any better?

'You don't understand,' she said. 'I have a child.'

He knitted his brows together and took a step back.

'My sister has her.'

'Once a French whore!' he snapped, and she could see the disgust in his eyes.

She wanted to offer him something but he ignored her outstretched hand. She shook her head. 'Trần, I'm sorry but you have to let me go.'

'I do not have to do anything,' he said, clearly upset and not attempting to hide it. 'I have a mind to inform the authorities that you are here.'

'The Vietminh isn't in charge yet. As far as I know the authority is still French.'

'Hanging on by a thread. You have time to change your mind.' His face softened and a shadow from the past slipped back; just for a second, there was a trace of the old Trần.

'We can be happy living together above the shop,' he said.

She shook her head. 'You aren't listening. I have a baby. I have no desire to be a docile Vietnamese wife.'

He went over to the window and threw open the shutters. A terrific banging and clattering rose up from the street accompanied by the sound of angry voices, the noise exploding into the room, assaulting her. She rubbed her eyes, then used her hands to shield them from the light.

'It will be best if you give me the silk shop,' he said as he twisted back to regard her with sterner eyes.

'Much good a silk shop will do you when the regime is seizing everything,' she said. 'But I'll leave the keys and the deeds of ownership when I go.'

'I hope you will not be going anywhere.' He smiled. 'It will not last. Things will go back to the way they were. I've never been a proprietor before. We shall run the shop together. When the time comes. You will see.'

Fearing her feelings might show in her face, she tried to calm herself, but her body felt heavy and her heart was going way too fast. She needed to keep the atmosphere calm; not by agreeing, but not being openly defiant either. Much as she wanted to, she didn't dare slam the door in his face.

'Are you all right?' he said.

She nodded. 'How will you be able to keep the shop open?'

'I won't. Not at first. They will want everybody on the land or in large municipal factories. There will be no private trade.'

'Let me think about it,' she said. She leant back against the pillow and closed her eyes. There was nothing to be gained from crossing him. She hoped O-Lan would know how to tempt him away so that she could leave.

She felt rather than saw him kneel beside her bed.

'Nicole, I came back for you.'

She felt dizzy again. 'It was such a long time ago.'

'I told you I would come back for you.'

'You're crazy. None of this is real. But, please, I've said I'll think about it and now I have to sleep.'

Convulsed by grief, she turned her face to the wall and heard him creep out.

40

A series of loud thumps woke her. She had been dreaming of drowning in the river at Huế again, and as she came to consciousness she struggled for air. But this time it wasn't a dream: somebody was holding her tight. Terrified, she felt as if a large bird had spread its wings and was knocking at her ribcage. She hardly dared look, but forced herself to open her eyes, exhaling in relief as O-Lan's face swam into focus. Beyond the room the light was failing and her friend was framed by the glow from one small lamp in the corner. She could see O-Lan had a finger to her lips and was looking wide-eyed. Once Nicole nodded, she released her grip.

'You were thrashing about in your sleep,' O-Lan whispered. 'I didn't want you to shout out.'

'What's happening?'

'You have to leave.'

Nicole lifted her head. 'Vietminh agents?'

O-Lan grimaced. 'No. Hanoi is falling apart. It's the Vietnamese army deserters. The ones who've been with the French fighting the Vietminh.'

Nicole pulled herself up as a great noise erupted, like the sound of people banging pots and pans.

'What?'

'It's householders trying to summon help from the police. It won't work.'

A loud crash made them jump and clutch each other.

'Thugs,' O-Lan said with a withering look. 'But if they find you, you will never get out of here. They are angry with the

354

French for losing the war. Now their own lives are at risk from the Vietminh.'

Horrified, Nicole stared at her friend.

'They're in your shop now. They've already held two people at gunpoint in the street.'

'French?'

'Vietnamese, but supporters of the French regime. Once they've gone, I'll take you back to the shop. They won't go in twice. They're looting and stealing everything they can.'

'Won't they come here too?' An awful sense of dread crept up on Nicole. If they came and found her here she'd never have any chance of seeing her daughter again.

O-Lan shook her head. 'They came while you were asleep.'

Nicole's heart leapt in her throat. 'And they didn't come up here?'

'No. They know I am a cousin of Trần. They will not dare touch me. But I have to get you out before Trần gets back. He's out at the moment.'

'He wants the deeds and the keys to the shop.'

'You can leave them with me. He'll be back at midnight. You must both be gone.'

'Both? I don't understand.'

'Mark is here.'

Nicole's heart almost buckled, it raced so fast. 'He's alive?' She glanced around, as if Mark might suddenly appear as an apparition out of the shadowy corners of the room.

O-Lan smiled. 'He's not here now. When he found out you were not in France he went to your villa, and when you were not there he came looking for you here. He's coming back later.'

'He's alive,' Nicole repeated, hardly able to take it in. 'He's really alive?'

O-Lan nodded.

Nicole felt a leap of energy and sprang upright. She had hoped and prayed that he would be spared, but now that she knew he had been, the feeling of joy was overwhelming. Every nerve in her body seemed to burst into life. She had tried to stave off the longing she'd felt, tried to numb herself to the pain that had settled in her chest, but now energy was coursing through her veins as she thought of his hands, his face, his bright blue eyes. There was not a part of him she couldn't recall; not a part she didn't want to see and touch again. He was alive. Alive.

She grinned at O-Lan. 'Lucky it was you who saw him and not Trần.'

'I told him Sylvie has your daughter. He knows we are friends. He is going to help you find your sister.'

Nicole felt heat prick her eyelids and, as tears sprang to her eyes, she held out a hand.

'Mark will drive my cousin's motorbike. I told him you had been sick. All you have to do is cling on. Here is the money I managed to raise.' She gave Nicole a little packet.

Nicole reached over to hug her.

'Sorry it's not more.'

There was a loud crash from next door like furniture being tipped over. Nicole looked at her friend, wide-eyed.

'Don't worry, you'll be in Haiphong before daybreak. You are not too far behind your sister.'

'Is the road safe still?'

O-Lan grimaced. 'It's a risk you will have to take.'

As they waited for the commotion from next door to stop, Nicole's hopes were raised in a way she could not have imagined. Now all they had to do was leave that night. With Mark's help she would find Sylvie and Celeste; it would all come right and she'd be with her beautiful daughter again. The thrill of it ran through her and she felt like shouting out in relief but then she hesitated. O-Lan must have noticed the flicker of anxiety on her face as she tried to ignore the little voice in her head that told her Sylvie might have decided not to go to France at all. But when O-Lan squeezed her hand, Nicole felt her friend's strength. It would be all right because it had to be.

When they felt safe enough to move, they set off by slipping out of O-Lan's house at the back, and entering via the alley behind Nicole's shop. It was a clear night and the sky was glittering with stars. They stood in the courtyard together where it was hard not to think of all the times they'd had together; the laughter, the meals they'd shared sitting outside soaking up the last of the sun, and the hard times they'd been through too. It was clear to Nicole that O-Lan was remembering the exact same things and, for a split second, she didn't want to go. A sound from O-Lan's place drew their attention. Nicole froze.

'Trần?'

'No. A door I left open I think. I must leave you now. Mark has the keys for the bike. I will leave the shed unlocked.'

'Won't Trần be angry?'

'Yes. I will have to tell him you stole the bike.'

They grinned at each other. Nicole held her friend's hands and squeezed. 'Thank you for everything.'

'I am your friend, Nicole.'

'The best friend I've ever had.' Nicole knew she'd probably never see O-Lan again and wanted to say more, but the look in O-Lan's eyes said it all.

She nodded. 'You too.'

'As soon as it gets dark Mark will come, and you must go. Make sure it is well before midnight.'

Nicole nodded. 'I can't believe this is the end.'

'Think of it as a start, as well as an end. I hope you find your sister quickly. Kiss the baby from me.'

Nicole closed her eyes. The tears backed up, stinging her

lids, until she forced herself to open her eyes and brush the dampness away. She gave O-Lan one last hug, and after they had stepped back from one another she watched as her friend walked to the door leading to the alley. Just before the door, O-Lan turned and signalled goodbye. Nicole felt a wave of sadness but raised a hand, then with shaking fingers opened the courtyard door to her shop and slipped in.

Inside the shop the thugs had thrown her precious bales of silk to the floor. She picked her way across in the dark and began putting some of them back on the shelves, but then resigned herself to letting them be. There was little point. She stood and gazed around her, hardly able to believe all her hard work and love had come to this. The fever had faded but her legs still felt weak, so she went upstairs to lie on the bed to wait for Mark. It was damp and cold up there but she closed her eyes and listened to the sounds of the night: the hoot of an owl, the flurry of wings, a child crying in its sleep. This would be the last time she'd ever be in her silk shop.

41

In the half-light of the shop the first sight of Mark flattened her. With feline caution he had padded up the stairs, but she had not been sleeping and, with eyes wide open, was keeping watch. Her skin prickled with the agony of anticipation and, when she got to her feet, she felt so light she feared she'd float off before he even reached her. She saw his tall shape at the top of the stairs, he held out his arms and she ran to him. He scooped her up and stroked her back; comforted by the warmth of his body at last so close to hers, she sobbed silently into his chest. Everything she'd been through since she had last seen him, every doubt, every hope and every fear, threatened to pour from her.

When it had finally passed, he held her away from him. 'So? Like that then!'

'I thought you were dead.'

'It's over now, Nicole. I'm sorry it took me so long.'

He explained that when he'd returned from Russia he'd expected her to already be in France. He had called Lisa who'd told him that she'd received a letter from Nicole but that was all. So he'd gone to the Duval villa where, finding the garden door locked, he'd climbed over the wall.

'The back door to the conservatory was wide open, so I went in and saw everything in chaos. I knew you were untidy,' he said, 'but this was something else.'

She laughed. 'I left rather quickly.'

His face grew serious. 'I was terrified I'd lost you. But something told me to look for you here.'

'But your job?' she said. 'How is this possible?'

'I've made arrangements.'

She wanted to know what had happened in Russia, but when she began to speak, he held up a hand to silence her. 'Let's not pick it over now. Let's gear ourselves up for the bike ride of our lives. Agreed? All that matters now is that we slip away without Trần knowing, and we get on that road.'

She nodded.

He studied her face. 'You are feeling well enough for this?'

'Of course. It was only a fever. I would have had to go on my own tonight anyway.'

'You look pale.'

'You can't see me properly in this light. I'll be fine.'

He pulled something out of his pocket. 'Here, eat this,' he said as he handed her a squashed cheese roll from out of a paper bag.

'I'm not hungry.'

'When did you last eat?'

She didn't reply.

'I thought not. Now eat. You'll need your strength. Have you got something warm to wrap round you?'

She laughed. 'I have a shop full of somethings. Or at least the somethings that haven't been sold or stolen.'

They lay on the bed for a delicious few minutes, his fingers tangling in her hair as he stroked it. She breathed in the salty, citrusy smell of him and thought of her daughter. The fragility of their present happiness was clear, but she tried not to focus on the danger ahead. The minutes spooled out as he held her so close that she could feel his longing was as strong as her own.

He had brought a rucksack with him and she added a change of her own clothes to his things before leaving the shop by the outside staircase to the courtyard and then out via the alley. She glanced up, glad to see the sky had clouded over. When she reached for his hand she felt his energy flood through her.

'All set?' he whispered.

They crept over to O-Lan's, where they found the shed door unlocked. In fact, O-Lan had cleverly broken the lock to make it look like theft. Nicole prayed her friend would be safe and that Trần wouldn't take his anger out on her.

Mark hugged her one more time, then spoke in a low voice. 'Ready?'

This was it. Every part of her was bursting with the desire to see Celeste. The love was absolute. Full of hope, she gave him a squeeze. 'She looks like you, Mark. You should see the sparkle in her blue eyes when something makes her chuckle.'

'I can't wait to see her.'

They walked the bike through the empty streets surrounding the shop and it looked as if it would be easier than they expected. But, about half a kilometre further on, a voice rang out somewhere behind them.

'Halt!'

They couldn't see where the voice was coming from, but it sounded like a French patrol.

'Take the bike and the rucksack. Get down that alley fast,' Mark whispered and pointed in front of them. 'Stay there. I'll distract them. I'm hoping they only heard us, and didn't see us.'

Once Nicole had rolled the bike into the alley, she watched Mark go off in the opposite direction, whistling nonchalantly and walking with an ambling gait as if he was drunk.

After he turned the corner, she was unable to see him or the officer, and could only hear what they were saying.

'Officer.' It was Mark's voice. 'S'nice evenin'.'

'There is a curfew. You need to come with one of my men.'

'Just on m'way home.'

'What are you doing this side of the city? I heard you with somebody else. Who was that?'

'I –' He paused.

The muscles in her neck and shoulders tensed. She waited for a moment but, worried Mark had run out of ideas, could stand it no longer. Leaving the motorbike, she undid the top buttons of her dress, ruffled her hair and left her wrap behind. Stepping out of the alley, she ran over to where the officer was confronting Mark. She giggled repeatedly and spoke in rapid French.

'Officer, I am so sorry. We both had too much to drink and, oh dear, but I was feeling sick and my boyfriend –' she draped an arm round Mark – 'he thought I needed some fresh air. He's American and leaving Vietnam. I wanted to be with him before he goes. We thought it would be quiet here, near to the lake, where we could be alone. You know what I mean. We weren't causing any trouble. Just lost track of time. On our way back home now.'

The man put up a hand to stop her and looked at them dubiously. He yawned and pointed at the route they should take. 'Very well. But don't you realize it's dangerous? Now out of my sight, the pair of you. The French quarter is that direction. Get back home and keep out of trouble. Hell is about to let loose in Hanoi.'

Nicole struggled to control the feeling of relief as she and Mark walked away, arms wrapped round each other. The trouble was they were now heading in the opposite direction to where Nicole had left the motorbike. 'What if they find the bike?' she whispered.

'You left it out of sight?'

'Yes.'

'We'll skirt back. The patrols are moving around the city. With any luck they'll not see it.'

For fifteen tense minutes they waited before creeping back,

holding to the shadows and concealing themselves wherever they could.

It still took too long and Nicole's nerves were stretched to breaking as fear surged through her. At every sound they froze. This section of the city wasn't quiet even in the dead of night, and at one point Nicole imagined others crawling around the streets, all desperate to engineer an escape. Eventually they reached the right alley.

'It's down there,' she said.

'I can't see.'

'Behind that shop.' While Mark went down to look, she leant into the shadow of the shop door, feverish with anxiety that the bike might not be there. When he appeared a moment or two later wheeling it beside him, she felt suddenly weightless. They'd got away with it.

'We can't start it up here, Mark,' she whispered. 'The patrol will still hear.'

'We'll push it a little further, but we can't take the risk of leaving it too long. There are other patrols. Here's your wrap. Can you take the rucksack too?'

She nodded and slipped her arms through the straps. A few minutes later, outside a Vietnamese temple shrouded in darkness, he turned to her. 'Okay?'

She nodded, they shared a brief kiss, and then Mark sat astride the bike. She climbed up behind him, wrapping her arms round his middle and leaning in.

'Hold tight,' he said.

As he revved, the bike sprang into life and they headed for the road to Haiphong. Until they reached it, Nicole would be nervous. Instead, she tried to think of her life in Hanoi: of her family and of Lisa, of her shop and her friend O-Lan. Even with the dust stinging her eyes she kept them open, wanting one last look at the city as they sped by.

Once they arrived at the open road, Mark gave a great shout. Like a warrior going into battle, she thought, and laughed at herself for being fanciful. With her cheek nuzzled against his jacket she breathed wool smelling vaguely of dust and grease. She twisted back to look as the city receded. Overjoyed that they were going to follow Sylvie, together, she also wanted to say goodbye.

'Adieu, Hanoi,' Nicole whispered, 'adieu.' Her words scattered in the wind as she gazed into the empty road ahead.

The bumping speed of the ride and the throbbing of the engine meant they arrived at Haiphong exhilarated, but extremely tired. There had been no road mines, no stopping at outposts, nothing more than the usual potholes. It had been as easy as they could have hoped, but as dawn gradually revealed what lay ahead of them, it began to rain, and Nicole felt anxious again.

A sea of makeshift tents stretched as far as the eye could see. Mark told her the US Naval Task Force had been mobilized to assist the evacuation of thousands of refugees.

'Refugees,' she said. 'Is that what I am now? A refugee?'

'I guess so. It's called "Operation Passage to Freedom". The demand is so high the French asked Washington for help, so the US Department of Defence brought in the navy.'

'How will we ever find which ship she's sailing on in this?'

'We need to find one of the American naval officers in charge.'

They plunged into the great tide of grey and spiritless refugees. All morning they asked everyone they met if they had seen a woman answering Sylvie's description, but grew more and more disappointed at the lack of information. People without tents were huddling together against the rain and if anybody had seen Sylvie it was clear they had too much to worry about to remember or care.

But in the afternoon Nicole spotted a woman a few metres ahead of where they had stopped to rest, a woman with Sylvie's build, and carrying a baby.

'Celeste,' she cried out, 'at last.'

She felt a huge burst of relief and, blood pumping through her body, she shouted her sister's name. The woman did not turn round and when Nicole reached her she saw it wasn't Sylvie at all, but a much older woman. She burst into tears, the pain of it eating away at her hope.

'We'll never find them,' she said as Mark held her.

'Don't give up. We'll keep searching. Someone will know something. We have to keep looking.'

'And if we don't find them? They've probably already sailed.'

'We'll head for France anyway.'

She nodded. Throughout the tented city, the smell of sickness and damp permeated the air. She tried to remain positive but her courage was fading. Disconsolate-looking people dragged their feet as they wandered up and down the muddy aisles between the tents, and whenever a ship's horn blew, there were angry shouts and yells. The sound of crying children tore her apart. She could picture the shoving and pushing in the rush to get on the ships and, terrified that Celeste might have been hurt in the scrum, she clung on to Mark; they couldn't risk separation or the crowds would swallow them instantly.

It took a while, but they eventually found an officer.

'This is just the beginning,' he said. 'You're lucky to be here early.'

'This is early?'

'The ships sail to Saigon. We are currently evacuating civilians, but soon it will be all the soldiers and members of the French army from North Vietnam.'

She turned to Mark. 'Sylvie said they were taking out officials and army only.'

Mark gave a sigh of frustration.

'Either way,' the man continued, 'we don't have enough ships.'

'So what's going to happen to all these people?'

'We'll get them moving in time. Those who survive the camp that is. Our US boys are renovating cargo vessels and tank carriers. Doing repairs en route from bases in the Philippines.'

'How long does it take to get to Saigon?'

'Almost three days.'

'What about ships sailing for France?' Mark asked.

The man frowned. 'That's more difficult. The rumour is the French air force will be running a mass emigration and their navy will be assisting. Only as far as Saigon, I believe, though there may be liners sailing for France from Saigon. There could be one or two sailing direct from here, but I have no concrete information.' He gestured at the chaos around them. 'You'd need to ask the French authorities.'

Nicole looked at Mark. 'Do you think she might have gone south to Saigon on a US ship and not straight to France? She might even still be there.'

'She might,' Mark said, and turned back to speak to the officer again. 'Are there lists?'

'We've tried. Basically people are registered and we pile them in wherever we can. Many don't have identification. As I said, we'll soon be evacuating troops as well as citizens. If the woman you want is on a French ship, we wouldn't have a record of her.'

'She had a baby with her. The baby may have been ill.'

'There are a lot of sick babies.'

'Please?' Nicole begged.

'Look around you. Before long tens of thousands will be waiting and it will swell to hundreds of thousands. The diarrhoea has been through the camp like wildfire. But there's a Catholic hospital and crematorium. If she's French, why not ask there?'

A crematorium. The words rang in her head.

He gave them directions and, as they ploughed their way through the filth of the muddy walkways, the smell of human sewage grew strong. Nicole, gripped by fear, could not speak. Celeste had been ill. What if she had died in this terrible place?

Mark sensed her despair and reached for her hand. 'Stay strong,' he kept saying. 'Stay strong. Keep believing.'

When they reached the hospital they could see it consisted of long rows of tents strung together with rope and lit by a series of oil lamps. A man in a grey coat was busy snuffing them out and the smell of burning oil drifted over.

Mark went across and explained the situation. The man scratched his head. 'Everyone is fighting for limited shelter, food and medicine, let alone places on the ships. I've only just arrived, but one of the nurses might know.'

He waved a tall woman across.

'You are French?' she said as she came over and held out her hand to Mark.

Nicole stepped forward. 'I am French. I have a French passport.'

'But you look . . .'

'My mother was Vietnamese.' She held out her hand with her passport in it. 'Nicole Duval. I am looking for my sister, Sylvie Duval. She –'

'She came on ahead,' Mark interrupted. 'She had a baby with her.'

'Celeste. She wasn't well.'

The nurse frowned. 'I don't recall the names. With insufficient sanitation and water, there are constant outbreaks of disease. I've seen too many babies.'

She turned to go but Nicole put out a hand to stop her.

'Please. She has red hair. The baby. Reddish hair.'

The nurse shook her head. 'I'm sorry.'

Nicole stared at the ground, feeling as if it was about to swallow her.

'Hold on,' the woman said.

Nicole glanced up and felt a flicker of hope when she saw the woman was frowning.

'And blue eyes?' she said. 'Yes, I remember. So unusual.'

'Is she alive? The baby?' Nicole whispered.

'Very much so, although it was touch and go. Her mother wanted to get her on to a ship that morning, but I told her without medical treatment the child would die. She was dehydrated so we kept her on a drip here.'

'Sylvie Duval was not her –'

Mark touched her arm and interrupted again. 'Do you know if they managed to get on a ship?'

'There is a French ship sailing for Saigon today. It's only recently docked. I believe she was hoping to get on that.' She patted Nicole's hand. 'If you hurry you should catch up with your sister.'

'How do we get tickets?'

'You don't, you go with your French passport. As long as there are spaces, you'll be able to embark.'

By the time they found the French liner, Nicole felt so winded she could barely walk; the fever had drained her more than she'd realized. As she glanced around she saw the people at the dock now stood a dozen deep and the queues were still swelling with new arrivals. Frightened they might become separated, she gripped Mark's arm as they approached a tent set up at the dockside to register evacuees. She showed her passport and was told to hurry as the ship would soon be sailing. But an argument developed as the French officer told

Mark he was required to board an American ship. Nicole's heart plummeted as Mark waved her away.

'Get on the ship,' he said. 'Quickly. Go on!'

She hesitated, but was being pushed forward by the people crowding behind her. She called out to Mark. 'If we are separated, go to Paris. Find my father in Le Marais, Rue des Archives, or go to Lisa.'

People were now pushing past, grabbing at each other to gain a better place in the queue. She couldn't stand to be separated from him again, not after everything they'd been through, and tried to hold back, but was forced to take a few steps as people surged forward, carrying her with them. She had no choice and began moving with the crowd.

As she slipped deeper into the throng of people waiting to board, the jostling became more desperate. She glanced around and saw she was not the only one close to tears; they were the lucky ones, the ones who would probably get away, but many would be left behind and she knew it was not only her world that was breaking. She gulped back her tears. She had no idea what might lie ahead and she would far rather have faced it with Mark, but if it was not to be, she would do it alone; her love for Celeste would drive her on. The wall of noise grew more frantic as people huddled in teeming ragged groups, barking orders at each other and endlessly counting to ensure all the family were together; their fractured voices revealed their terror of separation, their shadowy eyes showed their fatigue. People were carrying children, cases, bundles of clothes, even pots and pans.

When the narrow steps were just ahead of her, she took a deep breath. This was it. Once on the gangway there could be no going back.

'Nicole!' she heard Mark call.

She twisted her head and saw him squeezing past people,

who shouted out in frustration and anger. The feeling of relief hammered in her chest.

'Typical Frenchman!' he said. He paused and then had to yell to be heard. 'He only let me through when I told him we're to be married in a fortnight . . . so what do you say?'

A cheer broke out and, for that sweet moment, hope returned.

After about an hour, the ship began to slip away. Nicole stood on the deck with Mark and watched as the liner left the shores of Vietnam. Giddy with the bitter-sweet intensity of her feelings, she held on to Mark, and knew she'd never return. She had loved her country, but she was consoled by the knowledge that people mattered more. Her daughter, her sister and the man who would be her husband. She would never forget O-Lan's generosity, but it was time to say the last farewell.

There were a huge number of people on board. Nearly two thousand, they found out later. But they had three days to look and if Sylvie was on the ship they would surely find her somewhere. It took several hours to locate anyone in authority, and as they searched they talked.

'I wrote, you know, but didn't hear back.'

'I found two letters, with some money, but only recently. Sylvie had hidden them.'

'Dear God, why? I feared you hadn't received them but it didn't occur to me that your sister might intercept them. And then it was months before I could get back to Vietnam. I did try to phone but it wasn't easy.'

'I think she disconnected the phone too.'

He shook his head. 'I was so worried about you and the baby. I found our man in Moscow, but he was badly injured and that slowed our progress getting out of the country.'

The danger he must have been in while in Russia caught at

her throat and she clutched hold of his arm as if to stop them ever being ripped apart again.

When they finally caught up with a French officer, he told them a passenger list had been compiled as people boarded, and was now held below, but they couldn't be absolutely sure of the accuracy. Only those with French passports or special clearance would be allowed to continue on from Saigon to France.

'This ship does sail to France then?' Nicole said as an immense feeling of hope swept through her.

'Indeed. Why not come along to my office?'

They followed him down slippery metal stairways to a lower deck, and a drab room painted green, where he opened a ledger.

'I'm looking for my sister, Sylvie Duval.'

'Very well,' the man said as he scrutinized the list.

Nicole could feel her nerves tighten. What if Sylvie was not on this ship?

After about ten minutes, during which time nobody spoke and the atmosphere was very strained, he stopped and tapped a name on the page. 'Sylvie Duval and her child, Celeste.'

'She said that? Her child?'

'Yes, it's here in black and white.'

Nicole showed her passport and also Celeste's birth certificate with Mark's name on it too. The man raised his brows. 'So, not her child?'

'No. Her niece. Do you know where they are on this ship?'

'The ship isn't policed but ask any of the women who are looking after children. They keep their eyes open. They'll know more than anyone where people are to be found.'

Nicole felt dead on her feet, but still they went on. They would ask every single person on the ship if they had to. Mark forced her to eat the bread and soup provided free, and then they carried on looking.

A day and a half later, they got a lead.

A young French girl told Nicole that a woman and child answering the description had gone to the upper deck. They had needed air. The baby was pale and her mother thought the sea air might put the roses back in her cheeks.

As they climbed to the deck, Nicole heard the seabirds screeching and the ship's timbers creaking as the sea slid around them, a wild empty place that seemed to go on for ever. Worse even than the bottom of the river, it felt as if she'd reached the world's end. She glanced up at a sky the colour of iron, and froze.

'I'll go first, shall I?' Mark said.

Nicole saw at once that he was right. There was no knowing how Sylvie might react. She walked on, allowing him to lead the way. While below deck many were seasick, few had braved the icy winds above. A sailor was attempting to stack crates and another was staggering to keep his balance as he wound ropes to secure them. The rest of the crew had stayed safely below. Nicole struggled to remain upright and felt the thump of the water as it slammed against the sides of the boat. A wall of water surged over the railings. They both drew back and waited for it to subside. They scanned the deck. Nicole spotted Sylvie at the same moment Mark did. Elated by the mixture of hope and relief that poured through her, Nicole had to force herself to remain still by gripping the salty edge of a lifeboat.

Sylvie stood with her back to them, leaning on the railings and gazing out to sea, Celeste cradled in her arms.

'Sylvie Duval,' she heard Mark say. 'Is it you?'

Nicole gasped at her sister's ravaged face as she whipped round. Her clothing was ripped and her hair looked matted, as if it hadn't been combed in days. A flurry of fearful thoughts flipped through Nicole's mind.

'How are you?' he said.

Sylvie stared at him. 'What are you doing here?'

'Going to Saigon and then France. Like you, I imagine.'

Sylvie drew back and leant against the rails. Her eyes darted about as he took a step forward and then she turned back to the ocean again. For a horrible, terrifying moment Nicole pictured Sylvie dropping her baby into the water. The fear felt so real she almost shouted out, but instead tightened her grip on the lifeboat until the skin of her knuckles turned blue.

Mark stepped closer. 'Would it be all right if I held Celeste?'

Sylvie glanced round and Nicole immediately saw there was something really wrong with her sister. Her expression was blank as if she were looking with sightless eyes.

'I promise I won't hurt her.'

'I'm looking after her.' Sylvie glanced over the rails at the sea again, then passed the child to Mark.

'Thank you.' He stepped away from the rails.

Sylvie followed him. 'She has been ill, but she's better now.'

'I'm glad to hear it. But you don't look too well, Sylvie.'

Nicole could bear it no longer, and stepped towards them. Sylvie seemed startled by the sound and spun round.

'I looked after her. I promise.'

Nicole went closer. 'I know you did. It's all right. We're here now.'

The air, drenched with the smell of salt and fish, hit the back of Nicole's throat. Her confidence wavered and she felt as if she was being pulled into the ocean surrounding them. She squeezed her eyes shut and dragged herself out of it.

Sylvie frowned. 'I don't seem to be able to remember . . .'

The tone of her voice had been neutral and Nicole took another few steps towards her sister. Then she halted, horrified by something inexplicable in Sylvie's hazel eyes.

'Come on,' she said to Sylvie. 'Come with me now. It's all right.'

The silence hung between them, broken only by the

occasional shriek of a seabird. Nicole watched her sister's face. Something was dreadfully wrong. Sylvie glanced away and then back at Nicole but did not move.

'I looked after her.'

'I know you did.'

Nicole couldn't bear to see the despair in Sylvie's eyes. She heard a rumble in the distance and fixed her own eyes on the clouds, holding on to such complex feelings she barely knew how to comprehend them. Despite everything that had gone on between them, she loved her sister and hated to see her so broken.

She turned from Sylvie for a moment and went over to Mark who, with a look of amazement on his face, was still cradling their daughter. She felt her heart flip at the sight of them together.

'I didn't know she would be so beautiful,' he said, his voice hoarse with emotions she could only guess at.

She nodded and for a moment couldn't speak.

'Don't you want to hold her?' he said.

She swallowed the lump in her throat. 'I do. More than anything in the world I do, but I'm shaking so much I think I might drop her.'

He held Celeste with one arm and put the other round her shoulders. 'Come on. We'll find somewhere to sit down on the lower deck. It'll be safe there and you'll be able to hold her for as long as you need.'

'In a moment.'

As the sky turned even wilder the ocean heaved again and a cold rain began to fall. Nicole turned and went back for Sylvie, who was still standing in the exact same spot.

'Come now, Sylvie,' she said, holding out a hand. 'You can't stay out here. You'll catch your death. Come with us.'

Epilogue

Eighteen months later – November 1955, Paris

Nicole's father lived in a top-floor flat in a crumbling gothic corner building in Le Marais, Paris. He'd bought it for the view, he said. So far above the street, he could see for miles and didn't need to pay attention to what was going on below. Though his mobility wasn't as limited as she had expected, Nicole was relieved that the cranky old lift still functioned. Standing on the balcony, she glanced down at the street. On the opposite corner stood a hairdresser's salon but, in this area heavily frequented by prostitutes, that wasn't what caught her attention: it was the extraordinarily bright hair colours of the women going in and out. Her father didn't care. With his favourite cafe for his morning hot chocolate, a fresh food market on the next street, plus a boulangerie and a boucherie close by, he was content, which, considering his previous attachment to Vietnam, surprised Nicole. But this simple lifestyle seemed to suit him and his health had improved.

With the help of an excellent Parisian doctor, Nicole's health was now completely restored. It had taken longer than she'd expected, but Mark had always maintained she'd underestimated how ill she'd been after that perilous journey south, and how vulnerable she'd been after her time in prison. She leant on the intricate filigree railings surrounding the balcony and gazed at Paris, wanting to fasten the image in her mind.

'Mama,' a voice called out, and Celeste came racing out after a ball, the strawberry-blonde curls tumbling around her face, her blue eyes sparkling.

'What have I said about playing ball out here?'

She looked so thoroughly at ease, so happy and pleased with herself, and luckily seemed to remember nothing of the past. Nicole laughed, picked her up and swung her round. Celeste loved it and begged for more, but it was time.

'Go and play with Grandpapa. I must finish packing.'

Celeste ran back into their sitting room and her grandfather helped her clamber on to his lap where she blew kisses at him. Nicole followed her daughter through.

'I shall miss you, little one,' her father said as he kissed the child's cheek.

'You will visit us,' Nicole said.

She didn't blame him for the past now. What would be the point? They had all made mistakes – some dreadful ones – and, not without tears, they had sorted out most of their differences.

'I will miss you too, Nicole,' he said.

'*Moi aussi, Papa.*'

'Will you speak French to Celeste?' he said. 'Not just English?'

She nodded and glanced at her watch.

Mark would be arriving soon and they planned to head south to visit Lisa at her little house in Narbonne. Nicole felt a thrill of anticipation at the thought of being with her old friend again after all this time. After that, a flight to London, and then on to Washington in the USA. Mark's new job in security, thankfully not as a member of the CIA, gave Nicole the financial support to launch her fledgling silk business; she was already working with a Parisian fashion house.

The door bell sounded and her father spoke into the grille. Mark had been incredible since they'd caught up with Sylvie on the ship, though at times Nicole had thought they'd never make it home, especially when Sylvie appeared to sink into a terrible internal darkness and had remained silent throughout the voyage. Nicole sighed at the memory. The fact that Sylvie was now receiving treatment for the emotional problems that had, since childhood, dogged her life, had to be a good thing, but it was distressing that Sylvie now lived in a long-term hospital. They all prayed for her recovery. And before leaving for the south, Nicole had decided to take Celeste to visit her aunt.

Sylvie was living a few kilometres from Saint-Cloud, and about fifteen kilometres from the centre of Paris. As châteaux went, this one was not so grand, and had been used as a residential hospital for some time, but as you approached along the curling wooded driveway, you could see it still retained an aura of charm. From her previous visits, Nicole knew that the shabby interior, with its dusty rooms and neglected air, didn't bother Sylvie. This peaceful, spacious building was just what her sister needed.

Nicole had arranged to meet Sylvie outside and as she, Mark and Celeste made their way round the side of the building to the back, they passed a few people sitting at tables quietly reading, and others dozing in the sunshine. A large terrace extended right across the back of the château, overlooking lawns and flower beds now looking wintery and bare. She couldn't see Sylvie at first, then spotted her sitting on a bench fronting a small lake, about fifty metres away. All alone.

Feeling taut inside, Nicole stood for a moment, struggling with her mixed emotions: the fear of what Sylvie might yet do if she reached a vanishing point, but also huge relief that her sister was, at least, still there.

With her back to them Sylvie didn't hear their footsteps as they swung Celeste between them. The child had been warned not to be noisy and it was amusing to watch her attempting to suppress her glee at seeing her aunt again. When they were within ten metres of Sylvie, Celeste pointed at her. They let her go and she raced across to Sylvie, who lifted her up and hugged her.

Then she turned, nodded at Nicole and put Celeste down again. 'Here,' she said. 'I have some bread in this bag. Why don't you feed the ducks while I talk to Mummy? Your daddy will go with you.'

The breeze got up and a gust ruffled the surface of the water. Celeste reached up for the bag, then Mark took her hand and they wandered down to the water's edge. With plenty of ducks bobbing about, Celeste chattered excitedly as she picked out her special favourite.

'How are you?' Nicole said, and held out her arms to her sister, who looked aged by fatigue and despair.

They embraced briefly.

'Will you sit?' Sylvie said.

Beyond the lake the wind whipped up the fallen leaves of the oak trees. While Nicole felt Sylvie slip in and out of the past, they sat in silence. Celeste and Mark were still laughing at the ducks and the sight filled her with love, but she didn't know how to make this meeting with Sylvie bearable.

'So you are going to America?' Sylvie said, and glanced at her hands where they lay folded in her lap. Quiet, obedient hands, that gave no hint of the turmoil she had been going through. Her nails were clipped short, as was her hair.

'It's for the best. And when you are well I want you to come and stay.'

Sylvie sighed and the tension between them softened. 'Maybe.'

'So how are you? You didn't say.'

As if waking from a trance, Sylvie drew back her shoulders and gazed around her. 'I'm not sure. At times I feel quite mad, and it's hard to sort what happened from pure imagination. But other times I feel happier and calmer than I ever have. Being here is good.'

'It must be hard, though.'

'It is hard to look at oneself clearly.'

Their eyes met and at that moment a rare glimpse into her sister's soul shook Nicole. 'You like to sit here close to the lake?'

'I love the water.' Sylvie paused, hesitated for a moment longer, frowned and brushed off a fly that had landed on her knee. 'What about you? Do you still dream of drowning?'

Nicole felt the cold on her cheeks and realized she was intensely aware of her sister's every move. 'Not so often now.'

'You must be happy.'

She noticed an odd expression on Sylvie's face, a reckless look that disturbed her.

'I have something I need to say,' Sylvie said. 'It's about Huế. It was my idea to go out in the boat, not yours. I lied and told them it was you. I'm sorry.'

'It doesn't matter now.'

Sylvie grew agitated and began to rub her hands together. 'Everything matters. Don't you see? Some things have to be said. It's what I'm learning. All the things I thought didn't matter . . . well they do. And I'm sorry.'

There was a short, uncomfortable silence.

'It was my idea that you should jump into the water too.'

Nicole felt a chill as her sister spoke. After all this time, to hear Sylvie admit that she had wanted her to drown was more than she could bear.

'I knew it was deep.'

'Sylvie, I'm not sure I . . . you don't have to do this.'

'I do. I wanted to maintain the illusion that you were the one who always caused the problems.'

They both stared at the lake and watched a gull skim across the water.

'Do they remind you of Huế? The gulls?' Sylvie said.

That day came racing back. Nicole could see the sun spanning the entire horizon and the stream of silvery bubbles of her breath. The terrifying feeling of sinking had never diminished and she felt the heat of tears pricking her lids.

'You wanted me to drown.'

Wide-eyed with shock, Sylvie shook her head. 'No. Did you think that? Really, no. You mustn't cry.'

Nicole frowned, feeling uncertain. Sylvie reached for her hand.

'Nicole, I tried to save you. As soon as I saw you were in trouble, I jumped in too. I held on to one of the boat's ropes with one hand and kept on trying to reach you with the other. I wanted you to see that I was there and that you weren't on your own.'

'When I dream of it I always see your face. I thought . . .'

Nicole gulped and there was a slight pause as she listened to Celeste's happy shrieks and her laughter at the ducks squabbling over bread.

'I thought you pushed me under.'

Sylvie seemed to fold in on herself.

'Are you all right?'

Sylvie nodded. 'I couldn't reach you, so I screamed for help. A fisherman dived down. When he brought you up I thought you were dead. He pumped your chest, you spluttered, water spurted out and, thank God, you were alive. But when I think of what so nearly happened . . .'

Nicole could hardly take it in.

'I would never have forgiven myself.'

'I thought you wanted me dead.'

'I resented you, yes, but never that. I was so frightened. I knew it was my fault but I lied about the whole thing. Told Papa it was all your idea. Told him I'd said we mustn't jump in. I'm so sorry.'

Nicole warmed Sylvie's icy-cold hand in her own.

'It's in the past. I'm glad you told me, but let's leave it back there now, shall we?'

Sylvie nodded. 'I miss it, you know. Hanoi. Huế. Our old life together.'

'I miss it too.'

Sylvie's face dissolved and for a moment it looked as if she would collapse into tears, but then the old Sylvie came through and she held up her head. 'We have to carry on, right?'

Nicole reached for her other hand too and her sister gave her a bleak smile.

'I wanted to secure my place in the world back then. It seemed to be the only thing that mattered.' She let go of Nicole's hands and reached for a brown leather-bound book lying beside her on the bench. 'Here,' she said. 'Take this with you. It will tell you everything you need to know.'

'About?'

'About you. And me. Our childhood. How it was when our mother was alive. I want you to know everything. I never could bear to share her before.'

'Are you sure?'

'I want you to have it.' As she passed the book to Nicole, her hands were trembling.

At that moment Mark and Celeste came up to the bench. The sisters both stood.

'I think we should be heading off now that Celeste is flagging,' Mark said, and held out a hand to Sylvie. She took it, squeezed, then let go.

'Will you come round to the front to wave us off?' Nicole asked.

Sylvie shook her head. 'I find goodbyes too difficult.'

The sisters hugged again and then Sylvie picked up Celeste, kissed both her cheeks and, with unshed tears in her eyes, put the child down.

'We will see you,' Nicole said.

They began to walk away but as they neared the house Nicole twisted round to gaze at the figure of her sister still in exactly the same position as they had left her. In air that smelt of wintery dampness and smoke, Sylvie raised a hand and waved, looking so terribly alone it was all Nicole could do to stop herself rushing back and gathering her in her arms.

As they left the château behind, Nicole gazed out of the car window and thought of Vietnam. After the fall of the French garrison at Dien Bien Phu on 8 May 1954, the Geneva Accord was finally signed in July the same year. People in Paris asked them how they had lived their lives back then. How could they live not knowing if they were going to die? How could day follow day? Meal follow meal? Sleep follow sleep? She would tell them you did what you had to. Just as they'd had to in Paris during the German occupation.

But she was so glad they had decided against returning to Saigon since, as part of the Geneva agreement, the country had been divided into North and South Vietnam. The Vietminh, now known as the Vietcong, were in power in the north, but a battle was brewing for control of the south. When it came, and she and Mark were both certain it would, the war would be between the communists in the north and the Americans. But Vietnam would always be part of Nicole, and it devastated her to think there might be more bloodshed.

She thought of their lovely old house beside the Perfume River in Hué. The river was deeper in colour in her memory than it was in reality, but in her mind she was still watching the birds fly over the river; back and forth they went, ducking and diving. And Lisa was still sitting on the back steps lighting a Gauloise. The happiest and the saddest of times. For her it would always be the most beautiful place on earth.

Over time, though the rest of what happened in Vietnam would not be forgotten, it would be laid to rest. It had to be if they were to move on with their lives. It hadn't been easy for those who were left behind, and stories reached them about how the people were now learning what it meant to live under the yoke of rigid communism. She prayed O-Lan was safe.

So who was she now?

She was Nicole Jenson Duval, half Vietnamese, half French, married to a Russian-American and, at last, no longer searching for where she belonged. In the end she didn't have to choose one part of herself over the other, as she once thought she'd be forced to. Soon her thoroughly mixed-race daughter would live in America. She crossed her fingers and hoped the world would change enough so that her daughter would never be faced with having to make that kind of choice either.

So that was the end. Or was it the start? Perhaps, as O-Lan so wisely said, it was both. Nicole could never have imagined what had happened to her sister. The ground had shifted beneath their feet and their relationship had changed. But an image came back of being together when she was about five and Sylvie must have been ten. Sylvie was holding her hand as they dipped their bare feet in the cool river. All her life Nicole had felt the loneliness of being different, but now she knew Sylvie, in her way, had been desperately lonely too. It was the terrible agony of isolation she'd seen in her sister's eyes when they were on board the ship.

After Mark parked the car – they had some shopping to do before leaving for the south – the three of them walked along the narrow Parisian street. Mark and Celeste went into a patisserie but Nicole stopped outside and opened her sister's journal. Then she took a deep breath and read the first sentence.

I am Sylvie Duval. This is the story of me and my little sister, Nicole.

She knew she and Sylvie would always be connected in the way that sisters were, but couldn't read any more and felt her eyes brimming with tears as she closed the book. There were always two sides to every story, but she would have to save Sylvie's for another day.

Acknowledgements

Once again I'd like to thank my agent Caroline Hardman. Her brilliance has made my entire writing adventure possible, from her clever editorial suggestions to her support on all other matters, large and small. She introduced me to my terrific editor and publisher, Venetia Butterfield, and I couldn't have asked for better. Venetia has maintained her faith in my writing from the start, but I'm also indebted to the entire team at Penguin who have been super fantastic as they always are. My publicist, Anna Ridley, accompanies me on trips to the BBC, making the whole thing fun instead of terrifying, Celeste Ward-Best and Stephenie Naulls show me the way on social media, and Lee Motley makes the covers look beautiful. But I also want to thank the sales, distribution and rights teams who have all worked so tirelessly. The one thing I've come to realize, above all else, is that bringing a book to publication and beyond takes a whole raft of people. I am grateful to every single person who has contributed to this process, and to all the wonderful bloggers who carry on such sterling work. I also want to mention the people who have bought my books. Thank you so much. Experience Travel organized a great tailor-made research trip to Vietnam and I have to thank Nick Clark for that. Finally, I really do have to applaud my husband, Richard, who gets me through the up and downs of writing a novel with endless cups of tea, good ideas, technological support and delicious meals. He has been preparing me for my next adventure – in India – by increasing the use of chilli! I feel very lucky indeed to have his, and my much loved family's, support.

These are some of the books I found useful during my research:

A Dragon Apparent, Norman Lewis, Jonathan Cape, 1951

Daughters of the River Huong, Uyen Nicole Duong, Ravensyard Publishing, 2005

Derailed in Uncle Ho's Victory Garden, Tim Page, Touchstone, 1995

Hanoi: Biography of a City, William S. Logan, University of New South Wales Press, 2000

Hanoi: Traces of the Old Days, Phuong Dong Publishing House, 2010

Indochine Style, Barbara Walker, Marshall Cavendish International (Asia), 2011

Paradise of the Blind, Duong Thu Huong, US edition, William Morrow & Co., 1993

The Sacred Willow, Duong Van Mai Elliott, Oxford University Press, 1999

Uniquely Vietnamese, James Edward Goodman, The Gioi Publishers, 2005

How I wrote *The Silk Merchant's Daughter*

When I'm thinking about a new book my first task is to choose a location. The settings and location are significant, not only because I love to bring a landscape to life and transport my reader to another time and place, but also because the place itself has to impact on the characters. Because I was born in the East, I am constantly drawn to explore the countries of that region: the Indian sub-continent, South East Asia, the Far East. It's a powerful drive inside me, partly due to the fact that after nine years in Malaya, we came to live in England and I missed my childhood home terribly. So far I've written *The Separation*, set in Malaysia, and *The Tea Planter's Wife*, set in Sri Lanka when it was Ceylon.

For *The Silk Merchant's Daughter*, I chose French Vietnam as a setting because I wanted to write about the difficulties faced by a mixed-race character as she attempts to define her identity. I also wanted to explore a different colonialism; one that wasn't British. In the early 1950s Vietnam was caught in a struggle between the French, determined to hold on to their hugely profitable colony with its abundant raw materials and agricultural products, and the equally desperate Vietminh, in their bid to achieve independence. The French defined their purpose in Indochina as a 'civilizing mission' and, like the British and other colonial powers, they did build schools, hospitals and roads but, as far as I can tell, colonialism was always really about profit. So my main character, half-French half-Vietnamese Nicole, has a foot in both sides of what was to become a war. A war that almost rips her apart and that, against all the odds, the Vietminh win.

The Silk Merchant's Daughter wasn't an easy book to write, firstly because the history of Vietnam is incredibly complex around the time frame I was contemplating. My aim was to explore the way Nicole is pulled in different directions, so I needed a time when that was most likely to occur. I learnt that the period between the end of the Second World War and 1954 (when the French eventually lost the final battle with the humiliating defeat at Dien Bien Phu) was a time when being mixed race was less accepted. After the terrible Japanese invasion during the Second World War, both French and Vietnamese became more suspicious and less tolerant.

After choosing the place, the next challenge is to read up on the history and make copious notes. I enjoy researching a period of history that's new to me, but the real test is to determine the best way to bring my chosen period alive. I want to give my readers a cultural and atmospheric read but also a gripping story. Everything I uncover at this stage will add to the book's authenticity, and I enjoyed reading about the history, the food, the fashions and, perhaps most of all, the architecture. But I must never forget that the story has to take precedence.

After that I'll outline a plot for the entire novel. I don't go into great detail at this stage, but I start putting myself in my main character's shoes. As the process of writing continues I want to know more and more about Nicole: what she feels, what she fears, what she loves and what she hopes for. She doesn't know where she belongs and neither did I when I came to live in England all those years ago, so it wasn't difficult to empathize with her plight. Once I have an idea of who she is, I then create the cast around her, particularly the Duval family and the tensions within it, heightened by the world they live in; a world where the French are losing their grip on Indochina.

I like to visit the country I'm writing about if I can and Vietnam was no exception. I had never imagined that I would go to Vietnam but, once I'd decided I would, it was enormously exciting. I still hadn't clarified a story plan when we stepped on the plane and I was hoping that the country itself would provide me with answers.

In fact, it didn't prove to be quite so simple. We started off in a dreadfully cold and damp Hanoi. I had chosen not to go in the hot season, but I hadn't expected a chill so profound that it seeped into my bones. I barely slept that first night. The next day I'd hoped to find evidence of the French colonial era: the graceful buildings, wide avenues and smart hotels. Some of it was still visible but much of French Hanoi had been built over, sometimes literally. Hanoi was such a fragmented hotchpotch that at first I found it frustrating. But gradually I found what I was looking for and began to see evidence of the past everywhere. The most beautiful avenue of unspoilt French villas was where the Communist Party leaders lived. You were not allowed to stop the car or even to take pictures, though I did so discreetly, using my phone through the car windows. I also took tons of photos at the Museum of the Revolution, including some of the methods of torture the French regime had used. Unfortunately, while trying to climb some railings to obtain a better shot of a faded French villa, I got stuck and dropped my phone on the other side of the railings. My husband was dispatched to find a handy branch to hook it back out while I kept watch. The Communist Party are everywhere, or so they'd like you to think. Anyway, the phone was damaged and I lost all my photos so I got my just desserts.

After Hanoi we went to Hoi An – a UNESCO world heritage site – but so touristy that it was deeply disappointing. It is actually a wonderfully preserved village and I had thought to use it as a location in my book but the crowds put me off. The old cultured and formal Vietnam was still there but only in isolated pockets.

Which left me with Huế and a gorgeous restored hotel overlooking the Perfume River where we stayed. I loved it. This is where the Duval family come from and I found it beautiful and mystical. The hotel had once been the mansion of the French Resident for that province. We had views across the Perfume River, which we crossed by boat, and we visited the Forbidden Purple City where the Emperor had held court until it was burnt down in 1945, though now extensively restored. After a wonderful car ride, up and over a mountain, including visits to tiny rural villages and a terrific view of the countryside, I'd seen enough to make a real start on the book as soon as I got back home. At least the sights and smells of Vietnam were firmly in my head, if not in my photographs!

Finally, I reached the end of the novel. It was the end for the French, too. They never believed they would lose the war with the Vietminh but, like the Americans after them, they got that wrong. Looking back, it seems to me that it was inevitable that Indochina – like India, Ceylon and Malaysia – would achieve independence. And that leads me to my next stop: India, where my next novel will be set.

For me, finally bringing a novel to completion and seeing it on the shelves is the most satisfying experience of all, and I hope you have enjoyed reading the result in this novel about Nicole, the silk merchant's daughter.

Dinah Jefferies